"I'm pregnant."

Pregnant? What the hell?

Nash stared at Lily, knowing full well she wasn't lying. After all, she looked just as freaked out as he felt, and what would she have to gain by lying to him? She didn't know his identity, didn't know who he truly was or how something like this would be perfect blackmail material.

In Lily's eyes, and the eyes of everyone else on the estate, he was a simple groom who kept to himself and did his job. Little did they know the real reason he'd landed at the Barrington's doorstep.

And a baby thrown into the mix?

Talk about irony and coming full circle.

* * *

Carrying the Lost Heir's Child
is part of The Barrington Trilogy:
Hollywood comes to horse country—and the
Barrington family's secrets are at the

CARRYING THE LOST HEIR'S CHILD

BY
JULES BENNETT

® and ™ are trademarks owned and used by the trademark owner and/or its licensee. Trademarks marked with ® are registered with the United Kingdom Patent Office and/or the Office for Harmonisation in the Internal Market and in other countries.

Published in Great Britain 2015
by Mills & Boon, an imprint of Harlequin (UK) Limited,
Eton House, 18-24 Paradise Road, Richmond, Surrey, TW9 1SR

© 2015 Jules Bennett

ISBN: 978-0-263-25246-0

51-0115

Harlequin (UK) Limited's policy is to use papers that are natural, renewable and recyclable products and made from wood grown in sustainable forests. The logging and manufacturing processes conform to the legal environmental regulations of the country of origin.

Printed and bound in Spain
by CPI, Barcelona

National bestselling author **Jules Bennett**'s love of storytelling started when she would get in trouble as a child and would tell her parents her imaginary friends were to blame. Since then, her vivid imagination has taken her down a path she'd only dreamed of. And after twelve years of owning and working in salons, she hung up her shears to write full-time.

Jules doesn't just write Happily Ever After— she lives it. Married to her high school sweetheart, Jules and her hubby have two little girls who keep them smiling. She loves to hear from readers! Contact her at authorjules@gmail.com, visit her website, www.julesbennett.com, where you can sign up for her newsletter, or send her a letter at PO Box 396, Minford, OH 45653, USA. You can also follow her on Twitter and join her Facebook fan page.

To Gems for Jules—
the best street team an author could ask for!
You all are so amazing and supportive. I love you all!

One

The masculine aroma. The strength of those arms. The hard chest her cheek rested against…she'd know this man anywhere. She'd watched him across the grassy meadows, dreamed of him…made love to him.

Lily Beaumont struggled to wake and realized all too quickly she didn't have a clue how she'd gotten here.

Or more to the point, where was "here"?

The straw rustled against the concrete floor beneath her. She lay cradled in Nash James's lap, his strong arms around her midsection. What on earth had happened?

"Relax. You fainted."

That low, soothing voice washed over her. Lily lifted her lids to see Nash's bright blue eyes locked on hers. Those mesmerizing eyes surrounded by dark, thick lashes never failed to send a thrill shooting through her. No leading man she shared the screen with had ever been this breathtaking…or mysterious.

But, she'd fainted? She never fainted.

Oh, yeah. She'd been walking to the stables to talk to Nash…

"Oh, no." Lily grabbed her still-spinning head. Reality

slammed back into her mind, making her recall why she was in the stables. "This isn't happening."

Rough, calloused fingertips slid away strands of hair that had fallen across her forehead. "Just lie still," he told her. "No rush. Everyone is gone for the day."

Meaning the cast and crew had all either gone to the hotel or into their on-site trailers. Thank God. The last thing she needed was a big fuss over her fainting spell, because then she'd have some explaining to do.

Just a few short months ago Lily started shooting a film depicting the life of Damon Barrington, dynamic horse owner and a force to be reckoned with. The Barrington estate had become her home away from home and the quiet, intriguing groom whose lap she currently lay in had quickly caught her attention.

Before she knew it, she'd been swept into a secret affair full of sneaking around, ripping off clothes and plucking straw pieces from her hair...which led her to this moment, this life-altering moment when she was about to drop a major bomb in Nash's life.

All the trouble they'd gone through to keep their escapades a secret were all in vain. No way could this news stay hidden.

"Nash." She reached up to cup his face, the prickle of his short beard beneath her palm a familiar sensation. "I'm sorry."

His brows drew together, worry etched across his handsome, tanned face, and he shook his head. "You can't help that you passed out. But you scared the life out of me."

Lily swallowed, staring at such an attractive, spellbinding man could make a woman forget everything around her... like the fact that she was carrying this man's child.

"Are you feeling okay?" he asked, studying her face. "Do you need something to eat?"

Just the thought of food had her gag reflex wanting to

kick in again. Weren't pregnant women supposed to be sick in the mornings? What was this all-day nonsense?

Lily started to sit up, but Nash placed a hand over her shoulder. "Hold on. Let me help you."

Gently, he eased her into a sitting position as he came to his feet. Then he lifted her, keeping her against his firm, strong body the entire time. Strong arms encircled her waist again and Lily wanted to seek the comfort and support he was offering. This might have been the first tender moment between them, considering anytime she'd come to meet him after dark they hurried to the loft where their passion completely took control.

How on earth would he react to the news? She was still reeling from the shocker herself, but she refused to keep this a secret. He had a right to know. She honestly had no clue what Nash would say, what he would do. A baby didn't necessarily affect his line of work. Hers, on the other hand…

She'd been burned so badly before and had fought hard to overcome the public scandal that ensued. How would he handle being thrust into the limelight?

Lily groaned. Once the story broke, the press would circle her like vultures—and they would make her private life a top headline. People were starving, homeless, fighting wars and the media opted to nose their way into celebrities' lives and feed that into homes around the world rather than something that was actually newsworthy.

Lily loved being an actress, loved the various characters she got to tap in to and uncover. But she hated the lack of privacy. A girl couldn't even buy toilet paper without being spotted. Lily prided herself on being professional, doing her job and doing it well, and staying out of the media's greedy, sometimes evil, clutches…a nearly impossible feat.

"You okay now?" he asked, his breath tickling the side of her face.

Nodding, Lily stepped away, immediately missing the warmth of his body, but thankful the dizziness had passed.

Over the past couple months she'd actually come to crave his touch, miss him when he wasn't near her. She should've known then she was getting in over her head where this virtual stranger was concerned. Their passion had swept her into a world she'd never experienced before. How could any single woman turn away from a man who touched her beneath the surface, who looked so deep within she was certain he could see in to her soul?

A physical connection was something she could handle. But all of those nights of sneaking around, of giving in to their desires had caught up with them. Now they would have to pivot away from the sex-only relationship and actually talk about the future…a future she'd never expected to have with this man.

With her back to him, Lily tried to conjure up the right words, the words that would soften the blow, but really was there a proper way to tell someone they were going to be a father? No matter how gentle the words were, the impact and end result would still be the same.

"Nash—"

Before she could finish her sentence, Nash took hold of her shoulder, eased her around and framed her face with his firm hands. Hypnotized by those vibrant blue eyes, she said nothing else as his mouth claimed hers.

And that right there was the crux of their relationship. Passion. Desire. Instant clothes falling to the floor.

Some might have said having a secret affair in the stables on a film set was not the classiest of moves, but Lily didn't care. She'd been classy her whole life…now she wanted to be naughty. The secret they shared made their covert encounters all the more thrilling.

Who knew Hollywood's "girl next door," as they'd dubbed her, had a wild side? Well, they'd caught a glimpse of it with the scandal, but she had since reclaimed her good girl status. She certainly had never been this passionate with or for a man. Definitely not the jerk who had used her and exploited her early in her career.

Before she'd become a recognized name, she'd fallen for another rookie actor. He'd completely blind-sided her by filming her without her knowledge. Their most intimate moments had been staged; everything about their relationship had been a lie. After that scandal, Lily had to fight to get to where she was now.

Nash's arms enveloped her and Lily was rendered defenseless as his mouth continued its assault on hers. Her arms slid up the front of his shirt, taut muscles firm beneath her palms.

He eased back slightly, resting his forehead against hers. "You sure you're feeling okay? Not dizzy anymore?"

"I'm okay," she assured him, clutching his T-shirt.

Nash's lips nipped at hers. "I missed you today. I kept seeing you and Max together. It was all I could do to ignore the way his arms were around you. His lips where mine should be."

Chills spread over her body. Tingles started low in her belly and coursed throughout. That hint of jealousy pouring from Nash's lips thrilled her more than it should…considering this was supposed to be a fling.

"We were acting," she murmured against his mouth. "You know we're playing a young couple in love."

Lily had wanted to play the role of the late Rose Barrington since news of the project had first spread, and having Max Ford as the leading man was perfect. She and Max had been friends for years…so much so that he was like a brother to her.

Nash's hands slid between them, started peeling down the top of her strapless sundress.

"If Max weren't married with a baby, I'd think he was trying to steal my time with you."

Baby. Just the word threw a dose of reality right smack-dab in the middle of their minor make-out session.

Lily covered Nash's hands with her own and eased back. "We need to talk."

Vibrant eyes stared back at her beneath heavy lids. "Sounds like you're breaking things off. I know we never discussed being exclusive." Nash attempted a smile. "Don't take my Max joke so seriously."

Shaking her head, Lily took a deep breath and pushed through her fear and doubts. "I didn't take you for the jealous type. Besides, I know what this is between us."

Or, what it had started out being.

"Oh, baby, I'm jealous." He jerked her against his body. "Now that I've had you, I don't like seeing another man's hands on you, but I know this is your job and I love watching you work."

"I can't think when your hands are on me," she told him, stepping back once again to try to put some distance between temptation and the truth.

A corner of Nash's devilish mouth kicked up. "You say that like it's a bad thing. Because I'm thinking plenty when my hands are on you."

Smoothing a hand through her hair, Lily tried to form the right words. Since seeing the two blue lines on the stick this morning and confirming what she'd already assumed, she'd been playing conversations on how to break the news over and over in her mind. But now it was literally show time and she had nothing but fear and bundles of nerves consuming her.

"Nash…"

Abandoning his joking, Nash's brows drew together as he reached for her once again. "What is it? If you're worried about when you leave, I don't expect anything from you."

"If only it were that easy," she whispered, looking down at his scuffed boots, inches from her pink polished toes.

Nash was a hard worker, so unlike the Hollywood playboys who always tried to capture her attention. Money and fame meant nothing to her—she had plenty of both. She preferred a man who worked hard, played hard and truly cared for other people…a man like Nash.

This wasn't supposed to happen. None of it. Not the deeper feelings, not the lingering looks that teetered on falling beyond lust and certainly not a baby that would bind them forever.

"Lily, just say it. It can't be that bad."

She met and held his questioning stare. "I'm pregnant."

Okay, maybe it *could* be that bad.

Pregnant? What the hell? Suddenly he felt like passing out himself.

Nash stared at Lily, knowing full well she wasn't lying. After all, she looked just as freaked out as he felt and what would she have to gain by lying to him? She didn't know his true identity, or how something like this would be perfect blackmail material.

In Lily's eyes, and the eyes of everyone else on the estate, he was a simple groom who kept to himself and did his job. Little did they know the real reason he'd landed at the Barringtons' doorstep.

And a baby thrown into the mix?

Talk about irony and coming full circle.

"You're positive?" he asked, knowing she wouldn't have told him had she not been sure.

Lily nodded, wrapping her arms around her middle and worrying her bottom lip. "I've had a suspicion for several days, but I confirmed this morning."

Well, this certainly put a speed bump in all the plans he had for his immediate future here at Stony Ridge Acres. Not to mention life in general. A baby wasn't something he was opposed to, just something he'd planned later down the road… after a wife came into the picture.

"I have no idea what to say," he told her, raking a hand through his hair that was way longer than he'd ever had. "I… damn, I wasn't expecting this."

Lily kept looking at him as if she was waiting for him to explode or deny the fact the baby was his. Of course, she could've slept with someone else, but considering that they'd been together almost every night for nearly the past two months, he highly doubted it.

Besides, Lily wasn't like that. He many not know much about her on a personal level, but he knew enough to know she wasn't a woman who slept around. Despite that whole sex scandal she'd endured years ago, Nash wasn't convinced she was some crazed nympho.

But he also wasn't naive and he wasn't just an average groom, so he needed to play this safe and protect himself from all angles.

"The baby is yours," she stated, as if she could sense where his thoughts were going. "I haven't been with anybody since months before I even came here."

"I thought you said you were on birth control."

"I am," she countered. "Nothing is foolproof, though. I'm assuming it happened that one time we…"

"Didn't use a condom."

One time in all those secret rendezvous he had thought he'd put one in his wallet, but they'd used it already. They'd quickly discussed how they were both clean, amidst clothes flying all over the loft floor, and they'd come to the mutual decision to go ahead… Thus the reason for this milestone, life-altering talk they were having now.

Emotions, scenarios, endless questions all swirled through his mind. What on earth did he know about babies or parenting? All he knew was how hard his mother worked to keep them in a meager apartment. She'd never once complained, never once acted worried. She was the most courageous, determined woman he'd ever known. Traits she'd passed down to him, which gave him the strength to carry on with his original plans, even with the shocking news of the baby. He would not let his child down, but he had to follow through and take what he had come for.

"I don't expect anything from you, Nash," Lily went on as if she couldn't handle the silence. "But I wasn't going to keep this a secret, either. Secrets always become exposed at the wrong time and I felt you deserved to know. It's up to you whether you want to be part of this baby's life."

Secrets, hidden babies. Wow. The irony kept getting harsher and harsher as if fate was laughing at him. This hurdle she'd placed in front of him really had him at a crossroads. What started out as a fling had now escalated into something personal, intimate…anchoring him in for the long term. Because now he couldn't keep pretending to be someone he wasn't, unfortunately he couldn't come clean with his identity, either.

He wanted to give his child, and Lily, the absolute best of everything. Even though Lily wasn't financially strained, Nash would be front and center in his child's life in every single way. How the hell could he do that without her discovering his identity?

Damn it. He'd never, ever intended for her to be hurt, but he'd passed the point of no return and now the inevitable heartbreak lay in the very near future.

She was never supposed to know who he really was. She was supposed to be gone well before he revealed himself. But now she would be part of his life forever and there was no escaping that hard fact.

"I would never leave you alone in this, Lily." He stepped forward, sliding his hands up over her smooth, bare shoulders. His thumbs caressed the edge of her jaw as an ache settled deep within him, knowing he would cause her even more pain. "How are you feeling? I assume the pregnancy is why you passed out?"

"I'm feeling okay. I've been very nauseous for several days, but this is the first time I've fainted." Her eyes sought his as a smile tugged at her unpainted lips. "I'm glad you were there to catch me."

"Me, too."

He still craved her, ached for her, even with the stunning news. Nash slid his mouth across hers, needing the contact and comfort that only she could provide. When he'd go back to his small rental cottage at night, he'd long for her even though he'd just been intimate with her. Nash had never been swept into such a fast, intense affair before.

And his attraction had nothing to do with her celebrity or her status as one of Hollywood's most beautiful leading ladies. Lily was genuine, not high maintenance or stuffy. Nash honestly admired her. The fact that she was sexy as hell and the best lover he'd ever had was just a bonus.

Her lips moved beneath his, her arms wrapped around his neck as her fingertips toyed with the ends of his hair. Even though they'd been secretly seeing each other for a couple of months, their passion had never once lessened. This woman was so responsive, so perfectly matched for him that he simply couldn't get enough.

Right now they had more pressing issues to deal with… not to mention the ones he had to face on his own.

Damn it. He'd wanted to keep her out of his own sordid affairs and keep things strictly physical. But now Lily discovering the truth about him was unavoidable. There was no way he could avoid the crushing blow that would eventually come down. He could delay the bombshell, weigh his options, because he didn't just have Lily and a baby to think about…he had another family to consider.

Stepping back, Nash studied her, processing just how vulnerable she was right at this moment and knew the end result of his lies would be the same. Once she figured out who he was, she would want nothing to do with him. There was no way in hell he'd be absent from his child's life, though, which meant Lily couldn't be rid of him no matter how much she would come to hate him.

"I'll walk you to your trailer so you can pack your things."

Lily jerked back. "Pack my things?"

"You're coming to stay with me."

Lily completely removed herself from his touch and crossed her arms over her chest. "Stay with you? Why on earth would I do that?"

"So I can take care of you."

Laughing, Lily shook her head. "I'm not dying, Nash. I'm having a baby."

"My baby," he corrected. "I want you with me, Lily."

"How am I going to explain why I'm living with you and not in my trailer? Nobody knows about our affair."

Nash shrugged. "I don't care what they think. I care about your health and our baby."

"Well I care," she all but shouted, throwing her hands to the side. "The media is just waiting to publish something juicy on me. Don't you understand that I have a career, a life, and I can't throw it away because you want to take charge? I've worked too hard to overcome the reputation Hollywood first gave me. I'm no longer the wild child of the industry. I'm respected and I'd like to keep it that way."

Fine, so he was thinking selfishly, but still, he refused to let her go through this alone. Just the thought of his mother being in this position once upon a time had his stomach tightening. Besides, this was Lily. She was a drug in his system and having her close by at all times would only feed their sexual appetite even further.

Maybe he needed to rein in the testosterone. But only for now and only because he refused to back down. He would still find a way to keep her close whether she liked it or not. Yes, he wanted the sex, but now that there was a child involved…he wanted to be right there every step of the way for his son or daughter.

"Fine. I'll come stay with you."

Lily raised a brow and tilted her head. "Seriously, Nash. I'm fine. I'm not going to do anything but sleep and work."

"That's what concerns me," he retorted. "You're getting tired and you're pushing yourself because the film is almost finished. You passed out, for crying out loud."

"I can't stop working."

Moments ago he'd been ready to take her up to the loft. Now he was struggling with how many more lies he would have to tell before this was all over.

Horses shifted in their stalls behind him, the sunset cast a bright orange glow straight through the wide-open stable doors. The setting epitomized calm and serenity...too bad the storm inside him was anything but.

"What about after you're done filming? What will we do about the baby?"

And there it was. The ultimate question that wedged heavily between them, but he had to throw it out there. He had to know what her plans were. He wasn't ready for a family by any means, but considering he and Lily lived on opposite sides of the country, they needed to figure out how they could both be in this child's life.

Lily smoothed her hair away from her face, turned away from him and sighed. "I don't know, Nash. I truly don't know."

They had time to consider how to deal with the baby. For now, Nash needed to stick with his original agenda and nothing could get in his way. He'd done enough spying, enough eavesdropping to calculate his next move.

He'd had many reasons—professional and personal—for taking on a new identity. But the main reason was the horses he needed from Damon. Those horses were the final pieces in the stable he'd spent years creating. He would move heaven and earth to get them.

As he watched Lily, her worried expression, her still-flat belly, Nash came to the realization that the truth he'd come here to disclose had nothing to do with Lily. Yet, because of a decades-old secret, Lily and his baby might pay the price.

All he had to do was figure out a way to get Damon to sell him the horses, go back to his own estate and keep his child in his life.

One monumental obstacle at a time.

Two

Well, she'd lost only part of the battle. She wasn't going back to Nash's place, but he was escorting her to her trailer. And she was almost positive he intended to spend the night.

A thrill shot through her, but would their cover be blown? He'd promised to be up and in the stables working before sunrise so he shouldn't be spotted. She didn't want him to think she was ashamed, far from it. Unfortunately, her reputation was always at stake and after the scandal from years ago, the press would love to see her "backslide" into bad girl mode. She refused to give them any fodder.

Nash knew of the sex video that had been leaked and he knew how sensitive she was about her privacy. Being a very private, secretive person himself only made their hidden affair the perfect setup. They'd been able to sneak around on the private grounds for months now.

Thankfully, the press wasn't on-site because of the security who kept them outside the gates. Still, she worried. What if a member of the crew spotted them together? What if they leaked a story? She couldn't endure another scandal, she just didn't have the energy to fight it, and she wouldn't put her mother through that again.

"Relax." Nash squeezed her hand. "Nobody can see us. It's dark."

He was right. Nobody was around, but she was used to being in the loft of the stables where she was sure no one would see or hear them. Right now, walking across the Barringtons' vast estate to head toward her on-site trailer, Lily just felt so exposed. Their footsteps were light and all was quiet except for an occasional frog croaking, a few crickets chirping and a horse neighing every now and then. They were utterly alone.

Before discovering the baby, Lily had wanted to talk to Nash about her feelings…feelings that had grown deeper than she'd expected. They'd both agreed that everything they shared was temporary and physical, but somewhere along the way her heart had gotten involved. She didn't want to open up now or he'd probably think she was just trying to get a husband to go along with the baby to keep the gossip at bay.

With Nash's rough fingers laced through hers, Lily had to admit she loved the Neanderthal routine when he'd gone all super protective of her. She'd known from the moment she met Nash that he was a man of power, of authority.

Her stepfather had been a man of power, too, waving his money around to get what he wanted. Nash was different, though. He was type A, without all the material possessions. He appealed to her on so many levels; she just wished they weren't facing this life-altering commitment together when they barely knew each other.

Yes, they were compatible in bed—rather, in haylofts— but that didn't mean in her realistic, chaotic world they would mesh well. Added to that, she didn't know if *she* could handle having her passionate nature back in the public eye. Any serious relationship she took out in the open was subject to being exploited.

When they stepped into her trailer, Nash locked the door behind him. The cool air-conditioning greeted them. A small light from the tiny kitchenette had been left on, sending a soft glow throughout the narrow space.

Nash's heavy-lidded eyes met hers. She knew that look, had seen it nearly every night in person, then again in her dreams later. He could make a woman forget all about reality, all about responsibility.

This was the first time he'd been in her trailer and she realized just how broad and dominating his presence truly was. A shiver of arousal slid through her.

"We really should talk about this," she started, knowing she had lost control of this situation the moment she'd agreed to let him come back to her trailer. "I want you to know I didn't trap you."

"I know." He closed the gap between them, barely brushing his chest against hers. "I also know that I want you. I wanted you before you broke the news and I still do. A baby doesn't change the desire I have for you, Lily."

Oh, mercy. When he said things like that, when he looked at her like that...how could a girl think straight? Just one look from beneath those heavy lids framed by dark lashes had her body reacting before he could even touch her. This was why they had to sneak around. No way could she be in public with this man when he looked at her like he was ready to eat her up, and she knew she had that same passionate gaze when she looked at him.

He smelled all masculine and rugged, and pure hardworking man. A man who was gentle with animals and demanding as a lover was pretty much her greatest fantasy come to life. A fantasy she hadn't even known lived within her until she'd met Nash.

"Maybe we shouldn't be doing this," she stated as his fingertips slid up over her chest and started peeling away the elastic top of her dress. "I mean, we have a lot to talk about, right?"

Nash nodded, keeping his focus on his task. "We do,

but right now you're responding to my touch. I can't ignore that. Can you?"

His gaze met and trapped hers. "Unless you're ashamed to have the groom in your trailer."

Lily reached up, squeezing both of his hands. "I've never, ever hinted that I'm ashamed of you, Nash. I'm just not normally a fling girl and whatever we have going on is nobody else's business. That's all. I'm not hiding anything else."

A brief shadow crossed over his face and Lily wondered if she'd imagined it for a moment because just as fast as it came, it was gone.

"I can't deny you," she whispered. "How can this pull still be so strong?"

Nash dipped down, gliding his mouth over the curve of her neck, causing her head to fall back. The rasp of his beard against her bare skin always had tingles shooting all over her body. On occasion he'd trimmed his beard back, but thankfully he'd never fully shaved, because Lily figured she was ruined for smooth faces forever after being with Nash.

"Because passion is such a strong emotion," he murmured as his lips trailed up her neck. "And what we have is too fierce to sum up in one word."

In no time he'd yanked her dress down to pool at her feet. Lily kicked it aside as he quickly worked her free of her strapless bra and panties.

He reached behind his back and jerked his T-shirt up and over his head, tossing it to the side. Those chiseled muscles beneath a sprinkling of dark hair on his chest didn't come from working out in some air-conditioned gym. Nash's taut ripples came the old-fashioned way: from hours of manual labor.

"I love how you look at me," he muttered as he lifted her from the waist and crossed to the end of the trailer with the bed.

He lay her down and stood over her, whipping his belt through the loops of his jeans. Lily didn't know what on earth they were doing. Okay, she knew what they were doing, but wasn't this a mistake? Shouldn't they be discussing the baby? What their plans were for the future?

But when his weight settled over her, pushing her deeper into the thick comforter, Lily relished in the feel of his hard body molding perfectly with hers. Right here, this was the feeling she'd come to crave—the heaviness of him pressing into her in a protective, all-consuming manner.

Nash was right. *Passion* was such a simple word for the intensity of what they shared. But what label did it have? The impulse with which they'd jumped into an affair had overwhelmed them both. They'd never given anything beyond sex another thought.

The truth was, she had feelings for Nash, feelings she didn't think she'd have again for another man. Could she trust her feelings to stand up to public scrutiny? Could she rely on anything she felt that stemmed from a hidden affair?

Giving up her mental volley of trying to have this all make sense, Lily raked her fingers up his back and over his shoulders as he settled between her thighs. Nash had a way to make her forget everything around her, make her want to lock away the moments in time she shared with him. As he entered her, his mouth claimed hers and Lily had no choice but to surrender. Why did every moment with this man make her feel things she'd never felt before?

Nash's hands slid up her sides and over her breasts as her body arched into his. In no time her core responded, tightening as Nash continued to move with her.

After he followed her lead and their bodies stopped trembling, he lifted her in his arms, tucked her beneath the covers and climbed in beside her.

"Rest, Lily." He reached over and shut off the light. "Tomorrow we'll work this out."

Did he mean he'd still try to get her to move into his house? Although his dominance was a turn-on, she wouldn't let him just start taking charge simply because of the baby.

She was still in charge of her own life. Besides, being intimate with a man and living with him were two very different things.

As much as Nash was coming to mean to her, she still had to face reality. She was going to be done filming in about a week and she had a life in LA to get back to.

So where did that leave them?

Well, what a surprise. They'd ended up with their clothes off again and nothing was discussed or planned.

On the upside, she wasn't nauseous this morning…yet.

As she headed toward the makeup trailer, her new agent Ian Schaffer stepped out of one of the cottages on the Barrington estate. Ian had initially come out to the movie set in hopes of getting Lily to sign with his agency, and she did, but then he had gone and fallen in love with one of the beautiful Barrington sisters.

Sweet Cassie, the gentle trainer, and her precious girl, Emily, were both part of Ian's life now and family had never looked so adorable. Ian caught her eye and waved as he headed her way. At some point she'd have to discuss her own family situation with Ian and what this meant for upcoming films…especially since he was already getting several scripts for her to look over.

Too bad none of those movies called for a pukey pregnant heroine. She'd so nail that audition with her pasty complexion and random bouts of profuse sweating.

"You have a second?" he asked.

"Sure." Lily shifted so Ian's height blocked the morning sun. "We're heading into town today to shoot a scene near the flower shop, but I'm not due in wardrobe for a few more minutes. What's up?"

"I have a really good script that came through yesterday I'd like you to look at it." Ian rested his hands on his hips and smiled. "I know we've only worked together for a few weeks, but you had indicated that you'd like to try something different, maybe break away from the softer, family-style roles and into something more edgy. Are you still up for that?"

Lily tilted her head and shrugged. "Depends on the role and the producer. What do you have for me?"

"How would you feel about playing a showgirl who is a struggling single mother?"

Lily froze. "Um…yeah, that's quite the opposite of anything I've done before."

Oh the irony. Showgirl? By the time the movie started filming Lily figured her waistline would be nonexistent. As far as the single mom aspect? She honestly had no clue. Nash claimed he wouldn't leave her, but he'd only been aware of the baby for less than twenty-four hours. Once reality set in would he still feel the same?

"Lily?" Ian eased his head down until his gaze caught hers. "You all right? You don't have to look at the script if that's too far outside your comfort level, but I will say the producers are amazing and the script is actually very well plotted. Aiden O'Neil was just cast as the opposite lead."

Aiden was a great guy, an awesome actor and would be a joy to work with again. But how could she accept this role knowing she couldn't commit to the grueling hours of exercise and perfecting her body that, no doubt, Hollywood would require in order to portray a showgirl?

Lily's eyes drifted over Ian's shoulder and landed on Nash. Now that was a leading man…and he'd sneaked out of her trailer without her noticing. He'd promised to be gone by morning, and he was, but still she'd been a little disappointed not to be able to wake up next to him. Yes, she was quickly losing control over her feelings for Nash and she feared she'd have a hard time keeping them tucked against her heart.

Ian swiveled, glanced across the estate and turned back to Lily. "I'm not sure why you keep hiding what you two have going on."

Lily jerked her attention back to Ian. "Excuse me?"

Shrugging, Ian smiled. "I won't say anything, and honestly I doubt anyone else has picked up on the vibes you two are sending out."

Lily wasn't sure if she was relieved or afraid that someone else knew about her and Nash. Old images of a video she'd thought private played through her mind. That was another time, another man. Nash was trustworthy...wasn't he?

"What is it you think you know?" she asked, crossing her arms over her chest.

"I caught you two in a rather...comfortable embrace about a month ago. I was looking for Cassie and you and Nash were in the stables. I didn't say anything because I know you value your privacy and it was nobody's business what you two do in your downtime."

Lily had thought for sure no one would've spotted them at night and after hours. Thankfully it was only Ian who most definitely had her best interest at heart. As her agent, he didn't want any bad press surrounding her, either. The limelight would stay directed elsewhere, for now.

Blowing out a sigh, Lily nodded. "I don't know what is going on between Nash and me, to be honest. But just keep this between us, okay?"

Ian smiled. "You're my client, and I'd like to think, friend. We all have secrets, Lily. I won't say a word."

Speaking of secrets, she had a doozy. But for now, she would keep the pregnancy to herself. This was definitely something she and Nash needed to work through before sharing the announcement with any outsiders. They were still riding the sexual high, the excitement of being so physically attracted to each other, she had no clue how to discuss something so permanent with him. They were facing a relationship she didn't think either of them was ready for.

"You sure you're okay?" Ian asked.

Pulling out her most convincing smile, Lily nodded and turned to head toward the wardrobe trailer. "Fine. Just ready to relax after this shoot is over."

"Well, when you get a chance, come find me. I'll let you

look over those scripts." He fell into step with her. "I believe the single mom part would be perfect for you, but that's going to depend on how comfortable you are with playing a show-girl. I also have a part that is set in a mythical world, and that also involves bearing a great deal of skin because from what I can see, the women all wear bikini tops and short skirts."

Lily refrained from groaning because here she was, just discovering her pregnancy and already having to choose be-tween her career and her personal life.

How would she juggle this all when the baby came? Even-tually the world would know she was pregnant, then she couldn't keep Nash a secret any longer—couldn't keep her feelings for him a secret. Sooner rather than later, their re-lationship—whatever it became—would be out front and center.

How would he cope? How would they get through this? As a couple? As two people just sharing a child? With the depth of her feelings only growing stronger, Lily worried she was in for a long road of heartache.

Three

It was after midnight and Lily hadn't come to him. He'd spent the night in her trailer, in her arms. So why wasn't she here?

Turning off the lights in the stables, Nash kept to the shadows of the property and headed toward the back of the estate where Lily's trailer sat. He told himself he just wanted to check on her to make sure she was feeling okay. Nash refused to believe he was developing deeper feelings for her. He couldn't afford to be sidetracked right now, not until his plan was fully executed.

He climbed the two steps and glanced over his shoulder to double-check he was alone before giving her door a couple taps with his knuckles. When she didn't answer, he tried the handle, surprised it turned easily beneath his palm. Even with security, keeping the door unlocked wasn't smart. You never knew what length the crazies would go to in order to snap a picture of a celebrity. Money held more power than people gave it credit for.

"You need to keep this locked," he told her as he entered. "Anybody could walk right in."

Lily sat hunched over the small dinette table, papers

spread all around her. When she glanced up at him, tear tracks marred her creamy cheeks.

Fear gripped him as he crossed the small space. "Lily, what happened? Is it the baby?"

Raking her hands through her long, dark hair, she shook her head. "No, no. The baby is fine."

A slight sense of relief swept through him, but still, something was wrong. He'd never seen such fierce emotions from the woman who always appeared so flawless, so in control…except when she surrendered herself to him and she unleashed all of that pent-up passion.

"Then what is it?" he asked, sliding in beside her on the narrow booth.

Her hand waved across the table. "All of this. I'm looking at the future of my career, yet I have no clue what way to go. I'm at a crossroads, Nash, and I'm scared. There's no good answer."

Nash wrapped his arm around her and pulled her against his side. He'd grown used to the perfect feel of her petite body nestled next against his. What he wasn't used to was consoling a woman, delving into feelings beyond the superficial. This was definitely out of his comfort zone and he absolutely hated it. Hated how he'd allowed himself to get in this position of being vulnerable with the threat of being exposed before he was ready.

More than anything else, he hated lying to Lily. She didn't deserve to be pulled into his web of deceit and lies, but now that she was pregnant, there was no other option. He'd already put his plan in motion and he wasn't leaving until Damon Barrington gave up the horses and Nash disclosed his real identity to the man. Nash couldn't wait to see Damon's face when the truth was revealed.

But now he had Lily and a baby to worry about. He sure as hell didn't want innocents caught in the mix. Things had been so simple before, when Lily planned to wrap up filming and go on her way. Everything in her life from this moment on would revolve around their child and he had to figure out a way to make this right…he just had no clue how.

Angst rolled through him at the thought of his own mother feeling even an inkling of what Lily was going through. And his mother had been all on her own. No way would he ever let Lily feel as if she didn't have him to lean on. He wasn't looking for that traditional family, but he wouldn't abandon what was his.

For so long it had been just Nash and his mother. She'd always put his needs first, rarely dating, never bringing a man to the house until Nash was in his late teens when he got engaged and eventually married. She'd always made sure her two jobs covered their bills and a few extras.

In short, she worked her ass off, purposely setting her own needs aside until Nash was old enough to understand and care for himself.

He didn't want to see Lily struggling as a single mother, juggling a career and a child.

Added to that, she was pregnant with *his* child. It would take death to tear him away from what belonged to him. Did he love her? No. Love wasn't in the cards for him, wasn't something he believed in. That didn't mean he didn't already love this child they'd created. Now Nash had to make sure once she discovered the truth, she wouldn't shut him out.

He knew how she loathed liars, how she'd been betrayed by a man in her past. Surely she would see this situation was completely different.

"What are all these papers that have you so upset?" he asked her.

Lily rested a hand on his thigh, tapping a stack with her finger. "Scripts Ian gave me to look over for the next film. He's so excited because this will be our first film together, but everything here would be impossible for me to do until after the baby is born and that's if I get my body back. Hollywood is ruthless when it comes to added pounds."

He kept his opinion about Hollywood and their warped

sense of "beautiful" to himself. Not all women needed to be rails to be stunning and added pounds didn't take away from a woman's talents. Lily was a petite woman, but she had curves in all the right places.

"Why don't you tell Ian that none of these will work for you?"

Lily lazily drew an invisible pattern over his jeans with her fingertips. "I need to tell him about the baby. This has to be my sole focus. My career will have to come second for a while. I only hope I'm not committing career suicide."

Nash smiled and stroked away a strand of hair from her eyes. "I highly doubt this will kill your career. Ian will understand, I'm sure."

Lily scrubbed her hands over her face. "This is my life. I don't know anything else. What do I know about being a mom?"

About as much as he knew about being a dad.

She slid out the other side of the booth and grabbed a bottle of water from the fridge. Nash watched as she twisted off the cap and took a long drink. An overwhelming sense of possession swept through him. This sexy, vibrant woman would soon start showing visible signs of their secret affair.

"You can't keep pushing yourself right now, Lily. It's best you relax."

Her eyes darted to his. "I don't need you coming in here and telling me how I should be reacting. My life is mine alone, Nash. Yes, you're the baby's father, but I need to figure out what to do here. Even if I take some time off, I'm still in the spotlight. I don't want…"

She bit her lip and glanced away. In the soft light casting a glow in the narrow space, Nash saw another fresh set of tears swimming in her eyes. Damn it.

"You don't want the media to know," he murmured.

After a slight hesitation, she nodded, but still didn't meet his gaze. He climbed out of the seat and came up behind her, cupping her shoulders and easing her back against his chest.

"They're going to find out, Lily. What you need to do is make sure you always stay in control." Sliding his arms down, he covered her flat stomach with his hands, still in awe that a life grew inside there. "Don't let them start the gossip. I'm sure you have TV interviews scheduled. Make a big bombshell announcement then. You'll take the wind right out of the press's sails."

Lily turned in his arms. Her eyes met his as she blinked back tears. "That may be the best plan of action. But, I need to tell my mother first."

Her mother. They'd never discussed their parents. That topic usually meant a relationship was building. He and Lily hadn't planned on building on anything. They were enjoying their time together, not thinking of tomorrow.

Tomorrow, however, had caught up with them and smacked them in the face with a good dose of reality.

The fact they were bound forever now sent a bit of uncontrollable fear sliding through him. Whether either of them liked it or not, they were about to delve into personal territory.

Lily could talk about her mother all she wanted. That was most definitely an area in his life he wasn't ready to reveal.

"Does your mother live in LA, too?"

"No, she lives in Arizona in a small, private community that's run by an assisted living facility. She has her own home on the grounds and she's very independent, but if her health gets bad or as she gets older and needs care, she's already set."

Lily stepped back and crossed her arms. "I don't tell people where she is because I want her to have a normal life and not be hassled by the media."

Nash didn't want another reason to be drawn to Lily, but damn it she was protective of her mother. How could he not relate to that? Nash would do anything for his mother…which was why he was still harboring his secret instead of bursting through Damon's front doors and laying it all out on the line.

Part of Nash wished he'd never kept this secret about his life, wished he'd just confronted his past immediately and moved on. But he'd wanted to protect his mother and wanted to move cautiously without making rash decisions. Lily was a different story. He'd seen her, he'd wanted her. Now, here they were, pregnant and discussing parents.

Irony shot at him from so many angles he could hardly keep up. He had been a secret baby, and Lily was expecting a baby that had to remain a secret for now. The best course of action for him would be to complete his original plans and confront Damon.

"Are you going to see your mom as soon as you're done filming here?" he asked.

He needed her gone. He needed her away so he could have a face-to-face with Damon and not have Lily right there witnessing his confession of every single lie he'd told since meeting her. There was no way he could avoid the outcome, but he could at least soften the blow if she weren't present for the bomb he would drop.

He wanted so much, from Damon, from himself…from Lily. In the end, he would have it all. He hadn't gotten this far in his life by sitting idly by and watching opportunities pass. He reached with both hands and took what he wanted.

"I just need to think." She rubbed her head and sighed. "I need to find a doctor. I have no idea where to go. Obviously I should look in LA, but I won't be back there for a while."

"I'll find you one." When she quirked a brow, he added, "I know people in the area. You need a checkup and then you can see a doctor when you get home."

Assuming she went back home after filming wrapped up. Hell, he had no idea what her plans were. Honestly, all they'd managed to work out was how well they fit together intimately. Any discussion beyond that would be a vast change of pace.

"Just get me a name," she told him. "It's going to be nearly impossible to get in and out of a doctor's office here without word getting out about my condition."

Nash's mind was working overtime. He couldn't say too much or she'd know something was off about him and who she believed he was. She had to keep thinking he was just a groom until he could tell her otherwise. The last thing he needed at this point was her, or anyone for that matter, getting suspicious. Still, money talked and he'd use any means necessary to get her the proper care she needed while she was here.

"I bet we could get a doctor to come here, secretly," he offered. "People can be silenced for a price."

Lily's eyes widened. "You're not paying someone to keep quiet. I know how this works, Nash. We just need to find someone who can be discreet."

From her tone and the worry filling her eyes, Nash knew she didn't like the idea of him spending his money on her health care. Little did she know how heavily padded his accounts were. Even if they weren't, even if he did only make groom's wages, he'd spend every last cent if that meant proper care for his baby.

"I'll take care of it," he assured her. "You won't have to worry about a thing."

Lily leaned her shoulder against the narrow kitchenette cabinet and stared at him. "There are so many layers to you," she muttered. "You're all casual and laid-back, yet sometimes you're all business and take-charge. Makes me wonder who the real Nash is."

She'd barely scratched the surface. All too soon those layers would be peeled back one at a time, revealing things that would change lives forever.

Forcing himself to relax, he hooked his thumbs through his belt loops, intending to keep playing the part of groom. "Which Nash do you think I am?"

With a shrug, Lily continued to stare. "I'm not sure. You

just seem more, I don't know, powerful and composed than I thought you'd be about the baby."

In one stride he'd closed the space between them, snaked his arms around her waist and leaned over her so her back arched. "You saying I wasn't powerful when we were in the loft?"

Lily's hands slid up his chest. "Oh, you were powerful, but you didn't have that serious tone you just used."

Nash eyed her mouth, then traveled back up to her eyes. "Trust me, when it comes to someone I care about, I'm very serious."

Lily's tremble vibrated his entire body. He couldn't let her know anything about his real life, but at the same time he had to use his influences to keep her near, keep her and the baby safe. Everything in his life was at stake—things he hadn't even considered a possibility were now major markers on his journey. He'd started down this path with one vision, now suddenly there were forks in the road. Still, he had to stay on track because no matter which way he went, hearts would be ripped apart. Two life-altering secrets would shatter the trust he'd built with everyone around him over the past couple of months.

Even with the odds drastically stacked against him, with the devil in the corner mocking him, Nash had no intention of failing. He'd have it all: the horses, a family, his baby.

Four

"What do you mean he's still not accepting our offer?"

Nash glanced behind him, making sure he was still alone. He'd stepped out of the stables and around the side where he was sure to have privacy when his assistant had called.

Damon Barrington may technically be his boss here, but Nash had a surprise in store for him.

"I know what they're planning," Nash said in a low tone. "I know exactly what he's willing to let go of and what he wants to hold on to. What the hell will it take to get him to sell to me?"

"I think that's the issue," his assistant replied. "You know how he feels about you. He may sell to someone else."

Nash raked a hand through his hair. Yeah, he knew how Damon felt about him. They'd been ongoing rivals in the horse industry and for the past two years or so, but they'd pretty much used their assistants to handle all business dealings between them. That gap in time had only aided in Nash's covert plans. All he'd done was grow a beard, grow his hair longer and put on old, well-worn clothes. Sometimes the easiest way to hide things, or people, was right in plain sight.

Nash had wanted to purchase several of Damon's prize-winning horses, knowing the mogul was set to retire after this season, but Damon kept refusing. Nash needed those horses, needed the bloodlines on his own estate because he'd not been faring well in the races and losing was not an option.

The most recent offer had been exorbitant and Damon still wasn't budging. Stubborn man.

Like father, like son.

"Let me think," Nash said, heading back toward the front of the stables. "I'll call you back."

He slid the phone into his pocket and rounded the corner. Stepping from the shade to the vibrant sun had him pulling his cowboy hat down lower. He needed to figure out what it would take to get Damon to sell those horses to him because Nash had never taken no for an answer and he sure as hell wouldn't start now.

Pulling the pitchfork off the hook on the wall, Nash set out to clean out the stalls at the end of the aisle. Tessa and Cassie had taken two of the coveted horses out for a bit which gave him time to think and work without distractions.

What if someone else called Damon's assistant and made an offer? Would the tenacious man consider the generous offer then if he knew the horses weren't going to his rival?

Nash shoved the pitchfork into the hay, scooped out the piles and tossed them into the wheelbarrow. He missed his own estate, missed doing the grunt work with his own horses, in his own lavish stables. But he'd left his groom in charge and knew he could trust the man.

Only Nash's assistant knew where he was and that he was trying to spy on the Barringtons in an attempt to buy them out. But even his right-hand man wasn't aware of the other secret that had Nash uncovered here. Nobody knew and until he was ready to disclose his full plan, he had to keep it that way.

If Damon hated him before, how would the elderly man feel once he discovered the real truth?

By the time the first stall was clean, sweat trickled down his back. Nash pulled his hat off, tugged his T-shirt over his head and slapped his hat back on. He didn't often take his shirt off during workdays, but the day was almost done and the heat was stifling. He'd even gotten used to the itchiness of his beard after endless hours of working in this heat.

After both stalls were ready to go, Nash put all the materials away. Damon kept a clean, neat stable—something they had in common.

Nash didn't want to admit they had anything in common, but over the past several months since he had been on the Barrington estate, he'd seen Damon many times, seen how he treated his family, the crew filming there. But Nash hadn't allowed himself to get swept into that personal realm. He was here for a job, both as a groom and as a businessman.

Nash's last order of business was sweeping the walkway, ridding it of the stray straw and dust. The chore didn't take long, but had him sweating even more. He pulled the T-shirt from his back pocket and swiped it across his neck and chest.

"Have you ever thought of doing calendars?"

Nash jerked around to see the object of his every desire standing in the stable entryway, the sunlight illuminating her rich hair, her curvy build.

"What are you doing here?"

"Is Cassie around?"

"She's out riding." He took a step closer, since no one was around and he couldn't resist. So, he'd actually found one thing he had absolutely no control over. "You all right?"

With a soft smile, she nodded. "Yeah. I have a short break between scenes and I needed to ask her something."

Fisting his shirt, Nash crossed his arms over his chest. "Care to elaborate?"

"I'm asking her what doctor she used while she was pregnant, if you must know," she whispered.

"I already found out and you have an appointment." He'd had to do some sneaky digging, or rather his assistant did, but he'd been able to find the doctor in town who Cassie had seen for her pregnancy. "I was going to tell you this evening because I wasn't sure of your schedule today."

Her eyes raked over his bare chest and he didn't mind one bit being the recipient of her visual lick. "Keep looking at me like that and people are going to know more about us than we want them to."

Her eyes snapped up to his. "I can't even think when you're working like that," she muttered, gaze darting back down to his bare chest. "But thank you for arranging the doctor. When is he coming?"

"*She* will be here on Thursday."

Lily nodded. "That will be great. We're supposed to finish filming Thursday, but they may have something else for me to do last minute. I'll make sure I'm free, though."

"We're meeting at my house so there's no question as to why she's here."

"Taking control again?" A corner of Lily's lips kicked up into a grin. "This once I don't mind and if we were alone, I'd show you how grateful I am for you taking care of this."

Damn, his body responded immediately and he couldn't wait to get back to her trailer. "We'll be alone later and I'll let you."

At first all the sneaking around had been exciting, thrilling. Of course, that part was still arousing, but they basically knew nothing about each other. All he'd wanted was to confront his past, secure his future and now he was dealing with a whole new future.

Lily was an amazing woman, there was no denying that fact. But that didn't make him ready to settle down and play house, either. Could he see himself with someone like her? Considering they only knew each other in the bedroom, sure. Reality might be a different story.

Why the hell was he thinking like this? They were having a baby, that didn't mean they had to register for monogrammed towels.

"Hey, Lily."

Nash turned to see the beautiful Barrington sisters as they led their horses into the stalls.

"Hi, Cassie, Tessa." Lily walked around him, sending her signature scent of lilac straight through him. "I had a break from filming and thought I'd come see you guys since I rarely get in here."

Good save.

Nash went on with his duties, trying to ignore the feminine laughter of the three women in his life…only two of them had no clue just how close to him they were.

He'd created a complete and utter mess and he had to gain control and figure out how the hell to keep his plans and deception from blowing up in his face.

As much as he didn't want to admit it, he'd come to care for this family. Even though he hadn't let them in beyond work, he knew these sisters, saw the love their father had for them, witnessed bonding moments when they thought no one was around.

They were a family. A tight-knit, perfectly woven-together family. And when Nash ended up besting Damon, Nash had no clue where that would leave him in the family tree.

Ridding her body of her meager breakfast of dry toast was not a promising start to her day. It was the final day of shooting and Lily just wanted to crawl back into bed and tell the crew to do the scene without her. With her stomach revolting, she didn't care that she was the female lead, she just wanted to lie in her bed and die, because she was positive that's what was happening.

She was already fifteen minutes late for hair and makeup. She was never late. Some actors and actresses had a reputation for being divas while filming, often times making the rest of the crew wait on them, but Lily had prided herself on being professional. Her time wasn't worth any more than any other person's on set.

She slapped her sunglasses on, hoping to hide the dark

circles until she got to the makeup chair. She'd had enough energy to throw on her strapless maxi dress and flip-flops before heading out. But her mind wasn't on filming. Besides the baby, Lily was seriously starting to worry about her and Nash.

Her and Nash? Why did they instantly click like a couple inside her mind?

Because that's the way her mind—and her heart—had started leaning. The man exuded strength, not just in his physical job, but with everything he did. Since he found out about the baby he'd been ready to control every aspect of this pregnancy, to anticipate her every need. And, as much as it pained her to admit it, his dominating presence only deepened her attraction to him.

There was so much to the man and she wanted to discover it all. She completely trusted him with her body, now she wanted to see if she could trust him with more.

What did he want? Did he want more with her? If he did, would he be able to handle the very public life she led? One worry after another cycled through her head.

The overcast clouds were about as cheery and pleasant as she felt at the moment. She really hoped the first trimester passed quickly and she was a textbook case pregnancy because, while she was excited about the little life growing inside her, she was so over feeling carsick, as if she was riding a roller coaster and spinning in circles all at once.

Adding all of that to the uncertainty about Nash and what move they would take next was about to break her.

"I was just coming to check on you." Ian fell into step beside her. "Everything okay?"

Tears pricked her eyes. Was everything okay? Not really. She was pregnant by a man she knew little about and she was falling in love with him. That chaotic mess had somehow become her life and she had no clue how to sort out all these emotions to make sense of things.

Ian stared at her, waiting on her to answer. Shoving her

hair away from her shoulders, Lily blinked back tears, thankful for the sunglasses.

"I wasn't feeling very well this morning."

He gripped her elbow and pulled her gently to a stop. "You're looking a little pale. Are you okay?"

Lily sniffed and shook her head. "No, I'm not, but I will be."

Ian's brows drew together as he glanced around, then focused back on her. "You're crying. That's not okay. Did something happen with your mom?"

"No, my mom is fine."

Lily reached beneath her sunglasses and swiped the tips of her fingers at the tears just starting to escape. Why couldn't she control her emotions? She just wanted to wrap up this day of filming and go back to her trailer where she could think of how to gently let Nash know she was developing stronger feelings for him.

"If you're sick, maybe I should see about putting your scene off. A few more hours shouldn't make a difference."

A few hours? She needed a few weeks, or months, depending on how long this state of feeling like death lingered. Of course by that time she'd resemble a whale which would totally knock her out of playing Rose Barrington.

"A few hours won't make a difference, but thanks."

She sniffed again, desperately needing a tissue. Wow, if the paparazzi could only see her now. Sniffling, crying and looking like pure hell. They'd make up something akin to Starlet Hooked on Drugs or The Girl Next Door Reverts Back to Her Wild Days as their top story.

"Does this have to do with Nash?" he whispered. "You seem really upset for just not feeling well. Did he do something?"

Hysterical laughter burst through her as more tears flowed. Yeah, she was officially a disaster and she was totally falling apart in front of her new agent. An agent who had flown all the way out here to convince her to sign with his agency…the poor man was probably reconsidering his decision even though in the short time they'd been official, they had come to think of each other as good friends.

So instead of letting him continue to think she'd gone completely insane, she blurted out, "I'm pregnant."

Ian's eyes widened for only a second before he wrapped his arm around her shoulder and pulled her into a friendly hug.

"I assume this is Nash's?"

Lily nodded against his shoulder and held on to his arms. "Nobody knows. Please keep the news to yourself until I tell you otherwise."

"Of course." He gave her shoulder a slight squeeze, then stepped back. "Is this why you haven't gotten back to me on either of those scripts?"

His smile warmed her and she nodded. "I'm so torn. I have no clue what work you can find for me and I just don't know how I'll manage with being pregnant or even what will happen when the baby comes."

Ian kept his grip on her shoulders and tipped his head down to look her straight in the eye. "Listen, this news is a shock to you now, but you are a strong woman. Actresses have babies all the time. You will do just fine and I've no doubt I'll find work for you. Never worry about that. That's my job. Okay?"

The strong wind had her hair dancing around her shoulders. Lily shoved the wayward strands behind her ears. "I need to get to hair and makeup. I'm really late now. Thanks for understanding and for keeping my secret."

Ian dropped his hands. "You go on. I'm going to see Nash because he's been shooting death glares at me from the stables since we stopped to talk."

Wrapping her arms around her waist, Lily smiled. "He's a bit protective."

"Looks like a man in love to me."

Love? No. Lust? Yes. They weren't near the stage for love to enter the equation—well, she was teetering on the brink. Their sexual chemistry was completely off the charts, though.

"Tell him I'll see him later and that I'm fine," she told Ian. "He worries like my mother."

With a soft chuckle, Ian nodded. "Will do."

Ian walked toward the stables and Lily paused briefly to stare at Nash. Even from across the wide concrete drive and the side yard, she could see the stone-solid look on his face. That wasn't jealousy. What did he have to be jealous of, anyway? Yes, they were having a baby together, but they'd still made no commitment to each other.

Why shouldn't they try for more? Why couldn't she just tell him what she wanted? She wasn't asking for a ring on her finger. This innocent baby wouldn't be caught in the middle. Lily wanted her child to have security and the love of both parents whether they were together or not. She had to figure out how Nash felt about her beyond the sexual aspect.

But she had a feeling she knew how his mind worked. A man like Nash wouldn't let go of anything that belonged to him and since this baby was his, she knew he wouldn't let go of her, either.

This could be an opportunity to see if she was ready for something long-term with the man who had literally turned her world upside down.

Five

Nash had no idea how nervous he had been about this appointment until he closed the door behind the doctor once the checkup was done. Now he and Lily were alone in his rental house which was only a few miles from the Barrington estate.

The baby was healthy with a good, strong heartbeat. Lily's blood pressure was a bit on the high side and the doctor warned about too much stress and urged her to rest for the next few weeks until the next appointment. Nash vowed silently to make sure Lily was relaxed, pampered and wanted for nothing as long as she was here. And she would stay here for the next few weeks…if not longer. They hadn't really discussed her living arrangements, but Nash wasn't backing down on this matter. His child would stay under his roof for now.

The movie had officially wrapped up yesterday and Lily was free. Which meant he had some decisions to make. This wasn't just about Nash and Lily anymore. An innocent baby would be coming into this world soon and would depend on his or her parents to provide a stable, loving home.

When he stepped back into the living room, Lily was reclining on the leather chaise in the corner, pointing the re-

mote toward the flat screen hanging above the stone mantel.
He may be using this home as a prop for his plan, but that
didn't mean he couldn't decorate it according to his style
and his needs, just on a smaller scale. His designer had done
quick work before Nash moved in and everything was perfect for a single groom who splurged only on a few necessi-
ties. A large television was a necessity.

When Lily had mentioned how nice his home was, he'd
indicated the place came already furnished. A small lie piled
atop all the others he'd doled out since he'd put his plan into
motion. At this point, what was a white lie about decor in
the grand scheme of things?

Lily's vibrant eyes shot to his, a smile spread across her
face as he approached. "I know I should still be scared,
or nervous, or whatever, but I'm just so happy the baby is
healthy."

Resting his hip next to her bare legs on the chaise, Nash
settled his hand on her calf and rubbed from her ankle to
her knee. "There's no rule book that states you have to feel
a certain way."

Lily rested her head against the arm, her hair falling over
her shoulder, framing her natural beauty. This was how he
preferred her. Not made up for a shoot with perfectly sprayed
hair, but fresh-faced, hair down and wearing a casual dress.
He loved how she didn't worry about her looks, didn't fuss
with herself just because she came from the land where ap-
pearances were more valuable than talent.

Small-town life suited her and Nash wasn't immune to
the fact he was starting to like how well she blended into his
world...or the world he'd created for his charade.

How would she look in his real home? In his grand master suite that had a balcony overlooking the fields? The need
to make love to her beneath the dark sky slammed into him.
He wanted her on his estate, not in the rental home that was
merely a prop for a life that wasn't even his.

"I'm pretty calm right now." She rested her hand on his

thigh, her dainty pink polish striking against his dark denim. "The film is done, the baby is fine."

Lily's hand came up, her fingertip traveled over the area between his brows. "Why the worry lines?"

Where to start? Did he confess now that he'd lied about his identity all along? Did he tell her he had more money than she ever thought possible and that this house, even his name, was one giant cover to keep him trudging forward with his master plan?

Did he truly want to see all that hurt in her eyes when he came clean about his life, that nearly every single thing he'd ever told her had been false?

Damn it, he hated he'd become *that* man. Hated that he would inevitably crush her. He didn't want her to look at him in disgust, but the moment would come and there wasn't a damn thing he could do about it. All he could do was stall, earn her trust outside of the bedroom.

Whether he wanted to face the fact or not, his feelings for her were growing deeper and damn if that didn't complicate things even further.

He'd thought getting her out of his system, then out of his life after the film was over, would be a piece of cake. His secrets could've remained just that from her and he could've revealed them once she was gone.

Yet here he was, tangled in his own web of lies, becoming more and more restricted with each passing day, each new lie, and finding himself sinking deeper into a woman he knew only intimately.

"Just worried about you." And that was the absolute truth. "With your blood pressure on the high side, I just want to make sure you take it easy."

Her hand slid over his stubbled cheek. "I'm taking it easy right now."

Easing forward, craving more of her touch, Nash slid his hand up over her knee, beneath the soft cotton dress and over her thigh. "I intend for you to take it easy until your next appointment."

Lily stilled, her hand falling into her lap. "Nash, I can't stay that long. I have a life in LA, a job, my mother is in Arizona...I can't just stay here and forget all of my obligations."

"You can take a break," he insisted. "You heard the doctor. A month off will be good for you and you don't have another film to get to, right?"

Lily shrugged, her eyes darting to her lap where she toyed with the bunched material of her dress. "I can't stay here with you, Nash. This baby is real. I can't just play house."

"You can." His eyes held hers as he leaned closer, nipped her lips and eased back. "You can stay for today." He nipped again. "And tomorrow."

He wasn't ready to play house yet, either, but he also wasn't letting her go.

"Reality is so hard to face when you're touching me," she murmured against his lips. "I don't even know what to do next."

Nash eased back and winked. "I've got a good idea."

"Does it involve the kitchen?" she asked with a crooked grin.

Giving her thigh a squeeze, Nash leaned back. "I thought you were nauseous?"

"Right now I'm starving."

Nash came to his feet and glanced down to her. The way she all but stretched out over the chaise, her dress hitched up to near indecent level, her hair spread all around her, she was sexy personified and had no clue the power she held.

And she was pregnant with his child. He never imagined just how much of a turn-on that would be.

Mine. That's all he could think right at this moment and the revelation nearly had his knees buckling

"What are you in the mood for?" he asked, trying to focus.

"Grilled cheese."

"Grilled cheese? Like bread, butter and a lot of fatty cheese?"

"You saying I can't have that?" she asked, quirking a brow as if daring him to argue.

"Not at all." With a laugh, he held his hands up in defense. "I'm just shocked that's what you're asking for."

"Grilled cheese is just one of my weaknesses," she told him. "All that gooey cheese and crispy bread."

Something so simple, yet a fact he hadn't known about her. Which just proved he really didn't know much about the mother of his child except how to excite her, how to get her to make those sweet little moans, how to make her lids flutter down just before she climaxed.

"One grilled cheese coming right up," he declared, quickly heading toward the kitchen before he took what he wanted, which was Lily all laid out beneath him.

He was serious about wanting her there, wanting her to stay with him until they figured out a game plan. So that meant he needed to take the time to learn more about her and not just how fast he could peel down those strapless sundresses she seemed so fond of.

As much as he wanted to learn about her, he was terrified she'd be wanting to learn more about him.

Which begged the ultimate question. Did he come clean or continue this farce for as long as possible?

Ever the gentleman, Nash had put her bags from her on-site trailer in his guest bedroom. He was giving her the option of staying in a room by herself or sleeping with him.

This baby had them taking every step carefully, moving from a hot, steamy affair into something more…calm.

Lily slid her hand over her still-flat stomach and took in the cozy bedroom with its pale gray walls, dark furniture and navy bedding. The fact that she was pregnant with his child and trying to figure out where to sleep was really absurd.

Lily turned, smacking into the hard, firm wall of Nash's

chest. His bare, gloriously naked, tanned, taut muscular chest. Would she ever tire of looking at this man? Would her body's fierce response always be so overwhelming? When she was with Nash she couldn't think, let alone figure out a future or make decisions. He aroused her, made her ache and crave his touch, and he'd managed to start working his way into her heart. Strong, firm hands gripped her bare arms in an attempt to steady her as her eyes held on to the tantalizing view before her.

"I'm going to assume by the way you're looking at me that you're not sleeping in the guest room."

Lily's eyes traveled up to see the smirk, the dark lifted brows. "Did you parade in here half-naked on purpose to sway my decision?"

With his focus on her lips, the tips of his fingertips slid over her sensitive breasts and down her torso to grip her hips and pull her flush against his strong body.

"It wouldn't take much persuasion to get you in my bed," he murmured against her lips. "The decision up to you."

She never grew tired of his hard body against hers. Lily flattened her palms against his chest. "I'd love to sleep in your bed, but I need you to know that I have no clue what's happening between us. I mean, I know I have feelings for you that go beyond sex. And that was before the baby. I don't know what to do now and I have no clue how you're feeling."

Great, now she was babbling and had turned into that woman who needed emotional reassurance. She'd also exposed herself a bit more than she'd intended.

Shaking her head, she slid her arms up around his neck and laced her fingers together. "Never mind. I'm not looking for you to say anything or make some grand declaration. I guess I'm just still scarred from trusting the wrong man a long time ago."

Of course she'd redeemed herself, but Lily had no doubt if she slipped up the media would be all too quick to resurrect that footage her then "boyfriend" had taken of her in the bedroom.

"You can trust me," Nash told her, sliding his hands up and down her back. "I know you're worried about the future, but you can trust that I will always take care of you and our baby. Never doubt that."

The strong conviction in his tone had her believing every word he said. "You must've had some really amazing parents for you to be so determined and loyal."

A sliver of pain flashed through those icy blue eyes. "My mother was the strongest woman I've ever known. She's the driving force behind everything good in my life."

"And your father?"

Nash swallowed as he paused. Silence hovered between them and Lily realized she probably should just learn to keep her mouth shut. But she wanted to know more about Nash. He was the father of her child, for pity's sake. They were bound together for life and eventually, little by little, they had to start opening up. "I never knew my father."

Lily's heart broke for him as she smoothed his messy hair away from his face. "I'm sorry. My father passed when I was younger, so I know a little about that void."

Click. Another bond locked into place and her heart slid another notch toward falling for this man.

"So it was just you and your mother, too?"

That scenario would've been better, actually. After all she and her mother had lived through, being alone would've been for the best.

"No." Lily slid from his arms and went to her bag to pull out a nightgown. She hated discussing her stepfather. "My mother was a proud woman, but we were pretty poor and she ended up marrying for financial stability."

A shrink would love diving into her head. The stepfather had virtually ruined her for any man with money and power. Settling down with someone as controlling as that wasn't an option. Lily would rather be alone than to be told how to live her life.

Lily kept her back to Nash as she pulled her strapless maxi dress down to puddle at her feet before she tugged her silky chemise on. For now her sexy clothes still fit.

"She probably wouldn't have married Dan had it not been for me," she told him, turning back around. "Mom was worried how she would keep our house, keep up her two jobs and keep food and clothes coming."

Picking up her discarded dress, she laid it on the bed and crossed back to Nash. "He was a jerk to her. Treated her like a maid instead of a wife. Treated me like I didn't even exist, which was fine because I didn't want a relationship with him anyway. But I loathe him for how he treated my mother."

Nash pulled her into his arms, surrounding her with the warmth and security she'd hardly known. This sense of stability was something she could easily get used to, but could she trust her emotions right now? Passion was one thing, but to fully rely on someone else, to trust with her whole heart… she wanted that more than anything.

"He's probably sorry he treated you like that now that you're famous."

Lily laughed and eased back to look him in the eyes. "I wouldn't know. He left my mother several years ago, just as I was getting my start. He took all the money, even what she'd worked for. He was always a greedy money whore. Money never meant anything to me, still doesn't. It doesn't define me, but I saw the evil it produced."

Nash's arms tightened on her again. "Money isn't evil, Lily. It's what a person chooses to do with it that can be evil."

"Yeah, well I choose to keep my mother comfortable in a nice home that's in a gated community where she can have her privacy and not worry. Other than that, I don't need it."

"So if I were a rich man you wouldn't have looked my way twice?" he joked.

Lily laughed. "Oh, you still would've caught my atten-

tion. I've just always promised myself I wouldn't get involved
with anyone like my stepfather."

Nash squeezed her tighter. "Not all men are like your
stepfather."

"Don't defend him."

Nash's chuckle vibrated through her. "I'm not, baby. I'm
defending all of mankind."

Lily snuggled deeper into his embrace, wondering what
path they were starting down. The last time her passion had
bested her, she'd ended up across the internet, on the news
and every magazine willing to make money off her bad decisions. Karma had intervened and her ex hadn't made it
very far in the industry. She couldn't help but take a little
satisfaction.

Now her passion had cornered her again. This time the
consequences were far greater than a soiled reputation. She
was going to be in charge of another life. How long would
Nash want to be in the baby's life? Would he honestly be a
hands-on father? He hadn't grown up with a dad so perhaps
he truly did want to give this child a better life.

Lily hated all the unknowns that surrounded them, but
her doctor said she needed to relax and she would do anything to ensure a healthy baby. Maybe she hadn't planned
on a child, but the reality was, she was going to have one.
There was a little being inside of her right now with a heartbeat of its own, growing each and every day. Angry as she
may be at herself for allowing this to happen, she couldn't
deny that she loved this baby already. If that meant relaxing with Nash for the next several weeks or even months,
she wouldn't argue.

She'd wondered how they would work if they tried
for something more serious, more than just ripping each
other's clothes off at every opportunity. How would they
mesh together in reality?

Looked like she was about to get her chance to find out.

Six

He was screwed. Royally, utterly screwed. He'd wanted to open up to her, wanted to start paving the way for an honest relationship. Or at least some type of relationship, considering she was carrying his child and he was developing stronger feelings for her.

Nash still couldn't put a title on whatever they had going because all their "relationship" consisted of so far was hot, fast sex in a stable loft and a surprise baby. He didn't know what the hell the next logical step would be because nothing about the entire past two months had been logical.

But Lily deserved the truth and Nash was too much of a coward to give it to her. He'd had an opening last night when they'd been halfway clothed and just talking. Such an emotionally intimate moment hadn't happened between them before, but that moment slipped by about as quickly as he'd taken off her silky gown. Yet again, he'd let passion override anything else. His need to have her consumed him and he didn't even try to push it aside and reveal his secrets.

Desire was easier to deal with than the harsh realities waiting them both.

Even when she'd spent the night in his bed, he had time to open up. Yet here he was making breakfast on a Saturday morning like some domestic family man when so many secrets hovered between them.

Soon, he'd reveal the truth—or at least all he was able to.

Damn it. He wanted more from her than sex. He hadn't expected this…whatever "this" was. The fact so many lies lay between them only cheapened anything they would start to build together, but being stuck between the rock and the proverbial hard place was a position he'd wedged himself into. And he wasn't going to be able to come out any time soon.

How the hell was he supposed to know he'd start actually wanting more from Lily? He hadn't planned on a baby, hadn't planned on Lily being a permanent fixture in his life. Of course now she'd be part of his life no matter what, but beyond the baby, he wanted more.

Nash scooped up the cheesy, veggie-filled omelet and slid it onto the plate. After pouring a tall glass of juice, he headed toward the bedroom where he'd left Lily sleeping.

Gripping the plate and glass, Nash turned into the bedroom and froze in the doorway at the seductive sight before him. Those creamy shoulders against his dark sheets had his body responded instantly. He never had a woman pull so many emotions from him, have him so tangled in knots and have him questioning every motive he had for furthering his career.

But Lily had a power over him that scared him to death, because once she uncovered all of his secrets—and there were many—she'd never want to see him again. Now that he'd realized he wanted more from her, he also had another revelation—Lily would end up hurt in the end and because he was slowly opening to her, he would be destroyed, as well.

He had nobody to blame but himself.

Being cut from her life, from their child's life was not an option. She may hate men who used money and power to get what they wanted, but he wouldn't back down, not when his child was the central point.

Nash moved into the room, setting the plate and glass on the nightstand. Easing down onto the bed, Nash rested his hip next to hers. Those sheets had never looked better, gliding over and across Lily's curves and silky skin, making her look like a pinup model.

The urge to peel down those covers and reveal her natural beauty overwhelmed him. He'd gotten her from the trailer to his rental home. He was easing her into his life slowly. The ache to be closer to her exploded inside him. He had to touch her, had to feel that delicate skin beneath his rough hands.

Nash's fingertips trailed over Lily's bare arm, leaving goose bumps in the path. Even in sleep she was so responsive to his touch.

Lily stirred, her head shifting toward him, strands of dark hair sliding across her shoulder, and her lids fluttered open. For the briefest of seconds a smile spread across her face before she threw back the covers and sprinted to the adjoining bath.

Morning sickness. Nash hated that there wasn't a damn thing he could do to make her feel better.

He pushed off the bed and padded barefoot across the hardwood floor toward the bathroom. He reached into the cabinet beside the vanity, grabbed a cloth and wet it with cold water before turning to her. He may not be able to stop her misery, but he could at least try to offer support.

Nash pulled her hair back, reaching around to place the cold cloth on her forehead. Hopefully that would help the nausea.

"Go away, Nash," she muttered as she tried to take her hair from his grip. "I don't want you here."

Too damn bad. He wasn't leaving.

After a few more minutes, Lily started to rise and Nash slid his arm around her waist and pulled her up. Limp, she fell back against his chest, resting her head on his shoulder. The way her body fitted against his always felt so right, so perfect. Would he ever be ready to let her go?

"I'm sorry," she murmured. "This is not a side of me I wanted you to see."

Splaying his hand across her abdomen, Nash kissed her temple. "Don't hide from me, Lily."

She covered his hand with her own. "I just wish I knew what we were doing. Where we were going."

That made two of them. For now they had a baby to focus on and the passion that was all-consuming whenever they were close to each other. They may not have the ideal setup or even an idea of what to do next, but they had something.

"I'm not going anywhere," he assured her. "And you're going back to bed. You need to keep up your strength and I made you breakfast."

Lily groaned. "I can't eat. The thought of food makes my stomach turn."

"You'll make yourself even sicker if you don't get something in you."

Without a warning, he bent down, snaked an arm behind her knees and another supported her back as he scooped her up and carried her back into bed.

"You're really taking this role of caring for me to the extreme." She slid her arms around his neck and closed her eyes. "But I'm too tired to argue. When I feel better in a couple hours we'll discuss this caveman persona you've taken on."

Smiling, Nash eased down onto the rumpled bed. "I'll take the eggs away if you think you can't eat, but at least drink."

Nash took the plate into the kitchen and dumped the contents into the trash. By the time he got back to her, she was propped up against the headboard, sheet pulled up and tucked beneath her arms. The glass of juice was about a quarter of the way gone.

And she was holding his gold designer watch in her hand.

Her eyes sought his across the room. "This is a pretty nice watch," she told him, setting it back down on the nightstand.

Damn it. He'd completely forgotten he'd left that out.

"Thanks. It was a gift."

Not a lie. One of his own jockeys had bought that for him several years ago after a big win.

"For a groom you have a pretty impressive house, too," she said, settling deeper into the pillows. "You must be really good at managing money."

He knew she wasn't fishing, but he also knew he was treading a thin line here. He had to open up about some things or she'd really start to wonder if he was hiding things from her.

Stepping farther into the room, he shrugged. "I don't really have anything to spend my money on. I'm not married, I don't travel or buy lavish things. I work, I come home."

Okay, that last part was a complete lie. But he really was a good manager of money. Because he came from nothing, watching every dollar was deeply instilled into him at a young age.

"How you feeling now?" he asked, desperate to switch topics.

"Good. You know, I do plan on getting up, showering and possibly doing something today." She took another sip of juice before focusing on him as he sank down on the edge of the bed beside her. "Just want you to be aware that I don't plan on sitting on my butt for the next seven months."

"I'll take you anywhere you want to go."

Lily sighed. "I'd like to go into town. There were some cute little boutiques I saw when we were filming, but if I go, I'll be recognized."

Nash rested his hand on her sheet-covered thigh. "If you want to go somewhere, I'll get you there and you won't be bothered."

Quirking a brow, Lily sat her near-empty juice glass on the nightstand. "And how will you do that? Because I'd love to be able to shop for just an hour."

Keeping his plan of action to himself, Nash shot her a grin. "Consider it done."

With the slightest tilt of her head, Lily narrowed her eyes. "You're planning something."

Easing forward, Nash ran a fingertip down her cheek, her neck and to the swell of her breast. "I am. But your job is to feel better, take your time getting ready and just let me know when you're done. I have nothing to do today but be at your service."

Her wide eyes slid over his bare chest, a smile danced around unpainted lips. "Sounds like I better rest up for an eventful day."

Because his body still hadn't gotten the memo that he needed to chill, Nash came to his feet. "I'm going to clean up in the kitchen. Yell if you need anything."

He cursed himself all the way down the hall. Lust, sex, it was always there, hovering between them. She was pregnant with his child, which was a hell of a turn-on, but this wasn't the time to worry about how soon he could have her again. He had to find a way to lessen this instant, physical pull between them. They'd indulged in an affair for months and where had that gotten them?

Too much was at stake, too many lives hinged on his next move.

He needed to touch base with his assistant, needed to send a final offer to Damon Barrington because Nash refused to settle for anything less than he came here for. He had an agenda and he had to stick with it or he'd lose it all.

She had no clue how he did it, she really didn't care.

Lily strolled out of the last boutique with bags in hand and headed toward Nash's truck parked in the back alley. He'd gone in with her, even helped her shop and offered pretty good advice when she would try on things.

Who was this guy? She'd never met a man who actually added input on a woman's purchases. He didn't sit out in his truck, he didn't ask her if she was almost done and he didn't act bored even one time. In fact, in one store he found a blue dress which he threw over the dressing room door, telling her it would look great on her.

Guess what? He'd been right. Not only that, the dress was stretchy and flowy. Perfect for that waistline that would be disappearing in the very near future.

Still, she was trying to put a label on him and so far there were just too many layers. No way could such an intriguing man be narrowed down to just one appealing trait. She could only assume his eye for fashion, his nurturing side and his patience came from being raised by a single mother.

And it was his take-charge, powerful side that must have stemmed from wanting to care for his mother. How could she fault that? How could she even think he was anything like her stepfather? Control was one thing, being protective was another.

Nash pulled the passenger side door open, took her bags and placed them in the extended cab part of the truck before offering his hand and helping her up into the seat.

Lily smiled, her eyes level with his now. "Such a gentleman."

"My mama raised me right," he told her, grabbing the seat belt and reaching across her to fasten it. His hands lingered over her breasts as he adjusted the strap. "Better keep you safe."

"Well, my boobs are fine so you can stop," she laughed. "I take back my gentleman compliment since you just wanted to cop a feel."

Nash's flirty smile had her heart clenching tighter. "You wouldn't want some stuffy gentleman. You like the way I can make you lose control."

Standing in the open truck door, Nash's hand traveled over her leg to slide up under her cotton skirt. "Boring and mundane isn't for you."

Not at all. She always thought she wanted someone who was down-to-earth, more trustworthy than the jerk who exploited her innocence years ago. She never thought she'd find someone who was so laid-back, loyal and had the ability to set her body on fire with such simple gestures. Finding the complete package had never crossed her mind.

When she'd started the affair, she'd definitely gone for appealing. Now she was discovering there was so much more than she'd ever bargained for when it came to Nash.

Lily's breath hitched as Nash's fingers danced across her center. Instantly she parted her legs without even thinking. His mouth, just a breath away from hers, had her aching for that promise of a kiss. Never had she desired or craved a man with such intensity.

"Did you have fun today?" he asked, his hand still moving over her silk panties.

"Yes," she whispered. "What are you doing?"

His eyes darted down to where she was fisting her skirt with both hands. "Getting you ready."

"For what?"

Nash nipped at her lips before breathlessly moving across her cheek to whisper in her ear, "Everything I've ever wanted."

His confident declaration had her shivering. Her head fell back against the seat as her lids closed. This man was beyond potent, beyond sexy and quickly becoming a drug she couldn't be without.

Seconds later he removed his hand, smoothed down her skirt and captured her mouth with his. Lily barely had time to grip his arms before he eased back, his forehead resting against hers.

"You think I'm everything you've ever wanted?" she asked, worried what he'd say, but unable to keep the question inside.

"I think you're everything I didn't know I was looking for and more than I deserve."

Slowly, Nash stepped back, closed the door and rounded the hood.

Well, that was intense. Now she was achy, confused and had questions swirling around in her mind. There was no doubt he could turn her on with whispered words, the tilt of his head with that heavy-lidded stare or a feather-light touch. But she wanted more. The man obviously cared about her or he wouldn't have gone to so much trouble to get her in his home, get her out of the house without being seen by too many people and care for her while she'd been sick.

He didn't have to do all of that, yet he did, never once asking for anything in return.

Added to that, he'd just hinted at his deeper emotions and she had a feeling he had shocked himself with his declaration, if his quick retreat was any indication.

Lily wanted to uncover so much more because she honestly didn't know a whole lot about the man who would be in her life forever—one way or another.

As he maneuvered the truck toward his home, Lily adjusted the air vents. Summer was in full force and the sun beat right in through the windshield, making her even hotter.

As much as her body ached for his, she needed backstory, needed to know what made this impossible-to-resist man so captivating. While they were driving, this was the perfect opportunity to dig in to his life a bit more.

"Where did you grow up?" she asked, breaking the silence.

His hand tightened on the steering wheel. "Not too far from here."

"Have you always worked with horses?"

"Yes."

He wasn't as talkative as she'd hoped, but most men weren't. Still, he never seemed to open up about his past... which made her want to uncover all he held back.

"So you had horses growing up?"

His eyes darted toward her, then back to the road. "We couldn't afford them."

Lily laced her fingers together in her lap and turned to stare out the window as he turned onto his road. "Sorry if I'm prying. I just want to learn more about you."

"Nothing to be sorry about," he told her. "My mom worked for a farm so I was always around horses. We just didn't own any. I always swore I'd have a farm of my own one day."

He had a vision, dreams. He worked hard and didn't sit back and feel sorry for himself about what was missing from his life.

How could she not be intrigued by this man who was so opposite from any other man who'd captured her attention? Everything about Nash was different. There wasn't a doubt in her mind that he held on to his past because he was embarrassed. He was a groom, she was a movie star, but couldn't he see that she saw them as equals?

She'd had very humble beginnings and she'd tried to express how money meant nothing to her. All she wanted was a man she could trust and rely on. The fact Nash turned her inside out with his seduction was just icing on the proverbial cake.

When Nash pulled to a stop in front of his house, Lily hopped out and grabbed some bags while Nash took the others and headed up the porch to unlock the door. Once they were settled inside and the bags were dropped onto the floor inside the foyer, Lily turned to Nash.

"Do you mind if we talk?"

Tossing his keys onto the small table, he turned back to meet her gaze. "I'd hoped we'd be doing other activities. What do you want to talk about?"

Lily stepped forward and reached up to wrap her arms around his neck. Instantly his strong arms enveloped her, always making her feel safe, protected…loved. Could he love her? Was he even thinking along those lines?

"Anything," she said. "I just feel like all we do is get naked and I think we really have so much to discuss. The future, what we're doing, the baby. I still don't know much about you."

Nash pulled back, literally and figuratively, as he stepped around her and let out a sigh. "You know all you need to right now."

Lily turned and followed him into the living room, refusing to accept his evasive tactics. "I know you grew up around horses and that you are close with your mother. That's all."

Across the room, Nash rested his hands on the mantel, his head dropped as tension crackled in the silence between them. Something weighed heavily on those wide shoulders of his, something he didn't want her to know.

Was he worried she'd think less of him? Did he wonder how much he should share just because they had different pasts?

Dread settled deep in the pit of her stomach. Was he hiding something worse? Endless possibilities flooded her mind.

"Nash, I know you're keeping something from me." She eased farther into the room, skirting around the sofa and coming to stand just behind him. "You're scaring me with the silence. It can't be that bad, can it?"

She hoped not. Had her judgment been so off again? *Please, no. Please let it be something that is in actuality very, very minor.*

"You deserve the truth," he muttered, still gripping onto the mantel so tightly his knuckles were white. "This is harder than I thought."

Lily slid a hand over her stomach. What had she done? She stepped back until her hip hit the edge of the sofa arm. She gripped the back of the cushion for support.

What bomb was he about to drop and how would this affect the life of her and her child?

Nash turned, his eyes full of vulnerability and fear. Raking a hand through his hair, he met her gaze across the room. "Damon Barrington is my father."

Seven

She'd been played for a fool...again.

Her shaky legs threatened to give out. How could she be so foolish? Was she so blinded by men with pretty words and charming attitudes that she couldn't pick out the liars?

Damon Barrington, billionaire horse racing icon, was Nash's father? Her eyes sought his across the room. He hadn't moved, had hardly blinked as he watched her to gauge her reaction. So many thoughts swirled around in her mind she didn't know how she was supposed to react.

"You lied to me."

That was the bottom line.

Oh, no. Nash's father was a wealthy mogul and famous in his own right in the horse racing industry. How would the media spin this story once word got out who her baby's father was?

The muscle in his jaw ticked as he crossed those muscular arms over his chest. "Yes, I lied."

No defense? Was he just going to reveal that jaw-dropping fact and not elaborate?

Lily rubbed her forehead, hoping to chase away the impending headache. She wouldn't beg him to let her in. He either wanted to tell her or he didn't, but he better have a damn good reason for lying to her face.

"I honestly didn't want to lie to you," he defended, as if her silence had triggered him to speak up for himself.

A laugh escaped her. "And yet you did it anyway."

"Damon doesn't know who I am." In two long strides, Nash closed the gap to stand directly in front of her. Those bright blue eyes held hers as if pleading for her to hear him out. "To my knowledge he never even knew my mother was pregnant. I only found out he was my birth father several months ago and that's when I came to work for him. I needed to see what kind of man he was, needed to know if I even wanted to pursue a relationship with him."

A bit of her heart melted, but he'd still withheld information from her, pretending to be someone he wasn't.

"You're the son of the most prominent man in this industry and you didn't even think to tell me?"

Nash reached for her hands, held them tight against his chest as he took another step toward her. "When we first started our connection was just physical. You know that. But then I started getting more involved with you and I worried about disclosing the truth, but I also knew you'd be leaving at the end of the shoot. I wasn't going to say anything to Damon until you were gone and it never would've affected you. But now..."

Realization dawned on her. He'd had to tell her. But the fact of the matter was he only did so when forced to, and that hurt her more than she cared to admit.

"The baby."

Nash nodded, squeezing her hands as if he was afraid she would turn and run. "I truly never wanted you involved in my mess, in this lie, but things were out of my control."

Lily raised her brows. "Out of your control?"

"Fine." The corners of his mouth lifted slightly, showcasing that devastating smile. "I couldn't control myself around

you, but I could control how much of my life I let you in on.
I wasn't able to tell you before."

"Why now?" she asked, searching his face, finding only
vulnerability masked by a handsome, rugged exterior. "You
could've kept this to yourself until you talked to Damon."

He held her hands against his heart with one palm and
slid his other hand up along her cheek, his fingers thread-
ing through her hair.

"No, I couldn't. You've come to mean more, we mean
more, than I thought possible. I wasn't ready for you, Lily.
I've had this secret living in me, I couldn't just let anyone in."

His heart beat heavily against her hand and Lily knew that
him baring his soul was courageous and brave. He could've
kept lying to her, he could've gone to Damon first with this
bombshell, but he'd opened himself up.

"Besides," he went on, drawing her closer. "I need you.
More than I want to admit, and on a level that terrifies me.
No matter what's going on around me, in spite of all my is-
sues, I need the passion we possess. I need you, Lily."

Mercy, when he said things like that her entire body shivered, her stomach flopped as nerves settled deep inside her.
He wasn't lying now. No man had ever looked at her the way
he did. She saw the raw truth in his eyes. Saw how hard it
was to expose himself.

"I need you with me right now," he told her, nipping at
her lips. "I need to draw from your strength."

The man was twice her size, with his broad, muscular
shoulders, his towering height, yet he wanted her strength?
He humbled her with his direct, bold declaration.

"Are you going to tell him soon?" she asked, gripping
his shirt.

"I really don't know. Part of me wants to, especially now
that the film is done, the racing season is over and the girls
aren't under as much pressure."

Lily smiled, warming to the idea of Nash being part of
such an amazing family. "You have sisters. Nash, this is

such a big deal. You have to go to them. They deserve to know. If you want me to go with you, I will. I'll stay back, too. Whatever you want."

Encircling her waist with both arms, Nash pulled her close where her hands were trapped between them. "I'll go soon. But right now, I want to embrace the fact the mother of my child is in my house where there are no interruptions, no schedules to keep. You're supposed to be relaxing and I have the perfect spot."

She eased back, looking him in the eyes. "Don't keep the truth from me again. We're in this together and I can't be with someone I don't trust."

Those bright eyes held hers, the muscle in his jaw clenched and for a second she thought he was about to say something, but he simply nodded.

"Was that our first fight?" she asked.

Nash nuzzled his lips against her neck, his beard tickling her sensitive skin. "I guess so. We better go kiss and make up."

He walked her backward and Lily couldn't help but laugh as she found herself being drawn more and more into his world. Yes, he'd kept something monumental from her, but in his defense he was still working through the new information himself. She couldn't imagine finding your father at this stage in life and she couldn't blame Nash for being confused on how to respond and what steps to take. This was all new territory and they had to wade through it together.

They headed down the hall, his hands cupping her bottom as he led her into the bedroom.

"This is where you'll stay while you're here," he told her as he trailed his lips across her jawline and to her ear. "Clothing is optional."

A thrill shot through her. Being claimed shouldn't be so arousing, yet she found herself wanting Nash more and more each time he threw down that dominance gauntlet.

With a kick of his foot, the bedroom door slammed shut.

* * *

Nash jerked another bale of hay from the stack and moved it into the stable. Frustration and guilt fueled each aggressive movement. He'd lied to Lily, was still lying to her and had worked his way back into a corner he may never find the way out of.

He'd never forget the look on her face when she'd discovered he was Damon's son. But she only knew part of the truth. The rest of his secret wouldn't be so easily defended and the damn last thing he'd ever intended on doing was hurting her.

His plan was to reveal himself to Damon, figure out how the hell to get those horses and get back to his own estate. He was done living these lies, done hurting people he had been around for the past few months.

As much as the guilt ate at him, he still wouldn't leave without what he came for. Otherwise this whole journey would be in vain.

Sweat poured down his back as he stacked the last bale against the far wall. He'd called and checked on Lily several times today and each time she assured him she was fine and if she needed anything she'd call him. Still, he couldn't help but worry. Would he be like this the entire pregnancy? Always worrying?

Nash knew it wasn't just the pregnancy. Everything was closing in on him at once. He needed to confess now that the racing season was over and Cassie and Tessa were focusing on Cassie's new school. He couldn't wait for Damon to sell those horses to someone else.

Nash's assistant should've already proposed the next offer, now Nash just had to wait.

Waiting was about the dead last thing he wanted to do, but he hadn't gotten this far in life by being impulsive. Timing was everything in reaching your goals.

And timing would definitely play a major role in the next steps he took with Lily. It was like walking through a minefield. One wrong move and every plan, every unexpected blessing could all blow up in his face.

He'd spoken with his mother this morning and she was still worried about him exposing the truth, but Nash assured her he wasn't going to disclose everything, only that Damon was his father. Everything else…hell, he had no clue when to drop that bomb. Would Damon look closer and see the man who had been his rival for so long? They'd not been face-to-face in the business world in years and Nash knew he'd changed. Besides the hair, the beard and the clothes, Nash had done more grunt work on his own land, bulking him up quite a bit and changing his physique.

"You may be the hardest working groom I've ever employed."

Nash jerked around to see Damon striding through the stables. Fate had just presented him with the perfect opportunity…but was he ready to take it?

Damn it, this was harder than he thought. Before him stood the man who was his biological father and had no clue. How would he react? Would putting the fact out in the open change Damon's life? Would he care? Would he embrace Nash as part of the family?

In the past several months since learning the truth, Nash had played this scenario in his head a million times. Now that the perfect opportunity had presented itself, he didn't know how to lead into the life-altering conversation.

"Haven't seen you down here much lately," Nash finally said as he tugged off his work gloves and shoved them in his back pocket.

"The girls are done training, so that's freed up my time." The elderly man rested his hand on one of the gates to a stall, curling his fingers around the wrought-iron bars. "I come down more in the evening now. Been spending some of my days playing with sweet Emily."

Nash smiled. Emily was Damon's granddaughter…and Nash's niece. So many instant family members. Actually, with Ian marrying Cassie, that would make Lily's agent Nash's soon-to-be brother-in-law.

His head was spinning. Everything would start unraveling the moment he told Damon the truth, or the part of the truth that Lily knew.

Nash had no clue how Damon would react to having a long lost son, but he knew damn sure how he'd react if he found out the rest of Nash's identity. Epic anger like nothing Nash had ever seen, of that he was positive.

One step at a time.

"You going to be home later?" Nash asked, resting his hands on his hips.

Horses shuffled in the background, one neighed as if trying to chime into the conversation. Nash was starting to love these stables as much as his own. Damn it, he hadn't counted on getting emotionally invested in this place, this family...Lily.

What the hell was happening to him?

"Should be."

"Mind if I come back around seven? I need a private meeting with you."

Damon's silver brows drew together. "You're not quitting on me, are you, son?"

Son. The word was a generic term yet Damon had no clue just how swiftly he'd hit that nail on the head.

"No, sir."

"You've got me intrigued." Damon let out a robust laugh and nodded. "Sure. Come on up to the house about seven."

"Will Cassie and Tessa be around? They may want to be there, too."

He'd made a split-second decision to include his half-sisters. Honestly, Nash wasn't sure if Damon would want the girls to know, but Nash needed them to. The more time he'd spent here, the more he'd gotten involved in their lives and wanted a chance for a family.

"I can ask," Damon informed him. "You've certainly piqued my curiosity, so I'm sure they'll be intrigued, as well."

Nash swiped his forearm across his sweaty forehead, then rested his hands on his hips. "Great. I'll be up to the main house around seven."

If Lily wanted to join him, he wouldn't turn down her support. He needed her, and that wasn't weakness talking, either.

Besides, if he shared everything he could with her now, perhaps the blow that would inevitably come later wouldn't be so harsh. The only other woman he'd let close to him was his mother. Women in his life had come and gone, nobody really fit. Lily fit…as much as she could with all the jagged edges of his life he'd yet to smooth out.

Nash knew he had fallen into a hole so deep, there was no way out and he was starting to wish for things that could never be.

Eight

Lily resisted the urge to throw her phone, and she would pull the childish tantrum if she didn't have to go through the annoyance of getting a new one.

But she wasn't one to waste money.

For pity's sake, she was so sick of certain people in the industry—ahem, producers, actors, etc.—assuming that because they were a big name, she would jump at the chance to work with them. Then when she declined, the offer of more money really set her teeth to grinding. She couldn't be bought, something they found hard to believe.

Thankfully her agent, Ian, had called with the movie options and the ridiculous counteroffers. He was still trying to find her a film that could accommodate her expanding belly, but Lily wasn't sure how work would fit into the life she was envisioning with Nash. The baby was no problem. A relationship with Nash? How would he feel about Hollywood? There was no way she could stay away from the limelight and she knew he was a private man. He'd made no definite declarations to her, yet she found herself hoping everything would work out, because she truly wanted this amazing man in her life, and not just for the baby.

Swinging her legs around, she propped her feet up on the

leather sofa and settled back against the cushioned armrest. This relaxing nonsense was getting really old really fast and she had only been here a few days. If this lasted her entire pregnancy she would go insane.

Added to that, Nash was very attentive to her needs. Okay, wait, that wasn't a bad thing at all. But the man wouldn't let her do anything for herself. He insisted she take it easy and rest until her next appointment when the doctor would come and assess her.

Funny, Lily didn't recall agreeing to stay with him that long. Apparently he'd assumed she would just live here. That was definitely a talk they would be having soon. At some point she'd have to leave, to pack her things and go back to her life. She didn't want all of this uncertainty in her future.

And she was still reeling from the news that Nash was Damon Barrington's son. Even though her first gut reaction was anger, she had to give Nash the benefit of the doubt. The man was obviously torn. He was struggling with this new identity and working as a groom to get close to his biological father. How could she hold that against him?

He hadn't deliberately lied to her and she'd seen the turmoil he'd battled with over revealing the truth to her. What had he done before coming to the Barringtons' estate? Had he been a groom elsewhere? She assumed he worked with horses since he'd told her he did that as a child. Obviously love for the animals and hard work were in his blood.

Had she been in his shoes, she wouldn't have disclosed her secret to a virtual stranger, either.

Oh, how fate had other plans for them. Lily never would've dreamed she'd be living in Nash's cottage, pregnant with his child while he debated on when and how to drop the paternity bomb on the racing mogul.

The sooner the past came out, the better. Wasn't that true for any type of potential relationship?

The front door opened and closed seconds before Nash's heavy footfalls moved through the foyer. He rounded the arched doorway into the living room and offered her a half smile.

"You look like I feel." She rested an arm along the back of the couch, taking in his lean form as he propped a shoulder against the door frame. "Bad day?"

"I'm grabbing a shower and heading back to the estate." Nash ran a hand along his short beard, around to the back of his neck as he let out a sigh. "I'm going to tell him."

Lily jerked up, gripping the back of the couch. "Does he know you're coming back?"

"Yeah."

Lily couldn't believe he was ready to take this step. She knew he wanted to, but she had no idea he was doing it so soon after telling her. Had opening up to her released something else in him? Something that made him want to get his life in order before the baby came? And, dare she hope, for them to move forward together?

"Do you want me to come?"

Nash's eyes met her, his toe-curling smile spread across his face. "I would, but only if you're comfortable going."

Lily came to her feet, smoothing her simple cotton dress down her legs. Rounding the couch, she crossed the cozy living room. Encircling his neck with her arms, Lily answered his devastating smile with her own.

"I don't want to assume anything in any part of your life, Nash. I know our relationship has been a whirlwind, but I don't think you should go through this alone."

"Damn, I want to hold you," he told her, resting his forehead against hers. "But I smell like the ass end of that stable and I need a shower."

Lily laughed as she settled a quick peck on his lips. "I don't mind, you know. But, go shower. I'll throw on my shoes and pull my hair back real quick."

Nash's brows rose. "That's all you're going to do?"

"Uh, yeah, why?" Stepping back and narrowing her gaze, she crossed her arms. "Are you saying I need to change or put makeup on? I know you're used to seeing me all made up on set, but this is the real me, Nash. No fuss and kind of boring."

His hand snaked out, wrapped around her arm and tugged her until she fell against his chest. "I'm a much bigger fan of the no-fuss Lily. I'm just still surprised that you don't care about getting all made up to leave the house."

With a shrug, she laid her palms against his taut T-shirt. "I'm not like most women and I'm definitely not like most Hollywood women. I'm pretty low-key when I'm not working."

Nash's hands roamed down to cup her bottom as he pulled her hips against his. "That's a good thing. Now let me get in the shower and stop manhandling me or we'll be late."

Rolling her eyes, Lily laughed as he kept squeezing her backside. "Yes, of course. What was I thinking?"

As he moved down the hallway, Lily watched him go. The confident stride, the wide shoulders pulling the material of his sweat-soaked T was beyond sexy and his sense of humor only added to his appeal. She found they were growing more and more comfortable with each other outside the bedroom, not that their passion had diminished any, either.

Within thirty minutes they were in Nash's truck, making the ten-minute drive to the Barrington estate. Lily was nervous for him, but he seemed pretty relaxed with his wrist dangling over the steering wheel, his other hand lightly holding on to hers in her lap.

"So what happened with you today?" he asked, breaking the silence. "Are you feeling bad?"

"No, nothing like that." She glanced out the side window, taking in the beautiful farms with the acres of white fencing as far as the eye could see. "I've been on the phone off and on with Ian. He's still trying to find a part for me that will work with this pregnancy. There was one role that would have been a good fit, but I just turned it down before you got home."

"Turned it down? Why?"

"I'm not ready to commit to something long-term just now." She turned to face him, loving the comfortable feel of his hand wrapped around hers, loving even more how fast they were venturing beyond their physical connection. "Besides, the producer is beyond arrogant and he assumed I'd jump at the script. To be honest, if this was another time, with no complications, I would've sucked it up and taken the film."

"Then take it," he told her simply. "Don't let anything hold you back. If they want you, they'll work around the baby."

"I know they will." She wasn't so sure they would work around the fact that she was falling in love and had no clue where she would end up if Nash wanted a future. "It felt good to say no, though. Money is a big part of negotiating contracts, but he just flashes it like it's the red flag and we're the bull charging in after it."

Perhaps that sounded petty, but she wasn't one to be swayed so easily.

"I just have issues with people throwing money around, thinking that will buy them happiness or anything else they want," she went on. "My stepfather kind of ruined me for the rich type. That sounds strange coming from me with what I pull in per film, but I've never thrown my money around and I certainly have never tried to buy someone to get my way."

Nash tensed. "Not everybody with a lot of money is bad and sometimes they have good intentions but things can still go wrong."

Lily wasn't quite sure how to respond and she was quite frankly shocked that Nash was defending the upper class. But it wasn't worth arguing about and she held tightly to his hand as they pulled into the Barringtons' entrance. The wrought-iron gates, with a scrolling *B* on each side, were standing wide-open, inviting them in.

The long, picturesque drive leading back to the property, showcased the horses out in the pasture and led the way to the grand stone stable up ahead. Of course the family famous for their world-renowned success in the horse racing industry would have something that monumental in their lives front and center.

The months she'd spent filming on this farm and in the surrounding area were some of the best of her life. The small-town atmosphere, the intimate setting and getting to know the family of the story she was depicting was icing on the cake. She'd really grown close to Cassie, Tessa and Damon, and even their cook, Linda. The Barringtons might be small in numbers, but they made up for it in love and determination. Lily wanted that kind of family bond, craved it actually.

Her hand went to her flat stomach and she couldn't help but think ahead to the future about what life would be like with a child…and if the man beside her would be part of it.

"You sure you're ready to do this?" she asked when he pulled up in the circular drive and stopped near the front entrance.

Nash pulled their joined hands up to his lips, kissed the back of hers and gave her a big squeeze. "More than ready."

"What reason will you give them that I'm still here?"

Nash shrugged. "What do you want me to say?"

Lily prided herself on the truth, but she still wasn't ready to disclose her pregnancy to the world, yet. She also didn't want this to be about her or the baby at all. This was Nash's moment to possibly connect with a family he hadn't known existed.

And she was still unsure if she would be part of his family once they really sat down and talked about the future.

One monumental moment at a time.

"We can just tell them we met when I first started filming and became friends and I decided to hang around for a while and take a mini-vacation since the shoot was done."

Nash shot her his signature naughty grin. That sexy smile never failed to arouse her because she knew firsthand what that smile looked like as he rose above her just before he joined their bodies.

"I'm pretty sure they'll know we're more than friends," he told her.

"That's fine," she said with a shrug, realizing she truly didn't care.

She trusted this family to keep things private. They understood the way the media worked, considering they were celebrities in their own right with the Barrington sisters making history with their wins. Besides, she'd come to consider them friends and if she wanted to pursue something more with Nash, she needed to get used to opening herself to those that could quite possibly be a big part of his life.

"I'm just not adding any more information than that and I'm not bringing up the pregnancy. Besides, when you tell them the news, I'll be all but forgotten."

"You could never be forgotten." He smacked a kiss on her hand. "I'm not ready to let our little secret out, either. I like having you and this baby to myself for now."

Nash leaned across the center console, slid a hand along her jawline and captured her lips. Those soft, talented lips had been all over her body, yet when he kissed her with such tenderness and care, she couldn't help but wonder if he held back feelings and emotions he was afraid to express out loud.

Because his silent actions were screaming that he was falling in love with her. Heaven help her, she wanted him to be just as torn as she was. She wanted to know that as she entered into this unknown territory of what she felt could be true love, that she wasn't alone.

"Let's go," he murmured against her lips.

Nine

Nash couldn't let his mind drift to the conversation he had with Lily about her career and he sure as hell couldn't think about how his emotions regarding her were tying him up in knots. He was here for one reason and one reason only—to figure out what Damon Barrington would do with the paternity bomb Nash was about to drop.

"Well, we're all here." Damon smiled, crossing an ankle over his knee in his wingback leather chair in the living room as though he hadn't a care in the world. "I'm anxious to hear what you have to say."

Cassie and Tessa sat on the sofa, their matching bright blue eyes locked on his. Didn't they see it? Hadn't they noticed how they all had the exact same shade of cobalt-blue eyes? He'd purposely not worn contacts when he'd come to the estate, perhaps in hopes that someone would mention his eye color.

Nash sat next to Lily on the other sofa across from Tessa and Cassie. A rich mahogany coffee table sat between them, adorned with a perfect arrangement of summer flowers. The Barrington home was just as lavish and beautiful as his own…a home he was itching to get back to. A home he wanted to show Lily.

The Barrington clan had been surprised to see Lily, but had bought the friend story…or at least they hadn't questioned any further.

Even though Lily wasn't touching him, just her presence beside him was all the support he needed. Lily was his rock right now.

"I've really enjoyed my time working here," he began, fighting off the nerves that threatened to consume him. "I've gotten to know all of you and was able to witness history firsthand when Tessa won the Triple Crown. I celebrated even though I was here and not at the race. Being on the ranch during filming was pretty amazing, too."

"You sure you're not quitting?" Damon chimed in. "This sounds like a lead into a resignation."

Nash shook his head and offered a smile. "I assure you, I'm not quitting."

"Is everything okay?" Cassie asked, her brows drawn in.

The two women on the opposite couch were so similar, yet so different. Both had long, crimson hair and those striking blue eyes, but where Tessa was lean and athletic, Cassie was curvy and softer. Both were beautiful, dynamic women and he realized just how much he wanted to be part of their lives.

Damn it. He'd never let himself be vulnerable before. Business had always ruled his life and in that aspect he kept control gripped in a tight fist. His mother was the only person he'd ever let affect him emotionally. But, in a sense, he was also here for her. It was time the secret came out. She deserved to be free of any guilt or residual turmoil and he deserved to know where he stood in his father's life.

"Everything is fine," Nash assured them. Unable to stay seated another minute, he came to his feet and paced behind the couch. "This is harder than I thought."

Along the mantel sat photos in pewter frames, some pictures were of the girls as children, some of Damon's late wife, Rose, but they all depicted the family and the love they shared.

He'd missed out on all of that. But he couldn't blame his mother. She'd made the choices she thought best under the circumstances. Besides, what's done was done and now he just had to figure out the best way to deal with the facts he had…and still get all he wanted in the end.

"I need to start at the beginning." He turned to face them, rested his hands on his hips. "My mother used to work on this estate years ago. She actually worked here as a trainer before I was born."

Damon's eyes widened. "Other than Cassie, I've only employed one other female trainer."

Nash's heart beat so hard, so fast. He waited, letting the impact truly sink in as he kept his eyes on Damon's.

"Your mother was Elaine James?" Damon asked, almost in a stunned whisper.

Both Cassie and Tessa turned their eyes to their father. Nash waited, wanting to see how the events would unfold before he continued.

"Who's Elaine James?" Tessa asked before glancing back to Nash.

"She was one of the best horse trainers in the industry at one time," Damon told her, still staring at Nash. "I used her during a period when female trainers were frowned upon, but some owners snuck around that. She kept her hair really short, wore a hat and would come in early in the mornings and late at night to work with the horses."

Nash knew all of this, had heard his mom tell that same story over and over of how women were gentler and less competitive by nature so Damon had wanted a woman for the job.

"When my mother left here to take care of her parents, she went to work at another farm several hours away," Nash went on. He forced himself to keep his focus on Damon. Right now, nothing else mattered but gauging the older man's reaction. "It wasn't too long after she'd left that she realized she was pregnant with me."

Damon's gasp nearly echoed in the spacious room. Lily sat quietly with her hands in her lap, but Cassie and Tessa's eyes widened as if they were putting the pieces together.

"This can't be," Damon whispered, his eyes darting around the room frantically, then back to lock on Nash's. "You—"

"I'm your son."

There. He'd admitted half of the truth that had weighed heavily on his shoulders since first arriving here several months ago.

Now what? He honestly hadn't planned this far ahead. He'd definitely planned on the end result, but he hadn't factored in all the uncomfortable moments—and now was one of them.

Stunned silence settled over the room. Lily hadn't moved, she merely sat with her eyes locked on his as if silently sending him support. When his gaze landed on hers, she offered a sweet smile of encouragement.

"Nash, forgive me, but I'm going to need more proof than just your word," Damon finally said. "Where is your mother now?"

Nash came around the couch, taking a seat next to Lily again. Now that the secret was out, or part of it anyway, he could somewhat relax for the moment. But he still kept the upper hand.

"I don't blame you for not taking just my word," Nash told the older man. "My mom had a stroke about six months ago. She's doing much better now, but right after the scare, she confessed that she used to work for you and the two of you were…involved."

Nash refused to elaborate.

"Why didn't she tell me?" Damon asked, his brows drawn in, shoulders stiff. "Once she left, I never heard from her again."

Even through years of rivalry and more recently while

working here in a more personal setting, Nash had never seen Damon so stunned.

"When she left to take on a new role at another farm, she had no idea she was pregnant." Nash rested his elbows on his knees, lacing his fingers together as he looked from his half-sisters to his father. "From what she told me, by the time she found out and got the courage to come back and tell you, she was about eight months pregnant. She worried you wouldn't believe her, or that you would marry her just for the baby and she didn't want you to feel trapped. But she wanted you to know. She said she came back to town and all the buzz was about you and Rose and your recent engagement."

Nash recalled his mother's watery confession when she'd begged him to forgive her for not following through and going to Damon. She'd apologized for keeping Nash from his biological father and said that the years of seeing them as rivals in the industry had nearly killed her.

But how could Nash blame her or be angry? She was young, alone and scared. He sure as hell had no place to judge anyone keeping a secret.

"She told me she didn't want to ruin your relationship with your fiancée," Nash went on. "So she ended up having me and raising me on her own."

The words settled in the air and Nash had to fight to keep from reaching out for Lily's hand. He wanted her familiar touch for support, but more than anything he wanted to re-assure her that their baby would always know her place in a family.

Damon rubbed his forehead as if still processing all this information. "Did she ever marry?"

Was he asking as a man who once cared for Nash's mother or was Damon asking from a father's standpoint, worried about his son having a male role model?

"She did when I was about ten."

"Yet you still have her last name," Damon said, shifting in his seat. "Your stepfather didn't adopt you?"

This was the part of coming clean that was about to get tricky. He had to proceed cautiously because one slip of the tongue and all hell would break loose as the complete truth was finally revealed.

"He did," Nash replied. "I chose to still use my mother's maiden name."

Okay, that was a lie, but Damon couldn't know Nash's true identity…not until Nash was ready to share that fact. And the first person he owed the real truth to was Lily.

Wow, his priorities had definitely shifted since he'd first arrived at Stony Ridge Acres. When the hell did that happen? When did contemplating his next step automatically have his mind shifting to how Lily would react or how Lily would feel?

"So you've been here all this time…spying on us?" Tessa asked, her eyes narrowed as she took both hands and shoved her hair away from her face. "Why not say something right at first? Why the lies?"

Nash cleared his throat. "I wasn't sure I wanted to reveal the truth, to be honest. I've always worked with horses and before I could really make up my mind on how to handle the situation after I learned the truth, the groom position came open. I couldn't pass it up."

"You couldn't have told us who you were before now?" Cassie's eyes were softer, yet still guarded like her sister's.

Yes, he could've, but he'd been busy trying to buy out Damon's prizewinning horses and in his spare time he'd been getting naked with Lily. His priorities had taken a hard turn into unexpected territory.

"I understand this makes an impact on all of your lives," he began, choosing his words carefully. "I had to see if this was even a family that would welcome me, or if I should keep the secret and eventually just leave quietly."

Lily did reach over now and squeezed his hand. The gesture wasn't lost on the Barrington sisters whose eyes darted in their direction.

Nash didn't want to think how that silent action truly spoke volumes for how supportive Lily was and how, right at this moment, his emotions meant more to her than what other people assumed or thought. Damn it. He didn't deserve her loyalty, her kindness and innocence. He was lying to her and no matter how he justified it, no matter how he knew there had been no way around the secrets, he was still in a relationship with a woman who didn't even know his real name.

"And you've deemed us fit to be in your life now?" Tessa came to her feet, tugged the hem of her shirt down and crossed her arms. "I'm skeptical, for sure, but more than anything I'm a little hurt you basically spied on us."

Nash nodded. "I expected all of you to feel that way, but I had to do what was best for me and my mom. My stepfather is gone and I've taken care of her for years. I have to put her wishes and feelings above anything else."

"She was okay with you coming here?" Damon chimed in.

"She left that decision up to me," Nash informed him. "But she was worried that, at this point, I would disrupt your lives."

"I have a brother," Cassie whispered, her eyes filling.

"Cass," Damon warned. "We still need proof, though I'm pretty sure Nash is telling the truth."

"It's the eyes," Cassie said with a wide smile as she swiped her damp cheeks. "He's got our eyes."

Obviously not one to show emotions, Tessa turned to her father. "How could you go from his mother to our mom in such a short period of time?" she asked, throwing her arms wide. She still hadn't sat back down and Nash was pretty sure she really wanted to storm out. She was definitely the more vocal sister.

Damon eased back in his chair, his hands gripping the leather armrests. "Without getting into details you all probably don't want to hear, Elaine and I were attracted to each other, but we never fell in love or even mentioned a relationship beyond the physical. Once she left, I met Rose and love at first sight was something I had believed to be a myth until I saw her. We met one day, went on our first date the next and were inseparable. She was it for me."

Nash swallowed. His mother had pretty much said the same thing. She and Damon hadn't been in love, just young lovers having a good time. And they were from two different worlds, which was probably frowned upon at that time.

The beginning of his mother and Damon's relationship mirrored that of Lily and himself. Only Nash had every intention of a different ending.

"Your eyes," Tessa murmured as she slowly maneuvered around the coffee table and sat on the other side of him. "I knew when you first came here that there was something about you."

Nash nodded, trying not to get too wrapped up in these emotions that threatened to rise to the surface. "I saw it first thing, too."

He hadn't even realized until this moment just how much he wanted the girls and Damon to accept him. He may have more money than he would ever need or know what to do with, but there was one thing money couldn't buy…a family. And deep inside, that's what he'd always wanted.

"You really are my brother?" she asked, her voice cracking.

Nash smiled. "Yeah, I am."

"So what now?"

Nash shifted to focus back on Damon, who still had his silver brows drawn as if he didn't know whether to be confused or angry. This was another part of the plan that he'd have to tread lightly on because as much as Nash wanted to get those horses, he also wanted this family. He just had to figure out a way to cleverly capture it all.

"That's up to you," Nash told his father. "I love working here, but I understand if you aren't able to trust me right now."

"No," Cassie said, shaking her head. "You've proven yourself. Right, Dad? Nash is the hardest working groom we've ever had."

Damon nodded, easing forward in his seat. "You're more than welcome to keep working here, Nash. And, if you own any horses, feel free to house them here."

Oh, the irony. Between the double families, the Barringtons, Lily and his baby, and the horse ownership, Nash was spinning in circles and feared he'd have a hard time keeping all of his lies straight before he could present them in a justifiable manner.

"I actually don't have any right now," he told Damon, which was partially true. Nash's horses just weren't here locally.

"The groom position is yours as long as you want it." Damon came to his feet and Nash assumed that was his cue to do the same. "And if you get a horse, these stables are available to you anytime."

Nash stood before his father, the same man he was trying to buy out, and held out his hand. "I appreciate that."

Damon clasped Nash's hand and pulled him into a one-armed man-hug before easing back. The sadness in his eyes matched his tone. "I'm sorry about your mother. If there's anything I can do…"

"Thanks." Absolutely no way would anyone else take care of his mother. Nash was a bit protective of her and right now he wasn't ready to discuss her too much. "She's doing really well, actually."

Damon nodded and released Nash's hand. "You've certainly dropped a bomb I hadn't expected. I hope my stunned silence at times didn't make you feel unwelcome, I'm just still so shocked."

"I understand. I was shocked, too, but I've had several months to process this." Nash glanced down to Lily who was toying with the hem of her dress lying against her tanned thighs. "I think Lily and I will go and let you all talk things over in private."

He extended his hand to Lily and assisted her up. She presented a killer smile to Damon and patted his arm.

"You've really been blessed with this news," she told him. "Shocking as it may be, your family has grown and you've gained a wonderful son."

Damon embraced her and patted her back. "Rose would've loved you."

Nash knew Damon and Lily had bonded pretty well during the filming of Damon's life. Lily had played Damon's late wife and the two had often discussed the late Mrs. Barrington. Damon was all too eager to share stories and memories of his wife.

Guilt and a new set of nerves settled deep in Nash's gut. There was still one more piece of damning information he had to reveal. He'd grown beyond the man who initially settled in here to spy on his rival and to have a heated affair.

Now Nash wanted a family, both families, and he had no choice but to destroy any amount of progress he'd made. Once the truth revealed itself, any hope of having a relationship with the Barringtons or Lily would be gone.

"I just hope once the film is out, people will see how amazing this family truly is, and not just in the racing world." Lily made her way around the room and hugged Tessa and Cassie. "I'll be in town for a while," she informed them. "Perhaps we could go to lunch or something?"

Cassie smiled. "I'd like that. I assume we can find you at Nash's?"

Lily laughed. "Yes, but please don't let that get out."

"We'd never say a word," Tessa assured. "I'm glad you'll be here awhile. Now that Cassie and I have a little more free time, we could use a girls' day out."

Nash watched as the sisters he'd just inherited bonded with the mother of his child.

Failure wasn't an option. Not when he had this much at

stake. All he could do now was wait for his assistant to get back to him on whether or not Damon would take the deal. Until then, Nash was at a standstill and unclear of his next move.

Ten

Insomnia was a cruel, unwelcome friend.

Lily tried her hardest not to make too much noise as she searched the kitchen for her guilty pleasure. Unfortunately, Nash didn't keep cocoa or chocolate syrup on hand.

With the gallon of milk in tow, she closed the refrigerator door and thought how she could get her chocolate milk fix. Being a chocoholic was her downfall, right behind the grilled cheese. Hey, she could have worse addictions. Granted, food obsessions in LA were unheard of, considering women there opted to starve themselves so they were skinnier than their so-called friends. Lily loved food too much for all of that nonsense.

And she had a weakness for chocolate milk.

With a brilliant plan in mind, she jerked open the freezer and instantly spotted a gallon of chocolate swirl ice cream. Perfect backup in a pinch.

Grabbing the largest glass she could reach in the cabinet, Lily found a spoon and scooped a hefty helping of ice cream into her glass before she carefully poured milk over it. She saw nothing wrong with having a chocolate float at two in the morning. One good thing about the pregnancy, she could totally blame her crazy cravings on the baby. Of course, even when she wasn't pregnant she'd wake up in the middle of the night for chocolate milk, but nobody needed to know that.

Using the spoon, she stabbed at the hunk of ice cream at the bottom of the glass in an attempt to break some of it up into chocolaty goodness. She'd just taken her first sip when footsteps shuffled over the tile behind her.

Licking the milk mustache off her top lip, because she was a classy lady, Lily turned to see Nash looking very sexy and sleepy with his lounge pants sitting low on his narrow waist. His long, disheveled hair fell across his forehead and those bright blue eyes zeroed in on the glass in her hand before darting to the ice cream and milk on the counter.

Even with just the small light on over the stove, she could see the amusement overriding the tiredness etched on his face.

"Don't judge me."

She took another gulp and welcomed the coolness as it spread through her body. Who knew being pregnant turned on some sort of internal furnace?

"I don't even know what to say," he told her with a smirk. "Is this something you normally do?"

Lily leaned her hip against the center island. "When I can't sleep I usually get up and have some chocolate milk, but you didn't have any syrup so I had to improvise."

With a slight tilt of his head, his eyes instantly flashed with concern. "What's on your mind that you're not sleeping?"

Clutching her glass, Lily laughed. Where to start? "Everything at the moment."

Remaining in the doorway with his shoulder propped against the jam, Nash crossed his arms over his deliciously bare chest. Would she ever tire of looking at him? Touching him?

The fire that continued to burn between them wasn't all that had her wanting more with this intriguing man. He excited her in ways she'd never felt before, he made her feel as if she was actually meaningful to his life, as if he wasn't only with her for her celebrity status. And he was honest. She needed honesty. Coming from a land where lies flew as quickly as the wind, she needed that stability. She needed him.

Earlier tonight when she'd seen him vulnerable, baring his soul to a family that didn't know he existed had twisted something even deeper within her. There was so much more to Nash than she'd first uncovered and all she knew was she wanted to discover the rest.

"Talk to me," he murmured, that low tone washing over her. "I'm a pretty good listener."

He was good at everything…hence her hang-ups and torments.

"I'm just thinking." *Worrying.* "With Damon knowing who you are now, what will happen next with your life."

She took a drink, thankful for the prop in her hands and the comfort of her guilty pleasure. Having these thoughts occupy her mind was one thing, letting them out in the open was another. But here they were, surrounded by near darkness and silence where they would have no interruptions. Might as well lay out some of her concerns.

"That's not all on your mind."

Lily caught his stare from across the room. He knew her all too well. And here she'd worried they only knew each other intimately. For months everything had been so one-dimensional, which had worked perfectly for them until the shocking baby news. Even after that, though, they'd kept things physical, not delving too deep.

Everything about them had recently shifted. She knew his fears of opening up to Damon and the girls just as he knew her fears of the baby and her career. They were in this together, bonding, growing closer…and that scared her to death.

"I don't want this child to ever worry about where she stands with us." Lily slid her free hand over her stomach, silently vowing protection over her innocent baby. "I saw the torment in your eyes, Nash. I saw the vulnerability when you were talking to Damon. You're a strong man, but family is something that I can see you take very seriously. I guess I'm worried where we're headed, not just you and me, but this baby. I don't want her life torn between ours."

Nash moved farther into the kitchen. The closer he came, the bigger he seemed to get. Those tanned, bare, broad shoulders, wrapped over muscles from working hard on a farm, would make any woman's knees weak and toes curl. She was no exception.

His hand slid over hers on her stomach. "This child will never question how much we love her. No matter where we are, this child takes top priority."

Thrilled that his level of passion for protecting and loving this child was the same as hers, Lily smiled. But she didn't miss the fact he avoided the topic of them as a couple.

One day at a time. She still had months to think things through. Ian was totally understanding in her taking a bit of time off since she'd just wrapped filming and was coming to terms with the pregnancy. She couldn't be happier that she'd taken him on as her agent.

So while he was figuring out her next career move, Lily was trying to get a handle on her personal life and how she could keep her career, raise the baby and figure out her feelings for Nash. Whatever they had went beyond lust, beyond sexual, but she couldn't identify it quite yet.

Without another word, Nash took the cold glass from her hand and took a drink. Milk settled into his mustache before his tongue darted out to swipe it away.

She'd never been attracted to a man with a scruffy beard and unkempt hair before, but something about Nash had been intriguing from the second she'd met him. Lily had actually found his ruggedness sexy and a nice change from all the pretty boys in Hollywood who worried too much about their looks.

"You're right," he told her. "This is good."

Reclaiming her glass, Lily took another drink and made a mental note to go to the store for syrup first thing in the morning. A woman had needs, after all.

Speaking of needs, the way Nash's heavy-lidded eyes raked over her silky chemise made her shiver with arousal. She'd worried about staying with Nash because she'd been afraid all they would do was act on all this sexual chemistry they had instead of figuring things out. But staying with him had forced them to evaluate what was going on between them and open up a little more each day.

The sex was just icing on the proverbial cake.

Without a word, Nash took the glass from her once again, but instead of taking a drink, he set it on the counter. The clank of the glass on the granite echoed in the silence. His strong hands glided over her silky gown at her sides as he eased her closer to him. The warmth of his fingers burned through the thin layer of material.

"I know something else that cures insomnia," he murmured. "It's quite a bit more grown-up than chocolate milk."

With a firm hold around her waist, Nash leaned forward, sliding his lips over her jawline and down her neck. Trembling against his touch, Lily gripped his biceps and tilted her head back as he continued his path on down toward the slope of her sensitive breasts.

Nash cleverly reached up, easing the thin straps of the chemise down with just the brush of his fingertips. Lily lifted her arms, ridding herself of the straps and in a swift whoosh, the flimsy garment puddled at her feet, leaving her wearing nothing but his arousing touch.

Nash quickly took advantage of her state of undress and bent his head to continue his torture with those talented lips. Lily arched into him as he claimed her with only his mouth. While Nash thoroughly loved on her breasts with his hands and lips, she slid her thumbs into the waistband of his pants and shoved them down. A sense of urgency overwhelmed her.

Nash pulled away from her breast and before she could protest, he slammed his mouth onto hers. Wrapping her arms around him, she threaded her fingers through his hair and held him in place. Without breaking contact from her mouth, Nash lifted her off the ground, keeping her flush with his body.

Encircling his waist with her legs, Lily locked her ankles behind his back and clung tighter as he moved from the kitchen toward the hall. Lily clutched at his shoulders, angling her mouth to take the kiss deeper in an attempt to take some control. When he tried to break the kiss, her lips only found his again. She needed his mouth on her, needed that contact with a desire she'd not known before Nash.

He backed her into the wall before they made it to the bedroom door. Grabbing her hands from his shoulders, he plastered them beside her head and held her in place with only his hard, firm body.

"None of that," he whispered against her lips when she tried to capture his mouth again. "You're supposed to be relaxing, which means I'm in control."

Lily smiled, tilted her hips toward him, pleased when his lids shuddered closed as he let out a low groan.

"You would tempt a saint," he growled.

"I only want to tempt you."

Nash's eyes opened, focused on hers as he slid into her. Those cobalt baby blues demanded her attention, held her captivated as he set the pace. Lily couldn't look away if she wanted to.

Everything about Nash was demanding, yet attentive, bold, yet nurturing…in bed and out.

As her hips met his and her hands continued to grip his shoulders, Lily watched Nash's face. A myriad of emotions crossed before her eyes: determination, arousal, need…and love. She saw it as plain as she could feel him. The man loved her, but whether he was ready to admit it to himself was an entirely different matter. He had enough going on right now without professing his love to her.

Still, she couldn't help but feel a bit relieved that he may have developed such strong feelings for her. Because she had already started falling for the simple groom with a complicated life.

Lily continued to hold his gaze as she trembled with release, and as Nash followed suit, he didn't look away. Those bright blues stayed transfixed on her, sending a new wave of shivers coursing through her.

And when their tremors passed, Nash leaned his forehead against hers and whispered, "You're more than I ever thought I was looking for."

Eleven

Nash had no clue what the hell had transpired in the hall just moments ago, but as he lay holding Lily in his arms on the bed they'd shared for a week, he realized two things: one, she was more vulnerable than she wanted him to see; and two, he'd let some of his own feelings slip out when his guard had been let down.

He had to keep his emotions close to his chest. He couldn't afford to reveal just how fast he'd started falling for Lily.

She was right when she'd said family meant everything to him and that's why he had to remain in control. He had to grip tightly with both hands: the Barringtons in one and Lily and his baby in the other.

She shifted against his side, her hand drifted over his abdomen as she slid one smooth leg over his thigh. He'd carried her back to bed after they had frantic sex in the hallway.

Yeah, he was a real classy guy not being able to hold back long enough to take those few extra steps to get her into bed. She didn't seem to mind. Actually if her moans and nails biting into his shoulders had been any indication, she'd rather enjoyed herself.

As frantic and aggressive as they'd been together, something had passed between them…something silent, yet significant. He'd seen so much in her eyes and he worried what she'd seen in his.

Lying in silence for several minutes, Nash knew Lily wasn't going to sleep anytime soon.

"I'm sure you see the parallel in my mother's pregnancy and yours," he told her, breaking the silence. He glided his fingertips along her bare arm across his body. "You're not here because of that. You're here because I want you here."

Lily's body softened against his. "I know. I know we started off as just a private affair and suddenly we're both thrust into a world we have no clue how to face. One day at a time is all we can do right now."

Relieved that she knew that much, Nash wished he could tell her the rest. Wished he could fully disclose his identity. But telling her now would certainly murder any chance he had of being with her. He needed more time.

"But, I do need to make some decisions soon," she said after a minute of silence. "I can't stay in Virginia forever and avoid my responsibilities."

Forever. Was he ready to use such a word when thinking of them in terms of a couple? He'd never considered forever with one woman before, but something about Lily made him reconsider his list of priorities. She made him want to be a better man, not always putting business first and really focusing on life. But he'd already dived headfirst into this plan before he met her and, unfortunately, there was no turning back now.

Damn it. He'd had every intention of coming out of this charade unchanged and besting his rival.

"Have you told your mom about the baby?" he asked.

Her warm breath tickled his side as she blew out a sigh. "Not yet. This isn't something I want to just tell her over the phone. Besides, I'd like to go visit her, anyway. I try to get there between films."

Moonlight filtered through the crack in the curtains, slant-ing a soft glow across the bed. So many things raced through his mind, from the buying of Damon's horses to the baby, but one thing was certain. He couldn't let Lily go. He kept having images of her in his home, his real home, on his grounds and in his stables. She would fit in perfectly and his staff would be just as charmed by her as he was.

"What do you say we go on a picnic or horseback riding tomorrow...well, today." He stopped, wondering if that was even a possibility. "Are you even allowed to ride horses pregnant?"

She turned, fisted her hand and rested her chin on it. "I'm not sure, really. Are you asking me on a date?" she asked with a smile.

Smoothing her hair away from her face and shoving it behind her shoulders, he trailed a fingertip down her cheek. "Yeah. Kind of working backward, but what do you say?"

"I'd love to go on a date with you. Let's just stick with the picnic for now, okay?"

Why her bright smile and upbeat tone sent his heart into overdrive was beyond him. They were having a baby, they'd been intimate and she went with him to offer support with Damon. Now he decided to ask her on a date?

"If we have a big date planned, I better get some sleep," she told him around a yawn.

"Need more ice cream and milk?" he chuckled.

"Oh, no." Her delicate laugh filled his room, his heart. "Your way worked so much better to cure my insomnia. You wore me out."

Nash couldn't help but smile as he kissed the top of her head. "That's the idea. Now rest."

He pulled the thin comforter up around her shoulders and held her tight until her breathing slowed and her hand beneath his went lax.

Nash couldn't wait for the sun to rise, to get in some time at Stony Ridge, then go on a date with Lily. He needed her to see who he truly was before she found out about the other side to him. He needed her to see that there was so much more to him than his millionaire businessman and millionaire persona. He was still the man who tended to horses and enjoyed the simple ways of life.

But first, he needed to find out where Damon stood on selling those thoroughbreds. Little did Damon know, his newfound son was also his most hated rival in the racing industry.

"You've got to be kidding me."

Lily cupped her hand and scooped up the cool, refreshing water, playfully sending it in Nash's direction.

"Come on," she teased. "You're a country boy. Don't let a little creek water scare you."

After a filling picnic consisting of sandwiches, fresh fruit, lemonade and chocolate chip cookies, Lily had toed off her sandals and stepped into the brisk creek to splash and play around. Nash still lay propped on one elbow on their blanket, watching her with a huge, devastating grin.

"Oh, I'm not scared," he retorted as he sat up and pulled off his cowboy boots and socks. "It's you who should be scared."

Shivers raced across her body at his threat. She slid her toes gently over the creek bed in an attempt to avoid the sharp pebbles.

Nash came to his feet, reached behind his head and yanked his T-shirt off and flung it to the side. Oh, my. Those taut muscles all tanned and perfectly sculpted had her belly quivering. He knew how to fight fire with fire…he poured gasoline on it.

"Keep looking at me like that and I'll clear off that blanket in two seconds and make better use of it," he warned as he stepped closer to the creek.

At the edge, he stopped and rolled up his jeans. Lily propped her hands on her hips, loving this playful, relaxed day. With the sun high in the sky, the warmth of summer was in full swing and the country setting was just what the doctor ordered. Nash had told her about this creek that ran through the back of his rental property. It was simple, private and perfect for them. And from how he kept eyeing her in her short tank-style dress, she figured privacy was going to be to their benefit very shortly.

Would she ever tire of how he watched her? How his eyes seemed to drink her in, in one sweeping glance? Each time she caught him visually sampling her, her need for him sharpened even more.

"Damn, that's cold," he complained as he put one foot in. "You didn't tell me that."

Rolling her eyes, Lily laughed. "It's refreshing. Don't be such a baby."

"I'll show you baby."

He bent down, scooped up handfuls of water and trickled a stream down her bare legs. The coolness did nothing to ease the heat rushing through her. Everything with this man turned intimate and aroused her like nothing else she'd ever experienced.

He made her laugh, made her appreciate how a relationship between two totally opposite people may actually work.

And she found herself wanting that more and more each day. She wanted to be with a man who wasn't afraid to lean on someone else when he needed to, a man who could also protect and take charge without being overbearing. She wanted Nash.

Still bent down, his hands lingered on her legs, those bright eyes came up to hold her gaze. "You're right," he said. "This was a great way to cool off."

"You turn everything into sex," she laughed, even though she wanted him to rip her clothes off and have his way with her on the creek bank.

His hand stilled, that naughty grin widened. "I'm a guy. Of course everything is about sex. It doesn't help you're looking at me like you want to gobble me up."

Lily couldn't help herself. She took her foot and tapped

his chest with just enough force to send him butt first into the water. Crossing her arms, she tried her hardest not to double over with laughter as he glared up at her with a smirk on his face.

"Thought you needed to cool off," she quipped with a shrug.

"Oh, baby, I always need to cool off around you," he told her as he started to come to his feet. Water dripped off his hands, his thighs as he wrapped his wet arms around her and pulled her flush against him. "Don't tell me you don't want me for my body."

Lily's hands were trapped between them, so she laid her palms against his bare chest. "You have a very fine body, Nash. No denying that."

"Gee, you make a guy feel really wanted."

Lily slid her hands up to his shoulders, around his neck and laced her fingers together. "I think your ego needs bringing down a notch sometimes."

Those kissable lips offered up a sideways grin. "And you're the woman to do that?"

"That I am," she said. "I bet you've used this body to get what you wanted from women before. I can't blame you, though, you're a sexy man. All those muscles from manual labor, the scruffy, rugged beard and shaggy hair…you give off a sense of mystery. But I want more than the body, more than the seductive exterior."

She nipped at his lips, loving the sensation of his soft beard feathering over her skin. "I want to uncover the mystery," she whispered against his mouth. "I feel there's so much more to you than what you're showing me."

Nash stiffened in her arms, those bright eyes narrowed in on hers. "Be careful what you wish for," he told her. "What if you don't like what you uncover?"

What started out as playful had taken a turn into an area she wasn't sure about heading into. While she'd been half-joking, his tone implied he was dead serious. Was he implying there was something she wouldn't like about him? Was he hiding something else? Everyone had secrets, but the way he'd issued that warning, Lily couldn't help but wonder what he meant.

"How much more do I need to uncover?" she asked, swallowing the lump of fear in her throat.

Those strong hands on her back slid down to cup her backside. "You could spend a lifetime unraveling me."

Arousal slammed through her, but something else, something akin to love spiraled right along with it. Was he indicating he may want forever? Were they honestly ready for that type of talk?

All of a sudden black dots danced in front of Nash's face as the world tilted. Her heart rate kicked up and her stomach flipped with nerves as she broke out into a sweat.

Lily heard him call her name before her world went black.

Twelve

Cradling Lily in his arms and beating a path through the field and toward his house, Nash said a prayer with each step he took. One second he'd been ready to confess his life to her, the next she'd slumped against his body. A fear like nothing he'd ever known slammed into him.

Never before had Nash been so consumed with worry or gut-wrenching panic. She was pale, too pale. Those pink lips were white and she was deadweight in his arms.

As he reached his patio, Nash laid her down on the cushioned chaise lounge which was thankfully shaded by his house this time of day.

Lily's eyelids fluttered, her face turned toward him and Nash eased down beside her, smoothing her hair back from her face, which was starting to regain some color.

"Nash?"

"It's okay," he assured her, cursing his shaking hands. "You passed out on me. Just lie here for a bit. I'm going to run in the house and get my cell to call the doctor."

Her fingers wrapped around his arm before he could move. "No, please. I'm fine. I think it was just the heat."

"I want the doctor to come and make sure you and the baby are healthy." Uncurling her fingers from his arm, he brought her hand to his lips and kissed her palm. "I need to know."

He didn't wait for her to argue, it wouldn't matter if she did because he was up and in the house in seconds. As he placed the call, he went back out to Lily who was still lying down, now with her arms wrapped around her abdomen.

The doctor assured Nash he would be there within ten minutes. Sometimes money wasn't the root of all evil.

Nash's hand slid over hers. "Are you in pain?"

Shaking her head, Lily squeezed her lids together. A lone tear streaked out, sliding down her temple and into her hair. Nash eased back down beside her, swiping the moisture away.

"Talk to me," he urged, placing his palm against her cheek. "Are you hurting or still dizzy?"

She opened her eyes and stared up at him. "I feel fine. I just got scared. What if something is wrong? I mean, just because I feel fine now doesn't mean something isn't going on inside my body."

He shared her dread, but refused to be anything less than strong for her, for their baby. Had his mother gone through this type of fear and worry? Nash couldn't even fathom his strong, vibrant mother being alone and facing all this uncertainty without support.

"Everything will be fine," he assured her. "The doctor will give you a clean bill of health."

Her dark eyes filled as her chin began to quiver. Damn it, he hated being so helpless. What could he offer her right now but promising words and a shoulder to cry on? Even paying for the best doctor to be at their beck and call couldn't prevent something unexpected from happening.

Nash was used to getting his way, getting what he wanted, whether it be through his power or financial control. But this child and this woman he was coming to deeply care for couldn't be handled in the same manner as his business dealings.

The fact he was putting them above everything else, even his end goal, should tell him he was falling in deeper and deeper with this Hollywood starlet.

"What are we doing?" she asked, her voice trembling. "How can we raise a child when we live on opposite sides of the country and our lives are so different?"

Nash knew enough about pregnancy to know that her hormones were all over the place and with the scare she'd just had, Lily's mind was going into overdrive. Treading carefully with each word was the only way to keep her calm.

"Right now, all we're going to think about is relaxing because our baby is depending on us to keep her safe."

That misty gaze held his. After a moment's hesitation, Lily nodded and smiled. "You're right. As long as she's healthy, we can figure out the rest."

Nash slid her hand between both of his and squeezed. "You know we keep referring to this baby as 'she'?"

Lily's smile widened. "I know. Honestly I don't care what the sex is, but something just tells me this will be a girl."

The image of a baby with Lily's stunning, natural beauty gripped his heart. No matter if the baby had his bright blue eyes or her dark features, Nash knew one thing, this baby would be loved, would know her place in the family and would want for nothing...and he didn't just mean monetary things, either.

After the doctor had come and gone, giving Lily a clean bill of health, Nash had still insisted she lie around and do nothing. Absolutely nothing. This hero act was sweet for about five minutes, but she was really getting tired of him jerking around to see if she was okay with every move she made .

Lily settled deeper into the propped pillows behind her back and crossed her ankles. She probably should warn Nash she didn't plan on staying in this bed the entire time she was here. Tomorrow she would get up and do...something.

Her phone chimed on the nightstand and Lily glanced over to see a text from Ian. She hadn't checked her phone since this morning, considering she'd planned on a more fun-filled day she hadn't wanted to be interrupted. But when the events had turned more worrisome, she'd not even given work a second thought.

Reaching for her phone, she quickly read his text.

Did you get my voice mail?

Lily went to her messages and listened, her heart thumping as she realized Ian was presenting her with a role made for her and she had to make the decision rather quickly. As in, by Monday morning.

After she listened fully to his message, she fired back a text stating she'd listened and she was definitely interested and he would have a decision by tomorrow night. She didn't go into details of her day's events because even though he knew she was expecting, he didn't need to worry she couldn't do her job.

As she was pondering the role and how wonderful the opportunity would be for her, Nash rounded the corner with his phone in hand.

"Still feeling good?" he asked, coming to stand beside the bed.

"I hope you don't think I'm lying in this bed for months," she informed him. "I'm going to have bedsores."

Nash lifted her legs and sat down, placing her feet across his lap. "Yeah, well we had one outing and you went out like a light. I don't think my heart could take too much more of that."

His heart. That was an area they'd yet to explore. She honestly wanted to know what was in his heart where they were concerned.

"I just got off the phone with Damon."

Lily perked up. "Did he call you?"

Nash smiled. "Yeah. He wants us to come out to the estate for lunch tomorrow. You don't have to if you don't want to. Don't feel obligated."

Lily sat straight up. "First of all, that's a little hurtful that you think I wouldn't want to. Second, if you're not comfortable with me around your new family, just say so. I know you're wanting to get to know them and I'm still an outsider."

Nash slid his hands up her legs to her thighs as he gripped her and leaned forward. "I want you there. Never doubt that I want you with me. I didn't want you to feel like I was dragging you through my family drama right now."

"Fair enough." The fact he wanted her there spoke volumes for the direction their relationship was headed. "Are you going to tell them about the baby?"

Nash's thumbs slid back and forth over her bare thighs, making this conversation hard to focus on. But she realized he wasn't even paying attention to the gesture when he sighed and shook his head.

"I'm not sure," he said. "I want to leave that up to you since we're not ready for the media to get wind of it."

"Well, Ian knows, so Cassie may, too. Although he did promise to keep the information to himself."

Lily thought about the Barringtons, about how dynamic this family was and how the media tended to hound them, too. They would understand the need for privacy, especially when an innocent baby was involved. A close-knit family like that knew all about loyalty and protecting those around them.

"I don't mind if we tell them," she said, pleased when his mouth split into a wide grin.

"Seriously?"

"Sure. That will give everyone something positive to discuss, something that takes the edge off the intensity of you shocking them with your identity."

The smile on his face faded, the muscle in his jaw clenched. Something she couldn't identify passed over his eyes.

"You all right?" she asked, wondering what she'd said that had him so worried.

He blinked, and an instant transformation had his smile returning. "I'm good. Just thinking about how I'll fit into Damon's life now, I guess."

Framing his face in her hands, Lily held his gaze. "You'll fit in perfectly. You all already have a love of horses, it's in the blood. Things will all work out, you'll see."

His dark brows drew down as if some worry still plagued him. "I pray you're right."

"That was wonderful," Lily declared as she sat her napkin on the table. "Thank you."

"My pleasure," Damon replied with a smile.

Nash hadn't known what to expect when coming for lunch today, but so far he was pleasantly surprised at how easily he and Lily had slid into the family role…as if they were a real couple coming to his parents' for a gathering.

With Ian, Cassie and Cassie's little girl on one side of the long table and Tessa and her husband, Grant, on the side with Nash and Lily, Damon sat at the head like the grand patriarch he was.

The confident man had no clue he'd just hosted his rival.

Nash wished more than anything he and Damon weren't at odds in the business world. Nash hated lying, hated being someone he wasn't just to get the prizewinning horses to complete his breeding program. He hadn't worried about this when he'd first come onto the scene.

He had Lily to thank for that bout of conscience. When he'd set out to get the inside scoop on Damon's plan after the racing season, Nash had been ready to steal, lie and cheat to get what he wanted. But Lily made him want to be a better man.

Nash had also gotten to know Damon on a more personal level and the elderly man wasn't too different from Nash. They both knew what they wanted, and both went after it full force…how could Nash fault that? Damon wasn't the man Nash had originally thought.

Damon had a passion for the sport, just like Nash. The man cared for his family, would do anything to protect them. Nash hadn't seen that side of him years ago in the circuit. All Nash had known was how ruthless Damon could be. And, honestly, Nash had actually recognized how alike he and his father were.

Trouble now was, Nash was already wrapped so tightly in his own lies. He still wanted those horses, still needed desperately to breed them with his own back on his estate. He'd not had the best seasons lately and he had to do something.

Lily's hand slid over his leg under the table. "You okay?" she whispered.

Pushing away thoughts of business, Nash patted her hand. "Yeah."

"Nash, I'd like to talk with you a moment if you don't mind taking a walk down to the stables with me," Damon said, not really asking. A man like Damon Barrington didn't ask.

"Of course," Nash replied, wondering what the man would want to discuss in private. Had he found out the rest of the truth? Doubtful, but the possibility was always there.

"You're not seriously going to talk work are you?" Tessa asked.

"Not at all." Damon came to his feet and handed his plate to Linda who had just come into the dining room. "Ah, thank you. But I would've taken my own plate in."

Linda, the house cook and all around amazing lady to the family, laughed. "Of course you would've. I trained you years ago."

"Go on," Lily gestured to Damon and Nash. "I'll help clean up."

Both Tessa and Cassie both chimed in their refusal for Lily's help, but Lily stood and started gathering dishes anyway.

"I think we should pitch in, too, Ian," Grant spoke up as he scooted his chair back. "I don't know about you, but I don't want to face the wrath of my wife if I let Lily do all of this."

Reaching into the high chair, Ian pulled Emily out and tucked her firmly against his hip. "Actually, there's a smell coming from our section over here and I'm pretty sure I'm on diaper patrol. You enjoy wrapping up the leftovers, though."

Lily couldn't help but get a bit choked up at the easy way this dynamic family all meshed together so beautifully. What would it be like to live here, to have that connection every day? She had her mother and they were extremely close, but Lily wondered how raising a child in LA and bouncing him or her around from film set to film set would affect the outcome of her child's life.

"Lily?"

Nash's soft tone, his easy grip on her elbow had her turning. "I'm sorry, what?"

She realized the entire room was now staring at her. Great. She'd thought they'd all scurried out, apparently not.

She'd given off the image of a professional actress when she'd been filming on set here for months, but now they were all looking at her as if she'd sprouted another head.

"I asked if you were okay." Ian stared across the table at her and seeing him holding his stepdaughter had Lily smiling and nodding.

"I'm pregnant," she blurted out.

Nash laughed. "Way to break the news, sweetheart."

Inwardly cringing, she turned to him. "Sorry. I'm botching things up here."

He took the stack of plates from her hands and kissed her cheek. "You're fine."

Lily glanced around the room to the stunned faces. Only Ian was smiling and threw her a wink and a nod of encouragement.

"It's okay," she told them with a smile as she blinked back the tears. "Nash and I are both excited about this. While we certainly weren't planning on a baby, we are thrilled."

"A son and a new grandbaby on the way all in one week?" Damon asked as he puffed out his chest and grinned. "This calls for a major celebration."

"How about Wednesday?" Cassie suggested with clasped hands and a wide smile. "That's the fourth. We could have fireworks, grill out and make a big night of it."

Lily's head was spinning as the Barrington sisters started planning, then Linda came in, heard the news and chimed right in on everything she could make, too. As she babbled on, she bustled around the table, took the plates from Nash's hand and kept right on planning without missing a beat.

The moment went from her instant onslaught of tears to a chaotic meshing of voices chattering over each other.

"I think they're excited," Nash leaned over and whispered in her ear.

Damon came around the table and settled his hand on her shoulder. "Congratulations, Lily. I'm really happy for you guys."

Lily couldn't help the lump of emotion that settled in her throat. Nash's newly minted father was already welcoming her and the baby into the family. This was everything she'd ever wanted to give her children…a sense of belonging.

"Thank you."

Nash's hand slid over the small of her back. "We want to keep this private for now," he informed his father. "Lily is taking some time off and staying with me until we figure out the best course of action. If the media gets hold of this news before we're ready…"

"I understand completely," Damon nodded. "If you need anything, let us know. Privacy is something we value here. I promise to only keep Nash a few moments in the stables and then we'll be back and we can continue this celebration."

Nash leaned down, placed a kiss on her cheek. "I'll be back in a bit," he murmured before following Damon and the other men from the room.

Lily looked up to see, Tessa, Cassie and Linda all smiling

at her. Damn it. She wished she could label her relationship with Nash because she didn't want to bond and fall in love even more with these amazing women if it wasn't going to be long-term.

Now that Nash had come clean with his family, would he want to get closer to them? Surely he wouldn't want to just pack up and follow her back to LA. But, she had a job, a life there that she couldn't ignore.

She loved her job, not so much the lack of privacy, but digging into roles and bringing emotion to the screen. She still hadn't decided whether to take the film Ian had sent her way and she had to discuss things with Nash, too.

Lily needed to know what he was thinking, what he was feeling before she fell any deeper in love with this family.

But she was afraid it was too late for that.

Thirteen

Nash entered the stables, like he had many times before, but this time Damon walked silently at his side. The fresh, familiar smell of hay and leather greeted them, while a couple of the horses peeked their heads out to see who their new visitors were.

A tug on Nash's heart irritated him. He couldn't think of this estate as home or as a place where he would be welcome once Damon found out the truth. But he truly loved these grounds, these horses.

"Man-to-man," Damon started as he moved easily down the center aisle, his cowboy boots scuffing against the concrete. "How nervous are you about this pregnancy?"

Nash laughed. "That's not at all what I thought you'd say once we got down here. But, between us, pretty nervous. Not about the baby, and I know Lily will be an amazing mother. The worry more centers around the fact I want her to have a healthy pregnancy."

Damon stopped in front of the stall that housed Don Pedro, Tessa's prizewinning horse that had helped her secure the coveted Triple Crown and put the Barrington sisters in the history books as the first females to accomplish such a feat.

"It's rough being the man in this situation." Damon rested his hand on the top of the half door. "You're used to fixing things, being in control of everything in your life. I know when Rose was pregnant with our girls, I was a nervous wreck until she delivered. But once I held that baby in my arms, I knew for certain I'd never let anyone or anything hurt them if I could prevent it at all. I'd sell my soul to the devil himself to keep my girls happy."

Be careful what you wish for.

"Lily has had a few dizzy spells and she was told to relax and take it easy to keep her blood pressure down, so right now that's all I can concentrate on." Nash reached out, sliding his hand up the stallion's velvety nose. "So, I'm sure you didn't bring me down here to talk babies."

Damon took a step back, crossed his arms over his chest and nodded. "I want to make you an offer."

Intrigued, Nash continued his slow caress of Don Pedro's soft hair. This was where that power and control came into play. No matter what Damon said, Nash had to remember that he held the upper hand, not his father. And it was how Nash chose to play his hand that would determine both of their futures and any relationship Nash hoped to have.

"Tessa and Cassie retired, as you know. Cassie has plans to open a school for physically challenged children here and Tessa will help when she's available. She and Grant have discussed moving." Damon's gaze shot straight to Nash's, held there and demanded full attention. "I've been offered an excessive amount of money for several of my horses and I've yet to take an offer."

It took every bit of willpower Nash had not to laugh. He knew all about those offers…and the fact they'd been turned down.

"I know we just discovered each other," Damon went on. "But I'd like to offer Don Pedro to you. I've thought about this since you were here the other night and I know a gift hardly makes up for missing your entire life, but you're the best groom I've ever had and this is the best horse we've ever had. I'd like you to have him."

Nash barely caught himself before his jaw dropped. Control. He had to remain in that mindset. Damon Barrington was handing over such a remarkable horse? A horse that could pull in more money than any other at this point in time?

"I never expected that," he said honestly.

Here all this time Nash had been dishing out offer after offer only to be rejected and now Damon was hand delivering the horse right to his rival. Had he admitted the paternity months ago, would Damon still have given Nash the horse once the season was over? Or had Damon just come to know Nash well enough to know he would take care of the animal like the royalty Don Pedro was?

The fact that Nash had deceived a man he'd actually come to care about weighed heavily on his heart and his conscience. This would not end well…for anybody.

"What did Tessa say?" Nash asked.

Damon waved a hand, then reached out to stroke the Thoroughbred's neck. "She was well aware we'd be selling him after the race and she's on board. I'm selling a couple, actually, if Cassie can part with them. We all get attached, but that girl is so emotionally invested it rips her heart out to let them go after she's trained them."

Nash glanced at the horse in question, one of his main motivations for coming here. The end goal was in sight, but that last shred of truth still remained wedged between Nash and all he wanted. His goals had changed somewhat, but he still wanted Don Pedro. He just didn't know that he was comfortable using deceit to achieve that end anymore.

"I'm sure you could get a great deal of money for him from other owners who want to breed him," Nash said after a moment. "Are you sure you just want to give him away?"

"I could sell him, sure, but racing was never about money to me." Damon stepped away from the stall and crossed the aisle to show some affection to a horse named Oliver. "I had a passion for riding when I was a young boy. My mother was single and couldn't afford to give me a horse, so I would take lessons at a local horse farm in exchange for working in the barns. It was hard work, but I learned the love of the sport and saved every single penny I ever received because I was going to buy my very own horse."

A slice of guilt slashed right through Nash's heart. Hearing Damon talk of his childhood, wondering how much more their lives mirrored each other, Nash turned to face his father.

"I know hard work," Damon continued, resting his elbow on the edge of the door. "I know it pays off and I want to reward you for all you've done here in a short time. I realize you came here to technically spy on us, but I have to admit, I would've done the same had I been in your shoes."

That damn lump of remorse settled in his throat, making it nearly impossible to swallow. Nash had never expected to have a bonding moment with Damon and he sure as hell hadn't thought he'd nearly get choked up over it. But here Damon was sharing a part of his past, proving why Nash should take the free gesture of love.

Damn it.

Nash glanced back to the coveted stallion in question. Could he seriously go through with this? Just take the prize-winning horse and move on? Everything he'd wanted was right within his reach; all he had to do was grab hold.

What would Damon say once he learned the truth? Deceiving the man was initially the plan, but, now that Nash had actually spent time here and gotten to know this family, he cared for them in a way he never would've imagined.

Turning down this gesture, however, would require an explanation Nash wasn't quite ready to disclose yet. So he tightened the web he'd woven around himself and turned back to Damon.

"I'll take good care of him," Nash said with a smile that didn't quite come from his heart.

Damon's shoulders relaxed as his lips curved into a grin. "Anything for my only son."

The guilt knife twisted deeper, leaving Nash more vulnerable than he'd ever thought possible. He'd officially become the man he never wanted to be. Because in the end, he would tear apart the relationships he'd just started to build, relationships he realized he wanted more than anything.

He hadn't even known how much he longed for a family until he came here. Then when he'd discovered the baby another layer of need was added. So here he was, his heart overflowing with family bonds and relationships and in one second that all could be wiped right back out of his life.

Right now, he had to figure out a way to reveal the truth in the least damning way because that tight fist he'd had gripping all he wanted was slowly coming apart and he could feel the control slipping from his grasp.

Lily didn't remember laughing so hard in such a long time. Having an impromptu girls' day was beyond fun and quite a departure from the cattiness of the women in LA. Lily really didn't have good girlfriends back home and being here with Cassie, Tessa and Linda almost felt as good as being with her own mother.

"So what do you think for desserts?" Linda asked, crossing her leg over her knee and propping her notepad up on her thigh. "So far I only have the main course. What's your favorite dessert, Lily?"

"She's a fan of chocolate."

Lily jerked her head toward the doorway where Nash stood looking all scrumptious in his black T-shirt pulling taut across his wide shoulders and those well-worn faded jeans hugging narrow hips. His gaze zeroed right in on hers.

"I believe chocolate milk is high on the list," he added, his tone dripping in sex. "Ice cream will do in a pinch. Right, Lily?"

Lily suppressed a shudder. The man knew exactly how

to turn her on in a room full of people without so much as stepping into her breathing space.

"Why don't we do sundaes?" Linda asked, oblivious to the sexual tension.

Cassie laughed. "Emily will love that."

"I'm always up for anything chocolate, too," Tessa chimed in, pushing her hair back over her shoulder.

Lily smiled, excited to be pulled into the Barrington family like she belonged there. "Sounds like a great night. What can I bring?"

"Yourself." Cassie leaned over and patted Lily's leg. "Linda gets offended if we try to bring anything to a party she's throwing. And we've learned she's the best and anything we make won't compete so we just let her have at it. Bring Nash and an appetite. That's all."

Lily glanced to Linda who was rigorously jotting down notes, her lips thinned, her eyes narrowed. This woman was all business when it came to meal planning. Lily knew from being on the set that Linda loved to feed a houseful of people and she was an amazing chef.

"Sounds good to me," Lily said around a yawn. "Sorry, I'm so tired lately."

"It's the first trimester," Cassie told her with a soft smile. "You'll regain some energy soon."

Nash came to stand in front of her and extended his hand. "Why don't I get you home? It is getting late."

Glancing out the window, Lily realized the sun had all but set. They'd been there most of the day and time had flown by.

She took his hand and came to her feet. "This was so fun. Thanks for having us over."

"You're welcome here anytime," Tessa told her. "Feel free to come any time Nash is working. We can always use another female around here."

"Good thing the guys aren't nearby to hear that," Linda said as she rested her pad and pen on the coffee table. "But, I agree. Come by anytime."

After saying their goodbyes, Lily and Nash headed home.

Home. Had she really started thinking in terms of his house as her own? She'd spent the majority of the day being welcomed into his newfound family, she was having his baby and her feelings for him were growing stronger every single day.

Yeah, she was starting to feel as if this was home. LA seemed so far away, as if a lifetime had passed since she'd been in her spacious condo. Just the thought of going back to the lonely space depressed her. She'd never fallen in love with a place—or the people—she'd visited on location before like she had at Stony Ridge. Part of her never wanted to leave, the other part had to be realistic and see that she couldn't stay forever. Her job didn't allow her to set roots.

So how could she raise a baby with a man who lived here? How could she leave the man she'd fallen for in such a short time?

Tears pricking her eyes, that tickle in her nose and clogging of her throat had become all too familiar sensations lately. Her hormones were raging all over the place, just like everything she'd read said they would. She sniffed, turning to glance out the window so Nash wouldn't see her sniveling like some crazy, unstable woman…which she was, but still.

"Hey." He reached across the truck console and gripped her hand, giving a reassuring squeeze. "You all right?"

Lily glanced over, catching his quick look her way before he concentrated back on the two-lane country road. "I love it here," she found herself saying. "I mean, it's so nice, so laid-back. And today I felt like a normal person."

Nash's soft chuckle filled the cab. "Sweetheart, you're going to have to clarify that last part."

Staring down at their joined hands, his so large and tan and hers so delicate and pale, she tried to find the right words to make him understand.

"I'm always treated like a celebrity everywhere I go," she began. "I don't mind the pictures, the autographs, that's all fine and comes with my job. But that's just it. I do a job and that's what it is to me. I don't see myself as someone on a level above anyone else. Today everyone treated me like I was just a family friend, they welcomed me into their home and I had a fun time without worrying about work or the pettiness that comes along with the industry."

Nash continued to drive, not saying a word, and Lily started to feel a bit silly.

"I'm sorry," she finally said. "That all probably sounds ridiculous. I'm already worried about the media hounding me when I return to LA. They hover all over, even going through my garbage to get any morsel of gossip they can sell. I have no clue how to resolve that unless I do what you mentioned and make an announcement during a live interview. But this town, these people are so amazing. I'm comfortable here and it's just going to be hard to leave."

There. She'd said it. She really wanted to know how he felt on the matter and it was past time they discussed where they were headed. She was kind of glad her rambling led them down the path to a topic they'd danced around for over a week. The uncertainty of her immediate future was starting to really cause more anxiety than she should be dealing with.

"Do you want to stay?"

That low tone of his produced the loaded question she'd been asking herself.

"I want to know what you want."

Such a coward's answer, but she needed to know where he stood, needed to know what was on his mind because up until now they'd only talked seriously about his past and they'd had amazing sex. That was all well and good…better than good, actually, but there was so much more to be brought out in the open.

"I want you to be happy." He gripped the wheel tighter with one hand and continued to hold hers with the other as he maneuvered the truck around a series of S curves. "I want our baby to be healthy and I want us to build on what we've started."

"And what have we started?" she prompted.

She wanted him to label their relationship. Okay, maybe that sounded immature of her, but baby or no baby, she found herself wanting to be part of his world, wanting to see what the long-term outlook could be for them.

Nash turned onto his road, then into his drive before he pulled to a stop, killed the engine and turned to face her. The porch light cast a soft glow into the cab of the truck and his bright eyes seemed to shine amidst those dark, thick lashes.

"You want me to lay everything out for you?" he asked, grabbing her other hand and holding on as if his life depended on this moment. "I want you to figure out what makes you happy. Do you want to go back to LA and have the baby? Do you want to stay here until the baby is born and then see what happens? I'm not asking you to choose between the baby and your career, I'd never do that. But whatever you decide, you better make damn sure I'm part of that plan because I want this, us, a family. I'm going to take what I want and I'm not backing down."

Nash tugged her forward and claimed her mouth like a man starving for affection and staking his claim. With their hands tightly secure in her lap, Lily opened for him, relieved that he'd declared how he wanted to be with her and a bit aroused at the demanding way he'd all but marked her as his own.

Nash and his powerful mannerisms never failed to make her feel wanted and—dare she say—loved.

But she just realized she hadn't brought up the job opportunity Ian had presented her with. She had until tomorrow night to give him an answer.

When Nash eased back and looked her in the eyes, Lily knew she had an important decision to make. And this time her career move would affect the man she'd fallen in love with.

Fourteen

Lily had changed for bed, washed her face and pulled her hair back into a low, messy bun. She hadn't seen or heard a peep out of Nash since they got home. He'd come in, tossed his keys on the entryway table and told her he'd be back inside in a bit.

That was over an hour ago. She'd given him space, but what was bothering him right now? He'd been so open in the truck, then it was as though he waged some inner war with himself and he shut her out...again.

Was he having doubts about what he'd revealed to her in the car? Was he still caught up in the whole Barrington saga? Perhaps he was worried about the baby. Or maybe it was whatever Damon had discussed with Nash in the stables. Nash hadn't even mentioned the man-to-man talk and she wondered if she should ask about it or just let him decide if he wanted to open up.

Whatever had him closing her out right now, she wished he'd let her in. He only opened up to discuss his superficial emotions, but when it came to his fears Nash was a private man.

Well, too bad. If they were going to try to make this work, they needed to have an open line of communication at all times. The best of relationships struggled sometimes and they already had so many strikes against them. She refused to let go of the one man who made her feel like love was a great possibility and there was a chance for a happily-ever-after.

Wearing only her simple short blue tank-style gown, Lily padded through the house and slid open the patio door. Thanks to the light above the door she could make out Nash sitting out in the yard on a cushioned chaise lounge beneath a large old oak tree.

The warm summer evening breeze slid over her bare skin and for the briefest of moments she considered going back inside and allowing him the privacy he seemed to want. She didn't want to be that nagging woman who was always trying to get her man to open up. Even though Lily ached for Nash to talk to her, she hoped he would do so on his own.

Before she could make a move, Nash glanced her way. Even in the dim light, she saw the angst in those stormy eyes. The man held so much inside, all that worry he could be sharing with her. She knew he didn't want to upset her and he wanted her to be completely relaxed. But, how could she relax when she was constantly struggling with her own emotions and wondering what was on his mind that seemed to always put that worried look on his face?

Without a word, Nash extended his hand in a silent invitation for her to join him. Stepping from the warm, smooth concrete into the cool, soft grass tickled Lily's toes as she made her way through the yard.

When she slid her hand into his, he maneuvered her around until she sat on his lap, her legs over his thighs and her feet brushing the top of the grass. Her head fell against his shoulder, a move she'd become so comfortable with.

Nash's deep breathing combined with the crickets chirping in the distance had Lily smiling at another layer of the simple life she absolutely loved. Relaxing here would be no problem at all. And raising a child in this calming atmosphere would be a dream. Perhaps she could live here. Why not? Who said she had to live in LA? She was well-known, her agent shopped scripts for her and she would have to go on location regardless of where she lived.

When Ian scheduled her live interview, she could confess her pregnancy, open up about the man she'd developed a serious relationship with and explain they are keeping things private and had purposely kept away from the limelight.

Could the solution be so easy? So within her reach?

"Sorry I disturbed you," she told him, breaking the silence. "I started getting worried when you didn't come back inside."

Nash's arms tightened around her waist. "I lose track of time when I sit out here."

"I can see why." Lily trailed her fingertips along his tanned, muscular forearm. "So quiet and peaceful."

He flattened his palm against her belly, spreading his fingers wide. "How's our girl?"

"Safe and healthy."

He turned his head slightly to kiss her forehead. "And you? How are you feeling?"

"Hopeful," she answered honestly.

The rhythm of his heartbeat against her shoulder nearly matched hers. There was so much going on inside her, so many unanswered questions, but there was something she had no question about.

"I love you," she whispered into the darkness. His body tensed beneath hers. "I know we've really gone about everything backward and I don't expect you to say anything back. But I have to be honest with you because I need you to know how serious I am here."

When he remained silent a little piece of her heart crumbled. While she didn't expect him to return her feelings, she'd had a thread of hope that he would. She wanted to know how deep he was in with her, but he continued to be a man of mystery, because she never could get a good grasp on exactly how he felt.

Oh, he'd said he wanted to be with her, but that didn't necessarily mean love. And she so wanted a family, a real family. She didn't want to settle for less…and she *wouldn't* settle for less.

When the silence became too much to bear, Lily started to push off Nash's lap, but those strong arms around her tightened. "Don't go."

On a sigh, she closed her eyes and leaned back.

"You're everything, Lily," he said after a minute had passed. "I had no idea what my life had been missing until you came into it. But I'm still working through some things, still struggling with my identity."

The fact that she was worried about herself had guilt coursing through her. Nash had a great deal of life's obstacles thrown at him all at once.

"I want to give myself to you completely." His hands covered hers over her stomach as his soft, raw words washed over her. "I want nothing to come between us. This baby we've made is a blessing and I'm not taking our little family for granted. I just need some time to come to grips with everything and get things in order for us."

Easing up, Lily turned in his arms. Tears flooded her eyes. "Oh, Nash. There's nothing you need to get ready for us. I'm sorry I put you on the spot, but I couldn't keep the truth from you any longer. I think I started falling in love with you the moment you first swept me up into that loft."

Cupping her cheek with one of his rough, calloused hands, Nash's eyes zeroed in on hers. "I don't deserve you."

"You deserve everything you've ever wanted," she retorted with a smile as a tear slid down her cheek.

With the pad of his thumb, he swiped the moisture away. "I hope I get it."

Lily laid a kiss on his lips before shifting to lie against him once more. "Am I hurting you?"

"Never."

He may not have been able to give her the words she wanted to hear, but she knew he loved her. All those demons he battled internally kept him from speaking the truth, but Lily knew in her heart that Nash was in love with her.

"I have a film opportunity," she told him. "I think it's a good choice."

His body stilled beneath hers. "Are you going back to LA?"

Lacing her fingers through his, she settled their hands in her lap. "Not yet, but I will have to for a bit if I take the role. I would actually do the entire film there. I also still need to go see my mom, too."

"What's the role?"

Lily laughed. "Something I've never done before, actually. It's an animation and I'm pretty excited about the prospect because I think this will be a really big hit."

Nash stroked his thumb across the back of her hand. "And what does Ian suggest?"

"He said it's perfect, especially since I can record in a studio and not worry about my growing tummy." Lily turned her head to look up at Nash. "But I wanted to discuss this with you before I gave him my answer."

Piercing blue eyes met hers. "When does he need an answer by?"

"Tomorrow night."

Lily's heartbeat quickened. She'd never discussed her career with anyone other than her agent before. Never had anyone else to consider when making a film choice. This new territory was interesting and slightly nerve-racking.

"Do you want to take the role?"

"I think I do."

Nash shifted in the chair, causing her to sit up and look down into his eyes.

"What would you do if you weren't pregnant and you

didn't know me?" he asked, sliding his hand over her bare thigh.

"I'd take the role."

With a squeeze to her leg and a sexy, rugged smile, Nash nodded. "Then that's what you should do. I don't expect you to recalculate your life, Lily. You still need to do what makes you happy."

A weight she didn't know she was carrying was lifted off her shoulders. "Ian said recording wouldn't start for a couple months, but he's getting me the script to look over. Aiden O'Neil is going to play opposite me."

"Wasn't he the guy in one of the scripts you just turned down?"

Lily nodded. "He declined after he heard I wouldn't do it. He's a good friend, like Max. And this will be a good change of pace for me. Hey, no hair and makeup, either."

Nash laughed. "You're stunning no matter what you have on." Those eyes darted down to her lips as his fingers trailed up her thigh and beneath the cotton gown. "Or don't have on."

The man could get her body to respond with the simplest words or lightest of touches.

"You know you're the only man I've let get this close to me since the scandal." She trembled as his hand continued to glide over her skin. "I never thought I'd get this close to someone again, let my heart be exposed to the chance of being ripped apart."

Nash's looked at her seriously. "You humble me, Lily."

"If you want to try to make this work, you're not going to be able to avoid the media. Not once the pregnancy is out there."

The muscle in Nash's jaw ticked. She knew he didn't want to be thrust into the public eye. Resting her hand against the side of his face, rubbing her thumb along his bottom lip, Lily leaned in and whispered, "Take me inside and make love to me."

In one swift move, he had her lifted and turned to straddle his lap. Then his hands were lifting her gown to her waist. Lily leaned forward and clutched his shoulders as he worked the zipper on his jeans.

"Or not," she added as he threw her a crooked grin.

"I don't want to wait," he said, easing a hand between her legs to stroke her until she thought her eyes would roll back in her head. "Do you?"

Lily shivered, holding on tight to him so she didn't fall. "No," she whispered as he continued to torture her. "Please, Nash."

She'd come out here wearing a flimsy nightgown, sans underwear and she thought he could wait to get inside the house? Hell no. Nash wanted her here, now.

He also wanted to not discuss how the media would hone in on them. The last thing he needed was being identified before he could fully disclose the rest of his life.

The little moans escaping her, the way her hips rocked against his hand and seeing her eyes closed, head tilted back as he pleasured her was nearly his undoing. Not to mention the perfect distraction for both of them.

Damn it, he owed her so much…a debt he could never repay because while she was freely handing out her love, he was still betraying her by keeping a lie bottled inside.

The thought of having her walk out of his life once she learned the truth would be the equivalent of taking a knife to his heart. Because he loved her. God help him, he did. And when she'd whispered those sweet words to him, it had taken all of his willpower to remain silent.

He couldn't tell her he loved her, not when there was such a heavy lie that still hovered between them. He could only show her how much she meant to him. Once he revealed himself, after he'd talked with Damon one more time, Nash would truly open up and tell her every single thing she deserved to know.

Nash removed his hand, gripped her hips and eased her down onto him. Making love to Lily with the warm summer breeze embracing them like lovers, Nash wrapped his arms around her and tugged her toward him, capturing her mouth. Her fingers slid into his hair, sending him another reminder that he was living a lie. The longer hair, the scruffy beard, the rental home…all of it was a lie.

All of it, except for the fact he loved her, loved this baby and wanted a lifetime with them both.

As her body started to tremble, Nash felt himself losing control. She broke the kiss, looked him in the eyes, just like when they'd been in his hallway.

Those dark eyes held his as her body tensed. "I love you," she told him as her body broke.

And as Nash followed her over the edge, he wished he could repeat those words back to her.

The food had been amazing and now the entire Barrington clan was gathered on the back lawn, waiting for the fireworks show that Damon had no doubt shelled out a pretty penny for, considering they'd planned this impromptu party very last-minute. But when a man had his financial padding, he could afford to snap fingers and plan such niceties with little notice.

Blankets were lying side by side and some front to back creating the effect of an oversize outdoor carpet. Ian, Cassie and little Emily sat on one blanket. Another quilt had Grant and Tessa all snuggled together. Lily was nestled between Nash's legs, her back leaning against his chest. And surprisingly Damon and Linda were on a quilt together, laughing and…whispering?

Was something going on there?

Nash smiled. Good for Damon if he was seeking happiness. He'd been without his wife for so many years, concentrating on raising his family and climbing to the top of the horse racing industry.

Nash rested a hand on Lily's stomach. He would do the same thing for his child. Nash wanted to give his baby, and Lily, everything they deserved and more.

She'd already made plans to visit her mother this coming weekend. Nash figured while she was gone, he could have a heart-to-heart with Damon and come clean with him.

He kept telling himself he was waiting on the right opportunity. No other time would work to his benefit except while Lily was gone. He could only hurt so many people at a time without crumbling himself. And he had to remain strong or he'd never be able to fight to keep what was his.

When the first spark and boom lit up the sky, Emily squealed and jumped to her feet. "Look! Look!"

Nash watched the adorable toddler with bouncing blond curls. Her infectious laughter had everyone watching her reaction as opposed to the show in the sky.

"She is precious," Lily said.

Cassie grinned. "Thanks. I was afraid the noise would scare her, but obviously not."

With each colorful burst, Emily clapped or jumped up and down. Nash caught Tessa's glance to Grant, a smile tugged at her lips and Grant's hand came around to her stomach, as well.

Interesting. Looked as though they had their own announcement to make.

Yeah, he needed to finish revealing his identity sooner rather than later because he wanted to be part of this family with no lies hovering between them. If they would accept him after all was said and done. He also had to have a long talk with his mother. Lily wasn't the only one who needed to share news about her pregnancy. Nash hadn't wanted to tell his mom over the phone, either.

"I'm going to grab a bottle of water." Lily came to her feet and looked down to him. "Want anything?"

A do-over? A chance to make this all right from the beginning? A lifetime to make it up to her?

"I'm good," he told her. "I would've gotten your water for you."

Lily laughed. "I'm perfectly capable of getting my own water."

As she moved around him, he saw Tessa hop to her feet as well and head in Lily's direction. Within seconds, Cassie and Linda followed.

Emily settled onto Ian's lap and Damon turned toward the others. "Looks like our ladies have deserted us."

The fireworks continued, the thunderous sound filling the warm night.

"I'd say Tessa is telling our news," Grant replied with a wide grin.

"She told me this afternoon," Damon said, his smile matching Grant's.

Ian's head bounced back and forth between the two men. "Well? Do I get to know what's going on?"

"We're having a baby, too," Grant said.

Ian leaned over and slapped Grant on the shoulder. "That's awesome, man. Congratulations."

Nash nodded in agreement. "I'm happy for you guys."

"I'm sure they're all back there chatting about babies and pregnancies," Damon said, leaning back on his hands. "Linda has treated my girls like her own since Rose passed. I'm sure she's all over Tessa, asking about her eating habits and if she's resting enough."

"Oh, I'm making sure of it," Grant supplied. He raked a hand through his hair and sighed. "But her emotions are all over the place."

"Dude, they're not going to settle down anytime soon," Nash informed him. "Lily can go from crying to laughing in seconds."

Ian smoothed Emily's curls down, as they kept blowing in the wind. "Cassie has been wanting another baby," he said. "I'm sure all this baby talk will only speed up the process. We'd discussed waiting another year."

"My family is growing." Damon beamed, glancing up when Linda came back and settled down next to him. "These are exciting times."

"Indeed they are," Linda said as she patted Damon's leg.

Oh, yeah. Something was definitely going on there.

Cassie, Tessa and Lily came back and took their seats. Lily clutched her water bottle and leaned back against him.

Nash leaned over and patted Tessa on the arm. "Congrats on the baby."

Tessa lit up, just like Lily did when they discussed their baby. "Thanks. I'm so excited."

Chatter ensued as the fireworks came to an end. An hour later they were all still discussing babies, due dates, baby showers and growing families. Emily had long since fallen asleep in Ian's arms and Nash felt a tug on his heart. He couldn't wait to cradle his own child to sleep, to know that he was a comfort and security for someone.

Lily tipped her head, kissed him slightly on the lips. "Thank you for bringing me here."

"I didn't bring you," he replied, hugging her tighter against him. "Your movie brought you here."

She ran her hand along his arm. "You know what I mean. You've included me in your life, in your new family even though we're still new ourselves. I feel like I belong here, like I belong with you. You don't know how much that means to me."

Yeah, he did. He knew she valued family just as much as he did. He knew she wanted their baby to have that special bond.

But would Nash sever that bond once he revealed himself?

Nash kissed the end of her nose and squeezed her tight again. "You deserve this."

And he just had to find a way to convince her he wasn't purposely deceiving her and that she belonged there. She belonged with him.

Fifteen

Taking the first step in getting his life back under control was long overdue. He loved Lily. There was no denying the fact anymore. Now with her in Arizona visiting her mother, he was at the Barrington estate about to confront his father and put one hell of a kink in their newfound relationship.

He should've let this out earlier, but he'd just not been ready. Since falling so hard for Lily, Nash knew putting it off any longer would be an even bigger mistake. Starting now, he was going to set things straight and take control of his life.

Here all this time he'd thought he'd been in control. He'd only been controlled by his own lies and selfishness.

Nash paced the living room. He'd already gone into the kitchen and said hi to Linda, who was washing up dishes from breakfast. She'd invited him to stick around for lunch, but Nash didn't make any promises. He highly doubted he'd be welcome at that point.

Nerves curled deep in his gut and a vulnerability he hated to admit he had threatened to consume him. But he wouldn't back down. He wouldn't take the coward's way out.

"Nash, I was surprised to hear from you today." Damon crossed the room and Nash came to his feet. "Not that you aren't welcome anytime. What brings you here on a Saturday morning? Is Lily with you?"

Nash shook his head. "She went to visit her mother in Arizona. I needed to talk to you about something important."

Damon laughed and smacked his hand on Nash's shoulder. "Last time you said that you announced you were my son. What else could you have to tell me?"

Raking a hand through his long hair, hair that he couldn't wait to cut off so he could get back to looking like himself, Nash gestured toward the chair. "You may want to have a seat."

Damon's smile faltered. "Is something wrong with your mother?"

"No, no. She's fine." Nash sank to the sofa, resting his elbows on his knees. "I actually drove down to see her yesterday after Lily's plane took off. She's excited about the baby."

Nervous chitchat would only postpone the inevitable for so long. He'd come here on a mission and he refused to let nerves take over.

"I actually came to tell you that I can't accept Don Pedro from you."

Damon's silver brows drew in as he eased forward in the leather chair. "If you're concerned about the money I could make by selling him, don't be."

Shaking his head, Nash clenched his fists. Damn it, he hated this. "I know you're not concerned with the money. I know this because I've been offering to buy him for nearly three months now."

Confusion settled onto Damon's face as the elderly man drew his brows together in confusion. "I'm not following you."

"You've been getting phone calls from Barry Stallings."

Damon's back straightened. "How do you know this?"

Holding firm to his courage, Nash leveled Damon's gaze. "Because Barry is my assistant."

Damon stared, studied for a minute, then gasped as realization dawned on him. Jerking to his feet, he started shaking his head.

"How can this be?" he whispered, as if to himself. "You—you're…what the hell game have you been playing? The long hair, the beard. You're a bigger man than I remember. Then again I haven't seen you in person in years. How long have you been planning to come here and spy on me? Was the son angle just a convenient reason? Or are you even my son?"

For once in his life, Nash remained seated, wanting Damon to feel in control. Nash had never relinquished power to anyone before, and certainly not to his longtime rival, but right now, rivalry was gone and this was about so much more.

"I haven't lied about the fact I'm your son," Nash began. "I did find out when my mother had a stroke several months ago."

"Jake Roycroft is my son." Damon's jaw clenched. "So, you came in deceiving us from day one with this fake name, long hair and a beard. Your clothes are all worn and even your truck is dated. You sure as hell thought this betrayal out down to the last detail."

There was no other angle to look at it. Damon was dead-on.

"I did," Nash confessed. "I wanted to come in, find out what you had planned for your horses after retirement. I needed a prizewinner to breed with mine and I wanted the best.

"Finding out I was your son was like a slap in the face," he went on, putting everything on the line for the family he'd come to love…the rival he always thought he'd hate. "I couldn't believe it. But my mother's gut-wrenching confession was all the proof I needed. She'd kept the truth from me, from you, because she knew it would tear us up. She'd watched this feud for years, but when she had her stroke, she couldn't keep the secret anymore."

"And what was your plan when you first arrived?" Damon

asked, his tone anything but that of a loving father or the cheerful man who'd walked into this room moments ago.

Now Nash did rise. He needed to pace, needed to get out of here, but he had to stay and continue to unravel this damn web he'd caught himself in.

"I was hoping if I got a good idea of what your plans were for the horses, I could get my assistant to offer enough money to take them."

Nash crossed to the mantel where a new photo of Tessa, Cassie and Damon sat. The trio stood in front of Don Pedro after the historic win of the Triple Crown. Nash hadn't been there, he'd been here at Stony Ridge taking care of the other horses.

Other photos showed Rose holding her two young daughters in front of a waterfall, a teen Tessa atop a Thoroughbred, Cassie in a ring with another horse. The family was tight and Nash wondered if he'd ever truly be able to break in where he longed to be.

"I was also battling whether or not to tell you the truth about being your son." Nash turned back around. Damon hadn't moved, except to cross his arms over his chest. "But the more I got to know you all, the more I learned as the film was being shot, I realized you weren't the enemy I knew over the years. You were a ruthless businessman to me, but with your family…you were a different person."

Nash refused to succumb to those damn emotions that he was nearly choking on. He wouldn't show weakness, not now. Remaining strong was the only way he would get through this.

"Between sneaking around with Lily and battling how to tell you who I was, I was torn. I decided to tell you everything after the film crew left, after Lily and I were finished and after you'd hopefully sold the horse to my assistant."

Damon's eyes narrowed. "That all changed when Lily became pregnant. Right?"

Nash nodded, disgusted by the look of hatred he'd put in Damon's eyes.

Being cut off from the Barringtons would kill Nash, but he would take it like a man. He'd done all of this to himself and had nowhere else to place the blame. Every downfall that was about to happen was nothing less than what he deserved. Nash just prayed the people he'd come to care about had mercy on him.

"Have you been lying all this time to Lily?" Damon asked.

The man may as well have punched him in the gut. Nash rested his hands on his hips, glanced away and nodded.

"So she knows you're my son, but she has no clue you're a millionaire with your own estate, your own spread of horses," Damon repeated as if to drive that knife deeper. "She thinks she's fallen in love with a simple, hardworking, honest groom. You waited until she left town to confront me and, what, you expect this to all be tidied up for when she returns?"

Damn it, why did that explanation make Nash sound more like a bastard than a man who'd started off with good intentions?

"I'm telling her everything when she comes back," Nash replied, forcing himself to hold Damon's angry gaze. "I love her. I didn't come into this expecting to get wrapped up personally with anybody at all, least of all Lily. Then our affair started and spiraled out of control. Then I got to know you all even more and I started wanting more than what I came here for. I started out with a goal to get Don Pedro at any cost. Now, though, I don't want him. I just want Lily, I want my father. You have all the power. You can cut me out of your life or we can try to make this relationship work."

Damon continued to stare through that narrow gaze.

"I understand if you don't want anything to do with me." Nash had laid it all out there, had even offered a meager defense. Now he had to finish up and get the hell out before he started sobbing like some damn fool. "I wouldn't blame you for cutting me out of your life. I mean, I haven't been part of your life for very long, so you could just go back to the way things were before I ever came around. Nothing would change for you, really."

Linda stepped into the doorway. "Damon—"

"Not now, Linda."

She moved farther into the room until she was standing beside Damon. "Don't make a decision you'll regret later."

Nash jerked his attention to the elderly woman who was gripping a kitchen towel in her hands, her knuckles white. He'd never guessed he'd have an ally in any of this, but having anybody at all on his side was a blessing he didn't deserve.

"Linda, you don't know what you're talking about," Damon said between clenched teeth. "This is between me and Nash. Damn it. Jake."

"Nash is my real middle name," he replied, as if that made any of this easier to swallow.

Linda laid a hand on Damon's arm. "I know you're hurt, but if you'll put your pride aside for two minutes, you'll see he's hurt, too. And, he's still your son. That's something he never had to reveal."

Damon's eyes flashed toward Nash's. Odd, now that everyone had been calling him Nash for months, he'd come to think of himself as Nash, the groom, as opposed to Jake, the billionaire.

"I don't want to make this harder for you," he explained. "I wanted to get everything out and I did. I'll go and leave the next step up to you."

Leaving with so much hurt between them, leaving with so many questions still left unanswered would kill him. But Damon needed to come to grips with this just as Nash had. Realizing his rival was also his father had taken Nash months to digest and he couldn't expect Damon to do so in the span of a few minutes.

Silence filled the room as Damon continued to stare at

Nash in disbelief. Linda still clutched the towel as her eyes darted back and forth between the two stubborn men.

"You know how to reach me." Nash raked a hand over his jaw, the beard he'd become so familiar with bristling beneath his palm. "I won't contact you again."

Damon said nothing as Nash headed toward the foyer, but there was one last thing his father needed to know. One last bit of his heart he'd lay on the line, even though he would surely damn himself later for being so open and vulnerable.

Gripping the door frame, Nash turned to look at his father for what would probably be the last time. "For what it's worth, I enjoyed the past several months. I'd wondered about my father my entire life and even though I was shocked that it turned out to be you, I wouldn't trade my time here with you and the girls for anything."

Those threatening emotions choked him as Nash headed out the door, leaving Stony Ridge and his father behind.

That part was over, and as hellish and gut-wrenching as it had been, Nash knew what had transpired between his father and himself was absolutely nothing compared to the hurt and the anguish that awaited him when Lily returned. The thought of causing her pain was killing him.

She deserved to know the truth once and for all. And he deserved nothing less than watching her walk away. Now he had to figure out a way to keep the inevitable from happening.

Sixteen

Being away from Nash for a week had been harder than she'd thought. She'd loved seeing her mother again, but she truly missed the man she'd fallen in love with. Lily found herself missing the Barringtons, as well.

In the two weeks she'd been gone her little belly had pooched out just enough to have her smiling and gliding her hand over the swollen area. Not a drastic change to anyone looking at her, but she noticed and she had no doubt Nash would notice. That man knew her body better than she did.

She'd been careful not to wear anything tight, plus she donned sunglasses and a hat when traveling through the airport. The last thing she wanted was anyone finding out about the baby before she could make an announcement.

Nash's idea of her dropping the bomb before the media could speculate was brilliant. With the Barrington film getting buzz already months before release, Ian already booked her a one-on-one interview with a popular TV anchor. And perhaps by then she'd have some other news to share…maybe even a ring on her finger. Dare she hope that Nash was ready to follow her confession with one of his own?

Lily had changed her flight to a day earlier. She hadn't been able to wait to get back to Nash, to have him see how her belly and their baby had grown. She wanted his hands on her, wanted to share this moment, silly as that may sound.

Lily had rented a car at the airport, eager to surprise Nash since he thought he'd be picking her up the following morning. As she pulled up next to his old truck in the drive, she smiled and killed the engine.

The porch swing swayed in the breeze, as did the hanging ferns. This cozy home was perfect for their family. Images of her lavish condo in LA flashed through her mind and Lily knew that second that she didn't want her child growing up in a town with so much chaos. This porch would be the perfect play area for a toddler, the wide drive would serve as the place where their child could ride a bike or make chalk drawings. The expansive backyard just begged for a swing set complete with slide and maybe a sandbox.

When Lily looked at this house, she didn't see it as Nash's home anymore, she saw it as their future. Even though he was just renting it, she had fallen in love with it and wanted to stay. Perhaps if she offered the owner a fair price he'd sell to them.

One goal at a time, she promised herself as she stepped from the car. A light drizzle had accompanied her drive in and now the rain started falling a bit harder, faster as she made her way to the front door. The luggage in the car could wait. Her need to see Nash couldn't.

The front door was unlocked, such was life in the country, and another reason she wanted to raise her family there.

As soon as she stepped over the threshold, she smelled that familiar, masculine scent that could only be associated with the man she'd fallen in love with. She'd missed that smell, missed the feel of his body next to hers as she slept, missed the way he would hold her, look at her, bring her a random grilled cheese when she hadn't even said she was hungry.

And her body ached to touch him again. She'd gone so

long without sex before meeting Nash, but since that first time with him, she constantly craved more. Nash was it for her.

No longer did she fear the media and what they would say. They'd talk regardless and half the "news" was made up stories anyway. No, she knew Nash would be by her side; he wouldn't let her go through any of this alone. She was that confident in their newfound relationship. They'd come so far from the frenzied affair in the loft. Even their passion had reached another level of intimacy.

"Nash," she called as she stepped into the living room and clicked on a lamp. Dusk was settling outside and the promise of a storm was thick in the air. "I'm home."

Footsteps from the back of the house had her turning toward the hall. The sight of him shocked her, leaving her frozen in her place and utterly speechless.

The sight of him wearing only a pair of worn jeans riding low on his hips and nothing else but excellent muscle tone was enough to have her go silent and just enjoy the view. But, it was the clean-shaven face and the new haircut that had her doing a double take.

Those piercing blue eyes surrounded by thick, dark lashes were even more prominent now. His hair was wet as if he'd just gotten out of the shower. He froze, resting his hands on his hips. Apparently he was just as surprised to see her as she was about his transformation.

"You're early," he stated, brows drawn in. "Is something wrong?"

"Everything's fine." Lily took a step forward, then another until she'd closed the gap between them. Reaching up to cup his face with both hands, she studied this new Nash. "Why the change?"

Not that he looked bad. The Nash with the beard and unkempt hair was rugged and mysterious. This Nash with the square jaw and chiseled cheeks, with more emphasis on those mesmerizing eyes was flat-out sexy and intriguing.

"I needed to," he told her, taking her hands in his. He

kissed her palms before placing her hands on his chest. "It's the first step in getting where I need to be, where we need to be."

Lily couldn't stop taking in the sight of him. Who knew a dark beard and disheveled hair could change someone's appearance so much?

Those worry lines between his brows had deepened and the haunted look in his eyes hadn't been there when she'd left.

"Something's wrong." The feel of his quickened heartbeat beneath her hand confirmed her suspicions. "Talk to me."

Releasing her hands, he slid his own around her waist and pulled her against him. When he froze and jerked his gaze down, Lily smiled.

"I grew a little," she explained, lifting her oversize T-shirt to expose her slightly rounded belly. "One morning I just woke up and there it was."

She wondered how he'd react to her new shape, but when both of his hands came around to cover the swell, Lily knew he was just as excited about their growing baby as she was.

Nash dropped to his knees, laying his forehead against her stomach as his thumbs stroked her bare skin. The thought that this child could already bring such a strong man to his knees was so sexy.

Lily threaded her fingers through his much shorter hair. "I've missed you so much," she whispered.

The first rumble of thunder shook the house, rain pelted the windows harder now. Nash glanced up at her, a storm of his own flashing through his expressive eyes as he came back to his feet and gathered her against him.

He tilted his face against her neck, his lips tickling her skin and sending jolts of need streaming through her…as if she needed any more encouragement to want this man.

"I've needed this," he murmured. "Needed you."

Lily wrapped her arms around his bare waist. "You'll always have me, Nash. I'm in this forever, but you keep holding back. When will you open up and let me in? Finally see that what we have only gets stronger each day?"

Nash pulled back, and lightning flashed through the window, illuminating his handsome, yet troubled face. "I've always known how strong we are, Lily. I've never doubted it, never once thought what we had wasn't real. I didn't want to admit it at first because I knew you'd be leaving and I was going to have to say goodbye, so I was protecting myself. But you mattered to me the second I made you mine up in that loft."

Her body trembled at the memory even though she had a sinking feeling there was more to what he had to say.

"You're right, I've been holding back." He stepped away, raking a hand down his smooth jaw. "I never intended for you to get caught in this war I made with myself. I figured once you were gone and we parted ways you'd never have to know."

Chills crept up her spine. What was he about to confess? Was he married? Did he already have children somewhere? Was he dying? The endless questions swirled around in her head until she thought she'd pass out.

Gripping the back of the sofa, Lily met his gaze head-on. She wasn't about to cower now. Whatever he was on the verge of telling her obviously was tearing him up, too. If they were going to be a couple, they needed to face the crisis together.

"You said that about Damon being your father," she told him. "Is there another secret you've kept from me?"

"I need you to know I never meant for you to be affected by this."

Wrapping her arms around herself to ward off the tremors overtaking her body, Lily held her ground. She didn't move, didn't blink. Whatever this was, it was bad.

"You also need to know that I love you," he continued. "I fell in love with you before you told me about the baby. I've wanted to tell you, wanted you to know."

When he stepped forward and reached for her, Lily took a step back, holding her arms out to her side. "Don't. Don't preface whatever bomb you're about to drop with love and think that will fix this. You're picking an awfully convenient time to express the feelings I've tried to get you to share for a while now."

Nash nodded, drawing in a shaky breath. "You're right. You deserve more than what I've given. Just promise you'll hear me out before you make any decisions regarding us, our baby."

"Just tell me!" she yelled, fear spawning her outcry.

The lights flickered, but came right back on as thunder and lightning filled the night. How apropos for everything that was taking place inside this house, inside her heart.

"My real name is Jacob Nash Roycroft. I'm known as Jake to nearly everybody." He took a deep breath and let it out. "I'm not a groom, I'm a horse owner myself. All of this was a setup to spy on Damon."

Air left Lily's lungs as she stared at the man who was quickly becoming a stranger right before her eyes. "Why?" she whispered.

"Damon Barrington has been my rival for a couple of years now." Nash glanced down, raking a hand over his head before he lifted his tormented eyes to meet hers again. "We both own racehorses and I knew he and his girls were retiring. I wanted to go undercover so I could see how to get some of his prizewinning horses because he wouldn't sell them to me. I also wanted to see him as a man outside of the business world. I didn't even know going in if I would tell him about being his son. Every single day I battled this and before I knew it, we were in an affair and by then I was in too deep."

Everything he told her weighed heavily on her heart. He'd lied to her from the beginning. He had his own horse farm, he was a racehorse mogul.

Which meant he had money. Plenty of money and he

was used to getting his way. Which would explain his take-charge attitude, his beautifully appointed home, the doctor who made house calls, no doubt because Nash had paid her a hefty sum.

There was no way to describe the level of hurt that spread through her, leaving her cold, empty. Everything she'd known…no, everything she'd felt had been a lie based on nothing but a man who was only looking out for himself. Anything she felt was for a man who didn't even exist…except in her heart.

"You bastard," she whispered, hugging her midsection. She refused to look at him, she wouldn't give him the satisfaction of seeing her broken.

"My name may be different and my bank account bigger than you thought." Nash's bare feet shuffled across the hardwood floor as he came closer. "But I'm still me, Lily. I'm still the man who wants to be with you. I'm still the man who fathered that child."

His palm cupped her chin, lifting her face so she had no choice but to look him in the eyes. "I'm still the man who loves you."

There was no way to stop the tears from spilling over. She didn't even try. She hadn't wanted him to see her vulnerable, but she'd quickly changed her mind. He deserved to see the results of his lies, his betrayal. He deserved to hurt just as much as she was hurting. If he loved her so much, then she'd hate to see how he treated his enemies.

Swatting his hand away, Lily pushed off the back of the couch and stood straight up. "Don't touch me. Never touch me again. You don't love me, you love yourself. I don't think you're capable of loving me, Nash…or whatever the hell your name is."

She'd thought being deceived years ago had been bad, but this was a whole new level of crippling pain.

She'd take public humiliation any day over having her heart shattered into so many pieces she feared she'd never find all the shards. She'd been so sure she could trust him with everything.

"Hear me out."

"No." There was no way she would listen to more lies. "I'm done here. You had ample time to tell me the truth, but you started everything off with a lie."

Her heart ached and she feared the cracks and voids would never be filled.

"You want to know what's worse?" she asked, her words wretched out on a sob. "I still love you. Damn you, I can't just turn off my feelings. I can't be cold to someone I care about and I never thought you'd be so heartless to me. How dare you make me feel again, make me think I could trust you after you know what I've been through? How dare you make me love, make me believe in a family I've wanted for so long?"

Nash's eyes shimmered and Lily had to steel herself from feeling any pity. She had no room in her heart for him…not anymore.

"Please, Lily." He started to reach for her again, but as soon as her eyes darted to his hand, he dropped it. "I'll do anything to make this right. Anything so you can see how I've changed since we started seeing each other. You need to know that you are the reason I changed, the reason I told everyone the truth. I did it all because I love you. I want to be with you with nothing between us. Tell me what I can do, I'll do it."

Even hearing him pour his heart out, bare his soul, Lily couldn't trust that what he said was true. How could she? For months he'd found it so easy to lie. Not only to lie, but to sleep with her, make a baby and pretty much set up playing house, all while lying straight to her face.

He was used to getting what he wanted and now that she was done, he was pulling out all the pretty words he thought she wanted to hear. Nothing could fix what he'd done, what he'd destroyed.

"I can't be here."

She pushed him out of the way and headed toward the foyer. She'd just scooped the keys to her rental up off the entry table and placed her hand on the knob when Nash, Jake...whatever, placed his hands on either side of her head and caged her against the door.

The warmth of his chest against her back had her sucking in her breath. Damn her body for responding to his nearness. Her heart was broken, but her hormones hadn't received that message.

"We can work this out," he whispered in her ear. "I can't lose you."

Lightning illuminated the sky, the electric flickered, once, twice. Darkness enveloped them, the silence mocked them. There was a time they would have made use of this raging storm, the power outage. Right now, though, they were strangers, back to square one. Because she definitely didn't know this man standing so close to her she could feel the breath on her cheek.

Being deceived once in a lifetime was enough, but this was the second man to lie to her face and make a complete fool out of her. And even though this time had been just the two of them, the pain and anguish was beyond intensified compared to the first time.

"Let me go," she whispered as her throat clogged with more tears. "Just...let me go."

One hand came around, cupping her stomach and Lily choked back a sob. "Never," he rasped, nuzzling her neck with his lips. "I'll never let go of my family. I'll give you space, I'll do anything you ask me to. But not that. I love you too much."

Lily shook her head, circled his wrist and eased his hand away. "You don't understand," she said, turning to face him, his mouth just a breath away from hers. "This is one thing you can't buy back. You can't control or manipulate with money or power. You're dealing with real people, real feelings. I hope you were able to get those horses you wanted to so damn bad."

She jerked on the door handle behind her, causing his hand to fall away. "And I hope losing me and this baby was worth it."

"You can't go out in that storm."

Lily laughed as the sudden wind whipped her hair around her face. "I'd rather face this storm than stay one more second with a man who thought he could keep my heart in one hand and his secrets in the other."

Jake stood on the balcony of his master suite looking out over the land on his estate. He'd sneaked into his own home after midnight as the raging storm died down. He couldn't stay in the rental cottage another second. Every room smelled like Lily, held memories of their passion. The few bottles and potions of hers she hadn't packed for her trip dominated the vanity space in the bathroom, her small clothes hung next to his in the closet and she'd left a pair of sandals by the back door.

He had nowhere else to go but home…a place he'd always wanted her, but where she would never be. The rain had reduced down to a drizzle, but he didn't care. He felt nothing. Not the cool rain, not the emptiness in his heart, not even a yearning to go to his own stables and look things over since he'd been gone for months.

There was nothing left for him now. On a mission to see his father, gain prizewinning horses and not hurt Lily, Jake had managed to damage everything he'd set out to obtain.

Money wouldn't buy his way out of this because Lily was right, he was dealing with people's feelings and all he'd done was trample all over them in his quest to be number one.

Droplets of rain ran down his smooth face and Jake swiped the moisture away as he turned to go back into his bedroom. The second-floor master suite was impressive in size, but that damn king-size bed dominating the middle of the floor mocked him. Sleeping alone would be hell. Knowing he'd never reach for her again, feel her curvy body against his or her soft breath as she slept…at least if she had her way about it.

But he hasn't been lying when he'd said he would give her space. He'd do whatever it took to get his family back. He knew she'd be hurt from the truth, he didn't blame her. He just didn't know how gut-wrenching seeing her emotional breakdown would be.

Jake jerked off his clothes and shoved them into the hamper in the corner of his room before heading on into the open shower. He couldn't sleep, wasn't even going to attempt it.

As he stood amidst all of the showerheads pelting him with scalding water, Jake wondered how much time Lily would take. He would give her space, but he'd be damned if he'd let her go without a fight and there was no way in hell he'd ever let his child go.

Jake flattened his palms against the tile wall, dropping his head as the water pulsed against his neck. He had a fight ahead of him, a fight he'd never had to take on before. Business, horse racing and training, that's what he knew.

What he didn't know was how to fix all the broken hearts he'd left scattered all over his life.

Seventeen

Lily felt like an absolute fool. When she'd left Jake's home three days ago, she'd not been thinking of anything but how to get away from him. There was only one place she could think of to go and here she sat in the Barringtons' kitchen, sipping orange juice and wondering what in the world she should do next.

"Honey, you're going to have to eat something," Linda said.

The woman had been an absolute comfort these past couple days. She'd not asked questions, she'd merely opened the home up and Damon had even told Lily she could stay as long as she needed.

Problem was, she needed support, comfort, a shoulder to cry on and she didn't want to admit it. But they had fussed over her; even Tessa and Cassie had come over to comfort Lily. They'd brought some clothes when they found out she'd left his house with nothing but the suitcase that had still been in the trunk of her car.

To be coddled and pampered wasn't why she had come, but she had to admit, nursing wounds with people who weren't going to stab you in the back was a refreshing change from her LA life. She could stay there—okay hide there—until she figured out what to do.

Today, though, her doctor was coming by the estate to give her a checkup. Since leaving Jake's house, she hadn't been feeling well. Of course, she'd not been eating a whole lot, either. She made herself eat for the baby, but in reality she probably needed more.

Insomnia had become an unwelcome friend, too. She was in a strange bed, alone and heartbroken, but she'd keep that to herself. The last thing she wanted was pity from anybody. All she wanted was to make sure her baby was healthy and then she needed to confront Jake. As much as seeing him again would kill her, she needed to discuss the baby. He was the father and there was nothing she could do to change that cold, hard fact.

"Maybe just some toast," Lily told Linda, trying to avoid eye contact with the caring woman.

"After the doctor leaves, I expect you to eat a full lunch." Linda put a piece of toast into the toaster and turned back around. "No excuses. You need your strength for that baby and to fight that stubborn man of yours."

"He's not my man."

Linda laughed. "Oh, honey. Of course he is. He made some major mistakes, but you love him. You just need time and so does he. He should suffer for what he's done, I agree with you there, but don't make any major decisions right now."

Lily took another drink and smiled. "I couldn't agree more about the suffering, but I don't think time will make this hurt any less. He lied to me, Linda. Twice. I can't forgive that."

The toast popped up just as Damon entered the kitchen. The man looked about as rough as Lily felt. His silver hair was a bit disheveled, the dark circles beneath his bright eyes proved he wasn't getting sleep.

Join the club.

"Sit down," Linda ordered. "I want to talk to you, too."

Damon jerked his gaze toward her, but Linda wasn't looking at his shocked expression as she was lathering a generous amount of butter onto the thick slice of toast.

The older man remained standing, crossing his arms over his chest. "Say what you want to say so I can get out to the stables."

As calm as you please, Linda crossed to Damon, pointing her finger in his face. "You are being pigheaded. I know Jake hurt you, that's understandable. However, have you thought about what you would've done in his situation? Would you have opened up to your greatest rival and bared your soul? No. You would've treated it like a business move. You would've been just as calculating and secretive."

Guilt churned in Lily's stomach. So many people were hurting all because Jake felt he'd had no other choice.

"Maybe I would've." Damon nodded slightly. "But we're not talking about me." His attention turned to Lily. "What about her? What excuse does he have for deceiving her?"

Linda's eyes softened as she took a slight step back from Damon. "She was an innocent bystander who got caught up in the family drama. Jake loves her, I've seen how he looks at her."

Linda smiled, resting her hand on Damon's cheek. "Just as he's come to care for you and all of us. He's hurting, too, Damon. Can't you reach out to him? See if there's any way you can work on this relationship? He's your son. You can't forget that."

Lily cupped her stomach with both hands, wanting this nightmare to be over, wanting to go back in time and make Jake open up to her. But he hadn't trusted her enough to let her in. Hadn't trusted what they had together to share his life in full.

"Why are you so hell-bent on being in Jake's corner?" Damon asked.

With a slight shrug, Linda moved to take Lily's now-empty glass and put it in the sink. "I'm on the outside looking in. I can see people I care about in pain and I don't like it. This family is too close and life is short. You above all people should know that."

Lily winced as Damon's shoulders fell, and he blinked his eyes as if trying to gain control of his own emotions. Linda had gone straight to the heart with that veiled hint at Rose's unexpected death.

The doorbell rang before anyone else could say a word. Lily was all too eager to step away from this emotional battle because beneath all of this chaos, Linda and Damon shared something much deeper than the standard employer-employee bond.

"That will be the doctor," Lily said as she escaped. "I'll get it."

Lily was anxious to see how the baby had progressed, eager to hear that sweet heartbeat that made the whole world seem perfect and right. She had to focus on her child right now. Her love life, or the love she'd falsely believed in, would have to wait because this innocent child came before lies, deceit and broken hearts.

Entering the open wrought-iron gate flanked by stone pillars, Lily steered her rental car into the long drive lined by pristine white fencing.

She couldn't believe she was actually there. Nerves had her hands shaking as she maneuvered up the drive toward the impressive two-story colonial-style home. White columns extended up from the porch, stabilizing a second-story balcony that stretched across the house. A separate three-car garage sat just behind the house, and off to the left of the drive were the massive white-and-green stables.

Horses out in the field swished away flies as their tails swiped back and forth. An old oak dominated the front yard, but the tire swing dangling from a sturdy branch caught her attention. Why would Jake have a tire swing on a tree? He was single and didn't have any children…yet.

The landscaping around the wide porch had to have been professionally done with the perfectly placed variegated greenery and pops of color from various buds.

She should have turned around. The house was too inviting and the last thing she needed was to be drawn into this part of Jake's world.

As easy as it would be for her to convince herself to turn around, she had things to discuss with him. They were bound forever, whether she liked it or not, and the doctor had expressed some minor concerns with the baby. Jake deserved to know. Unfortunately, she needed his help, too. As much as she hated to admit it, she couldn't impose on the Barringtons any longer. She'd been there nearly a week and, after her appointment, she knew she needed to stand strong and take control back in her life.

Lily stepped out into the summer heat and made her way up onto the wide porch. Colorful pots filled with various greenery decorating each side of the door made for a picturesque entry. Everything about Jake's home looked like something out of a magazine.

This was not what she'd expected at all. Jake's rental house had seemed homey, but that had been a stage, a prop in his game. His real home was just as inviting, if not more so.

Lily rang the bell before she could change her mind and race back to her car. Moments later a young lady, probably somewhere in her early thirties, answered the door. The beautiful woman with long, blond hair had eyes the color of emeralds and a pleasant smile. Jealousy punched Lily straight in the gut.

"Hello," the lady greeted. "Can I help you?"

Whoever this woman was…

No. Lily had left Jake, so what he was doing now was none of her business. But seeing that he'd moved on so fast only intensified the hurt she'd lived with for the past several days. Or had this woman always been here waiting on Jake?

"Wait…aren't you Lily Beaumont?"

Celebrity status strikes again. "I am," she replied, trying to find fault with the stranger, but her beauty was flawless. "Is Jake here?"

The young woman nodded with a smile. "He's down in the stables," she said, pointing across the way. "He won't mind if you go on down. He told us you may stop by."

Anger slid through her veins, gliding right through the hurt he'd caused. "Oh, he did, did he?" she asked, raising a brow. "Thank you."

Turning on her heel, Lily's sandals slapped against the concrete as she marched her way toward the stables. The heat was nearly unbearable and Lily had to focus on the open doorway to the stable. Once she had her say, she could get back in her air-conditioned car and cool down, then this wave of dizziness would subside.

Of course, trying to keep her blood pressure down was a bit difficult at the moment. How dare Jake alert…whoever that lady was that Lily would be coming by? What a cocky, ego-inflated—

The rant died a quick death in her mind when she stepped through the open door and found Jake shirtless, holey jeans riding low, sweat glistening over every bare spot her eyes took in as he cleaned out one of the stalls.

He hadn't seen her yet, which gave her the opportunity to appreciate the beauty of his body. Just because she was pissed at him for lying didn't mean she was dead. Jake had the sexiest body she'd ever laid eyes on…which is how she ended up in this predicament to begin with. Saying no to a man like Jake was impossible.

Stepping farther into the stables, she stopped halfway up the aisle and crossed her arms. "Don't you have a staff to do this for you?"

Jake jerked around, bumbling with the pitchfork in one

hand before he caught it with the other. Gripping the top of the handle, his eyes drank her in, his chest heaving from obvious exertion. Lily had to remember she was here for one reason only…and it wasn't to appreciate the beautiful male form standing before her.

"What are you doing here?" he asked.

Holding her ground, Lily shifted her stance. "Why are you acting surprised? Didn't you tell the pretty blonde that there was a possibility I'd come by?"

Damn it, she hadn't been able to hold back that stab of jealousy in her tone, and from his amused smirk he'd picked up on her green-eyed monster, too.

"She's my maid," he informed her, swiping his forearm across his forehead.

Lily rolled her eyes. "I don't care what she is. What you do in your time now isn't my business."

Silence settled between them until a horse shifted in its stall. She hated the uncomfortable cloud that seemed to hang over them.

"You do care," he told her, dropping the pitchfork into the stall. "You wouldn't be here if you didn't."

Oh, that ego she once found attractive was so damn maddening right now.

Tilting her chin and taking a step forward, because Lily knew who really held the power here, she stopped only a few feet from him and cursed herself when her eyes dropped to that sweaty, chiseled chest. She couldn't hold on to her control if she was being tempted by the devil himself.

"Actually I'm here because I just had a checkup." Lacing her fingers just below her stomach, Lily held his gaze. "She said my blood pressure is still high and I need to start taking precautions to keep it down. There's some concern with me and the baby, so she said she wants to see me again in two weeks instead of the usual four to make sure the condition is under control."

"Damn it." He raked a hand through his damp hair,

rubbed the back of his neck and met her gaze. "What can I do? I know I've caused you more stress, that can't be helping. Tell me what I can do to fix this."

The worry etched over his face almost moved her. But that worry was for the baby.

"Actually I'm not here to get help from you," she said. "I'm here to ask what you paid the doctor to care for me. I'm reimbursing you."

"Like hell you are." Jake closed the gap between them, the tips of his boots nearly touching her bare toes. Those bright eyes were now blazing, the muscle in his jaw clenching. "You're not paying me a dime. This is my baby, too."

"I had a feeling you'd say that," she muttered as a wave of dizziness swept through her. Lily closed her eyes for just a moment, waiting for it to pass before she opened and met his still-angry gaze. "So I'm at least paying half."

"I pay for what's mine," he all but growled. "I will take care of my family, no matter what the needs are. It's best you realize that now."

Black dots danced before her and Lily shook her head, wiping the sweat from the back of her neck. "Could I get some water?"

In an instant Jake's hands were on her shoulders, touching her face, brushing her hair back. His eyes instantly held concern and worry. "Are you dizzy?"

Damning herself for showing weakness the one time in her life she needed to be the strongest, Lily could only simply close her eyes and nod.

Before she knew what was happening, Jake had swept her up into his arms and was carrying her out of the stables.

"Don't," she protested, but even to her own ears the plea sounded feeble. "I just need water. I'll be fine."

Ignoring her completely, Jake reached the back door to his house and squatted down far enough to turn the knob. Once inside where the cool air-conditioning hit her, Lily was already feeling as if the world had stopped tilting so much.

Jake closed the door with his foot and took her straight to the living area where he laid her on the oversize leather sofa.

"Jake, is everything all right?"

Lily didn't open her eyes, but she recognized the female voice from the lady who had answered the front door. Tossing her arm over her eyes, Lily wished she would've just phoned Jake instead of coming there. She'd wanted to show him she was just fine without him, wanted to prove she could get along alone.

And here she was, flat on her back, depending on him and now his girlfriend/maid was taking part in Lily's humiliation.

"Could you get a bottle of water, please, Liz?"

"Of course."

The cushion next to her dipped and Jake's hand covered her stomach, then his fingertips were at the base of her throat. She missed those hands, missed how they could go from showing strength caring for horses to dominating her body in the bedroom.

"Your pulse is out of control."

"I just got hot," she defended, ignoring her betraying hormones. "Once I get some water and sit for a minute, I'll be fine."

"What have you eaten today?"

Shifting her arm to behind her head, Lily glanced up at him. "I had some orange juice and toast a couple hours ago."

His eyes narrowed. "Lily—"

"Mom said you wanted some water."

Lily jerked her attention just beyond Jake's shoulder and saw a young boy with honey-wheat hair tousled by the wind or just the lack of a comb. He came closer, extending the bottle to Jake.

"Thanks, buddy."

The boy smiled, showcasing a couple of missing teeth. "Hi," he told her. "I'm Tyler."

Lily couldn't help but smile back. The boy had no clue who she was and that was just fine with her. He was adorable, but Lily couldn't help but wonder who he was to Jake. The boy looked nothing at all like Jake, but he didn't resemble the lady he'd referred to as mom, either.

"Tyler is Liz's son," Jake informed her as if sensing where her thoughts had gone.

"Hi, Tyler. I'm Lily." She took the water from Jake and sat up a little higher as she uncapped the bottle. "Thank you very much."

"You're welcome."

He turned and ran toward the back of the house, obviously finding nothing exciting with the new arrival.

Taking a long drink, Lily welcomed the cool liquid as it slid down her throat. She needed to get out of Jake's house. The longer she stayed, the more questions she had and she really had no business asking them since she'd left Jake. Well, she physically left him. Emotionally had they ever truly been vested? When a relationship was built on lies it was really difficult to say who left whom first.

When she twisted the lid back on, Jake took the bottle and set it on the coffee table. "Lie down. I'll get you something to eat."

Remaining upright, she shook her head. "I'm not staying, Jake. I just need to pay you and I wanted to let you know about the baby and my appointment. I'll never keep secrets from you."

His shoulders fell and he gave a curt nod. "I deserved that."

Lily laughed. "Oh, Jake. You haven't begun to get what you really deserve."

"Then let me have it," he challenged, his chin tipped up now. "Say what you want, ask whatever you want. Don't shut me out, not when we have so much between us."

He was serious. He truly thought talking would place a bandage over the hurts and they'd go on their merry way to make a family and happily-ever-after. If she started on her rant of how hurt and angry she was now, she feared she'd never stop.

"Whatever we had between us was a lie," she reminded him. "No matter how much you wish you'd done things differently, you still chose not to come clean with me, with Damon. You can't claim to care about us when you hurt us so deeply."

Jake stared at her for a minute, his eyes penetrating straight to her heart. Smelling him, sitting this close to him, within reaching distance of his bare torso, was pure hell. She missed the man she knew, the groom. The man before her was a stranger, a millionaire, but still…he was the man she'd fallen in love with.

Jake jerked to his feet and walked out of the room, leaving Lily confused. He wasn't going to fight? Was he done here?

Seconds later he came back in and stood beside the sofa. "I know you hate me, I know you want nothing to do with me, but I have a proposition for you."

Lily stared up at him. "You've got to be kidding me."

He settled back down beside her, taking her hands in his. Lily tried to ignore how the simple gesture still made her heart beat faster, how she wanted to keep that familiar touch locked away forever. She wanted to tug her hands back, but she wouldn't be childish. Whatever he wanted to say, she'd hear him out. Fighting at this point was moot. The damage was done and she'd officially steeled her heart…okay, she was in the process of doing so, which was why he needed to stop touching her.

"Where have you been staying?" he asked.

"At Stony Ridge."

"I figured," he muttered. "I want you to stay here."

"I don't want to be here at all, let alone to stay."

"Give me one week," he pleaded, his eyes never leaving hers. "That's all I'm asking. One week for you to see the side of me I wasn't able to show you. After seven days if you still want nothing to do with me, I'll let you go. I will still want to be part of my baby's life, but I won't pursue you anymore. I just want you to see the man I've become, the man who loves you and wants to show you he's not the selfish bastard who originally came to Stony Ridge."

Lily needed to tell him the rest of what she'd learned at her doctor visit, but she hated admitting she needed anything from him.

When she remained silent, Jake squeezed her hands. "Don't listen to your mind, Lily," he murmured. "Listen to your heart. You even told me yourself that you couldn't turn off your feelings. I'm only asking for a week. Let me take care of you, show you how we could be with no secrets, no lies."

One week. It was a drop in the bucket compared to the time she'd already spent with him. But how would her heart be at the end of that time? Resisting him was hard on a good day and she had no doubt he'd pull everything out of his arsenal to win her back.

She just had to be smarter, stronger and remain the one in control. Jake couldn't know how much he still affected her.

"The doctor also told me I needed to stay off my feet and let others do things for me." Lily closed her eyes, sighed and refocused on Nash. "I can't keep imposing on the Barringtons. Looks like you get your wish. I'll give you one week, but that doesn't mean I'm falling back into the way we were before."

Liz chose that moment to step into the room carrying a plate and a glass. When she set them on the table, Lily laughed as Jake thanked her.

"Grilled cheese and chocolate milk?" Lily asked, quirking a brow.

"Your favorites."

Why did he have to be so damn sweet at times? This was the same man who purposely betrayed her. She had to remember that. Who's to say he wouldn't resort to those tactics again?

"You owe me nothing," Jake continued, picking up where he'd left off before Liz had come and gone. "But I'm willing to give you everything. I'm laying it all out there for you to see."

Determination poured from him; he was serious and he wasn't backing down. It's not as if he could break her heart any more than he already had, and at the end of the seven days she'd leave. She'd go back to LA or even Arizona to visit her mother and then on to the set to record the animated film she'd just signed on for.

Lily continued to hold his gaze. "I won't sleep in the same bed as you."

Jake opened his mouth, but Lily cut him off. "That's my nonnegotiable. I'm not here to play house."

His eyes darted to her lips, then back to her eyes. "Deal. But, do you really think you can be here any amount of time and not fall back into my bed?" He eased forward, laid his hands over her stomach and feathered his lips across hers. "Now who's the liar?"

Jake came to his feet, set the plate on her lap and walked out of the room. Her lips tingled from the barely there kiss and she cursed her body for the ache that spread through her, begging for more.

Only an hour into her seven-day stint. Why did she feel as though she'd just fallen right into his perfectly laid trap?

Eighteen

Lily had chosen the bedroom upstairs at the opposite end of the hall from Jake's. That was as far away as she could get.

Day one down. Only six more to go and she would be free to leave for Arizona to see her mother again before heading home to LA. The thought of going back across the country both thrilled and worried her. She was eager to get going on that animation film, but going back to all the shallow people, the chaos of daily living and the lavish lifestyles just didn't appeal to her anymore.

Last night before bed, Lily had sent off a quick text to Ian, letting him know where she was. More than likely the Barringtons knew, but she figured she should at least let her agent know what was going on.

Not that it was anybody else's business, but she didn't mind if Ian shared where she was staying. These were complicated circumstances, after all.

Lily was thankful for the adjoining bath and it would serve Jake right if she spent the rest of her seven-day term in her room. No doubt Jake would show up at her door with trays of food so she didn't have to get up. He'd take the bed rest seriously and he'd use it to his advantage—best she knew that going in. She was allowed to get up and move around, but for the most part, she was supposed to be down with her feet up.

She'd showered and changed into the dress Jake had picked out that day they had gone shopping. Damn it, he'd see this as a sign she was giving in. Little did he know most of her clothes were still back at the rental house and this dress just so happened to be in her suitcase…a suitcase he'd had Linda pack up and bring out to the estate. He was still taking control and she wasn't sure if she was warmed by the fact or ticked that he still felt he had a right to be in charge of her life.

Pulling her wet hair up into a clip, she slid on her flip-flops and made her way downstairs. Before she could hit the landing the doorbell chimed, echoing throughout the house.

When Lily hit the bottom step, she glanced through to the foyer where Damon stood, hands in his pockets and glancing around as if he was just as uncomfortable being there as she was.

Was he here to see Jake or her?

Lily remained on the steps as Jake's footsteps fell heavily on the hardwood floors.

"Damon," Jake greeted. "This is a surprise."

"I apologize for coming by so early," Damon told him. "Is there somewhere private we can talk?"

Jake nodded. "Liz is in the back making breakfast. We can go into the living room. Should I tell her to set an extra place at the table?"

Lily gripped the banister, feeling like perhaps she should slink back upstairs and not eavesdrop on this conversation. But she didn't move.

"I can't stay long," Damon replied.

Jake nodded, leading the way into the living area. Lily slid down and sat on the step, grabbing the slender post for support. Damon was here for one reason: he was either ready to forgive Jake or he was letting him go. A portion of Lily's heart broke for Jake. Even with all the lies and deceit, she worried how he would cope if he lost his father forever. Jake was a strong, determined man, but just discovering your parent and then losing him would be crushing.

"I'm not sure if I should be worried or glad that you showed up on my doorstep."

Damon let out a brief chuckle. Lily couldn't see the men now, but she imagined the elderly mogul shaking his head as she'd often seen him do when he laughed.

The silence fueled the tension. Lily's heart beat so fast, she couldn't even imagine how Jake or Damon were feeling right now.

"To be honest I'm not sure how I feel myself," Damon admitted. "Your latest bombshell really spun me around so fast I didn't know how to react. But I've had several days to think about it."

Nerves fluttering in her stomach, Lily closed her eyes and waited.

"I hate being played for a fool," Damon went on. "I hate that you were that clever and I was so blinded that I didn't see through the disguise and the act."

"Damon—"

"Hear me out."

Lily took in a deep breath sliding her arms around her swollen midsection.

"We were adversaries for so long and I know finding out I was your father was a blow you didn't see coming. Your actions were made out of fear first and foremost. But I also know you're driven to succeed. How can I fault a trait you obviously got from me?"

"I still went about this the wrong way," Jake said, his tone low. "Once I started caring for you, the girls and Lily, I should've said something immediately."

"Yes, you should've," Damon agreed. "But you didn't and what's done is done. I believe everyone should have a second chance and I believe that being without my son for over thirty years is long enough. Life is short."

More silence fell and Lily was dying to know what was happening in that room. She'd listened in long enough. As quietly as she could, Lily came to her feet and headed back up the steps. Once she'd closed herself in her room, she sank back against the door.

Damon had fully accepted Jake for who he was, obviously forgiving the lies and mistakes. Even though he didn't come out and say the words, Damon wouldn't be there if he hadn't.

Lily didn't know if she could be that forgiving. Yes, she figured eventually she'd forgive him. But forgiving him didn't necessarily mean she could let him back into her life, her heart again.

Lily had only been at Jake's estate a short time, and she struggled with her emotions for him every single moment. One second she wanted to talk to him, try to figure out if they could get beyond this hurt. The next second she wanted to leave, wanted to get away because she worried she couldn't trust her feelings.

She wished she had the right answer and prayed for a miracle to guide her to where she needed to be.

Naps while pregnant were beyond amazing. Napping was a luxury she couldn't afford when home in LA or on location filming, but here in Virginia where the pace was slower and she was ordered by her doctor to take it easy, Lily fully embraced a good afternoon rest.

Besides all of that, she was tired. Tired from the pregnancy, tired from the roller coaster ride they'd been on and utterly exhausted from worrying about the future of this child. After spending time on Jake's turf, she was mentally drained and ready to pull her hair out.

Sexually, the man frustrated her. She wanted him, no matter how much her heart still hurt. He'd given her space, he'd not touched her since that slight kiss when she'd first agreed to stay, and damn if that wasn't driving her out of her ever-loving mind.

He'd never even mentioned Damon coming by the other day. Was he keeping that to himself, as well?

As Lily came down the steps, she realized she'd slept much longer than she'd meant to. The antique grandfather clock in the corner of the living room chimed four times, echoing into the empty space.

Lily glanced around, noting the photos along the mantel of Jake with his arm around a beautiful older woman, more than likely his mother, photos of him with jockeys and horses at various winners' circles. In every photo he was smiling.

She'd thought that smile was devastating with the beard, but without it, she could fully appreciate the intrigue, the devilish attitude and the power behind the man.

Laughter and squeals sounded from the front yard and Lily moved to the wide windows, shifting the simple linen curtains aside.

The tire swing swayed back and forth, Tyler held on, his legs dangling out of the hole. And Jake was pushing him.

Lily couldn't deny how the scene clenched her heart. Jake wrapped his arms around the boy's shoulders and pulled back, pausing for a moment before giving another big send-off. The wide grin across Jake's face spoke volumes for how much the lazy evening activity delighted him.

He was going to be an amazing dad. No matter what had happened between them, Lily knew that Jake would always put his child first and be hands-on. But, she couldn't help but wonder about this unique relationship he seemed to have with his maid and her son. Another layer he'd kept from her.

The fact he'd never let her fully in was the main point in that sharp blade that had pierced her heart.

Liz suddenly appeared beside Lily. "Tyler adores him."

"The feeling seems mutual," Lily replied, watching Jake's face light up each time Tyler laughed.

"Jake has been a good influence for Tyler since my husband passed away."

Stunned, Lily turned to Liz. "I'm so sorry."

A soft grin spread across Liz's face, but she kept her gaze on her son. "It's been hard, I won't lie. My husband was a groom here for several years. When he was killed four years ago, Jake asked if I'd like to work for him. I didn't know much about horses, so he asked if I could cook and clean. I know he was just looking out for us, and I could never find a way to repay him because he didn't have to take on a widow and a young child."

Swallowing the lump of remorse, Lily turned her attention back to the front yard. So many facets made up this man. Some were bad: the lies, the betrayal. But the others were so good, so…noble, that Lily hated that he'd damaged his image just to get ahead in the horse industry. Had the breeding, the prospect of winning and generating more money been that important?

"I know it's not my business," Liz went on, shifting to face Lily. "I have no idea what's going on with the two of you, but if it matters, Jake has never brought a woman here before. I can see how much he cares for you."

"He does." She couldn't deny that, but that also didn't mean they were meant to be. "He went about showing me the wrong way, though."

Liz nodded and offered a genuine smile. "Just don't shut him down, yet. Okay? Give him a chance. He's all work and traveling to see his mom. But with you, I see a different side to him and he'd hate me if he heard me say this, but he's vulnerable where you're concerned."

Lily closed her eyes, trying to block out the honest words coming from a virtual stranger. "You care for him."

"Not in the same way you do," Liz corrected. "He and my husband were good friends and had a strong working relationship. But my husband was killed during a robbery. He'd been in the wrong place at the wrong time. Jake didn't hesitate to see to all of my and Tyler's needs. I think of Jake as a friend and a hero when I needed one."

A hero. Lily opened her eyes, her focus shifting instantly

to the man serving as a little boy's hero. A man who had faults and had hurt her so deeply she didn't know how to forgive him.

"I need to get back to cooking dinner." Liz started to walk away, but laid her hand on Lily's arm. "I just wanted to make sure you knew where I stood with Jake because he loves you. He's a powerful man, but you've brought him to his knees. You're in control here."

Liz's footsteps echoed through the room until there was nothing but silence once again, other than the ticking of the grandfather clock in the corner.

Dropping the curtain back in place, Lily went out onto the front porch. The beautiful wide porch with sturdy wooden swings at both ends just begged for a lazy, relaxing day. She took a seat, curled her feet up on the deep red cushions and propped her elbow up on the back, resting her head on her fist. The gentle sway relaxed her.

Lily continued to watch the interaction in the yard, thankful she hadn't been spotted yet. Jake had invited her to stay for a week, had wanted her to see the real man he was with no pretenses, no secrets.

She was already seeing a deeper side to the person she'd fallen in love with. But could she ever get past the fact he thought it was okay to deceive her? Who's to say the next time he wanted something he wouldn't lie to get it?

Between Damon's visit the other day and seeing Jake with Tyler, Lily found herself wanting more. She just worried they were too far gone to get back on stable ground to build anything that could match the fire they had before.

A light flutter in her stomach had her pausing, her hand cupping her belly. The odd sensation happened again and Lily knew she'd felt her baby. Their baby.

The doctor had told her the first feeling she'd get in her stomach would feel like butterflies floating around. The description was pretty accurate, considering that for just a second the shocking sensation had tickled. The movement had only lasted the briefest of moments, but enough to have her smiling.

When she glanced back up, Jake's eyes were on her, and Tyler was hopping out of the hanging tire and racing around to the back of the house. Lily's smile faltered. So much tension stretched between them, so many words that needed to be spoken, so much emotion needing to be released.

Jake made his way toward the porch, and with each step Lily's heart beat faster. He stopped in front of the swing, took her feet from the cushion and sat down, placing her legs across his lap.

"Don't," he told her just as she started to shift away. "Let's just pretend this is a normal day and we're enjoying this late afternoon breeze."

His warm hands gripped her ankles, holding them securely on his lap. She hadn't felt his touch for so long, she knew she'd missed it, but she had no idea just how much his warmth affected her.

"We're not normal people and this isn't just a normal family afternoon," she whispered, hating how true her statement was.

His fingertips trailed from her shin to the top of her foot, back and forth until she couldn't control the tremors that slid through her. That powerful, seductive touch of his would be her undoing.

Jake tipped his head just slightly, focusing those bright eyes right on her as he always had, as if he could see straight into her soul. "You always say you want to be a regular person, not the celebrity when you're off location. Relax, Lily. We're both simply going to be ourselves, nothing fake, no acting. Just Jake and Lily."

Jake and Lily. As if they were an official couple. But she didn't have the energy to argue and she would remain calm to keep her blood pressure down for their baby's sake. And she was done fighting...fighting him and fighting herself.

"I think I felt the baby move a bit ago." She hadn't thought about telling him, but the words tumbled out of her mouth before she could stop them.

Jake's eyes darted to her stomach, a wide grin spread across his face. "What did it feel like?" he asked, his hand pausing in mid-stroke over her leg.

"Like someone was inside tickling me," she explained. "It was faint. The sensations happened twice while I was sitting here watching you and Tyler."

He brought his gaze back up to hers. "How long were you watching us?"

"Long enough to know you two have a special bond."

"I love him," Jake said without hesitation. "I'd do anything for him."

Lily nodded. "Liz explained the situation. I can't imagine being a single mom."

The smack of reality hit her before she realized what she'd said. Jerking her legs off Jake's lap, she came to her feet. Crossing the wide porch, she rested her hands on the white railing at the edge of the structure.

"You won't be alone." Jake's hands slid around her waist seconds later. She hadn't even heard him get up and move toward her. "I'll never let this baby feel neglected and I'll never let you feel like you're doing it all by yourself. No matter what happens with us."

Lily dropped her head between her shoulders and sighed. "There is no 'us,' Jake," she whispered. "Letting you back in…I don't know if I could survive being hurt again."

Tears pricked her eyes behind her closed lids as his fingers splayed across her abdomen. "I'm not giving up on us, Lily," he murmured in her ear. "And I won't let you give up, either."

As much as she wanted to resist him and back up her words with actions, she found herself leaning back against his chest as a tear slipped down her cheek.

"I'm not leaning on you," she told him with a sniff. "I'm not weak and I don't need you. I'm just tired, that's all."

Rubbing her stomach with gentle motions, he kissed the side of her head. "I know, baby. I know."

Nineteen

Jake swirled the whiskey around in the glass tumbler. Staring at the amber liquid wasn't taking the edge off, but he didn't want to lose himself in the bottom of a bottle, either. Right now he needed a clear head, needed to process what the hell was going on with Lily.

Keeping his hands off of her the past few days had tested restraint he didn't even know he possessed. But being with her on the porch, witnessing such raw emotions from her had nearly broken him. The damage he'd caused her was inexcusable, yet she'd leaned on him for a moment and he'd taken that as a sign of hope. At this point, he was grasping at anything she'd throw out.

She'd eaten dinner with him, Liz and Tyler and had gone to her room afterward. He hadn't seen or heard from her all evening and it was nearly eleven. More than likely she was asleep, curled up in that four-poster bed he'd bought from an antiques dealer. The clear image of her dark hair spread all around the crisp white sheets had him clenching the glass before finally slamming it down onto his desk.

If he ever wanted a chance with her, he needed to be open about everything from his life to his emotions. He needed for her to see that he'd changed, he put her first and nothing would come between them again. He couldn't let more time pass without telling her exactly where she stood in his life.

Standing just outside her door, he pondered for a minute if he should wait until morning. She was supposed to rest, after all, but he couldn't. He'd given her space and it was time she realized just how serious he was about winning her back.

Tapping on the door with the back of his knuckles, Jake swallowed and tried to ignore his frantic heartbeat. Nerves consumed him, but being a coward now would certainly secure a future without the woman and child he loved.

The knob rattled just as the door eased open. Lily stood before him, her hair spilled over one shoulder, her eyes wide. Apparently she'd been just as restless as he had. A small light glowed from the table lamp beside her bed.

"Can I come in?" he asked. When she said nothing, he added, "I have some things I need to say."

He worried she would slam the door in his face, a definite right she had, but she opened the door a bit wider and he realized her slamming the door would've been a blessing. Now his penance was having this conversation while seeing her dressed in a silky chemise, the same one he'd slid off her body many times before.

Only this time, her belly rounded out the midsection and her full breasts threatened to come out of the lacy top.

He glanced to the unmade bed, the sheets all twisted in the middle. "I'm sorry if you were sleeping."

Lily shook her head as she sat on the edge of the bed. "I wasn't asleep."

Jake remained by the door because if he even took one more step into this room he wouldn't be able to keep from touching her. Between her tousled appearance and the inviting bed that mocked him, he seriously deserved a damn award in self-control.

But he was here to lay it all on the line. Never before had he done anything so important and so terrifying.

"Damon came by the other day," he began, shoving his

hands into the pockets of his jeans. "We've come to an agreement to work on our relationship."

Lily rested her hands next to her hips. "I know. I was coming down the stairs when he arrived. I listened for a few minutes, but came back upstairs. I'm sorry I eavesdropped. I couldn't make myself leave until I knew what he wanted."

Jake smiled. "It's okay. He said the girls were upset, but they understood my angle and they wanted to get to know their only brother. Damon actually invited me over this weekend for dinner."

Lily's smile hit on every nerve Jake had. He missed that smile, missed the light in her eyes…a light he'd diminished and was desperately trying to get back. He didn't just want that brightness back for only himself, but for her. He wanted her to be that vibrant woman he'd fallen in love with, the stunning light he'd met months ago.

"I'm really happy for you, Jake."

"He asked if you'd be joining me."

Lily's eyes widened before her gaze darted down into her lap. "I don't think that's a good idea."

"I told him I was giving you time to make your own decisions," he went on, not letting her refusal deter him from his goal. "I hadn't planned on telling you about his visit because I didn't want you to think I was trying to sway your decisions."

Her dark eyes came back up to his. "And aren't you?"

"Not by telling you his choice to give me another chance." Jake pulled his hands from his pockets, massaged the back of his neck and took a deep breath. "I've time, Lily. I told you to stay for a week and I've truly tried to keep my distance. Knowing you're here, within my reach, has been one of the hardest things I've ever faced."

"I know," she whispered.

That spark of hope he'd had earlier on the porch grew stronger at her quiet confession—apparently she'd been battling the same war. Jake took another step into the room, then another.

"Tell me you're ready to give up," he told her, damning the tears that threatened to clog his throat. "Tell me the thought of living without what we have is more appealing than fighting for us."

He didn't miss the way her fingers curled into the sheets on the edge of the bed, nor did he miss her shaky intake of breath.

Her silence was invitation enough to move closer, so close he knelt in front of her, taking her hands and holding them in her lap.

"Tell me that I've got no chance with you," he went on. "Because I won't give up on us as long as there's hope. I have to believe you're not ready to give up or you would've left here before now."

Lily's chocolate eyes filled as she bit her unpainted bottom lip. "I can't tell you that."

Relief flooded him, but he was still not in the clear.

"I know we have a lot to work through," he continued. "I know I deserve nothing, but I'm asking for everything. I want you in my life, Lily. I want us to be a family. I don't care if I have to live in LA part of the time and we can come here to get away. You call the shots here."

"I'm scared, Jake. I've never loved like this before, never been so hurt because of it."

Easing forward even more, he let her hands go and wrapped his arms around her waist as he looked up into her teary eyes. "I've never loved like this before, either. That's no excuse for hurting you the way I did, but I can swear on my life that I'll never hurt you again. I want a lifetime to love you, Lily. I want forever to be the man you deserve and the father our children deserve."

She threaded her fingers through his hair. "I'm risking everything by letting you back in."

"My heart is on the line, too," he told her. "If you walked

out again it would kill me. I love you, Lily. I know when I said it before the timing couldn't have been worse. But I love you so much I ache when you're not with me."

The smile that spread across her face had tears gliding down over her cheeks. "I love you, too, Jake."

Every bit of tension and fear left his body as he leaned his head forward, resting it against their baby. Lily's fingertips caressed the back of his neck as he breathed in her familiar scent.

"I won't keep anything from you again," he murmured as he lifted his head.

"I know. You've shown me the man you are. I want to give us another chance." She stared into his eyes, and his heart swelled with love at the light shining back. "I do have one stipulation, though."

"What's that?"

Her hands framed his face, stroked his jaw. "Maybe a little scruff? I fell in love with a rugged man who turned my insides out that first night in the loft. Maybe you could not shave for a while?"

Jake laughed. "Anything you want. Besides, I'll be too busy to shave."

"Oh, really?" Lily lifted her brows. "And what will you be doing?"

Jake's hands traveled up the silky chemise to the thin straps barely containing her breasts. "I plan on keeping you in bed for the next several days."

Her body trembled beneath his. "Well, the doctor did tell me to rest."

Sliding the straps down, he peeled the lacy material over her breasts and palmed her. "Oh, you'll rest. You can just lie there while I take very good care of you."

Lily's head fell back as she arched into his touch. "You have the best ideas."

Epilogue

The grounds were as immaculate as always. The early fall sun shining high in the sky beamed down onto the intimate ceremony. The handsome groom held the bride's hands as their smiles beamed off the other. There was nothing fancy, nothing over-the-top for this outdoor wedding. An arch covered with white buds and sprays of greenery covered the stone walkway, white rose petals sprinkled over freshly cut grass and a family surrounding the happy couple.

Reaching over, Jake took Lily's hand in his. When she sniffed and swiped at the moisture threatening to slip down her cheek, Jake squeezed her hand and leaned over.

"I love you," he whispered. The man knew just how to press on every single hormonal button she had. He palmed her rounded belly with his other hand. "I love her, too. I can't wait to make you my wife."

Lily tipped her head to rest on his shoulder as she watched the couple standing before her pronounced husband and wife by the minister.

Damon kissed his bride, sealing his bond with Linda. Only Tessa, Grant, Cassie, Emily, Ian, Jake and Lily were in attendance. The quaint family ceremony was perfect. Every detail taken care of by the Barrington sisters and

Lily. For once Linda didn't lift a finger. The younger girls had wanted her to just show up and enjoy her special day.

As everyone came to their feet, Jake pulled Lily into his arms. "I can't wait to marry you next weekend."

They'd opted to hold off on their own plans until Damon and Linda were married so everybody's focus and celebration wouldn't be torn. They'd also opted to marry just before her exclusive interview in ten days, which would reveal the pregnancy and her marriage all in one shocking swoop. At nearly seven months, Lily had more energy than ever and they'd just found out the baby was a girl…as they'd thought all along.

They'd both immediately known the name—Rose. How could they name their baby after anyone but the woman who, in a roundabout way, brought Lily to the estate?

While Lily loved how private she and Jake had been for the past several months, she was eager to introduce him to her world, to show everyone that true love existed and she'd found it.

They'd visited her mother and she and Jake had clicked perfectly. Lily couldn't be happier with how her family was growing, how she was being welcomed into the Barringtons as if she'd always been part of them. Damon had fully embraced Jake, as well. The two men were already power planning for the upcoming racing seasons. Just because the girls were retiring and gearing up to open a riding school for disabled children didn't mean Damon was ready to let go just yet. Especially with his son breeding Don Pedro. The families were truly meshing in every way.

Linda and Damon turned, moving from one family member offering hugs and smiles to another. So much happiness enveloped them. Each couple had fought through pain, through obstacles that could break most others.

With three more children in the Barrington clan taking off, Lily knew this dynasty was truly just getting started.

* * * * *

"Most people just call me Chance, since that's my name."

"Fine. So, why are you here…Chance?"

"Can I be honest with you?"

"I don't know. Can you be honest?"

Damn but that question hit a little too close to home. Good thing he was the poker player in the family.

He deflected her question with a wink and a little smirk. "I'll plead the Fifth on that one. You know what folks say—all's fair in love and war."

"Yeah, but which is this?"

"You tell me, Cassidy."

"You still haven't answered my question."

"Which one?"

"Well, you're a man, so we know you can't be honest. So that leaves the other one. Why are you here?"

"Ow. I lodge a protest in the name of men everywhere." He offered her another crooked grin and a wink as he added, "I came to see you."

"Why?"

Time to lay his cards on the table. "Because I want to take you to dinner."

***
Cowgirls Don't Cry
is a Red Dirt Royalty book—These Oklahoma millionaires work hard and play harder.

COWGIRLS
DON'T CRY

BY
SILVER JAMES

Published in Great Britain 2015
by Mills & Boon, an imprint of Harlequin (UK) Limited,
Eton House, 18-24 Paradise Road, Richmond, Surrey, TW9 1SR

© 2015 Silver James

ISBN: 978-0-263-25246-0

51-0115

Harlequin (UK) Limited's policy is to use papers that are natural, renewable and recyclable products and made from wood grown in sustainable forests. The logging and manufacturing processes conform to the legal environmental regulations of the country of origin.

Printed and bound in Spain
by CPI, Barcelona

Silver James likes walks on the wild side and coffee. Okay. She *loves* coffee. Warning: her muse, Iffy, runs with scissors. A cowgirl at heart, she's also been an army officer's wife and mum and has worked in the legal field, fire service and law enforcement. Now retired from the real world, she lives in Oklahoma, USA and spends her days writing with the assistance of her two Newfoundland dogs, the cat who rules them all and the myriad characters living in her imagination. She loves interacting with readers on her blog, Twitter and Facebook. Find her at www.silverjames.com.

To my dad, who taught me how to ride and all about cowboy honor, to my family for always believing in me, and to Charles, my editor, for his faith in my abilities, his enthusiasm and his patience.

One

Chance Barron always knew exactly what he wanted. At the moment, he'd set his sights on the attractive blonde sitting at the hotel bar.

The late-March blizzard had shut down Chicago O'Hare Airport, and he wasn't going anywhere in a hurry. The weather service predicted the storm would blow over by morning, and he'd be on the first flight back to Oklahoma City. In the meantime, there was a pretty little gal all alone knocking back martinis like water. She'd twisted her hair up on top of her head and secured it with something that looked like a chopstick. Her face remained angled away from him, but the graceful curve of her jaw and neck had him noticing her profile. The red jacket and black slacks showed fashion flair and, despite the snow, she sported boots with impossible heels.

He studied her like she was evidence in a hotly contested case and debated how to phrase his opening argument. She ordered another martini and when the drink was served, he watched her long fingers play with the plastic pick and all but gulped as her full lips slid over the ripe, green olive stuffed with a cocktail onion. His groin tightened as his mind conjured up sexy images. A one-night stand wouldn't hurt, and he'd certainly be in a better mood to deal with the old man when he got home.

Thoughts of his father, Cyrus Barron, intruded at the

worst possible times. Probably because he was a force of nature. Oil. Land and cattle. Politics and media. Name the pie, and Chance's old man owned most of it. Too bad he was such a jackass. He delighted in setting his spurs in the hides of his sons, and Chance was no exception. He had his own law firm, though the family was a big client. He certainly wasn't in charge of the ranch's breeding program but his father had sent him on a fool's errand looking for a stud colt that didn't exist in the state of Illinois. And now he was stuck in the Windy City during a freak March blizzard.

The waitress approached, an interested smile curling her lips. He declined her offer for a refill and handed her a crisp fifty dollar bill to cover his tab and tip. "Keep the change, hon," he drawled. He slid out of the booth and homed in on the bar—only to realize his quarry had escaped.

"Damn." His muttered curse was lost in the clatter of glasses and hum of conversation as he pushed toward the exit. She couldn't have gone far. He'd find her and argue his case for keeping each other warm tonight.

Cassidy Morgan leaned against the window in the hotel lobby, her cell phone pressed to her ear. Outside, fat cotton balls of snow drifted across her view—like staring into the heart of a giant snow globe. Dizzy and a tad claustrophobic, her equilibrium thrown off both physically and emotionally, she closed her eyes.

"I'm not going to make it in time, am I?" The words spoken quietly into the phone were ripped from the depths of her soul.

"No, darlin'." Baxter "Boots" Thomas didn't believe in sugarcoating things. "The doctors don't know how he's hung on this long."

She heard the muted sounds from the heart and respiration monitors beeping in the silence that followed on the other end of the line. And she recognized both the exhaustion and surrender in the voice of her father's best friend.

"Will you put the phone next to his ear? I know he can't hear me but…" Her throat closed, and she blinked hard to clear her vision. She pictured Boots's actions from the rustling sounds and then she heard his muffled, "Go ahead."

She talked. She reminisced. In the end, her voice broke and she cried. When her mother died of pneumonia, Cassie had been three, so young the emotional pain was lost on her. But this? This hurt far more than she had ever imagined it could. She wanted to be there. Wanted to hold his hand as he passed. He'd always been there for her. And she'd always managed to fail him, the disappointment in his eyes apparent to her every time she'd seen him over the past ten years.

Her father's voice whispered in her ear. "Cowgirls don't cry, baby. Ya gotta pick yourself up and ride."

She blinked against the stinging tears and felt his sharply indrawn breath all the way to her toes. Then silence. He was gone. That quickly. Two blinks of her eyelids, his sharply indrawn breath, and the great bear of a man who'd been her father existed no more.

"You okay, baby girl?" Boots was back on the line.

Cass dashed at her eyes with the back of her hand. Hell no, she wasn't okay. But she had to be. She had to take care of things. Whether she wanted to or not. "I'll be there as soon as possible, Uncle Boots. I'm stuck here until the blizzard lets up. Couldn't even get back to my apartment, so I'm spending the night in a hotel here at O'Hare." Her voice remained steady. She couldn't lose it. Not yet.

"I'll be on the first flight out in the morning. I'll call to give you my arrival time." She cleared the lump forming in her throat. "Will you call the funeral home for me? To pick him up. I… Don't let them cremate him until I get there, Uncle Boots. I…I need to see him. To say goodbye. Okay?"

"Sure, baby girl. I'll take care of it."

"You know where he stashed the good stuff. Go home and toast the stubborn old coot for me."

"Sure thing, sugar. Now get your tail home. We've got work to do."

"I love you, Uncle Boots."

"Love you, too, baby girl."

She tapped the red end call bar on her phone and slipped it into her pocket. *Damn, damn, damn.* How could she absorb the enormity of this event and not let it drive her to her knees? She closed her eyes against the prickle of tears. She didn't cry. Not in public. Hadn't she learned that from her dad? Cowgirls were tough. Well, dammit, she wasn't a cowgirl. Not anymore. Not for a long time. Cass continued to rest her hot forehead against the cool glass.

She'd left the ranch behind ten years ago. With dreams of making her mark, she'd chased life in the big city, where stars in the night sky were outshone by light from skyscraper windows, and the rumble of traffic sounded like far-off thunder.

Ranch life was hard. Early mornings. Late nights. Worrying about the weather—searing heat, freezing cold, too much rain or not enough. Early frosts. Diseases that could wipe out a herd in a heartbeat. Rodeo was even harder. Her dad had loved the rodeo. She had, too, once upon a time when she was a little girl insulated from the reality of it all.

Cass did not want to go home. She didn't want to say goodbye to the man against whom she measured every boyfriend. Even hurting him as she had, and regardless of his disappointment in the choices she made, he had continued to love her. And now her dad was gone.

She squared her shoulders and decided she needed to go to bed, despite the allure of another martini. Or a bottle of whiskey. Not that it would help. Booze wouldn't touch the ache in her heart, wouldn't numb the pain like a shot of Novocain administered to an abscessed tooth. That's what her heart felt like. A deep, throbbing abscess full of decay and vile selfishness. She hadn't been back home for a year. And now it was too late.

She reconsidered getting another drink. Or ordering a bottle from room service. She knew that wasn't the answer. Plus, there were other drawbacks. Fighting the crowd at the airport and dealing with things at home while nursing a hangover just didn't appeal.

Cass turned —and buried her nose in a starched white shirt.

"Easy, darlin'."

The man's large hands gripped her biceps and kept her upright despite the fact her knees had turned to jelly. She tilted her head to look up. Quite a ways up. She took in the chiseled jaw shadowed by dark stubble, eyes the color of amber and dark hair—thick, silky and worn just a little long so that it caressed the man's wide forehead and kissed the collar of his crisp shirt. She swallowed. Hard.

"I'm so sorry. I didn't realize you were standing there." At least she didn't stammer. Two points for her. But she cringed inside at how breathless her voice sounded. It was surprise. That's all. She didn't want or need the complication presented by this sexy man right now.

"S'okay, hon. I didn't mean to scare you."

She backed away from him and shook his hands free. "Scare me?" Her brow quirked as she lifted her chin. "I don't scare, mister." Now that she had a good look at him, her brows narrowed in speculation. "You look sort of familiar. Have we met before?"

Cass managed not to blush as those wolf-like eyes traveled over her body from head to toe and back again. A smile she could only describe as appreciative spread across his full lips.

"Honey, as beautiful as you are, I'm sure I'd remember." He held out his hand as if to introduce himself but was interrupted when the theme song from the old television show *Rawhide* emanated from his pocket, startling them both.

A look of anger flashed across his face, and he muttered something that sounded like, "Dammit, I'm busy."

Busy? She stepped back, putting more space between them. For an insane moment, she wondered if he was stalking her. She'd noticed a man in the bar watching her. This guy fit the general description even though the corners of the place were dark, and he'd remained in the shadows.

He fitted a smile on his face but was interrupted again. This time his phone erupted with the sounds of a siren. People stopped, turned and stared. She stepped back farther.

"That sounds like an emergency," she hinted.

Chance fumbled in his jacket pocket and found the blasted phone. He planned to cheerfully kill whichever brother had reprogrammed his ring tones. Stabbing at the screen, he growled, "What!" He held up an index finger to indicate it would be a short conversation, hoping she'd stay.

"Did I catch you at a bad time?"

Chance could feel his brother's smirk through the phone. "It's always a bad time when you call, Cord. Tell the old man not even he can control the weather. I'm stuck in Chicago until this freaking blizzard blows over."

Chance barely listened, his attention focused on the blonde. Something in her expression captured his interest. Every time she blinked, her lashes appeared to leave bruises under her eyes. He peered closer and noticed the dark circles marring the delicate skin. Sadness. That's what he saw on her face and in her eyes.

"Chancellor! Are you even listening to me?"

"No." Not even the use of his full name could distract him.

"Well, you better. He called a family meeting for tomorrow. Clay is flying in from Washington. The old man tried to send one of the planes for you, but every pilot on staff refused to fly because of the weather. Pissed him off to no end, but he couldn't fire all of them."

Chance resisted the urge to scrub at his forehead. The old man's temper and propensity for firing people kept Chance hip deep in fixing the messes made by his father. In fact, he cleaned up all the predicaments his family got embroiled in. It was his duty, according to Cyrus Barron, and part of the price to pay for being a member of one of Oklahoma's richest and most powerful families. The perks of being a Barron were many, so Chance paid the dues.

"I have a seat on the first flight out in the morning. Any clue about the hornet's nest we're walking into?"

"Trouble with a capital T. The old man's worn a path in the carpet from all his pacing. He keeps muttering something about 'that old bastard thinks he can outsmart me by dying' with a lot more choice cuss words sprinkled liberally throughout. He had a map spread out on the conference table, so I have the feeling he's in acquisition mode and isn't going to take no for an answer."

"So what else is new?" The rhetorical nature of the question was lost on Cord. Chance resisted the urge to hang up on his brother as he continued to watch the girl. He liked her looks, but the playboy side of his brain told him to run. The abiding sorrow in her eyes boded nothing but trouble—and entanglements. With his father on the warpath, he couldn't afford either one. He tuned back in to his brother's voice.

"It's not enough that Clay is a senator. The old man is bugging Chase to run for governor next year."

This was a conversation he didn't want a stranger to overhear. He turned his back and stepped a few feet away. "Chase? In politics? Oh hell, no. Trouble follows him like an ambulance-chasing lawyer. The old man must be losing his grip on reality."

"Hey, at least he's not after you or me, bro."

Chance snorted. "I had that conversation with the old man when I was twelve."

Cord laughed again, harder this time. "Yeah, I remember that. You couldn't sit a saddle for almost a week after he finished tanning your hide with that switch. And he got back at you by making you go to law school."

Chance turned around just in time to see his plans evaporate behind the elevator doors. He laughed as he saw the woman lean over to continue watching him until the doors closed. His intellect remained curious about her. His body had a more basic interest involving naked skin and sheets. He could still smell the scent of her perfume, or shampoo or simply her. Almonds, orange and a hint of cinnamon—the fragrance as distinctive as the woman. With a frustrated snarl, he focused on his brother's voice yammering in his ear.

"The old man is livid, Chance. I've never seen him like this. Not even when Tammy ran off with the foreman. I'm worried he's actually going to stroke out."

Chance rolled his eyes. Tammy was wife number six. Or seven. Half his father's age and built like Dolly Parton, she'd turned her charms on the ranch foreman and convinced him to take off with her. The Barrons owned the two major papers in Oklahoma so she'd threatened to go to the tabloids with fabricated family secrets. She would sink to that level to cause a scandal. As the family lawyer, Chance negotiated a monetary settlement to avoid the nuisance and filed the divorce papers while the ink was still wet on her signature.

"So what the hell's going on, Cord? You just cost me a roll in the hay. There'd better be a damn good reason for the old man's fit."

"Does the name Ben Morgan mean anything to you?"

Chance rifled through his memory. "Vaguely. Old rodeo cowboy, right?"

"That's him. The old man and Morgan butted heads a few times, including once over a woman."

"Aw, hell… Which one of the stepmonsters?"

"That's the funny thing. None of them. This was years ago. Before he married Mom."

Chance rubbed his forehead. "Damn, Cord. I know the old man is legendary for holding a grudge, but that's a little ridiculous."

"You're telling me? I'm the one he's been cussing the last few minutes, ever since he found out Morgan died tonight." Cord paused for a breath. "He's upset enough he forgot about your failure to find the colt."

"Now you're giving me grief about that, too? Come on."

"Hey, you know how he reacts to losing, little brother. The good news, he's distracted. There's some sort of legal BS involving this Ben Morgan guy. The old man wants you to wade through it. Thought I'd give you a heads-up so you don't walk in blind."

"Thanks for the warning. I'll fire up the laptop and do some research."

"I'll email the particulars. And Chance? Sorry if I messed up any sort of extracurricular activity you might have planned for later."

"Yeah, right. I can hear the remorse ringing in your voice. I'll head to the office straight from the airport when I get back tomorrow."

"I'll let you know if anything changes."

Chance tapped his phone and dropped it into his pocket. This whole trip had gone to hell in a handbasket, and now he was quoting the old man's clichés. That was so not a good sign. He glanced toward the bar. The waitress would get off sooner or later but after getting up close and personal with the blonde, his desire for any other woman waned—at least for tonight. In three strides, he reached the elevator and stabbed the button. He had work to do.

Two

Cass loosened her seat belt as the flight attendant announced the flight would be delayed. Seemed a passenger was running late. The economy section was packed, so it had to be somebody in first class. She rolled her head on her neck and listened as her vertebrae snapped, crackled and popped. Better to sound like a bowlful of Rice Krispies than suffer the headache that would follow.

She closed her eyes and tried to forget her situation. Going home was always hard—that's why she'd avoided it for so long, even though Boots had urged her to visit. And now with her dad gone—with things left unsaid and apologies not made, her heart hurt. She swallowed her guilt but it churned in her stomach like raw jalapeños. Cass forced her thoughts away from her dad. She'd say goodbye when she got to the funeral home, but until then, she'd just have to hope he had heard what was in her heart when she talked to him last night.

The pilot's voice echoed over the intercom, scratchy and hard to hear over the hum of conversations. Evidently, whoever they'd been waiting for had arrived, and they were finally ready for takeoff. She braced her feet against the floor and clasped her hands in her lap. Flying was not her favorite activity, especially getting off the ground and landing. She measured her breathing, concentrating on remaining calm, then remembered the scent of the guy in the hotel.

Leather and rain on a hot day. That's what he smelled like—an odd combination that evoked memories of her childhood growing up on the ranch and around rodeo arenas all over the West.

He'd been wearing a starched white shirt with a button-down collar, like a banker, but it was tucked into a pair of well-fitting jeans, even if they were pressed to a knife-edged crease. Her brow furrowed. He'd also been wearing boots. Not that people in Chicago didn't wear Western boots. Some of them even wore them "for real," not just as a fashion statement.

Her stomach dropped away as the plane rumbled into the cloudy skies, chasing all thoughts of the guy out of her head. The fuselage shuddered several times before she heard grinding as the landing gear retracted. The plane continued to climb at a steep incline, and the pilot mumbled something about weather and flying altitude that she couldn't really hear over the throbbing in her ears. She swallowed to make her eardrums pop, pushed back against her seat and returned to thinking about her close encounter.

Had the timing been different, she might have let the guy buy her a drink, just to see what percolated between them. He was sexy as all get-out. Tall. Muscular. His hands strong as they gripped her arms, but with a certain amount of gentleness. She wasn't petite by any measure, but he'd towered over her. He radiated heat, too, or maybe he just touched something in her that created heat. She hadn't been so intrigued by a man in ages. Then she remembered the reason for her trip, and all thoughts of the sexy encounter fled.

I'm sorry, Daddy. She offered the apology to the heavens, knowing it covered so much more than her wayward thoughts. Cass squiggled her nose, fighting the burn of tears. She couldn't cry. Not here. Not now.

Her dad's voice echoed softly in her memory, reminding her to be strong. She flashed back to the time she'd just

lost the final round of a barrel-racing event by mere tenths
of a second. That she'd lost to the reigning national champion, who was twenty years older didn't mean a thing. At
the age of seven, all she'd wanted was that shiny buckle
and the saddle that went with it for winning.

"No, Daddy. No time for tears. Cowgirls just get back on
and ride." Back in the present, she whispered the words in
the hopes that saying them out loud would make them true.
She hadn't been a cowgirl for ten years. Not since she'd left
home to attend college back East. Not since she'd taken the
job in Chicago. In fact, she'd only been on a horse a handful of times since then. She hated going home. Hated the
heat and dust, the smell of cattle manure.

She didn't want to be a cowgirl. She'd liquidate the
ranch, get Boots set up somewhere comfortable and haul
ass back to Chicago where she belonged. No regrets. It's
what her dad would expect her to do. She'd told him often
enough she'd never be back, never take over the ranch.

Those guilty jalapeños boiled and raged in her stomach
again. Returning to Chicago was the right thing. Really.
She conjured up the picture of her close encounter from
the night before in her mind, shutting out the remorse. His
chiseled face still seemed familiar, and she felt as if she
should know him. Was he an actor? Or maybe a professional cowboy? She nudged the feeling this way and that,
seeking an answer, but didn't find one.

The passenger in front of her shoved his seat all the
way back jostling her tray table so that the coffee, served
moments before by the flight attendant, sloshed out. The
man on her right in the window seat snored as his head fell
over toward her shoulder. She dodged him but bumped the
woman on her left. That earned her a scathing look. Cass
rolled her eyes and shrugged. She could only hope this
flight from hell ended sooner rather than later.

She gulped what little coffee didn't spill and passed off

the sodden napkin and cup to the attendant as she came back down the aisle. Feeling far too much like a sardine for comfort, Cass closed her eyes and tried to sleep. Thoughts of the handsome cowboy danced in her head. She was positive she knew him from somewhere. Since she didn't watch much TV, she discarded the idea he might be an actor. Could he be someone she'd met in college? Or, heaven forbid, high school? She didn't have the best memory for faces, but there was just something about the man.

Giving up any pretense of relaxation, she shoved her tray table up and fastened it with the little lever, using a lot more force than technically necessary. Then she stretched her legs under the seat in front of her and drummed her toes against the bottom of it. When the occupant twisted to stare at her over the top of the reclined seatback, she flashed the smile of a two-year-old brat. And didn't care. The man eventually turned around and since he raised the seat a few inches, she quit kicking.

More memories of her dad swamped her. Moisture filled her eyes, and her nose stung. She blinked rapidly and had to sort through more guilt. She was a terrible daughter. Her dad had died, and she couldn't be bothered to get there in time to say goodbye. If she never saw the ranch again, never saw Oklahoma again, it would suit her just fine. Yes, she was selfish. She admitted it. So there. Boots had begged her for months to come, and she'd stalled. Her dad had been too proud to call. And she'd been too proud to bend. Now it was too late.

When the tears finally came, Cass dashed them from her eyes with the back of her hand. Her elbow caught the arm of the passenger sitting on her left. The woman exhaled, the sound uncompromisingly disdainful as she shifted away from the contact. The guy on her right just snored, mouth open and drool threatening Cassie's wool blazer.

Already walking a fine line between anger and grief,

Cass lost control. "Well, pardon my tears." She didn't bother to keep her voice down. "My father died last night, and I was stuck in a freakin' blizzard and didn't get there in time. I'm on my way home to bury him. If my crying is too much of an imposition, you can just move your…self to another seat."

Around her, the hum of conversation petered off into silence. She could tell from the heat radiating off her face that she'd turned beet-red—a legacy from her mother. She flushed scarlet whenever she got mad, cried or laughed too hard. Yeah, that was Cassidy Morgan. She wasn't pretty when her emotions ruled. Unfortunately, that was a great deal of the time. At the moment, her emotions slammed her with a double whammy.

The woman stared, mouth gaping, left speechless by Cassie's outburst.

Cassie bit back any further retort, instead, settling back into her seat. She crossed her arms over her chest and stared stone-faced straight ahead, ignoring everyone.

Chance sipped his French roast coffee from a ceramic mug and skimmed the information on his laptop screen. He was learning all sorts of interesting things about his father he couldn't wait to share with his brothers. To hear the old man tell it now, he'd been born with a gold spoon up his… Chance reined in that thought and tried to scrub the image from his brain.

But back when Chance's mother was still alive, the old man had been all about hard work and scrabbling to put the Barron name on the map. Chance's research from the night before showed Cyrus had worked the oil patch, ranched and even been a rodeo rider on the side.

And he'd loved a woman named Colleen before he'd met and married Chance's mother, Alice. According to the papers at the time, Cyrus Barron had done a stint in county jail after a spectacular fight at a rodeo in Fort Worth. He'd put Ben Morgan in the hospital and ended the man's promising bronc-riding career. Colleen had turned her back on Cyrus and married Ben within weeks. Oh, yeah. The old man didn't hold a grudge; he got even. He'd been dogging Ben Morgan's steps ever since, throwing up roadblocks in an attempt to grind the other man beneath his boot heel. But Ben Morgan didn't have any "give up" in him. He'd made a life for his wife, first as a supplier of rodeo stock then as a horse trainer.

Chance rubbed the back of his neck. His father was a royal jerk. He couldn't even let the man have peace in the grave. The email from Cord first thing this morning had confirmed that Morgan had taken out a loan at a small bank—the bank recently purchased by a subsidiary of Barron Enterprises, and he'd used the ranch as collateral. The old man wanted Chance to stop off and pick up the file before coming into the office. Since he could no longer screw with Ben Morgan, Cyrus planned to screw with any heirs or successors his old nemesis might have by calling the note.

Yeah, leave it to his father to be four moves ahead of any opponent. Chance had to admire the old man's business acumen. He'd thought the acquisition foolish at the time and certainly not worth the hassle of the federal and state banking regulators' paperwork. Chance had hired a couple of experts in banking law to handle it because Cyrus had remained adamant. The old man wanted the bank. So they'd bought it. Chance knew why now. He tossed off a mental shrug. Barron Enterprises could afford it.

Closing the laptop, he held up his mug for a refill as the flight attendant hovered, a ready smile on her face.

"You know, I have layovers in OKC sometimes," she whispered. She wrapped one hand around his to steady the cup as she poured, a move he recognized as an excuse to touch him.

Chance glanced up. She was a brunette, in her late twenties, and her trim uniform fit in all the right places. The girl was just his type—female—but even as he smiled, another face appeared in his memory. The blonde from the hotel. His abdomen contracted, and his heart thundered for a few beats. He hadn't even gotten her name, yet here she was haunting him.

"Sorry, hon. This is just a quick trip for me." The lie flowed smooth as honey from his mouth. As disappointment registered on her face, Chance wondered what the hell had gotten into him. Why would he turn down a sure thing?

While it was unlikely he'd ever cross paths with the woman, he did have a brother who was a private investigator and ran Barron Security. He'd sic Cash on her trail. All Chance wanted was one night to get her out of his system. That's all it would take.

He shifted in his seat, glad the tray table and computer disguised his discomfort. He couldn't pinpoint why the woman had gotten under his skin but she had, like a burr under his saddle. He shoved thoughts of her away and opened his laptop again, hoping to concentrate on the task at hand. He had to squelch his libido and his uneasiness over what his father wanted—the combination made for an odd sensation in and of itself.

The flight attendant scurried toward the economy section. He leaned into the aisle to see what was happening. Three attendants hovered around a row of seats toward the back of the plane. Everyone with aisle seats had twisted to watch the commotion, too. He heard raised voices, but the conversation was too indistinct. Within moments, the situation calmed. He returned his attention to the problem at hand.

Once the plane landed, he was the first one off. With no luggage to retrieve, he headed straight for the parking lot. He stepped into the gentle March sunshine, glad he hadn't bothered to shrug into his heavy winter jacket. The storm pounding the upper Midwest hadn't dipped as far south as Oklahoma, and Chance was thankful. He hated cold weather. Of course, he hated hot weather, too. If he had his way, he'd live somewhere where the temperature remained at a balmy sixty-eight degrees year-round.

He dug out his car keys, hit the button for the auto-unlock and dumped his carry-on suitcase and laptop case in the passenger seat before settling behind the wheel. With a reckless abandon born from experience, Chance maneuvered his sleek, phantom-black Audi R8 sports car toward the parking lot exit. The car swooped down the exit ramp, slowing to a stop just long enough for him to pay the attendant.

Without looking for merging traffic from other lanes, he downshifted and gunned the powerful 571 horsepower V10 engine. A flash of rust in the corner of his eye and the sound of squealing tires had him handling the powerful vehicle like a race car to avoid a collision. Caught by the next traffic light, Chance glanced over at the beat-up old pickup in the next lane. He looked away then looked back. He didn't recognize the old man in the driver's seat but the passenger? Oh, yeah. It was her! The blonde from the hotel. She'd rolled down the window, and her glare could melt the metallic paint right off the Audi.

His windows were tinted dark, and he doubted she could see him. When the light changed, instead of accelerating the way he normally would, he eased off the clutch, making sure the clunker pulled ahead of him. He made a mental note of the license plate. Now he'd have a chance to sic Cash on her and move in for the kill after all. He grinned, unable to calculate the odds of seeing her again, especially here on his home ground. Excitement tingled in his fingertips. Life was looking up. Gunning his engine, he headed toward I-40 and the command performance he had to attend.

Three

"Did you see that idiot? He could have killed us!"

"City folks drive a bit faster, sugar. That's all. We didn't wreck." Boots turned his head and spit out the window.

"You shouldn't chew, Uncle Boots. That stuff's bad for you."

"It's the only vice I got left, Cassie, and I ain't gonna live forever. Give an old man some peace."

She ground her back teeth together but held her tongue. The seat cover—an old horse blanket—made her back itch through her cotton turtleneck. She'd shed her heavy jacket as soon as she'd stepped out of the terminal. Compared to Chicago, the fifty degree temperature in Oklahoma City felt positively balmy. The Australian shepherd sprawled on the bench seat between them yawned, and she absently scratched his ears.

"I want your life, Buddy. Nothing to do all day but nap in the sun and chase squirrels. And you don't have to put up with the stupid people of the world. You can just bite 'em or piss on 'em."

"You watch your mouth, Cassidy Anne Morgan. I won't have you corrupting this poor dog with such language. Ol' Buddy here is sensitive."

She rolled her eyes but reached over to pat Boots on the shoulder. "Yessir."

They rode in silence for several minutes. The old man

cleared his throat but didn't speak. A few blocks later, caught by another red light, he glanced at Cassie. "I'm gonna miss him, sugar." Buddy whined softly and shifted to lay his head on the man's thigh, as if to say he'd miss Ben, too.

Cass pressed her lips together and lost the battle with her tears. They streaked her cheeks even as Boots pulled a faded red bandanna from his pocket and offered it to her. She took it and dabbed at her runny nose, but the tears continued. She leaned her head against the window.

"Why didn't you tell me?"

"Tell you what, Cassie? I asked you to come home lots of times."

"You could have told me he was dying."

"I told you he was sick."

Her temper flared. "There's a big damn difference between sick and dying, Boots!" Her tears stopped as her anger surged.

"And there's a big damn difference between being too stubborn to come home and make amends and being too busy to worry about your daddy."

"He started it." She winced. That sounded so petulant. But it was true. Her dad had fought her plans the whole way. If she had to go to college, why wasn't one of the local universities good enough? Why did she have to go traipsing off where he'd never get to see her? She'd saved her barrel-racing money and made straight As to get an academic scholarship. Even so, she'd had to wait tables to make ends meet while in college. Then she got a job with the Chicago Mercantile Exchange. Granted, she was far from rich, but she didn't have to haul her butt out of bed at the crack of dawn to do barn chores. She didn't have to muck the manure out of stalls or round up cattle too stupid to seek shelter in a storm.

Boots made a choking noise so she glanced over at him.

His face shone with tears and his white-knuckled grip on
the steering wheel indicated how upset he was. She leaned
over the dog and placed her hand on his.

"You're right, Uncle Boots."

"Aw, honey. The two of you are so dang much alike.
Stubborn to the core. But he loved you. And he was proud
of you."

"No." She shook her head, unable to believe that. "No,
he wasn't. I disappointed him. I didn't stay here to help with
the ranch. I didn't get married and give him grandbabies. I
didn't do anything with my life that he wanted me to do."

"All he ever wanted was for you to be happy, baby girl."

Cass didn't know what to say. She knew in her heart
Boots was wrong. She'd disappointed her dad from the
day she'd turned eighteen, lost her virginity in the back of
a pickup at the National Western Stock Show and Rodeo
in Denver and decided she'd never get on a horse again.

The old truck rattled across a speed bump as Boots
turned it into the parking lot at the funeral home. He pulled
into a parking space and shoved the transmission into Park.
Neither of them moved. She did not want to get out and
walk inside that building. With its white-washed stucco and
blue shutters topped by a red-tiled roof, the place looked
more like a Mexican restaurant than a funeral home. Part
of her wanted to ask Boots to just drive away. The other
part knew that if she turned tail and ran she'd regret it for
the rest of her life.

Cass sucked in a deep breath and held it. Letting the air
hiss out slowly, she wiped her face and nose with the bandanna then stuck it in her pocket, just in case. "Okay. Let's
get this over with."

The doors on the old truck creaked as they opened.
Buddy jumped out after Boots, and he scolded the dog.

"Leave him be, Uncle Boots. He has as much right to say

goodbye to Daddy as anyone." She met him on the sidewalk and slipped her arm through his. "We can do this. Right?"

Boots patted her hand where it rested on his forearm. "You know what your daddy always said, sugar."

"Yeah. Often and loudly." She inhaled deeply again. "Cowgirls don't cry, they just get back on and ride. I really hate that phrase, you know."

He chuckled and gave her hand another pat.

Boots distracted the officious man who met them at the door while Cassie snuck past, Buddy at her heels. They were probably breaking some law but she didn't care. Buddy needed this goodbye as much as she did.

Alone in a private viewing room a few minutes later, Cass stared at what used to be her father. A sheet covered his body from shoulders to toes. There'd be no burying clothes or makeup on his face since he'd be cremated once she left. The funeral home had kept the body solely for her chance to say goodbye.

His face had thinned with the years, as had his hair. And the crinkles around his eyes looked like they'd been etched in wax. This...thing wasn't her father. He'd been full of life. Of laughter. And a few choice cuss words. She reached out as if to touch his hand but couldn't follow through. The cancer had stolen his vitality. The thought of her skin touching that cold facsimile of her dad made her stomach roil.

"Oh, Daddy." The words clogged up her throat as sorrow surged. "God, I miss you. I'm so sorry. I'm so sorry for everything. Please forgive me?" She closed her eyes against the salty sting, and her throat ached from swallowing her sobs. With her arms pressed across her stomach, she swayed with the rhythm of her grief. Something warm leaned against her leg, and Buddy's whine joined her choking sobs. She dropped one hand to rest on the dog's head, her fingers burrowing into the soft fur. "You miss him, too, Buddy. I know. What the hell are we going to do now?"

* * *

Chance sat in the bank's parking lot making notes as he talked to Cash on the phone. "So Ben Morgan has a daughter." An heir complicated matters, but he could file enough paperwork to keep the estate tied up until he could get the loan called. Morgan had been desperate so there was a balloon payment—due and owing on a date certain. "Do you have a name?"

"Cassidy. I've put a tracer on her. Oh, and speaking of, I have the information you wanted on that tag. Truck belongs to a guy named Baxter Thomas."

A memory nudged him again. "Where do I know that name from?"

"Ya got me, Chance. Want me to run his financials?"

"No. Just do a quick Google search. See what comes up." He drummed his fingers on the leather-clad steering wheel as he listened to clicking keys through the cell phone.

His brother's low whistle caught his attention. "Now that's interesting. Baxter Thomas is also Boots Thomas."

"The rodeo clown?" They weren't called that anymore—now they were called bullfighters, which was more appropriate to what they did inside the arena. Boots Thomas was a legend and anyone who'd ever traveled the rodeo circuit knew his name.

"That's the one. And according to this article, he and Ben Morgan were partners in a rodeo stock company." Cash whistled again. "And the plot thickens. Cassidy Morgan was a champion cowgirl back in the day, but she quit after winning the Denver Stock Show ten years ago. That's the year you and Cord won the team roping up there."

"Well, damn." Had he met her on the rodeo circuit? He couldn't put a face with the name so probably not. His rodeo career pretty much ended after that night. He graduated from college that spring and started law school soon after. He didn't have time to chase steers or cowgirls.

"Chance? Are you listening?"

He wasn't. "What?"

"There's a memorial service for Morgan day after to-morrow at the Pleasant Hills Funeral Home. As near as I can figure, it's a cremation. I suppose it'd be really uncool to serve her with the papers at the service."

"Ya think? Jeez, Cash, you've been hanging around the old man too long. What time is the memorial?"

"Ten in the morning. Why? You aren't thinking about actually showing up, are you?"

He didn't examine his motives very closely as he answered. "It might be a good idea to go. Just to get a feel for things." Business. This was just business. But he could do business without being a jerk—even if his father wanted to steal a ranch out from under his enemy's grieving daughter. He didn't believe in coincidences, but the odds of his mystery girl being Cassidy Morgan just kept getting better.

Armed with the information he needed, Chance started his car and headed home. He had plenty of time to get the legal papers filed. First, he wanted a shower and a change of clothes because he felt slimy all of a sudden. Like a royal SOB. He had plenty of time to get the legal papers filed.

He was about to act the world's biggest bully, all under the orders of the bastard who sired him. At a stoplight, he glanced at his reflection in the rearview mirror. "You are a complete slimeball, you know that, right?" He didn't blink at the accusation. He always told the truth, at least to himself.

Lost in thought, the light turned green, but he didn't notice until someone honked. He waved a hand hoping the car behind saw the gesture as an apology, and wondered why the hell that mattered. He was a Barron. If he wanted to sit through a whole light, he would. He accelerated through the intersection and put his thoughts on hold until he arrived at his condo. Thinking about stealing the ranch from Cassidy

Morgan would only make things worse. He barked a wry laugh. As if. He wasn't sure how they could get any worse.

Cassie wore black—suit jacket, matching skirt and heels—and felt out of place. Colorful Western clothes abounded, the room resembling a patchwork quilt—homey and warm, like the people who wore them. The small chapel was bursting at the seams with an array of folks—old rodeo hands, neighbors, the friends garnered from a lifetime of living. Death was just another part of all that living. Her dad once commented that suits were for marryin' and buryin', but nobody said they had to be black. She should have remembered that.

The front of the room looked like a field of wildflowers. No fussy formal arrangements. She didn't know the minister, but he seemed to know all about her dad. While short, his eulogy painted a vivid picture of the man. When he finished, he invited any who wished to share a few words or a memory.

Near the back, a man cleared his throat. Chairs scraped and creaked on the wooden floor, followed by the sound of heavy boots marching up the aisle. A big bear of a man, with a scraggly beard, a paunch overhanging the huge rodeo buckle on his belt and a chaw of tobacco in his cheek stepped forward.

"Ben Morgan saved my life some forty years ago. We were dang sure dumb back in our twenties. At the Fort Worth rodeo, I got hung up on a bull named Red Devil. Ol' Boots here was working the arena as a clown, and Ben rode the pickup horse. While Boots kept Devil occupied, Ben jumped off his horse, grabbed that bull by the ear and rode him down to his knees so the other boys could cut me free. Next thing I knew, I'm sitting on my ass in the dirt, and Ben is flyin' across the arena. That dang bull broke three of Ben's ribs but he got right up, dusted off his britches and went on with his job. He was a helluva man, and he'll be missed."

A chorus of yesses and amens followed the man back down the aisle. A woman approached the microphone next. She paused to offer her hand to Cassie and gave Boots's shoulder a pat. At the lectern, she turned a 100-watt smile on the congregation. "Most of y'all know me. For those who don't, I'm Nadine Jackson, and I own the Four Corners Diner. Ben came in most every day before he got sick. But all the regulars kept up with him through Boots. Ben'd give you the shirt off his back if you needed it. He didn't have deep pockets, but if a cowboy was down on his luck, Ben always had a few bucks to spare and dinner to share. My granddaughter called him the Louis L'Amour Cowboy."

She paused to let the chuckles from the crowd die down. "She's only eight, so I'm pleased the little darlin' even knows who Mr. L'Amour is. But she's right. Ben could've been a hero in one of those books. He was tall, rugged and believed in doin' the right thing no matter what. He was the kind of man a body would be proud to call friend."

Nadine turned her smile toward Cassie. "And you, honey? You was his pride and joy. He couldn't stop talkin' about you. Your buckles and trophies from back when you were a champion cowgirl, your report cards and your college graduation. 'My little girl is a college graduate, Nadine,' he told me. 'She's made somethin' of herself.'"

Cassie's ribs seemed to constrict around her lungs, and she couldn't breathe. Pain. There was so much pain in her heart. She gripped her hands together until her knuckles turned white. Tears prickled behind her eyelids, and she swallowed around the lump clogging her throat. *Oh, Daddy, I'm so sorry.* She sent the prayer winging into the cosmos, hoping her father would catch a whisper of it.

"I just have one more thing to say," Nadine continued. "The Four Corners is closed to the public today. I figure poor Cassie ain't in any shape to be hosting this herd at home, so I'm throwin' open the doors. Y'all come on by, grab a bite t'eat and reminisce some about Ben."

When no one else came forward, the minister speared Cassie with a long look. She sat for a moment to gather her thoughts and steel her emotions. Boots gave her clenched hands a little squeeze. She leaned over, kissed his cheek and stood. From the podium, she gazed out over the room and was struck once more by the bright colors and the kind, honest faces of her father's friends. They knew him so much better than she. He wouldn't want her wearing black on this day, wouldn't want her tears or her remorse.

Movement in the doorway caught her attention, and her breath froze for a moment when she thought she recognized the figure ducking out. Impossible. There was no way that man could have been the same one at the hotel in Chicago. The hair prickled on the back of her neck and she got a shivery feeling. Her dad would have said someone was walking across her grave. She shivered again, doing her best to ignore the premonition.

"Daddy…" Her voice broke, and she coughed to clear the frog in her throat. Feeling a bit stronger now, she tried again. "Daddy was full of sayings, most of them taken from Louis L'Amour books." She offered Nadine a tentative smile. "We have a whole wall of them at the house, and I grew up on their truisms. Dad also had a tendency to tell me, 'Shoulda, coulda, woulda, honey, just opens the door to regrets. That's the worst thing a person can do—live a life full of regrets.'"

She bit her lip and stared out the door where that mysterious figure seemed to be waiting in the shadows. "I should have been a better daughter. And I could have. Would I if circumstances had been different? I don't know. But I do believe Daddy wouldn't want me worrying about the past. He lived and loved life to the absolute fullest. We can honor him best by doing the same." She glanced over at Boots and was puzzled by the look on his face. Something was going on, something he didn't want to tell her. She'd pin him down soon.

"Thank you all for coming, for being my dad's friends. And thank you, Nadine, for your gracious offer of Four Corners. I never did learn to cook." She glanced down at the speckled gray-and-black box that held her father's ashes. "Hard to believe that a man bigger than life can be reduced to a little box like that. What's left of his body might be in there, but his spirit is riding free. Nothing could ever contain it. Not a hardscrabble life and certainly not death."

Cass stepped away from the microphone and was immediately enveloped in a big hug from Boots. Within moments, they were surrounded by well-wishers, despite her resolve to get to the lobby area to see if her imagination was playing tricks on her. The hairs on her neck rose again, and she could have sworn someone was staring at her. As surreptitiously as she could, she scanned the room, but no one triggered the sense of her being…hunted. She shivered.

"I need to get outside, Uncle Boots." She breathed the words out in a rush and added a few "I'm sorry, excuse me's" in her wake. Stepping into the balmy temperature of the early spring morning didn't quell the feeling of being stalked.

A man wearing a black Stetson caught her eye. He strode across the parking lot headed toward a massive Ford pickup. Broad shoulders tapered to a really fine pair of jeans— could it be the guy from Chicago? That wasn't possible. No way, no how. The shiver dancing through her this time had nothing to do with fear.

Chance escaped before she recognized him. Traffic wasn't heavy enough to curtail his thoughts, which left him wanting nothing more than a tall scotch and a cold shower. What in the world had possessed him to attend the memorial service? Who was he trying to kid? Cassidy Morgan. He was drawn to her like a honeybee to clover. Crossing paths with her in Chicago had been a fluke but now he knew where to find her.

Her face as she eulogized her father was far too reminiscent of her expression in the hotel lobby. He'd probably bumped into her right after she received the news about her father's passing. Chance didn't do vulnerable but this woman had an inner spark that drew him like a bull to a red cape. He wanted her, plain and simple—even if there was nothing simple about this situation.

His cell phone rang, and he punched the button on the steering wheel for the Bluetooth connection. He snarled into the hidden microphone, "What?"

"Dang, bro. Don't be biting my head off."

"What do you want, Cord?"

"Cash and I tracked down that stud colt the old man wanted. You're not going to believe where he is."

"Dammit. Does he want me chasing a horse or stealing a ranch out from under a woman who just buried her father?"

"Whoa, dude. Back up there a minute. That almost sounded like you've developed a conscience."

Chance rubbed his temple and gave up trying to talk and drive at the same time. He pulled off and realized he'd parked a block from the Four Corners. How the hell had that happened? He jammed the transmission into Park and leaned his head back against the headrest on the driver's seat. "Okay, Cord, so tell me where the damn horse is."

"Right here. The plot thickens, little brother. Ben Morgan bought that colt months before you headed north to track him down. He's been under our noses all along."

He sat up straighter. "The ranch and everything on it is collateral. The colt, too?"

"No clue, but Cash is pulling financials. I'll keep you

posted. In the meantime, the old man wants to accelerate things. Can you call the balloon payment immediately?"

"Our father is a real SOB, Cord."

His brother's ringing laughter filled the cab. "So what else is new?" Cord broke the connection before Chance could retort anything.

He stared out the windshield. "So what's that make us, big brother?"

Four

The screen door banged shut behind her. The room hadn't changed one iota in her entire life. She stopped short as countless memories washed over her.

Don't run in the house.

Don't slam the door.

No, you can't bring that baby skunk inside.

Boots sprawled in the worn wooden chair on the porch, Buddy at his feet. A small metal table separated his chair from its twin. Her father's chair. How many evenings had she worked on her homework at the kitchen table, listening to the two men talk through the open window? She passed off an icy glass of sweet tea to Boots then grabbed a third chair, a refugee from some 1950s patio set, and settled into it.

"What are you not sayin', Cassie?"

She'd put off this discussion for almost a week. So much for easing into the conversation. There was no way to soften her news, so she blurted it out. "I'm putting the ranch up for sale." When Boots didn't respond, she plunged ahead. "I don't need the money. Not really. I want to set you up with a little place closer to town. A place where you and Buddy and a horse and some cows can live and be happy."

She gulped down a breath and continued. "It's for the best, you know. I have a life in Chicago. A job. Friends. I left the ranch and never intended to come back, and I wouldn't know what to do with it and…and…" Her voice trailed off as she raised her gaze to meet his. "Say something, Uncle Boots. Don't just sit there staring at me like I've grown a second head."

"You can't sell the ranch."

"Yes, I can. It's mine." She snapped her mouth shut. Maybe it wasn't hers. Maybe her father had left the place to Boots. "Isn't it?"

"Sort of."

"What's that mean?"

"You're Ben's heir, but the place is in hock to the bankers."

"What did Daddy do, Uncle Boots?"

"He took out a loan, Cassie, to pay the medical bills. The note on the land is coming due soon."

She winced, shut her eyes and rubbed at her temples. "How much?"

"A bunch."

"Define a bunch, Uncle Boots." Money. This she understood.

"More than what your daddy has in the bank. More than what I have in the bank. And unless you've made a fortune I don't know about, more than what you have."

"What was he thinking?" The words burst from her mouth before she could stop them.

"He was thinking about paying his bills."

The censure in Boots's tone burned, but she deserved it. "I didn't mean that the way it sounded. But if Dad took out a loan, he must have had a plan. He didn't believe in being in debt." She tried to feel hopeful while waiting for that proverbial other shoe to drop.

"Cattle."

"Cattle?"

"Before he was diagnosed, he bought a herd of five hundred feeder calves cheap. Had them on grass all winter so they're fat and almost ready for market. Give 'em another few weeks, and they'll bring top price. Grass-fed beef is the big thing now, so those calves should make enough to pay off the balloon payment with plenty to cover the rest of his debts to the hospital and leave you a little start-up cash."

"Start-up cash? Did he really believe I'd come back here to stay? With him gone? Why would I do that?" She gulped and quickly added, "Not that I don't love you, Uncle Boots."

"You need to come with me." He heaved up out of his chair.

He limped going down the steps, Buddy close on his heels, and she remembered Boots was even older than her father. He had to be pushing seventy. Man and dog ambled toward the barn and a few moments later, Cass followed. She caught up and as they entered the dim environs of the wooden structure side by side, Buddy darted ahead. Boots paused to flip a light switch, though it didn't add much illumination to the space. Whickers greeted them, and a few horses stuck their heads over the stall doors to watch. She recognized her father's favorite horse, Red. A big sorrel with a white blaze, the horse neighed and stretched his neck.

"Your dad spoiled that dang pony."

Cass laughed and stepped over to the stall. Red nickered and stretched his nose toward her. She reached up, and his velvet lips nibbled her palm. "I'll sneak you a carrot later." She patted the horse's neck before glancing back at Boots. "So? You wanted me to see Red?"

He shook his head before tilting it toward the stall across the way. "Nope. I want you to look over here." He pointed to a stall across the barn. "Ben was a horse trader and that's what he did. Just for you."

Chance knocked on the door, but no one answered. Lights illuminated the windows and Boots's rusty old truck was parked nearby. He walked to the end of the porch. A glass of tea sweated on a metal table. Then he noticed the open door and lights glowing in the barn. He sauntered that way, rehearsing what to say. Whatever he said, his heart wasn't really in what he had to do, even as it tripped a couple of beats at the thought of seeing Cassidy again.

He stepped into the soft gloom of the barn and stopped dead in his tracks.

Cassidy was leaning over a stable door murmuring something he couldn't understand. The old man stood next to her. Damn but she looked fine in jeans and boots. The plaid flannel shirt tucked into those jeans enhanced every one of her curves instead of hiding them. All the blood in his head rushed south, and he had to lean on the barn door to keep from pitching over face-first.

Boots opened the stall door, then they both disappeared inside. Chance inhaled several times, adjusted the front of his jeans and stepped deeper into the barn so he could see what was in that stall.

"Good-lookin' colt you have there."

Cassidy jumped about a foot off the ground, whirled and gasped, her face draining of color.

"You!"

He stepped back in mock innocence. "Me?"

"You! From Chicago!"

He held his hands, palms forward, out in front of him. "Guilty. Though I have to admit Fate is being a lady today. I figured I'd never see you again."

"What are you doing in Oklahoma?" Her brow furrowed, and he decided her glare was one of the cutest expressions he'd ever seen. Then again, there wasn't much about this woman he didn't find attractive in one way or another. That seemed to be the Barron family curse—they all had a tendency to think with the wrong part of their anatomy when a pretty woman was involved. He was far from immune from the affliction.

"I live here. What were you doing in Chicago?" As if they were playing poker, he called her furrowed brows with a sardonic grin and raised her with a wink.

"I live there." She sounded accusatory.

In all honesty, he rather enjoyed keeping her off balance. "So what brings you to Podunk, Oklahoma?" Cassie bristled, and color suffused her cheeks. He wondered if the same thing would happen if she were sexually aroused.

"Were you there this morning? At the memorial service?"

She'd seen him, dammit, just as he'd suspected. Well, he had no choice now. "Yeah. Why?"

"Pardon me for being a bit…suspicious. You try to pick me up in the hotel in Chicago then you follow me here and show up at my father's funeral. What's wrong with this picture?"

"Whoa, darlin'." She was a sarcastic little thing and damn if he didn't like it. A lot.

"Don't call me that. I don't even know your name."

"My name is Chance—Chancellor."

"Well, Mr. Chance Chancellor, you just turn around and walk right on out of here. I don't know who you are, why you're following me and frankly, I'm not sure I want to know. Get out and stay out!"

He blinked as his mind whirled. She'd cut him off before he finished his introduction. And now she was making assumptions about his name. Was it possible she didn't recognize him? That she had no clue he was a Barron? He wasn't sure if that bothered him. Okay, it did, but it simplified matters. He could figure things out before she ever guessed what was going on. "Easy, there, girl. I can explain."

"Oh? Really? And I'm not a girl, either."

No, she was definitely all woman. Her eyes positively

sparked energy, like two aquamarines under the noonday sun, and he shifted his stance to hide the effect she had on him. This was *not* the time to be thinking about getting her between the sheets. She was already suspicious of him, so he needed to walk very softly to gain her trust, and for some reason, that seemed very important to him.

No, he didn't need her trust; he needed her cooperation. He'd handled negotiations far more delicate in his career. He'd get Cassie into bed to get her out of his system then he'd move on, taking the deed to the ranch with him. That was the plan, and he needed to stick to it. Crossing the old man was not a smart thing to do, not when Cyrus Barron wanted something as bad as he wanted this place.

Then Chance inhaled. The dusty-sweet scent of Bermuda hay mixed with the musk-and-leather smell of horses. Rising above those, he caught a whiff of Cassidy—almond and cinnamon dancing with an underlying citrus tang.

"Yo, dude! Out of my barn. Now!"

Like a retriever coming out of a lake, he mentally shook to clear his mind. No distractions. Eye on the prize. But as she stood there, hands on her hips, forehead furrowed and chin jutting stubbornly, he realized she would always be a distraction. And that made him very nervous. No woman had ever gotten under his saddle like this one. His mouth curled into a slow smile, and he watched the effect on her— the slight dilation of her pupils, the flare of her nostrils and the swell of her chest. Yes, he could distract her, too. Good. The playing field was a bit more level now.

A not-so-polite hack and spit had them breaking their staring contest to glance at Boots. Chance recognized him now. Would the old man recognize him? Of all the Barron boys, he stayed out of the spotlight the most. Maybe he could slide through this as "Mr. Chancellor" after all.

"You here for a reason, son?"

Cass watched the stranger glance toward the stall, and

she could almost see the wheels turning in his head. Yes, he was sexy as all get-out, but she didn't trust him as far as she could throw that hunky six-foot-plus frame.

"Yessir. I came to see Ben's colt."

"I don't think we've met. How'd you know Ben?"

She cut her eyes to Boots. He didn't sound too put out, but she knew him. He was suspicious.

"I helped him locate the little guy. I own his half-brother. Same sire but from one of my mares. I considered buying this colt but didn't want to breed that close to the same bloodline."

She shifted her gaze from one to the other as they seemed to play a game of verbal ping-pong. She trusted Boots's instincts and for now she'd just let him run with the conversation. In the meantime, she could study Mr. Chance Chancellor. Tall, broad-shouldered and with a propensity for starched jeans and shirts, he looked like a model. But his boots were comfortably worn, if highly polished, and he wore that black Stetson on his head as if he'd been born to it.

If he traveled the rodeo or horse-show circuit, she'd lay odds he left a string of broken hearts in his wake. The hat covered his hair, but she remembered it being shiny, black and long enough to curl across his collar like the fingers of a lover. And his eyes. Amber, almost feral when the light hit them just right. His face? Chiseled. She had no other description for him. His cheekbones bordered on too angular but didn't cross the line. Plain and simple, he was gorgeous.

A vague memory pecked at her like one of the speckled hens searching the straw on the barn floor for a bite to eat. He still seemed familiar, but she couldn't place him. She'd figure it out eventually. She jerked out of her reverie when the guy took her hand and gave it a squeeze.

"I'm sorry for your loss, Miss Morgan."

"Cass. Everyone calls me Cass."

Her nose flared as if she couldn't inhale enough of his

warm scent. Leather and rain—a fragrance both homey and… Her insides tightened, but she refused to acknowledge the tiny quiver in the pit of her stomach. Well, a bit lower than that if she'd be honest with herself. This guy was sex on a stick, there was no denying it. But why was she being nice to him?

"On second thought, until you can prove you were a friend of my dad's, you can just call me Miss Morgan."

He laughed. Audacious and arrogant of him, but the sound reverberated in the barn and even Buddy came over to investigate. He sniffed at the man's boots, growled a little and hiked his leg.

"Buddy, no! Bad dog!" Her face flamed. Mortified that the dog was about to mark the man, she stammered an apology until Boots cut through her embarrassment.

"That dog has always had a good sense of people." He stared at Chance unblinking and for a moment, Cass wondered if Boots knew something she didn't. Her gaze darted between the two men, and tension in the barn ramped up a few degrees.

Buddy sat at her feet but his hackles rose, and she could feel the low growl rumbling in his chest as he leaned against her leg. Her father's old dog definitely did not like this man and apparently, neither did Boots. So why were her girlie bits going all fangirl on the guy?

"I think it's time for you to leave, Mr. Chancellor."

He dipped his chin and made a move to touch the brim of his Stetson. The gesture seemed old-fashioned and almost endearing. *Whoa, girl. Rein in that thought!*

"Another day then, Miss Morgan, when you aren't so stressed out or busy. Again, my condolences." He walked away but paused at the barn door. "We will see each other again, Cassidy Morgan."

Oh, hell. That dang sure sounded like a promise, but she wasn't sure just what the man had in mind.

Five

The office door clicked shut behind his secretary, but Chance had already swiveled in his chair to stare out the window. Restless energy roiled in his chest, leaving him unsettled. He wanted to see Cassidy again. And not because he wanted to serve her with legal papers. He wanted to spend time with her. Take her out and show her off.

What was it about this girl that riled him up? She invaded his thoughts, danced in his dreams and generally kept him guessing. He should stay away from her. She was bad news, and the old man would be royally pissed if he caught the barest whiff that Chance held any interest in Cass beyond his father's desire to crush her.

Screw it. He wanted to hear her voice. He could always say he was scoping out the competition if anyone in the family caught him. No one had to know what he was really thinking. Or feeling.

Chance scrolled through his contact list to the letter M. Not for the first time in the past few days, his finger hovered over the entry for Cassidy Morgan. He wanted to hit that call button so bad but he always stopped himself at the last instant—and not because he worried what the family would say.

What mattered was what Cass would say. How could he explain knowing her cell phone number? He'd called the ranch's landline once, only to hang up before anyone answered.

He finally gave up, shoved the phone in his jacket pocket and headed for the parking garage. He'd just drive out and see her.

Besides, he needed to check up on the colt, since he'd soon be a Barron asset. That was a good excuse. He'd also told Cass he would see her again, and to be honest, he'd enjoyed her quick intake of breath and the flash of her eyes when he made that promise. A grin twisted one side of his mouth. What Barron didn't keep his promises, right? Exactly. His driving out to see her this morning was now a matter of family honor.

Cassidy sat forward on the chair and watched the pickup rattle across the cattle guard and head up the dirt drive. She was alone, but for Buddy. The dog stayed behind when Boots had left first thing to run errands. Surprised when Buddy didn't jump up in the truck, Boots had shrugged and headed off. Cassidy had spent the morning mucking out stalls and making phone calls.

The loan officer at the bank seemed to be dodging her calls and try as she might, she'd been unable to hire a cattle hauler to get the herd to the stockyards in Oklahoma City. Every company she called told her to call back when the calves were ready to haul. What did she know about selling cows anyway? The cattle would be ready in May or early June. April was just rolling around.

And now Mr. Chancellor was pulling up in her front yard. Buddy leaped off the porch and charged the truck, dancing and barking as the driver's-side door opened and six-foot plus of sexy man stepped out. Since she'd last seen him, she'd done her best to convince her libido that the man was not nearly as hot as she remembered.

Her libido doubled over in laughter.

"What're you doin' here?" She had to yell over Buddy's excited barks.

Her visitor waded around the dog's determined forays to keep him away from the house and smiled. "A man can't come see a lady just because?"

"I'm not a lady, and I don't believe for a New York minute that you ever do anything *just because*."

He pressed his hand against his chest. "You wound me, m'lady."

She rolled her eyes. "You are so full of it, dude, I'm glad I have my boots on." He laughed, and the sound did funny things to her insides.

"You going to make me stand out here in the sun, or can I come up and sit down?" The grin on his face challenged her as much as if he'd actually thrown down a gauntlet.

"Buddy, come." The dog responded to her instantly, but he never took his eyes off Chance. She returned to the little vignette of chairs and settled in her father's. She'd overcome her aversion and now sat there in the evenings, watching the sun go down and visiting with Boots. The dog hopped up into Boots's chair, and she chuckled. Sometimes, the Australian shepherd seemed almost human. She petted the dog and ignored the man as he clomped onto the porch and sat in the metal chair.

"Buddy looks like a little ol' cowboy sittin' there."

She glanced at the dog and laughed. His shoulders, chest and front legs were white. A black stripe circled his back and tummy and below that, his fur was speckled gray with black spots. His lower legs were tan, like he wore boots. A brown-and speckled-gray mask covered his eyes and ears.

"That or a bandit." She leaned back in her chair and stared at her guest. "So why are you here again, Mr. Chancellor?"

"Most people just call me Chance, since that's my name." The grin he flashed was devilish, and she wondered what thoughts were in his mind. "Fine. So, why are you here…Chance?"

"Can I be honest with you?"

"I don't know. *Can* you be honest?"

Damn but that question hit a little too close to home. Good thing he was the poker player in the family. Okay, honestly, he wouldn't want to play poker with any of his brothers. He deflected her question with a wink and a little smirk. "I'll plead the fifth on that one. You know what folks say, all's fair in love and war."

"Yeah, but which is this?"

"You tell me, Cassidy."

"You still haven't answered my question."

"Which one?"

"Well, you're a man so we know you can't be honest, so that leaves the other one. Why are you here?"

"Ow. I lodge a protest in the name of men everywhere." He offered her another crooked grin and a wink as he added, "I came to see you."

"Why?"

Time to lay his cards on the table. "Because I want to take you to dinner."

"Dinner."

"Yes, dinner. I know Boots goes to the Four Corners to eat. A lot. I figure you weren't kidding about being a bad cook. I'd like to take you out to eat. To a real restaurant." She folded her arms across her chest, and his eyes drifted despite his best efforts.

"Yo, dude. Eyes up here?"

Heat climbed the back of his neck. Was he actually blushing? He broadened his grin. "Sorry. A man can't help it when the view is so lovely." She snorted, and he laughed. He tossed a shrug of his shoulders into the mix and tried a boyish look on her. "The point remains. I'd still like to take you out."

"Like…on a date? A real date?"

"There's such a thing as a fake date?" She rolled her eyes again, and he couldn't tell if that was progress or not. "Yes, a real date. Dressing up and everything. A nice restaurant, maybe a movie after? Or we could go to Bricktown, hit some of the clubs?" Or maybe not. He'd be recognized there. Crap. He'd be recognized at any of his usual haunts. He needed a Plan B in a hurry. "Or we could go to my place, order in pizza and watch the Cubs game."

"Cubs? Are you kiddin' me?"

"Okay…White Sox?"

She looked disgusted. "Why do you think I'd be a fan of either one?"

"Um…you live in Chicago?"

"Yeah. But lifelong Cardinals fan here."

"Really? You *like* baseball?"

"Really. And I like *Cardinals* baseball."

"So, does that mean pizza at my place and the Cards on the big screen?" He liked that idea. His media room was that much closer to his bedroom, and he had every intention of seducing her before the date was over.

She snorted again. "How cheap do you think I am?" She eyed him speculatively. "Why should I go out with you?"

"I was attracted to you when we bumped into each other in Chicago. That hasn't changed."

Her lips pursed as she considered his offer; he wanted to kiss her but he'd remain patient. The time would come—sooner or later.

"Dinner at a nice place then a sports bar to watch the Cards." ❧

She looked so cocky he couldn't help but grin back. For a brief moment, he toyed with the idea of calling up the corporate jet and flying her to St. Louis for the game. As a minority owner, Barron Entertainment had box seats, though he seldom got the chance to park his butt in them. Doing so would blow his cover, so he nodded in agreement. "Dinner out then a sports bar to watch the game. I'll pick you up around five? Game starts at 7:30." He stood up, and she looked startled.

"You're leaving?"

"Yeah, I got what I came for." Her expression changed, and he would have missed the flicker of sadness if he hadn't been studying her reactions.

"Well, don't let me keep you." She didn't move to stand. Instead, her hand gripped the arm of the chair as if to keep her in it. She wore an expression of studied casualness.

"Can you make coffee?" he suddenly asked. She stared at him like he was crazy. "We've established you can't cook. Does that mean you're a Starbucks baby, or can you perk a real pot of coffee?"

"I make excellent coffee, thank you very much. Even Uncle Boots doesn't complain."

Uncle Boots? This was a story he wanted to hear. "Then go make a pot, woman. Prove it to me."

"Ha! I made one just before you got here. So there." She darted up and through the door before he could react.

A few minutes later, she returned with a tray loaded with a clean mug, sugar bowl, creamer and a thermal carafe. "I figure you take your coffee black, but I admit to a sweet tooth and a need for cream."

Coffee steamed in his mug, and he inhaled the rich aroma. After a hesitant sip, he nodded. "This is good, but how do I know you made it?" She flushed, her anger rising quickly. He loved eliciting that reaction from her and couldn't wait to see what she was like when he had her in his arms.

"You'll just have to take my word for it."

Sparring with her was fun. He couldn't deny it. Most

women were dazzled by his last name. Cass had no clue, luckily. If she ever found out that his father wanted to take the ranch, she'd hate him. She could hate him later—after he'd given her a tumble, after he got her out of his system.

He finished off the coffee in his mug and reached for the carafe. His hand collided with hers, and instinct had him wrapping his fingers around hers. "Nice," he murmured.

"Mmm," she agreed.

As they chatted the afternoon away, clouds gathered on the western horizon. The rising temperature played with the white, puffy cumulous clouds until thunderheads billowed and thrust angry fists into the humid spring sky. A few formed the classic anvil shape associated with violent storms. Whatever breeze there'd been died, and the humidity thickened to the point it was almost hard to breathe.

"I don't remember a chance of t-storms mentioned on the weather last night." Cass stood and walked to the end of the porch, scanning the sky. "I'll be right back. You can come in if you want." She slipped into the house, and he followed.

Not sure what he had expected, Chance decided this wasn't it. The furniture might have been new when Cass was a child. Now it looked comfortably shabby. A clunky TV perched on a wooden bookcase and occupied the center of one wall. A metal stand with a saddle that seemed to be in the middle of repairs sat next to it. A leather couch and two ancient recliners formed a semicircle around a battered wooden coffee table made from a slab of pine and two small wooden wheels.

Cass pushed the power button on the TV and waited for the picture to form. Sure enough, one of the local weathermen spouted warnings as he stood in front of a radar image.

"Looks ugly."

She nodded. "Yeah, and headed this way." She walked closer and tapped the TV screen with her index finger. "See that? Hail core. I need to get the horses into the barn."

"I'll help."

"No, that's okay. Buddy and I can do it."

"Cass, I know horses. I can help."

She tossed a one-shouldered shrug in his direction, ducked around him and banged the screen door as she left. He glanced down at the dog. She'd banged the door in his face, too. "Wonder what we did wrong, boy?" The dog woofed, and the desultory wag of his tail might translate to a shrug, too.

"Well? You two coming or what?" Cassie's voice carried through the still air, punctuated almost instantly by a clap of thunder.

"Time to get a move on, Buddy. C'mon, boy." He opened the door and held it as the dog zipped out and launched off the porch, a gray blur headed straight for Cass. Chance followed at a trot. By the time he caught up, lightning flickered in the sky, and thunder rolled. The horses milled around a field on the other side of the barn.

"Get the barn door," Cassie yelled, but the rising wind tore her words away. She pointed, and he waved. She climbed the fence as Buddy ducked underneath the bottom rail.

Chance jogged to the barn, ducked inside and shut the door before heading to the far end. He noted the stall doors were already open and padded with fresh straw. He lifted the iron bar on the back door and pushed it open on well-greased rollers. He cut his gaze between the growing storm and the woman and dog working the horses up toward the barn. It was poetry in motion.

In the near distance, a sheet of rain filled the space between cloud and ground, marching across dusty fields. The first fat drops splattered in the dirt at his feet. He stepped out, prepared to help, then realized he might cause more problems by spooking the horses. While he wanted Cass to hurry, he knew she couldn't. She and Buddy were working the small herd like masters, but the storm galloped toward them.

The rain hit hard, and she was drenched immediately. The horses saw the open door and dashed inside. Chance had just enough time to step into the shadows as they charged in, Buddy hard on their heels. He rolled the door partially closed, leaving enough space for Cass to slip through. She darted in, looking as if she'd just climbed out of a pool. Her hair lay plastered to her head, and her white T-shirt, with the fitting slogan of "Take This Job and Shove It," did little to conceal every lacy stitch of her Victoria's Secret bra. He found that intriguingly incongruous. Despite her claims otherwise, Cassie Morgan was a cowgirl—but a cowgirl in a frilly Angel bra.

Chance closed the door, and the gloom in the barn deepened. His eyes adjusted, and he noticed the horses sorting themselves out and heading into stalls, with a little help from Buddy. Cass walked up one side shutting stall gates behind them. Chance took the other side and did the same. They met at the far end, and Cass flipped the light switch. He really wished she hadn't. He couldn't take his eyes from her curves. He began to unbutton his shirt.

"Whoa. Wait a minute there, cowboy. Just what the heck do you think you're doing?"

"You're wet."

"Um…duh."

"I'm dry."

"So?"

"So, either you're really happy to see me or you're cold." She glanced down, and when her gaze met his again, her cheeks were flushed. Oh, yes. She'd be delightful in bed. "I'm offering you my shirt."

She glowered at him. "You hardly seem the type to offer a girl the shirt off your back."

He peeled it off and handed it to her, amused that her

eyes widened, and her lips parted slightly. He got the distinct impression she liked what she saw when she licked her bottom lip. Of course the gesture created an interesting reaction behind the buttons of his jeans.

"Here." He waved the shirt a little, but she didn't seem to notice. His smile broadened, and he leaned closer to drape it over her shoulders. "There you go."

"Thanks…"

His lips hovered inches from hers and if she breathed deeply, her very perky nipples would brush against his bare chest. His fingers tangled in her hair as he smoothed the wet strands back from her face. Her eyes dilated, and she inhaled. Her chest swelled, and that's all it took. His lips found hers. He held her head still as his teeth nipped at her mouth. His tongue teased the seam of her lips until they parted for him. She tasted like café au lait, and he had an insane desire to fly her to New Orleans for beignets. Right after he kissed her senseless and made love to her for the rest of the afternoon.

She pressed against him, and he felt her shiver. He dropped one hand so he could encircle her waist with his arm and hold her closer. Like a contented cat, she rubbed and purred, her mouth open now and accepting the forays his tongue made against hers. While he kept his eyes open so he could watch her, she closed hers, as if lost in the moment. He liked that; liked the idea of sweeping her away, overriding her senses and making her his.

Cass was every bit as sexy as he remembered from their encounter in Chicago. He'd wanted to invite her up to his room and would have if not for that damn call from Cord. Just as he'd wanted to do then, his hand dropped to her round ass and he discovered it fit, filling his palm and making him horny as hell.

"I want you."

"Oh? Really?" She bumped against his erection and chuckled. "I hadn't noticed."

He ground his teeth together. "I didn't figure you for a tease, Cass."

She planted her hands against his chest and pushed a little. He dropped his arms. "I don't tease, Chance, not about sex."

"What about love?" She tilted her head and stared at him, unblinking. Where the hell had that come from? He didn't know, but he sure was curious about her answer.

"There's no such thing."

"Ooh. Cynical little thing, aren't you?"

"Yup, I am. What about you, Chance? I bet women tuck their phone numbers into those tight jeans of yours all the time. You're all about the sex, and I just don't see anything even remotely resembling love in that equation."

She backed up a step, putting some distance between them, but not so far he couldn't touch her if he wanted. Instead, he hooked his thumbs in the front pockets of his jeans and waited. The flash in her eyes convinced him she was just getting started, and he was curious about how far she would push.

"You tried to pick me up in the hotel in Chicago. You *knew* you'd never see me again. A one-night stand, that's all you were after. That's all you wanted."

She jabbed her finger in his chest, and the nail pricked a little, but then her fingertip caressed the spot before trailing down a couple of inches. Cass jerked her hand back as if she'd been burned and jutted her chin. He worked very hard to keep a poker face because inside, he was grinning madly.

"I bet you've never had a girl say no to you."

Well, no. I'm a Barron. They want to sleep with me for the name if nothing else. That thought hit a little too close to home, though he couldn't figure out why it bothered him.

"I bet *nobody* says no to you, in fact. You just...you have that arrogant air of being all charmed and stuff. Like everything you touch turns to gold."

Pretty much. I'm a Barron, baby. It's genetic.

"Guys like you are a dime a dozen. Good-looking enough to be a male model, and you just skate by."

Not quite a dozen, darlin', unless the old man is hiding a few in the woodpile we don't know about.

"So why are you *here*? Why do you keep coming around?"

"Does this mean you aren't going out with me tonight?" He watched the flush creep up her neck, and he stepped toward her. Yes, he was a predator on the prowl, and she was his prey, but when she didn't back up, he had to give her points.

"What's that got to do with this discussion?"

"Discussion? Sounded more like a lecture to me, Cassidy. Why am I here? I came by to ask you out to dinner because I don't have your phone number. Why do I keep coming back? Because you're a damned attractive woman, and I want to get to know you. Is that so hard to believe?" He ignored the lie about her phone number, but all the other answers bounced around in his thoughts. And then the main one sucker punched him in the gut. *Because my father wants to ruin you, and I'm having trouble with that.*

She lowered her chin, and he didn't know if that was a good sign or a bad one. She blinked once. Twice. And a third time before her eyes narrowed. "Don't expect me to go all Sally Field at the Oscars here. I left my ego at the front gate. I don't trust you, Mr. Just-call-me-Chance. Not as far as I can throw you."

Cass paused to lick her lips, and that's all it took. He wrapped his hands around her biceps and pulled her to him. He kissed her, taking her mouth by storm. She resisted for a long moment then relented, her tongue teasing his lips this time. He could feel her heartbeat, and was thrilled it galloped as fast as his own. His pulse pounded in his ears, every bit as loud as the thunder outside the barn.

Her arms slipped around his neck, and he backed her up to the nearest wall without breaking the kiss. Heat flared between them, and he brushed his shirt off her shoulders. He could feel the rasp of the lace on her bra through her T-shirt.

"Too many clothes." He growled the words as he peeled the wet cotton over her head and then sealed his lips against hers again. One hand roamed down to stroke her thigh and just as he hoped, she rubbed her knee up his leg. He cupped her sweet ass and the next thing he knew, she'd wrapped those long legs around his waist. He couldn't breathe for a minute as the most intimate part of her cradled his erection.

Chance broke the kiss to gasp for breath and leaned his forehead against hers. "Baby, you are so hot but dammit, I want to make love to you in a bed."

She froze. "What?"

Well, hell. He was definitely thinking with the wrong head at the moment. "Yeah. Our first time. I want it to be right. I'd take you standing here just like this, but I want to take it slow. I want to watch you come apart in my arms before I sink in. I want to touch you and kiss you and find out just how many times I can make you come before you beg me to stop."

Six

What the heck was she doing? Cass couldn't think straight and wasn't sure she wanted to. Her wet bra chafed her sensitized nipples but instead of irritating, the sensation sent waves directly to the area of her body presently rubbing against Chance's fly. He was as turned on as she was, a definite plus, and the things he was saying left her panting. Some part of her consciousness didn't trust him, but her libido didn't care. He was sexy and hot for her. His body promised things to hers, and waiting was killing her. She'd never been known for her patience.

"Shut up and kiss me."

"Yes, ma'am."

"Talkin—mmmmmm."

His mouth took her breath away and cut off any more talking on her part, too. Chance pressed closer, his erection rubbing against her as he pushed her a little higher on the wall to change the angle. If they'd been naked, she'd be riding him hard and fast. Her tongue pushed his aside and thrust into his mouth. He gripped her head with gentle hands and dragged his mouth from hers only to trail his tongue down her neck and across her collarbone.

Cass sighed and arched her head back. She rested it against the wood behind her, leaving her neck exposed to his attentions. With a little space between them now, one of his hands cupped her. She inhaled sharply, which pushed her breast deeper into his palm. He groaned, and she tightened her legs around his waist, all but sealing them together.

"Want to taste you." His words burst out in puffs of his breath. "Want to touch you."

"Talking. You're talking again."

"I think there should be a whole lot more talkin' goin' on and a whole lot less touchin'."

Mortified, she gasped and stared over Chance's shoulder. Boots stood in the barn doorway, hands on his hips, his face perfectly blank. Chance hunched against her, and she tapped him on the shoulder. "Yo, dude...company?" She cut her eyes to indicate they'd been caught.

Chance glanced over his shoulder and flashed a wicked grin. "He doesn't have a shotgun, so I think we're safe."

She thumped him on the shoulder. "Put me down, Chance."

"You're the one with your legs wrapped around my waist, darlin'."

She felt heat rise up her chest and flood her face. With her hands on his shoulders for leverage, she unhooked her ankles and dropped first one foot then the other to the floor. Her knees threatened to buckle but with a gallant gesture, Chance supported her until she got her bearings. Dizzy, out of breath and blushing furiously, she managed to face Boots from behind Chance's brawny frame.

"Busted, Uncle Boots. I...sort of figured you wouldn't be back until after the storm."

"Storm's been over awhile, Cassidy." His expression didn't change—remaining stony with a spark of anger lighting his eyes.

"I got a little wet getting the horses in. Chance offered me his shirt." Of course, his shirt was on the floor, along with hers. That elicited a quirked brow from the older man. She sucked in a deep breath and reached for her inner adult.

"If you don't mind, Uncle Boots, we'll see you up at the house in a few minutes."

Boots glanced at his watch, stared at her then favored Chance with a scowl. "Five minutes or I'm coming back. With Winnie."

As the old man exited the barn, Chance cut his eyes to her. "Winnie?" His whisper raised goose bumps on her rapidly chilling flesh.

"Winnie is his Winchester shotgun."

"We'll be right behind you, sir."

A giggle burbled up from nowhere at Chance's quick reply, and she hissed out, "It's not like he'll make you marry me or anything."

The man in front of her stilled. Completely, totally, not-even-breathing stilled. As quick as a snake, his head whipped around, and his eyes bored into hers. She choked off another giggle and stared back, wide-eyed and startled.

"That's a joke, Chance." She reached for him but seeing his expression, her hands plummeted to her sides like rocks.

"Marrying me would be a joke?"

Cass pressed back against the wall. This was a side of him she'd never guess at, and one that scared her just a little. This was a man used to getting everything he wanted. "No." Her brain whirled as she searched for the words to get her out of this. Where had this intensity come from? Why did he look both angry and hurt? They hadn't even gone on a date yet—making out in the barn did not count.

"Shotgun wedding, Chance. That's the joke. Us getting married? You have to admit that's a bit far-fetched. We just met. And besides, just because I took a leave of absence from my job doesn't mean that I'm not going back to Chicago once I get the ranch squared away."

He trapped her with his hands braced against the wall on either side of her head. "What's that mean?"

"What do you think it means? I live in Chicago, Chance.

I have a good job there. Friends. A life that's not here on a ranch. I plan to sell Dad's cattle, settle his debts and sell this place if I can so I can take care of Boots. And Buddy. Maybe a couple of the horses. Find a couple of acres where they'll be happy." She lifted one shoulder in a negligent shrug. "I'm not a cowgirl."

"So…going out with me is basically a one-night stand for *you*?"

She furrowed her brow as he tossed her own words back in her face. His attitude totally confused her. "You're getting way ahead of yourself, Chance. Yeah, we generate some heat, but it's just sex." She stared at him, trying to read his expression. "Isn't it? We don't know each other well enough for it to be anything else."

He pressed closer, crowding her, and she almost got dizzy from lack of oxygen. Cass inhaled sharply, ducked under his arm and slipped into the tack room. She emerged wearing a windbreaker and bent over to snag her T-shirt and his work shirt, which she tossed in his direction. "I'll be ready at five if you still want to take me out. If you don't show up, I'll understand."

With as much dignity as she could muster, she pivoted and marched to the door. Luckily, Boots had left it open, and she managed to step outside without tripping. The storm was gone, the black, roiling clouds with jagged lightning pushing on to the east, leaving wet grass and mud behind. Buddy dashed past her and raced to the house, leaving her to follow a bit more sedately in his path despite the fact she wanted to run.

When she arrived at the house, her boots clumped on the wooden steps and across the porch. The porch door banged behind her. She could hear Boots rummaging in the kitchen. She headed straight to her room. A hot shower and dry clothes would give her perspective on things. She hoped. Because at the moment, she was completely clueless as to what had just happened.

Chance watched Cassie walk away. What the hell had come over him? He was not the possessive type, and a one-night stand was his hookup of choice. No ties, no needy females. So how had he gone from cocky cowboy to the one clinging and needing reassurance of the relationship? As Cass said, what relationship? Dammit all to hell. He needed to get her into his bed so he could get her out of his system. Plain and simple.

Only it wasn't. Neither plain, nor simple. The time had come for him to think about work, not the sexy woman driving him crazy. Besides, what did it matter? Cassie was going back to Chicago. She didn't want to stay here. She didn't want to be with him.

He rubbed the spot over his chest as he climbed into his truck. He didn't start it right away, but instead sat and stared at the window he figured was Cassie's bedroom. The place wasn't big. Hell, his condo had more square footage than the farm house. The furniture was old, dilapidated, lived in. Loved.

And there was his answer. That house was filled with love. A kind of love he and his brothers had missed out on growing up. Cassie was three when she lost her mother, but her daddy had loved her. And her Uncle Boots. For the first time in his life, Chance was jealous. It was an emotion that would take some getting used to.

He started the truck, backed up until he had room to turn around and headed toward the main road. He had a lot to think about.

Cassie waited until she heard Chance drive away before she kicked off her boots and peeled out of her wet jeans. The man was a player. She knew that with every feminine instinct she possessed. Serial daters. That's what her best friend in Chicago called guys like him. Hopping from bed to bed. Their smart phone containing a contact folder simply labeled "Easy." The last thing she needed or wanted was to hook up with an Oklahoma cowboy, even if he had a fine ass, gorgeous build and a face that could melt the South Pole. Cowboys wanted cowgirls, and she no longer fit that description.

Standing in her bra and panties damp from more than rain, she turned a slow circle. Her room. Which hadn't changed a bit since she left for college ten years before. Trophies and buckles littered the top of her dresser with a couple of framed photographs stuffed among them. In one, she stood next to Barney, her first horse. She barely reached the top of his front leg, despite the hat jammed on her head. She proudly held her first championship buckle, even though she hadn't even been big enough to mount Barney without a boost at the time. In another, she sat behind her dad's saddle, her arms around his waist. In a third, she posed with a saddle she'd won.

A tap on her door sent her scrambling for her robe. She shoved her arms through the worn flannel sleeves and tied it at her waist. "C'mon in, Uncle Boots."

The door swung open, creaking a little. "We need to talk, baby girl."

Cass nodded. "Let me grab a shower first?"

He nodded, turned and shuffled down the hall to the living room. She dashed to the bathroom. Though she would have preferred to stand there until the hot water tank emptied, she showered quickly and dressed in clean jeans and a fresh T-shirt. When she was ready, she went out to the living room and settled on the couch. Boots sat in his recliner looking uncomfortable. Cass wet her bottom lip with a nervous swipe of her tongue and felt way too much like a teenager caught making out.

"You still planning on selling out?"

Selling *out*? That sounded almost ugly, and disloyal—and not at all what she anticipated for a topic. "I'm not a rancher, Uncle Boots. I need to sell the place to pay Daddy's debts. And to give you a cushion so you can find a little place."

"This ain't about me, Cassidy. This is about you. About the heritage your daddy left for you. About who you are deep down."

She clasped her hands together and shoved them between her knees as she leaned forward. Staring at her bare toes, she gathered her thoughts. "I'm not a cowgirl, Uncle Boots. Haven't been since I left for college."

"Then why did you go round up the horses when the storm hit?"

"Because it needed doing."

"Would a city girl have gotten soakin' wet to move them into the barn?"

"Just because I knew what was the right thing to do doesn't mean I want to run this ranch."

Boots leaned back and stared out the front window. "Ben went lookin' for a colt. A very special colt. For you." He held up his hand when she started to speak, and his words cut through any argument she might offer. "Just hush up and listen, Cassidy." His eyes returned to the scenery outside. The silence stretching between them wasn't comfortable, but Cass remained quiet.

"Your daddy knew you didn't want to stay here. He hoped you would, but he knew deep down that you had to go off and see the world. He did the same thing." He glanced in her direction. "He lived on the road for a good many years. And then he met your momma. She put down roots here. Deep ones. Then you came along. So he settled down. He built this place fence post by fence post. At one time, Morgan-Baxter Rodeo Company supplied stock for all the big rodeos. Calgary. National Finals. Las Vegas. Denver. We even made it to Madison Square Garden one year. Your daddy was a name, honey. But he didn't want you to be a cowgirl."

Her mouth gaped open. "Well, you damn sure could have fooled me!"

Boots chuckled softly. "He wanted more for you. He wanted you to be a rancher. Or a trainer. Or a breeder. Even as a kid, you had an uncanny sense about horses, baby girl. But at the same time, he knew you had the same wander-lust in your blood he did. So he waited for you to get it out of your system. And then he found that colt. Legend's Double Rainbow."

Memory flared—her dad driving Cass in his truck as he explained her mom wasn't coming home and a double rainbow arching across the sky in front of them. She stared at the old man, confused. "He bought this stud colt just because of his name?"

Boots laughed. At her. "Honey, you know your daddy better than that. That little fella has a pedigree going all the way back to Leo." A sly look crossed his face.

She blinked, her mind skipping everything but the name *Leo*. "Wait…Leo? As in the foundation stallion?"

He nodded. "Yep. He found a colt with a bloodline that traces straight back to Leo."

"Holy cow!" Leo was a legendary quarter horse stud. He had produced racehorses, the finest performance horses and more than a few rodeo champs along the way. She leaned back, possibilities whirling through her mind despite her intentions. No. She had to think about Chicago. Her life was in Chicago. Not here on some dirt-road ranch. Wasn't it?

Her brow furrowed in consternation as another thought intruded. She leaned forward. "How the hell did he pay for the colt? I…I can't even imagine how much he's worth!"

"Your daddy was a born horse trader, baby girl."

She processed that statement, her chest tight with dread. She didn't want to, but she asked, "What did he do?"

"Your daddy had one of the finest collections of rodeo memorabilia anywhere outside of the Western Heritage Museum. Turns out Doc's former owner is a collector."

"Wait. Doc?"

Boots nodded. "The colt. They call him Doc for short."

She had to think about that a minute before the initials DR—for Double Rainbow—occurred to her. "Oh! Sorry. I'm slow. I'm still…Daddy had a collection?"

He laughed. "Neither of us would have called it that, but the attic and the loft in the barn were filled to the rafters with stuff. Your daddy was a pack rat. He never threw anything away. This ol' boy drove all the way down from Illinois towin' a big ol' trailer with the colt inside. He sorted all the boxes, loaded up his trailer and left Doc in trade. Ben figured it was a good deal." His eyes misted. "I think he knew he was dyin' but wasn't ready to surrender to the damn cancer. Ben probably figured neither of us would want to sort all that stuff."

Boots stared out the window. He didn't look at her as he continued. "Your daddy wanted to leave you something, baby girl. A legacy. A way to find your own roots, and he hoped you'd put those roots down here."

Cass sucked in a long breath and held it a moment to ease the tightness in her chest. It didn't help. Despite the burning tears filling her eyes, she managed to choke out the words. "I didn't know how bad he was, Uncle Boots. I should have come sooner."

"He didn't want you to know, hon. He even hid it from me for a long time. But gettin' ahold that little stud was his final gift to you. It's up to you, Cassidy Anne. What are you going to do with it?" The old man's eyes twinkled as winked at her. "And what are you gonna do about that young buck sniffin' around you in the barn?"

Seven

Chance pulled up in the yard and parked. He sat for a moment, feeling far too much like a high school boy on his first date. The fact they'd been caught all but *in flagrante delicto* in the barn that afternoon didn't bother him. But the look Boots had given him did. The old man knew who he was, but Chance could not figure out why he hadn't told Cass. He needed to have a little chat with Boots Thomas.

His cell phone chimed, and he glanced at the caller ID. Barron Security—Cash calling from the office. He answered with a blunt, "What's up?"

"I've been following up on the paper trail on that colt the old man wants."

Chance rubbed his forehead. He'd all but forgotten about the colt between his efforts to dodge filing the lawsuit to foreclose on the ranch and reining in his wayward thoughts about the woman he was supposed to ruin. "This couldn't wait until morning?"

"You're sitting at Ben Morgan's place, aren't you?"

"Dammit, Cash. Are you tracking me?"

"What do you think? Gotta love built-in GPS on the smartphones."

Grimacing at the virtual leash, Chance steered the conversation back the subject. "What about the colt?"

"Registration papers just popped up with the AQHA. Ownership's been transferred. To Cassidy Morgan. Makes me wonder how a horse the old man had in his sights suddenly pops up in her name, and that makes me curious about her interest in you, bro."

Chance considered the possibilities. He'd seen her face in the barn when Boots showed her the colt. She'd seemed surprised. If he ever had to play cards with someone, he wanted it to be Cass. She had the worst poker face in the world. Besides, how would she or her father know that Cyrus was after the same horse? The facts just didn't add up. Sure, women always had angles to get close to or take advantage of the Barron brothers. He didn't believe Cassie was one of them.

"Who signed off on the registration? American Quarter Horse Association doesn't require a principal to file the papers."

"Former owner, as her agent."

He pondered that information, still not convinced of her culpability. "Doesn't mean she knew it was happening."

"Why are you defending her, Chance? Wait, don't tell me. She's pretty, and you're a sucker for a damsel in distress."

"Shut up, Cash."

"Then why haven't you filed the paperwork dealing with calling in the loan and preserving the collateral?"

"Are you checking up on me?"

"Just following the old man's orders, big brother. Which is something you'd better start doing. He wants that land and the colt. Cassidy Morgan has both. You've been jackin' around too long and spending way more time sniffing around that little gal than in your office taking care of business. It's time to get in, kill two birds with one stone and get the hell out. Simple."

Simple? Chance closed his eyes and rubbed his forehead again. Nothing about Cassidy Morgan was simple. Nothing about this acquisition was simple. Once upon a time, life had been. He'd wanted to ride the rodeo circuit, then settle down to run the family cattle business and breed some excellent horses on the side. Unfortunately, the old man had different ideas. He'd steered each of his sons into a profession. A short bark of laughter escaped at the thought. Cyrus Barron didn't steer. He bullied, hammered, demanded and dragged his sons kicking and screaming all the way. His old man always got what he wanted.

Movement on the front porch caught his attention. Boots stepped to the rail, staring at him. "I gotta go, Cash."

"Just get it done, Chance."

Opening the door, he stepped out of the truck and met Boots halfway to the house. The older man squared off, hands on his hips, jaw jutting, looking a bit like a bulldog ready to defend his territory.

"I just have one thing to say to you, boy."

Chance bristled. No one, not even his father called him *boy*. "Then say it, old man."

"You hurt that little gal, I'll hunt you like the junkyard dog I know you are."

Chance rocked back, surprised by the direction this conversation had taken.

"I recognized you, Chance Barron, when you walked into the barn that first time. And I know all about the bad blood between her daddy and yours."

"Then why haven't you told Cass?"

"Because I haven't figured out your angle. Given what I saw this afternoon, maybe you do have feelings for her. That said, I don't have to like you, and I dang sure don't have to trust you." Boots glanced toward the house then looked him up and down. "You better tell her who you really are. She's just like her daddy—never could abide a liar."

"I'm not…" His voice trailed off. He wasn't a liar. He might not tell the whole truth, or he might bend it, but he didn't lie. Besides, he wasn't under oath. He lifted one shoulder in a negligent shrug. "Does it matter, Mr. Thomas? She's headed back to Chicago soon anyway."

"Maybe."

Chance stared, wondering about the cryptic reply. As an attorney, he was used to having all the aces up his sleeve. He'd been half a step behind since seeing Cass at that hotel in Chicago. "As far as I know, she intends to go back to her job. They won't give her compassionate leave forever."

The front door opened, and Cass stepped out. He stood transfixed, the conversation with Boots forgotten. Her blond hair looked like spun silk, and the light shining from the house bathed her in a halo. This was the first time he'd seen her wearing anything remotely feminine—besides those killer boots in Chicago. The skirt she wore hugged her hips and left her long legs in plain sight. A lacy turquoise tank left just enough of the rest of her to the imagination. He swallowed. Hard. Ignoring Boots, he stepped toward her.

"Wow." She smiled, and he gulped again. "You look terrific."

Her cheeks pinkened, and she dropped her gaze. When she looked up, her eyes twinkled and crinkled at the corners. "Happy to see you, too, cowboy."

He was so busted. She laughed at the expression on his face when he figured out what she meant. He *was* happy to see her. And she was happy to see him. She couldn't remember the last time a guy turned her on like Chance. Her breasts swelled as she inhaled. Just thinking about the kiss they'd shared had her all but panting. She cut her eyes to look at him and noticed his gaze dropped to her chest. She cleared her throat, and his head jerked up, his expression guilty as he met her eyes. She bit back a laugh. Busted again, but she didn't mind.

He made her feel sexy and desirable, so she made a bit

of a show when she fastened her seat belt. Oh, yeah. He noticed.

"So, where are you taking me to dinner?"

He had to lick his lips before he spoke. Yes, her outfit definitely had the desired effect. She'd been ready to make love to him in the barn. She was more than ready to explore that aspect of things as soon as they finished dinner.

He started the truck and maneuvered it back toward the road before he glanced over, gave her an appreciative smile and replied. "I thought we'd go to Old Chicago." She flashed a "you've got to be kidding me" face at him and he laughed. "You have to admit, it's fitting, all things considered."

Cass rolled her eyes but resisted sticking out her tongue. "Well, if that's the case, I should have dressed for comfort..." She liked teasing him.

"Actually, I thought we might head down to Bricktown. Since you haven't been home in a while, I think you'll be surprised."

"Any place in particular?"

He chuckled. "Well, Toby Keith's place makes great chicken-fried steak."

"And this is your idea of a big date?"

"You've never seen the size of that chicken fry."

She laughed. "Okay. We'll go eat at Toby's. I'm starved."

After dinner—which included chicken-fried steak the size of a plate—Chance suggested a walk along the Bricktown canal. Amazed, Cass stared at the renovated brick factory buildings, the lights, the bustle of the crowd. Boats cruised by, and she caught snatches of the drivers' patter as they pointed out the sights to those on the tour.

Chance held her hand as they strolled. Nerves had nothing to do with her excitement. This was all about the sparks of sexual tension first ignited in the barn. Yet if she was honest, there was something more. Something deeper. Heck yeah, this man turned her on, but at the same time she felt a connection to him. When she fantasized about being with him, it wasn't…sex. Oh, it was sexy. Sexy as hell, but it was more. She wanted more. She wanted to make love to him. She wanted to explore that tenuous bond developing between them.

Cass glanced up, realized he'd been watching her and had to resist the urge to fan her face. She really wished her face didn't betray her moods so easily. He squeezed her hand and tugged her closer to him. Stopping in the middle of the walk, they forced people to step around them. She didn't care.

She'd never been in love, didn't have a clue what it felt like. Lust? Oh, yeah. She knew all about that flash-in-the-pan heat that burned hot and fast between a man and a woman. And dissipated just as quickly. With this man, though, it was a slow burn like banked embers radiating heat. Cass raised her face, and he obliged her by dropping a gentle kiss on her lips.

They stared at each other, ignoring both snickers and rude remarks from the people they blocked. She wanted to get lost in his eyes, in his arms, despite the prickle of unease tapping on her shoulder. Her parents had loved deeply, and her dad's world had shattered when her mom died. Only three when it happened, she remembered the crushing sadness—even now. And she wondered. Was that why she'd never let go? Never fully trusted a man enough to let him into her heart?

Could *this* man be the one? She didn't know him. But she did. On some deep level, she recognized their connection. Not that she believed in soul mates or anything. But her parents' relationship had been soul-deep and abiding. And love at first sight, according to her mother's diaries.

Chance didn't move. He watched Cass, curious about

her thoughts. Emotions danced across her face, changing her expressions. Her soft gaze held him mesmerized. Time seemed to stop, and he was afraid to do anything that might break the mood. He wanted to capture the smile she offered him—hold it and save it in a wooden box where it would be safe. That smile was a treasure greater than anything in his family's bank vault.

A couple of college kids brushed past them and one of them muttered, "Get a room."

With the spell broken, Chance led Cassie back to the lot where he'd parked his truck, guided her inside and lingered a moment with the door open. He leaned in, and his lips brushed across hers.

"Now or never, darlin'. We goin' back to my place or am I takin' you home?"

"Your place." Not a moment's hesitation there. She wanted him—his hands on her bare skin, and hers on his. She wanted to explore him with her fingertips, learn his contours. She wanted to kiss him. All over. She remembered to breathe.

"My place." The words came out in a possessive growl.

The drive was a blur, but she vaguely noted it when he pulled the truck into some sort of garage. As he rushed her to an elevator, she caught a glimpse of a dark metallic sports car parked back in the shadows—one that looked expensive. The elevator doors slithered open, and he urged her inside. He was a condo cowboy, and that made her giggle. He arched a brow but didn't say anything, or kiss her. He'd snugged her close to his side right after he hit the floor button but made no other moves. She could feel his heartbeat against her arm, and his quickened breath ruffled her hair.

The doors parted, and they got out. Chance fumbled with the door lock but managed to finally get it open. He ushered her inside, kicked the door shut with a booted foot and grabbed her—not roughly, but with force. Again she was struck by the gentle strength in his big hands as they wrapped around her upper arms. He tugged her to him. Her breasts collided with the muscular wall of his chest as his lips sealed against hers. He kissed her hard, his mouth hungry and demanding, and he sucked her breath away before his lips gentled and he angled his head, nibbling her lips like they were dessert. He sighed—actually sighed—and kissed his way along her jaw. Her knees trembled, and his grip slipped from her biceps as his arms encircled her. Her arms snaked around his neck, and she tilted her head up for more kisses.

"Cards game?" His voice sounded a little breathless.

"What game?" So did hers.

Chance scooped her into his arms and carried her to the bedroom. She caught a glimpse of the city skyline out the window before he hit a button and the drapes slithered close. One small part of her brain, the part still semicoherent and sane, wondered at the high tech but he kissed her again, and all reason disappeared.

Undressing devolved into a frenzy of buttons, zippers and tossed clothes. Naked, panting for breath, they stared at each other, eyes roving appreciatively. Cass blushed and dropped her gaze for a moment. She wasn't a model by any stretch of the imagination. Curvy. A real woman, not a stick figure. That's what she was and despite Hollywood, she would embrace her body. She squared her shoulders and raised her head. The heat from Chance's gaze almost rocked her backward. He licked his lips while he clenched and unclenched the fists at his sides, as if he was struggling to hold them there to keep from touching her.

"You. Are. Even. More. Beautiful. Than I ever dreamed." Each word huffed out as he panted, with the last ones rushing out in a gasp.

Before she could react, he advanced. His arms slid around her, pulled her close so her nipples brushed against the fine feathering of hair on his chest. Her tummy bumped up against something long, thick and hard. She arched and rubbed against his erection, and he groaned against her neck, distracted from the kisses he'd been planting there.

"Keep that up, and I won't be able to. Keep up, I mean."

She chuckled. "I'm a firm believer in—" She couldn't get the last word out. He pushed her back against the bed until her knees buckled. He eased her down, his lips sealed on hers, and then dragged her across the linen bedspread. He didn't bother turning down the covers.

"You first." He positioned her legs, knees up, and spread them. He stared at her for a long moment, and she fought the urge to press them together. He stretched out, his head between her thighs. His gaze caught hers, held it, and then he growled again.

"Mine."

Cass arched off the bed as his tongue tasted her. She was already primed and ready and at this rate, she wouldn't last long. His fingers teased her as he lapped at her bud. Incoherent now, she could only utter muffled moans and little panting whimpers. Every muscle in her body quivered, and her hips danced beneath him until his long fingers gripped her thighs to hold her still. With the gusto of a connoisseur, he kissed and licked, his fingers tantalizing her.

He raised his head. "Come for me, baby. Show me what I do to you, Cass." He inserted another finger, and his touch taunted her.

"No…no…no…"

"Yes."

That one word was an order she eagerly complied with, her eyes squinting shut as emotions and sensations overwhelmed her. Pressure built in her middle and if she didn't pop that cork, she would shatter. In the end, that's what she did anyway. The power of her climax tossed her into a sparkling tunnel, and she rode through it for a full minute before she shattered.

Cass wanted to cry and laugh at the same time. She'd never had a climax that rocked her so deeply. Chance kissed her down there before trailing kisses up her tummy and between her breasts all the way to her lips. His arms cradled her, and he stroked down her back as his kiss gentled her raging emotions.

"I'd ask if it was good for you, but I already know."

She thumped his chest but it was a feeble blow. "Holy cowboy. That was…" She inhaled and her breath hitched a couple of times as little aftershocks zinged all the way to her fingers and toes.

He laughed—a deep, throaty sound like a happy growl. Her head found the niche of his shoulder and seemed to fit. She curled in at his side, her fingers ruffling the soft hair on his chest. There was just enough there to play with so she did. In comfortable silence, they held each other. She'd almost dozed off when she shifted her knee over his thigh. And encountered his arousal. She shivered, and goose bumps prickled her skin.

Cass skimmed her palm down his chest and across some amazing ridges that defined his abdomen. Forget six-pack abs. This guy was at least an eight if not a twelve. When her questing fingers encountered his erection, his hips arched, and he groaned.

"If you touch me now, I won't last."

Her face crinkled with glee. "Oh? I guess that means I have you at my mer—" She choked on the last word as Chance grabbed, flipped and settled his brawn on top of her.

"I want to be inside you. We'll play later."

"I don't ride bareback."

He reached into a drawer next to the bed and withdrew a shiny packet. "Neither do I. Do you want the honors?"

"Um…awkward. Nope. I leave it up to your expert hands."

He grinned, ripped the top of the packet with his teeth and…*oh, yeah*. He definitely had expert hands. Cass had never found this particular part of lovemaking sexy, but what he did with his hands left her panting and wanting more. He stroked himself as he stroked her, and she arched her hips.

"Anytime now, cowboy."

"Yes, ma'am."

That was the last coherent thought she had for a very long time. He sank in, and she gasped. He filled her comfortably and once in, he withdrew almost immediately. Her inner muscles clenched around him, and she wrapped her legs around his waist to keep him inside. She found the rhythm, matched and expanded it, and succumbed to the sensations surging along her neural paths. She hoped they didn't short-circuit her brain. Then she hoped they would. Then she just didn't care, totally lost in the sensation of Chance driving into her. The muscles on his back bunched under her hands, and she cinched her legs tighter, as if she were riding a bucking bronco. His breath whooshed out, and she swore she could feel him swell and grow larger. A switch triggered deep inside her, and she spiraled up and out of control.

They came together, and lights sparkled behind her closed eyelids. She shivered and felt an answering shudder from him as he pushed against her, riding slowly now as he milked the last bit of passion from them both. Sated, sleepy and more contented than she'd felt in…forever, she nuzzled his neck, smiling at the salty taste of his skin.

He kissed her temple and pushed against the restraint her legs formed around his waist. "I'm too heavy." The words came out mumbled.

She opened her eyes. He looked like she felt, and that

made her smile even bigger, but she unhooked her ankles. Her legs quivered and dropped like logs to the bed. He rolled to his side and pulled her close, one hand caressing her hip and thigh.

"I'd ask if it was good for you, but I'd have to form a coherent thought to talk."

He laughed and kissed her forehead. "Yeah."

"Spoken like a true caveman."

"Baby, if it got any better, I don't think I'd survive."

She propped up on her elbow and smirked. "You ain't seen nothin' yet, cowboy." She licked her lips in a show of bravado, relishing that his eyes tracked her tongue. She finished the gesture by tapping the tip of her tongue against her top lip, as if she licked something else entirely. His gratifying groan elicited a laugh. "Oh yeah, buddy. Just you wait. The night is young."

He smirked back. "Be careful what you ask for, darlin'. A challenge like that might just jump up and bite you on the ass."

Eight

Cass drowsed in Chance's arms, content but all too aware she needed to get up, get dressed and get him to drive her home. She had chores to do. Since coming home, she'd pitched in to ease the burden on Boots. He was older than her father, and while he looked hale and hearty, he was seventy. He didn't need to be wrestling bales of hay or mucking stalls. And truthfully, she really didn't want him to know she'd spent the night with Chance. Feeling way too much like a delinquent teen, she slipped out of the circle of arms holding her. Tiptoeing across the room, she shut the door to the bathroom before flipping on the light.

The reflection staring back at her from the mirror showed a woman who'd been well and truly loved. Swollen lips, a slightly abraded cheek—darn his shadow beard—half-lidded eyes and hair that looked like a windstorm had blown through. She ran cold water from the faucet and splashed her face. Using her finger as a toothbrush, she attempted to freshen her breath. But when it came to her hair, running her fingers through it only created more snags. Talk about a major case of bed head. Reluctant to rummage through his drawers or medicine cabinet, though denying her curiosity almost killed her, she flipped off the light and opened the door—only to run smack dab into a muscular chest.

"You're up early."

She tilted her head to look up at him. "Sorry. Didn't mean to wake you, but now that you are…I need to go home, 'kay?"

His eyes narrowed. "No, not okay. Why?"

"I have chores."

He blinked at her and rubbed a hand across his face as if clearing the last bit of sleep befuddlement from his head. "Chores?"

"Chores. At the ranch. Horses to feed. Cows to feed. Stalls to muck. You're a cowboy." She glanced around, curious now about the luxury condo. "Allegedly. Surely you've done ranch work before?"

He scratched his chest, an idle gesture that drew her gaze. She inhaled sharply, her nostrils flaring as his scent filled her. Musk, leather and something clean—like fresh laundry hanging on a clothesline on a hot summer day. She almost laughed at the thought. *No* one smelled like sunshine.

"Want to grab a shower? We can share, save time and water?"

"Do you really think the two of us in the shower will save time?"

"Well, we could do it with you sitting on the counter, but I sort of like wet and wild." He backed her into the bathroom and flicked on the light. "Won't be as thorough as I'd like, but it'll take the edge off."

He reached around her, turned on the shower and before she could protest, picked her up and stepped under the myriad jets. He set her down, grabbed a bottle of body wash and started in. By the time he finished, she was clean, sated and weak-kneed. Then again, so was he. Two could play that game.

She forked the last bit of new straw into Doc's stall and turned around. Chance stood there watching her. Tilting her head, she cocked her hand on a hip and gave him her best sassy smile. "See something you like, cowboy?"

"Mmm-hmm."

Cass had to admit he'd surprised her. He didn't drop her off. He'd parked his truck and insisted on helping. While she slipped into the house to change, he headed to the barn and with Buddy's help, turned the horses out into the pasture so they could clean stalls.

"Fancy meeting you here."

She glanced at the door. Boots, his expression inscrutable, watched them.

"Good morning, Mr. Thomas."

"Stayed out a little late, Cassidy Anne."

She realized she'd dropped her gaze so that her guilt now appeared obvious—and that Boots had ignored Chance. She raised her chin and met the situation head-on—by ignoring the insinuation. "Chores are done. Any coffee left?"

"There is. But I figured y'all might be in need of something more substantial. Breakfast at the Four Corners. My treat."

She glanced at Chance, bemused by the expression on his face. He stared at Boots, but the smile curving his very sexy mouth looked almost hostile. She opened her mouth to decline and suggest that even she could scramble eggs, but her stomach growled. Loudly. Chance glanced at her and chuckled.

"Guess that means we're doing breakfast. I'll get washed up."

He disappeared into the tack room, taking longer than he needed so he could sort through his emotions. Boots Thomas didn't trust him, and Chance needed to figure out why. The old cowboy knew who he was. Did the man also suspect why he was pursuing Cassie? He stared at his reflection in the broken piece of mirror stuck up above the sink. Why *was* he after Cassie? He told his brothers and father it was business. But last night turned it into something else entirely.

Hell, he was falling for the girl. That was a big damn joke on him. Chance Barron didn't fall for girls. Life with the old man convinced him that love didn't exist. Lust? Oh, yeah. Lust was dependable. But love? With Cassidy Anne Morgan?

"Damn, son. You are in so much trouble now."

Over the sound of running water, he heard Cass leave. By the time he joined Boots to lean against the hood of his truck, she appeared on the porch, ready to go. Buddy lazed in the shade. Boots moved to the passenger side and as soon as he opened the back door, Buddy leaped into the backseat.

"No, Buddy. Get out." Looking mortified, Cass ran to the truck and did her best to pull the dog out. "You can't go."

"It's okay." He'd opened the driver's door and leaned in to watch.

"But Chance, those are leather seats."

"So?"

"So?" Her mouth gaped. "Let me at least get a blanket or something."

"He's fine, Cass. Just get in the truck. I'm hungry."

Her mouth gaped a little wider as she read his expression—and his double entendre. The tips of her ears burned as she flushed, and she ducked into the back before Boots got a good look at her. Buddy occupied the seat behind him, barking and looking pleased.

Once they got to the diner, he'd have to keep a low profile and hope no one recognized him. Clay, as a US Senator, was always in the limelight and Chase made the tabloids on a weekly basis. He supposed Chase's position as CEO of the entertainment and real estate arm of the family empire invited that sort of attention. Chance, along with Cord and Cash, did his best to stay out of the public eye. Maybe he could pull this off. Even though he was senior partner of his own law firm, he made sure his associates were the ones on the news.

Cass hadn't been back to Four Corners since the day of her dad's funeral. The warm pressure of Chance's palm against the small of her back propelled her through the door. A bell jangled merrily, and heads turned. Jovial greetings rang out, and Boots stopped to visit with folks on the way to a booth by the front window. Nadine appeared with clunky ceramic mugs in one hand and a steaming coffee-pot in the other.

Chance settled beside Cassidy and as soon as his thigh brushed against her, it stayed. Moments later, a waitress appeared with glasses of ice water, cutlery setups rolled tightly in paper napkins and a metal pitcher of cream. Cass doctored her coffee from the jug, watching the thick swirls turn the rich sepia liquid in the mug to gentle café au lait. They ordered. They ate. And she leaned into the corner listening to Boots and Chance. As the old man quizzed the younger, she watched their expressions. Chance remained relaxed, deflecting or answering the questions with good-natured ease. Boots, cynical at first, relaxed, as well. She could almost see the moment he made up his mind about Chance.

Nadine returned frequently, perching beside Boots to chat, her laughter filling the awkward moments. Cass smiled but hid it behind her napkin. Nadine had a thing for Uncle Boots, and if she knew him at all, he was rather sweet on the woman, as well. To her knowledge, Boots had never married and she wondered why now. Her smile morphed into a yawn, despite the copious amounts of coffee she'd consumed.

"I think we need to get our girl home for a nap, Mr. Thomas."

"Call me Boots, son."

Cass stared from one to the other, feeling as if an iceberg had just dislodged from a glacier. She would no longer have to justify Chance's presence or dating him. The idea left her feeling dizzy. *Were* they dating? Or had last night just been a one-night stand? He'd stayed to help in the barn today, and he certainly didn't seem in any hurry to leave. She wondered again what he did for a living. It paid well, whatever it was, based on his truck and his condo.

Both men made a grab for the check, but Chance snatched it first. He left cash to cover both bill and tip on the table and slid out, offering a hand to her. A bit shy, she placed her hand in his. Strong fingers closed around hers and with a gentle tug, he pulled her to her feet. He refused to relinquish her hand, and weaving through the diner to the door proved awkward. But she didn't care. Not one for public displays of affection, this particular PDA made her feel all warm and fuzzy inside. Outside, Buddy appeared from around the corner. He barked and jumped up on her, making her laugh.

"Bacon breath? You are so busted, dog!"

Boots climbed into the backseat with the dog, and she rode shotgun. Chance didn't seem the least bit embarrassed to hold her hand on the trip home, nor to kiss her in front of Boots once they arrived.

"I'll see you soon, darlin'." His words whispered in her ear after the kiss.

Cass resisted the urge to ask when that would be. Clingy and needy were not two adjectives she wanted added to her personal bio. Instead, she offered a wry smile. "You know where I live, cowboy."

Chance sprawled in the overstuffed leather chair, looking far more at ease than he felt. He could see the reflections of his brothers' faces in the highly polished surface of the mahogany conference table. His siblings ranged against him on the other side—all but one, and his face dominated the wide screen monitor on the wall. Chance studied them. Phones were ringing in Clay's office and he looked not only distracted but uncomfortable, as well. Of those arrayed on the other side of the table, Cord was the only one who would meet Chance's gaze directly. Chase had his smart-phone out, thumbs flying as he texted or surfed the web or did something. Cash looked bored as he stared out the window over Chance's left shoulder.

"This feels an awful lot like an intervention."

"It doesn't have to be, Chance." As the oldest, Clay took the lead. He sighed, the sound not quite synced with his image. "I'm in the middle of the budget battle. I don't really have time for this petty squabble."

A burst of laughter erupted from Chase, and he paused in his texting. "You callin' the old man's squabble petty, Clay?"

"I am in this instance. Chance, you've stalled long enough. Just file the papers, foreclose on the place and get done with it."

"But you forget, Clay. There's a pretty girl involved. I think brother Chance is letting his little head think for him."

Chance glared at Chase and jumped in before his oldest brother could. "You're one to talk, bro. How many times have we bought *your* way out of woman trouble?"

With a negligent shrug, Chase focused once more on his phone. "Whatever. But I'm tired of these command performances. I'm in the middle of negotiations for a new resort property, and I damn sure don't need to be jetting back and forth."

Cash cleared his throat and sat up a little straighter. "Look, Chance, I know you like the girl. Hell, you've been with her almost every night since you got back from Chicago. I'm betting she's a pretty good—"

Before he realized what he was doing, Chance reached across the table and grabbed the front of Cash's shirt, his hand fisting in the folds of expensive Egyptian cotton. "Shut. Up. Cash. I know damn good and well you've been tracking me. That ends now. Today. You hear me? I'll handle this. In my own way and in my own time."

"No." The single word cut through the tense atmosphere. Cyrus Barron filled the doorway. "You will do this my way and in my time."

Chance released Cash and faced his father. The old man looked right through him. His heart pounded as anger surged up from his gut. "Why is this such a big deal?"

"It's a big deal because I say it is." Cyrus stalked the rest of the way into the room and stopped at the head of the table. He stared at his middle son, and his face twisted as if he'd stepped in manure. "That old bastard died before I could settle the debt between us so I'll settle it with his brat."

Wanting to pound his fists on the desk, or on his father's face, Chance clenched them at his sides and breathed instead. Forcing his anger down, he looked for the right argument. If the old man figured out Cass was important to him, all bets were off.

"Cassidy Morgan plans to sell the place and return to Chicago. She has a herd of cattle. Once they're sold, she can pay off her father's medical bills. We can buy the place from her with one offer and a certified check." He didn't back down from his father's glare.

Cyrus leaned over the table and jammed his finger into Chance's chest. It took every ounce of self-control to keep from breaking his father's finger.

"Ben Morgan double-crossed me and stole something important. I vowed then I'd ruin him. It may have taken me almost forty years, but by God I will have my revenge. Now sit down and shut up, Chancellor. You always were the runt of the litter." His father faced the monitor. "Clayton, you better have that damn Senate committee straightened out on the oil pipeline bill."

Chance sank onto his chair. Old taunts still hurt, but he wasn't that little boy anymore. He opened his mouth to continue the argument but snapped it shut as Cord delivered a shift kick to his shins under the conference table. He pressed his lips closed and glared at his father in silence.

"I've made a few phone calls," the old man continued. "That should take care of it. Don't screw it up, Clayton."

"No, sir. I won't."

Cyrus cast his gaze on his other sons and missed the grimace on Clay's face. Chance caught it, right before his father's eyes zeroed in on him again.

"As of now, Ben Morgan's brat will no longer have a way to get those cows to market." The cynical smile on his face spoke volumes. Chance braced for the other shoe to drop.

"We'll foreclose on the property, and she'll be left with nothing but a crapload of debt. Morgan's remaining medical bills are over fifty thousand dollars. We'll come in, sell off everything lock, stock and barrel and throw her and that old SOB Boots Thomas out on their asses."

Chance's gut roiled and he fought down a wave of nausea. What the hell was the old man doing? Cass had nothing to do with this ridiculous feud. His father was out to ruin a woman Chance cared about probably more than he should, given the circumstances. He bit his tongue and remained silent. He knew the old man too well, positive there was even more to come. His father pinned him with a cold stare.

"Quit stalling, Chance. I sent you to law school and let you start a law firm for a reason. Now get those papers filed. I want the foreclosure a done deal and everything liquidated." The old man's lips twisted into a parody of a smile. "Well, everything but Legend's Double Rainbow. That little stud colt will finally be mine, too." His father dismissed him with a negligent wave of his hand and turned his attention to the others. "Now, what the hell else have you morons managed to screw up?"

Chance tuned out the conversation, stewing in his own anger. He looked up to catch Cord studying him, his brother's expression both speculative and serious. He stared back. They were all chips off the old man's block and where Chance had once had some pride in that, now he wondered. Why the hell did he try so hard to win this man's respect? Forget love. Cyrus Barron only loved power and money. Yet Chance had spent his entire life trying to please the old bastard.

"Blood sticks together, boys. And you'd all better remember that. No one takes care of a Barron but another Barron. The rest of the world doesn't give a damn so why should we give a damn about them? Family is all that matters. You all clear on that?"

Silence reigned in the void left by the old man's departure. Even the phones in Clay's office had stopped ringing. Chase pushed his chair away from the conference table, stood and presented his backside to his brothers.

"Is there anything left?" He *whewed* dramatically as everyone chuckled. "Nice to know something's still there after that ass chewing." He turned back around and focused his gaze on Chance. "Do us all a favor. End this thing with the Morgan girl, get the job done and get the hell out of Dodge. There's not a woman alive who's worth the old man's wrath."

Chance remained still, staring at all of them in turn. "This doesn't bother any of you?"

Clay's exasperated voice issued from the monitor. "Since when did you go all noble, Chance? I don't have time for all this crap. Do your job." The monitor flickered to a blue screen.

Cash and Chase, like the twins they were, walked out

shoulder to shoulder without a word, leaving Chance and Cord at the table.

"What?" He glared at his older brother.

"Man, you have it bad." Cord shook his head from side to side, his expression solemn. "You really need to get over this girl."

"Why? Tell me why we have to destroy *her*?"

Cord leaned back in his chair and for a moment, Chance thought his brother would prop his boots up on the highly polished wood of the table. "Why not? It's what the old man wants. And what the old man wants—"

"The old man gets. Yeah, yeah. We've been saying that our entire lives, Cord. But what makes him right?"

Cord laughed, a deep, rolling laugh straight from the gut. "I never said the old bastard was right, Chance. But he is who he is. He's always run roughshod over anyone who got in his way. This time, it just happens to be a gal you have the hots for."

If looks could kill, as the old saying went, Chance's brother would have been BBQ. "Shut up, Cordell." He pushed to his feet and strode out the door, his brother's laughter following in his wake.

Nine

Chance chewed on the handful of antacids he'd just taken. Outside his office window, Oklahoma City spread out to the southwest like a crazy quilt of buildings, parks and river. Sunlight glinted off the fuselage of a plane lining up for a landing on a runway at Will Rogers International Airport.

The door opened behind him but he didn't turn until he heard a heavy body drop into one of the wingback chairs arranged in front of his desk.

"I don't really want to talk to you."

Cord tilted his head. "Fine. Don't talk. I just want you to listen anyway."

"Didn't you say enough downstairs?"

"No. I said what the old man wants to hear when he plays back the tapes of the meeting."

Chance pressed his palms on his desk and leaned forward. He glowered, hoping to cover up the despair he really felt. "Just toeing the family line then?" When Cord didn't reply, he sank into his desk chair. He closed his eyes and dragged the fingers of one hand through his once carefully combed hair. "Dammit."

"Is that all you have to say?"

"What do you want me to say, Cord? Let's trade places if you think this is so easy. Let me run the ranch and the oil company. You go to law school and do all this legal crap. You serve papers on a sweet little girl who's just trying to do the right thing. You sit in this chair and do the old man's dirty work."

"Wow. You might have a conscience after all."

Chance rolled his eyes. "Shut up, Jiminy Cricket."

Leaning back, Cord propped his booted feet on the desk. "Tell me about her."

"What's to tell?"

"Well, there must be something since she has you tied up in knots."

"She's sweet and funny and doesn't want to be a cowgirl."

"You forgot sexy, Chance."

"Yeah. She's that, too."

"I finally figured out how I know her."

Chance rocked forward, his eyes narrowed into a glare. "You know her?"

"Whoa, bro. Not in the biblical sense. Unlike you." Cord waggled his brows and laughed as Chance snarled. "Down, boy. That just confirms my suspicions. She was named the championship cowgirl at the Denver Stock Show the last year we competed. She looked mighty fine in tight jeans but way too young for me."

Closing his eyes, Chance leaned his head back and tried to relax. "When you called me in Chicago, I was trying to pick her up. I didn't know who she was then, Cord, not until I got home. She just wants to sell the place, pay off her father's debts and get on with her life." In Chicago. Without him.

"Damn, bubba. You have it even worse than I thought."

"Shut up."

"What are you going to do? If she finds out the old man is behind her troubles, she'll hate you."

"Is it too much to hope she doesn't find out? At least until I get her out of my system."

Cord rolled his eyes. "Get her out of your system? Yeah,

right. Like that's going to happen. You don't have a clue, Chance. She rode you hard, put you up wet and now she's got her spurs dug deep. If the circumstances were different, I might actually enjoy watching your fall from grace."

Chance raked his fingers through his hair again. "Our father is a real sonofabitch."

"Yeah. You got that right."

Cass stared at the pile of bills in front of her. She puffed out a breath and the straggle of hair hanging in her eyes danced. Picking up the checkbook, she sighed. No matter how many times she ran the numbers, there was way more owed than what was in the bank—even if she drained her savings account. She had to get those cattle sold, and she had to do it soon.

She called everyone on her father's list of cattle haulers. The answer remained the same.

"You're from the Crazy M? Sorry, we're booked solid."

"No, we don't have even one truck to spare."

"Sorry."

Everyone was sorry. Or not. But not one cattle hauler would accept a contract from her. She placed another call to the independent hauler her dad had used for years.

"I'm sorry, but I can't do a thing for you. It's a real shame, too. I thought the world of your dad."

"I can't believe that every trucking line in three states is busy hauling cattle."

The man on the other end of the phone line cleared his throat. The nervous sound made Cass wonder what was going on. "You don't have another contract, do you?" He cleared his throat again but didn't speak. "Why? If you thought so highly of my dad, why won't you haul the cattle for me?"

"It's not you, hon."

"Then what is it?"

"Not what. Who." She heard him take several deep breaths. "Look, I can't say anything more. I'm sorry. Things are what they are, and sometimes a workin' man has no choice. Please don't call me again."

The phone clicked and after a moment of dead air, a dial tone echoed in her ear. "Now what the heck was that all about?"

Boots looked up from his paper, the crinkles around his eyes looking sad. "I was afraid that's what was happenin'."

"What?" Her voice sounded sharper than she intended, but she was so frustrated she wanted to punch something. "Do you know what's going on, Uncle Boots?"

"It's a long story, honey, and I'm not positive, but I have a suspicion that a man by the name of Cyrus Barron has thrown a monkey wrench into things."

Everyone knew that name but she asked to be sure. "As in Barron Oil?"

"And Barron Land and Cattle Company."

"And Barron Entertainment?" Her voice squeaked a little.

"That would be him."

"But…why in the hell would he care about me hauling five hundred head of cattle to market?"

"I told you it's a long story, honey. There's somethin' maybe you need t'know about the Barrons…"

Before he could continue, Buddy jumped up and began barking madly. He hit the door and banged the unlatched screen open. A muffled voice greeted the dog and then boots on the wooden porch preceded a knock on the door.

"May I come in?"

Cassie's voice sounded resigned as she answered. "C'mon in, Chance."

He held the door and followed the dog inside. Her eyes looked bruised and something in his chest shifted. Chance glanced at the pile of papers in front of her before his gaze slid over to Boots. "Everything okay?"

"No."

Chance wanted nothing more than to take her in his arms. She looked so fragile…so *beaten*. "What's happened?"

Her frustration bubbled over. "I can't get anyone to transport my cattle to market."

He replied carefully. "It's spring. Everyone's shipping their feeder calves."

She shook her head, adamant when she added, "No. They don't have trucks available to *me*."

Chance cleared his throat and glanced away. "That doesn't…make sense."

"You haven't been talking to these people, listening to their lame excuses. I'm not paranoid." She thumped the table. "I've called everyone listed in Dad's files."

Cass blew out a huff of air that ruffled her bangs and slumped back the wooden chair. "I don't understand why. I mean…Dad had a great reputation. He always paid his bills. I can't even get the bank to call me back about the loan I told you about."

She snatched a handful of bills and waved them. "The hospital. His doctors. Even the funeral home. I can't pay anything until those cows sell. And if I can't get them to market, how the hell can I sell them?" Cassie looked so small and vulnerable Chance wanted to gather her into his arms. A tear spilled from her eye, and she scrubbed at her face, smearing it away. "And that's not the worst of it."

He gave up. Striding across the room, he pulled her into his arms and held her. "What else is going on?"

"I…" She shivered and he kissed her temple.

"It's okay, baby. I have you."

"My boss called. If I'm not back at my desk tomorrow morning, I'm fired. I have rent due on my place in Chicago, and bills, and I've spent almost everything in my checking account keeping things going here until I can get Daddy's estate settled."

Chance ground his back teeth together, anchoring his anger to keep it from spilling out. He wanted to hurt someone. His father. Her boss. Himself. He was every bit as guilty as anyone. When she pushed away, he dropped his arms.

"I'll be fine." Cass turned on her boot heel and marched to the door. "I need to get away for a while. I'm going for a ride." She held up her hand, palm facing them like a stop sign. "I'm going alone."

The screen door banged behind her, and Buddy nosed it. He looked back at the two men and whined. Chance walked over, opened the door far enough for the dog to slip through then let it close with a gentle bump. He watched the angry but broken woman stomp toward the barn and fought the urge to follow her, to take her into his arms and promise her that everything would be fine. As long as his father persisted in this vendetta, nothing would ever be fine for Cassidy Morgan. And now the other shoe had dropped.

"You know who's behind all this trouble with the cattle?"

Chance continued to stare out the door, refusing to look at Boots. "I have my suspicions."

"You gonna do anything about it, son? That little gal thinks the world of you, you know."

Would he? Could he? He'd spent his whole life in his father's shadow. As the family's attorney, he'd filed lawsuits and defended them, always putting Cyrus Barron and whatever Barron enterprise first. The old man was always right, and the whole world was wrong if they didn't agree.

Chance patted his pocket absently, hoping he'd slipped in the bottle of antacids. He hadn't.

Was Cord right? Was he finally developing a conscience? If so, it was a helluva time. He needed to be detached. Uninvolved. Cold. He'd meant to sleep with Cass, get her out of his system and walk away. But here he stood at the door of her house, watching her run away so she could cry alone. His father would crush her. And he could do nothing but stand by and watch.

"I have to go." He pushed open the door and stepped onto the porch.

"And here I thought maybe you'd grown a pair."

He couldn't even work up a smidge of righteous anger. The man was right. Cassidy Morgan had far more courage than he ever would.

"I'm sorry, Boots." He mumbled the words as he trudged down the steps. He didn't know if the other man heard him and didn't care either way. As he opened the door of his truck, he paused to watch Cass, riding the big sorrel bareback, charge out of the barn and race across the field toward a line of trees. What felt like a steel band constricted his chest, and his pulse hammered in his ears. Maybe he was having a heart attack. That would solve everything, so he almost hoped he was.

Chance climbed into the truck, knowing he was a coward. He glanced at the house where Boots stood in the doorway watching him. The best thing he could do was leave. Get out of Cassie's life. Do what he had to do. And then head to Vegas for a two-week binge of wild women, strong drink and lots of gambling. Except never seeing Cass again tore at his heart. The thought of touching another woman held no appeal. That left booze and poker, and he wasn't a big fan of either.

"I'm sorry, Cassidy Morgan. I'm sorry I'm not the man you deserve."

Ten

"No." Cass glared at the man sitting across from her in the booth at Nadine's diner.

"You aren't thinkin' this through, sugar."

"No, Boots. I can't take your money."

"Honey, your daddy was my best friend. He was more like my family than my own blood. And so are you. Family helps family."

Cass refused to look at his earnest face. Her untouched breakfast cooled on the plate as she drew desultory designs on the table from the condensation ring left by her ice water glass. "Sandra agreed to box up the stuff I want to keep and ship it, and then have a tag sale to dump the rest. I gave notice so I should get my apartment deposit back and the utility deposits will pay off the final bills I owe up there."

"You aren't going back to Chicago?"

She hated the hope she heard in his voice. She'd done a lot of thinking in the few days since her firing. She loved Chicago. Loved her job and her dinky apartment and the wind whistling off the lake so cold it could cut. She hated the heat and the dust and smells of living on the ranch. The dirty, back-breaking work. Didn't she?

"I can't afford it right now, Uncle Boots. Not until I get things settled here." She glanced up. "No. I'm still not going to take your money. You need it. Daddy wanted you to be comfortable. So do I."

"Honey, I don't need much. You're just as stubborn as Ben. Always gotta do it your own way."

She shrugged and dropped her gaze to the water doodles she'd made.

"What? My cookin' not good enough for you, Miz Cassidy Anne?" Nadine had appeared, coffeepot in hand, and her voice held not a lick of chiding. "You look like you lost your best friend, hon. You wanna tell ol' Auntie Nadine about it?"

Try as she might not to, she felt compelled to look up at the woman. Concern radiated in Nadine's expression even as the skin around her eyes crinkled from her friendly smile.

"Everything looks better with a full stomach and a cup of hot coffee."

"I don't think buttermilk pancakes will solve my problems, Nadine."

The woman shooed her over and plopped down on the booth's bench beside her. "But sometimes, talkin' things over with friends does. Boots told me a bit of what's goin' on. I'm sure sorry for your troubles. I know your daddy didn't figure on this crap happenin'. He was a planner, Ben Morgan was. Always one step ahead of life in his thoughts. We just need to do the same."

For a moment, anger welled up. How dare Boots discuss her business with a stranger! But then she saw the expression on his face, and things cleared up. Nadine wasn't a stranger. Not to Boots. He was sweet on the woman. And Nadine returned those feelings.

"Honey, your daddy had a passel of friends. He had an open hand when it came to helpin' folks. I'm sure they'd all step up to return the favor. You just need to figure out what it is you need."

"I need to get my friggin' herd to market." The words

erupted before she could think about them, her voice filled with all the anger and frustration she'd tamped down for a week.

A man at the counter swung around on his stool. "That's what cattle haulers are for."

Cass rolled her eyes. "Duh. But none of them will haul for me."

The man's brow furrowed, and he scratched his head, which set the John Deere cap on his head to dancing. "They locked you out?"

"Evidently."

"That don't seem fair."

She bit back another *duh*. "It is what it is. I still don't have a way to get the herd to market. If I use the old stock trailer at the ranch, I can only take a few at a time. Running them through the sale that way loses me money in the long run. I need a big ol' chunk of money to pay off everything." She didn't want to mention that she could barely afford gas for the truck.

Almost everyone in the diner turned to look at her, and she resisted the urge to bang her head on the table. A little boy perched on a stool at the counter continued to watch the TV above the cash register. An old black-and-white movie played across the screen. He tugged on his mother's sleeve and pointed at the screen. "Mommy, can I have cartoons?"

The young woman chuckled. "I can't believe you don't want to watch a cowboy movie, C.J. With John Wayne, no less."

The youngster offered a disgruntled expression and a deep sigh. "But...cartoons, Mom."

The man on the stool next to the boy winked. "Your mom's right, son. John Wayne and cattle on a trail drive is a classic Western story."

"Huh." The child scowled again before gazing at his mother impatiently.

Nadine slid out of the booth and headed for the remote control. "I think I can get the Cartoon Network, honey. Just give me a sec to find the right channel."

Cass twisted in her seat to stare at the TV before it flickered quickly through several channels and cartoons filled the screen. She shifted to stare at Boots. "No."

Boots looked perplexed as he returned her gaze. "No what?"

"I...nothing." She shook her head. "Just a really crazy idea. One that is way too far-fetched to ever work."

"I can see the wheels turnin', honey. Why don't you just tell me?"

She continued to shake her head, denying the wild scheme forming in her brain. "But..."

Nadine returned with a fresh pot of coffee and refilled their mugs. "Boots, you ever notice she gets that same look Ben got whenever he got a wild hair?"

"No. It's...there's no way. The idea is too ridiculous to even consider."

"Well, honey, if you don't tell us about it, there won't be a way 'cause we won't be able to help you figure out how to make it work." Boots sipped from his coffee mug.

Cass stared from one to the other. "A cattle drive." Nadine and Boots exchanged a cryptic look, and she sighed. "See? I told you it was ridiculous. There's no way we could do a trail drive from the ranch to the stockyards."

"Why not?"

Her jaw dropped. "Because, Uncle Boots. Half of Oklahoma City stands between the Crazy M and the stockyards. Not to mention a couple of major interstate highways."

"You know, that just might work." The man in the booth behind her tapped her on the shoulder. "You'd need some permits and stuff but you could move 'em along section line roads. Wouldn't have to touch many busy streets at all."

Were they not listening? She still wanted to bang her head on the table. This was too crazy to even contemplate.

"Anybody got a map?" Another man dragged a chair over and planted his beefy body at the end of the table. "We could draw out the route right now."

"No. Just…stop. It's just Boots and me. We can't handle five hundred head. And it's…what? At least twenty miles to the stockyards? We can't push cattle more than five maybe ten miles a day tops. There'd be no place to stop at night. No place to water them. I…thank you. All of you. But I… it won't work."

Her audience grumbled but turned away, returning to their own business. The idea was simply too preposterous to even consider. She drank her coffee, completely unaware it held neither cream nor sugar. There had to be another way. She just needed to figure out what it was. Maybe she'd call Chance. He'd disappeared after her outburst, but he'd called and left voice mails on her cell phone since then, asking how she was doing. He was a cowboy. And smart. Maybe he had some ideas that would help.

Late that afternoon, she clicked off the phone rather than leave yet another voice mail message for him. Boots was down at the barn working with the colt, and Buddy lay in a puddle of sunshine streaming through a window. He woofed, and his paws twitched as he chased something in his dreams. She dropped beside him on the floor and buried her fingers in his thick fur.

"Am I crazy, Buddy? I mean like totally insane? There's no way we can drive those cattle to the stockyards. The logistics alone are…I can't even wrap my brain around what would be involved. No. I can't do this. There's got to be another way. I'll go to the bank tomorrow and park myself outside the president's office until he meets with me." She nodded as if to punctuate her resolve. "He'll have to talk to me. Have to listen to me. And I'll work something out." Bending, she brushed her cheek across the top of the dog's head. "I have no choice, Buddy."

The dog whined and licked her chin. "I'm glad somebody still loves me."

"I'm glad somebody still loves me." Chance flashed his legal assistant a smile. "Thanks for staying late."

"I stay late every night. Say what you mean." She waggled her index finger at him, the other hand on her hip. "Why, thank you, Heidi, for taking all the heat from my family, for not making me talk to them."

She was right, but he sure hated to admit it. Even so, her attitude made him grin. "You are worth your weight in gold, Heidi."

"I'm getting that in writing so I can hold it over your head come bonus time." She leaned on his desk and closed the folder he'd been staring at for the past hour. "Shut it down, boss. Go home. Or go out. Go do something besides sit here and brood."

He kicked back in his desk chair and fiddled with the expensive pen in his hand. "You're on her side."

She laughed—long and hard. "Of course I'm on her side. Your father is an absolute alpha hotel."

Heidi's husband was retired military, and she tended to reduce terms used in the vernacular to their military equivalent. "Yeah. But what else is new?"

She stared at him, both hands on her hips now. "Really? You have to ask this question?" She rolled her eyes when he remained silent. "You, boss. You're what's new. The way you're looking at this situation, the way you're reacting.

This girl's gotten to you. Why her after all the other stuff your old man has done, I don't know. But you've changed."

He shook his head. "No. No, I haven't, Heidi. If I had, I wouldn't be sitting here with these papers on my desk."

Heidi snorted. "Yes, you have. The old Chance would have filed the paperwork the first day and served the girl at her daddy's funeral. The old Chance would not sit here stewing over what an alpha hotel his father is, and the old Chance would not care one whit that he was following in his old man's footsteps. But here you are." She shook her head and started to wag her finger one more time but resisted. "I'm going home. Turn out the lights when you leave, boss."

In the silence following her departure, Chance swiveled his chair to stare out the window behind his desk. The Barron Building, all forty stories of it, dominated the skyline. From his view on the thirty-sixth floor, the southwestern expanses of the metroplex unfolded before him. He picked out the historic Farmer's Market building and beyond it, Stockyard City. The phone on his desk rang, but he ignored it. It was still ringing when his cell phone started. He didn't have to check his caller ID. At least one brother would be calling, probably two. Or worse, Cassie's number would stare back at him.

He'd done what they wanted—distanced himself from her. He listened to her messages—for a while at least—craving some tiny connection to her. Then he had to delete them without listening. Her voice tore his heart to shreds, and it took every ounce of self-discipline to keep from driving to the Crazy M to claim her.

Why did he have to choose between his family and the wonderful woman who'd captured his heart? But he knew the answer whenever he looked in the mirror. Take away everything else, he was a Barron. Through and through. Dammit. And when it came to women, being a Barron guaranteed the lady in question would get hurt.

* * *

Cass wore the same austere suit she'd worn to her dad's funeral. The sleeves bunched a little, and she realized all the physical labor she'd done lately had changed her body—slimmed some of the curves and packed on muscle. That wasn't a bad thing.

An office door opened, and she sat up straighter, but the woman who emerged ignored her, walking straight to the front of the bank.

Cass settled back against the uncomfortable chair and wondered again why she was doing this. She hated the ranch. The life didn't suit her at all. She wanted to sleep late on the weekends. Go out to dinner. Work in an office where her friends gossiped about the latest celebrity breakups and makeups, the hot new television show, the ugly dresses on the red carpet. Except she didn't care about those things. Not really.

Another door opened and she leaned forward, peering down the long hallway. A man stepped out and headed away from her. She glanced at the wall clock above the receptionist's head. Eleven o'clock. Two hours she'd waited. So far. The loan officer had already passed her up the chain to the bank president—who was stalling her. Surely he would leave for lunch. If she couldn't get in to see him before, she'd grab him on his way out.

At 12:15, a pizza delivery guy showed up with eight boxes. Pepperoni. Onions. Tomato sauce and baked cheese. The scents blended together, and her stomach growled. Offices emptied, the occupants all rushing down the hall to what she figured was a conference room. A security guard arrived and sat at the receptionist's desk. He glowered at her from time to time.

At four, she was thirsty, hungry, in desperate need of the restroom, but unwilling to give up. The man had to go home sometime. The phone on the desk buzzed, and the girl picked it up.

"Yessir... No, sir. Hasn't moved... Sitting here all day... Yessir." The receptionist covered up the speaker end of the receiver. "Mr. Leonard can't see you today. You might as well go home."

"I'll stay in case he has a cancellation in his schedule. And I'll just be back tomorrow. Tell him I'm not going away."

The girl sighed dramatically, swiveled her chair so that her back was turned and whispered into the phone. A door at the very far end of the hall opened. "Mr. Leonard can give you ten minutes. But that's all."

Cass jumped to her feet and all but jogged down the hall. Leonard sat behind his desk looking distinctly uncomfortable. He'd rolled his sleeves down but they looked rumpled, and he'd made no pretense at straightening his tie. His florid face glistened with a sheen of sweat despite the cold air venting from the overworked air conditioner.

"I can't help you," he began without preamble.

"How do you know? I haven't asked for anything."

"I know what you want, Miss Morgan. Your father owes this bank two hundred and fifty thousand dollars, give or take some interest. Are you prepared to pay that amount today?"

"I can't. I need an extension."

"The matter has been referred to legal counsel for collection and foreclosure on the assets and is no longer my responsibility."

She'd been ready to launch into her argument when the import of his statement sank in. "Wait... What? Foreclosure? But the papers—"

"Ms. Morgan, loan payments were deferred to a balloon payment at the end of the loan period. If you are prepared to pay the full amount due and owing, the bank will halt the collection proceedings. If you aren't, then the matter is out of my hands."

"You can't just do things like this."

"I not only can, young lady, but it's done. This bank is not in the habit of buying cattle, and that is essentially what we would have to do since your father defaulted on the loan." He leaned back and rocked, his fingers laced across his ample belly. "I work for the bank. The loan is in default. Filing suit was the financially sound action for this institution. The matter is out of my hands."

"But…" She sat, stunned and speechless.

"Your time is up. You need to leave, Miss Morgan, or I will call security and have you removed."

"But…"

He leaned forward and tapped a button on his phone. "Call security to my office."

Cass glared at the man but rose from the chair. "My daddy trusted you."

She spun on her heel and marched out with her head held high, brushing by the startled guard. He shadowed her all the way to the parking lot and waited until she climbed into Boots's beat-up old truck, started it and drove out of the parking lot.

"So much for the friendliness of small-town banks," she groused.

At the next stoplight, she dug her cell phone out of her purse and dialed. The incessant ring echoed from the speaker. "C'mon, Chance. Pick up. Please…"

"You have reached my voice mail. You know what to do."

Yeah, she knew what to do. Why the hell was she depending on the jerk anyway? He sweet-talked her, wined her, dined her and jumped her in bed and then he no longer had time for her. Well, fine. She didn't need him. She didn't need anybody.

A horn honked and startled her out of her thoughts. She focused on driving until she got to a little place next to the highway. It wasn't the Four Corners but the scent of BBQ wafting through the truck's open window made her drool and her stomach gnaw on itself.

Inside, the wooden-planked walls looked grimy and smoke-stained, but the food still smelled heavenly. Antiques and old pictures littered every surface. She ordered ribs and fries, heaped her plate with onions, dill pickle chips and jalapeños, and sat down at a little table in the corner.

She bit into the first rib and almost moaned. Plastic squeeze bottles held different sauces and ketchup. Experimenting with the various flavors, she found a mix she liked, dragged the rib through the puddle of sauce on her plate and devoured it.

As she finished off the last of the homemade apple cobbler and ice cream, Cass realized this would be the last time she splurged. She had less than a thousand dollars in her checking account. The ranch account had enough to pay the bill at the electric co-op. The propane company had told her they could wait, and she had almost a full tank at the house anyway.

No job. No income. The loan was due, and she had no clue how to pay it. A headache formed between her eyes, and she rubbed her forehead. Why did she even care? She hated the ranch. Didn't she? Hated Oklahoma. But not a certain man who lived here.

She could just walk away. Not look back. Leave Boots and Buddy and—she nipped that thought. She did not want to think about Chance. About leaving him. Her life was in Chicago. Not here. Wasn't it? She didn't want to deal with the tangle of emotions Chance conjured up. Why hadn't he returned her calls?

People gave up and walked away all the time. But she wasn't a quitter. Her daddy would be spinning in his grave—or in that little box holding his ashes—if he could hear her thoughts.

I don't raise quitters, honey. You wipe those tears, get back in that saddle and ride. You're a Morgan. Show 'em what you're made of.

"Oh, Daddy," she murmured. "I miss you. What am I going to do?"

Something clattered back in the kitchen, and she jerked her head at the sound. Broken glass and spilled food. Yeah, that was a terrific sign from heaven. She glanced out the window but a photo beneath it caught her attention. Faded with age, it showed a group of cowboys on horseback. A herd of cattle milled behind the riders. Leaning closer, she peered at the legend on the photo. *1944—Calvin Barron and hands deliver herd to Oklahoma City National Stockyards.*

"That was quite a day."

Cass jumped and jerked her head around. An old black man in a stained apron chuckled. "The war was on and gasoline was bein' rationed. Old Mr. Barron, he had him a herd of prime cows and no way to get 'em to market. The gov'ment wanted them heifers to feed the army, but them ol' boys had to figure out a way to get 'em to the stockyards to put 'em on the train."

Dizzy as ideas whirled in her head, Cass felt as if she was on the verge of discovering something important. Then the name clicked. "Wait. *Old* Mr. Barron?"

"Yes, ma'am. Mister Cal was the current Mr. Barron's daddy. Mr. Cal was sure anxious t'get those cows to the railhead. Story goes they were all sittin' around drinkin', and those boys decided they'd have an old-fashioned trail drive. So they did. Took 'em nigh on two weeks but we pushed that herd from Mr. Barron's ranch up on the North Canadian River and right down into the stockyards. The newspaper came out and took pictures. Some radio guy from back East came out to interview folks."

Cass glanced at him. "Wait… You said *we*? You rode with them?" She leaned closer to the picture, studying it.

He tapped the back corner, and she squinted at the grainy photo. She could just make out a chuck wagon in the background. A man with dark skin stood beside it while a little boy waved from the wagon's seat.

"My pop was the chuck wagon cook, and I got t'tag along. That was quite an adventure for a kid like me."

She smiled and resisted the urge to kiss his cheek. "Thank you."

The crinkles smoothed from his face as his expression turned curious. "For what?"

"For your excellent BBQ. For coming out here to talk to me. For…for giving me the faith that maybe I can do what needs to be done. I gotta go!"

She dashed out to the old truck, climbed in and pulled out her phone. Cass stared at it, gulping in long breaths as she attempted to quell her excitement. "Daddy, we might just be able to pull this off. With a lot of help." She'd give Chance one more…chance. She chuckled at the irony, but was barely able to breathe around the anticipation. When she got his voice mail, she didn't care. Her enthusiasm bubbled over as she left a garbled message, not even aware when it clicked off automatically.

Eleven

Chance's fingers curled into fists as he stared at his phone. He'd resisted the urge to answer, but had to listen to this voice mail, had to hear her voice. The message…hurt. She burbled with excitement, the words rushing like a stream tumbling over rocks.

"Saw the banker finally. Sorry sonofagun. He said the bank's foreclosing, Chance. But it doesn't matter. I can get the cattle to the stockyards. I know I can. You won't believe what happened. You know Cyrus Barron? Jeez, that man has more money than Midas. Anyway, I found out something tonight. You won't believe this. His father did a cattle drive. In the forties. During the war. I can—" The phone cut off.

He couldn't breathe. His chest felt like a boa constrictor had wrapped around him, squeezing all the air out. For a minute, he thought she'd found out about his father. When she continued babbling and her excitement level ratcheted up a notch, he'd tried to listen but the pounding blood in his ears muted any sound. He hit the replay button and listened again, prepared this time.

Cattle drive? During the war? What the hell was she talking about? And more important, what relevance did it have now? He grabbed his phone and hit a speed dial number.

"Oh? So now you decide to talk to me?"

"Shut up, Cord. She knows the bank is foreclosing."

"Does she know why?"

"I don't think so."

"You don't *think* so?"

"I don't know, Cord, and I really don't care. She called, really excited, and the way she said the old man's name, I don't think she knows. But I need some information."

"About what?"

"About some cockamamie idea she got from somewhere. Do you know anything about a Barron cattle drive?"

"Dude, seriously? The old man pushing cows?"

He heard the clacking of a computer keyboard. "No, not the old man, Granddad Cal. In the forties, during the war."

"Huh. Color me impressed. There's a big file on it in the *Oklahoma Chronicle*'s morgue. Hang on a sec and I'll forward it to you. To make a long story short, Granddad Cal had a crapload of cows to sell and because of gas rationing, he decided to herd them from the ranch to the stockyards. The thing got a lot of attention. According to the file, it was even featured in a newsreel at the movies. The last cowboy. That sort of thing. Bottom line, he got the herd to market and made a killing. Army paid top dollar. Drove those steers straight into box cars and shipped 'em off to Chicago for slaughter. Why? What's this got to do with the Morgan situation?"

Chance stared out the window wondering the same thing. "I don't know. Yet. I'll keep you posted."

"Nice to have you back on board, bro. Now get the paperwork finished. The old man wants the notice of foreclosure served pronto."

His brother's words echoed in his head. *Nice to have you back on board.* But was he? He needed to see Cassidy. Find out what harebrained stunt she was planning. And then he'd talk her out of it. He'd make a few calls. Get her another job in Chicago. His heart hammered at the thought. Was that what he wanted?

It would be the simplest solution. She'd go back to Chicago. Their relationship, if it could be called that, would be over. She would no longer be a burr under his saddle, and she'd never know that his family—that *he*—had betrayed her. There was only one problem with that plan. He didn't want her to go. He wanted her to stay. And he wanted her to care about him. Like he cared about her. There. He admitted it. He cared about Cassidy Morgan. He shouldn't. Didn't want to. But he did. No matter how many calls he ignored, how far away from her he stayed, his heart betrayed him. He was a coward, despite the fact he loved her. Admitting it to himself should make him feel better. It didn't. He felt like the biggest bastard on the planet. She deserved a better man, a man worthy of her.

"Dammit all to hell. How did my life get so complicated?"

Staring at the open folder on his desk, he sighed. Family was everything. Blood was thicker than water. All the clichés his father hammered into his sons as they grew up in his shadow came back to haunt him. He wanted to do the right thing. But what was it?

Boots stumbled out of his room and headed straight for the coffeepot. Nosy, Cass watched him. He walked back to the table and peered curiously at the maps. "You look a little peaked this morning, Uncle Boots. Bad night?"

He muttered something under his breath and she thought she caught the words, "honky tonk," "dancing," and "that fool woman."

She bit her lip to hide a smile. "Yeah…gotcha. None of my business. I suggest we institute a don't-ask, don't-tell policy around here when it comes to our social lives."

He growled and sipped his coffee. Then he tapped a finger on the map. "You planning a trip?"

Cass pushed back from the table, snagged her own mug and took a sip. She grimaced but swallowed the cold coffee. She headed to the sink to dump the contents and pour a fresh cup. "Sort of." She returned to the table, sat and gestured for Boots to join her. "We need to talk."

"No luck with the banker, I take it?"

"None. The bank is foreclosing unless I pay off the loan on or before the due date.""

He stared at her a full minute, his expression never changing before he asked, "You gonna explain the maps?"

She inhaled and rushed on. "For the cattle drive. It's been done before. Granted, it was almost seventy years ago but Calvin Barron…" She would have missed his expression if she hadn't been so intent on watching him. "What?"

"Nothing. Go on."

She knit her brows, puzzling through his reaction but continued doggedly. "I'll need permits. I plan on going to the commissioners of Canadian and Oklahoma Counties today to find out. Unless you need the truck?" She batted her eyes at him. "You know, to go to the Four Corners or…something."

He muttered under his breath, and she had to choke back a laugh as he blushed beneath his tan. "Take the damn truck. I have fence to ride." He pushed back from the table, the chair legs scraping against the scarred linoleum.

Cass paused to throw her arms around the old man's neck as he sat in his recliner. "This is going to work, Uncle Boots. I just know it!" The only damper on her enthusiasm was the fact Chance still hadn't called her. She alternated between concern and anger. If he'd blown her off, he could have been man enough to say so instead of keeping her dangling. But she was enough of a worrywart to wonder if something bad had happened to him. "Maybe Chance will help out, too."

"I hope so, baby girl." He muttered something under his breath that sounded like "for your sake."

Cassie kissed the top of his head, wondering at his words. Chance would call. She argued with herself, ending with the final insistent word as she muttered, too. "He will."

The next afternoon, Cass rode toward the barn, Buddy trotting beside her horse. Her sleeve was torn, and a few bloodstains spotted the frayed fabric. She'd stretched a strand of barbed wire too taut, and it had wrapped around her arm when it snapped. She'd have to make a trip to a clinic to get a tetanus shot. Her last booster was long out of date. Hot, sweaty and physically worn out, she wasn't looking forward to trekking into town.

As she neared the metal structure, something moved inside, and Buddy took off at a run. His excited barking reached her, and she nudged Red into a trot. Her heart skipped a beat when she recognized the man who stepped into the sunlight. Chance. She'd all but given up on him. He hadn't returned any of her calls. Her traitorous heart galloped at the sight of him, a stupid grin spread across her face and she laughed like a giddy girl on her first date.

He shaded his eyes and raised his hand in a rather tentative wave. She resisted the urge to wave madly back at him as she reined Red to a walk and then stopped the big horse several yards away. After dismounting, she did her best to ignore her emotions and the man creating havoc with her pulse rate.

"Gee, fancy meeting you here." She was so proud of herself. Just a hint of sarcasm and no breathy sigh.

He stepped closer and reached out, but she wasn't sure whether he meant to touch her or take the reins. "Cass, we should—what the hell?" He grabbed her arm, his hand gentle despite the urgency in his grip. "What happened?"

She tugged her arm, but his fingers didn't relinquish their hold. "I had a fight with a string of barbed wire. I won."

"Well, it doesn't look that way to me. You're bleeding."

"No, I'm not. It's dried. Mostly."

"We need to get you to the ER."

"No, *we* don't. In case you've forgotten in your rather noticeable absence, I was fired. That means no more insurance. That means I can't pay an ER bill."

"When was your last tetanus shot?"

"Long enough ago that I need one. But not at the ER. I can't afford five hundred dollars for a stupid shot. One of the drugstores in town has a clinic. I can get a booster there."

"Get up to the house and clean out the wounds. I'll put Red up and then come help."

She blew out a breath and her bangs, even though they were sweat-damp, danced from the force. "I'm a big girl, Chance. I can doctor myself and drive to the clinic."

"Driving what? The tractor?"

She leaned around him and glanced through the barn. Boots's pickup was gone. "Oh…"

"You. House. Now. I'll be up after I take care of Red, and we'll go to the clinic." He held up his hand, palm facing her. "No arguments."

Huffing and muttering under her breath about his bossiness, she relinquished the reins and marched through the barn. Buddy trotted beside her until she arrived at the far door; then the dog abandoned her to go back to Chance. "Traitor."

Two hours later, her arm properly bandaged and sore from the injection, Cass sat in a booth across from Chance at the Four Corners. A mound of mashed potatoes smoth-

ered in cream gravy perched next to a chicken-fried steak.
Fried okra and more gravy appeared in separate bowls on
the girl's next trip.

"Do I need to cut up your meat?"

She jerked her chin up and glared across the table. "I'm
not helpless, Chance. I am perfectly capable of cutting up
my own chicken fry." To prove her point, she grabbed the
knife and fork and proceeded to carve off a bite. She even
managed to hide her grimace when her upper arm throbbed
with pain from the action.

They ate in silence, though Chance watched her every
move. Self-conscious, she took little bites and made sure
her mouth stayed closed as she chewed. As the waitress
cleared her plate, she met his gaze.

"What?"

"Hmmm?" He seemed distracted, his eyes watching
her mouth.

"I guess you've been really busy. Or something?" Her
inner skeptic was back, front and center. Then an emotion
she couldn't decipher slid across his face before he shuttered his expression. She never wanted to play poker with
this man. He reached across the table and covered her hand
with his. She did her best to ignore the frisson of desire
ignited by his touch. As much as she wanted to stay angry
with him, she melted inside whenever he looked at her.

"You can't be serious, Cass."

Confused, she stared at him. "Serious? About what?"

He nodded toward the cash register and the bulletin
board hanging on the wall beside it. "A cattle drive. Really?"

She swiveled in the booth to see. Sure enough, her flier
asking for volunteer drovers was displayed in front of them.
Turning back to Chance, she readied for battle. Here she'd
been all "ooey-gooey" about being with him again and now
this? The dismissive tone of his voice set her off.

"How else can I get the herd to the stockyards? I can't hire a hauler. I talked to the sale manager. He said if I don't bring them all in at once I'll lose major money. And frankly? At this point, I can't afford to lose another dime."

She combed frustrated fingers through her bangs, wincing as she flexed her biceps. So much for him understanding and wanting to help. "I'm out of time, Chance, which you'd know if you ever listened to your voice mail." She watched as the arrogant facade he'd worn crumbled a bit. Maybe she could play poker with him after all. Score one for her.

"I've been busy, Cass. I'm…sorry."

A snort erupted—half bitter laugh, half the sound of derision it was meant to be. "Busy? Well, guess what, cowboy. Me, too. I'm hanging on by my fingernails. I'm stuck with a ranch I never wanted in the first place but all my options were ripped out from under me. I have no choice. I walk away with nothing after a forced liquidation sale, declare bankruptcy and hope to hell I can live in the homeless shelter until I can find a job."

He opened his mouth to protest, but she cut him off. "I don't own a car, Chance, so I can't live in it. Nadine has been after Boots forever. If he has any sense, he'll marry her and move in with her, and take Buddy, Red and Lucky with him. My other option is to stay and fight. I'm not paranoid, but I'm really starting to wonder. The bank decides to foreclose. There's not a cattle hauler in three states that'll talk to me. I lose my job." She ticked off the points on her fingers.

"The market is prime right now, and I've got Grade A beef on the hoof, grass-fed and tender. Daddy gambled everything on that herd. I can't let him down. I can't turn tail and run, as much as I'd like to just find a hole, crawl into it and die. I wasn't raised that way."

She paused for a breath, struck silent for a moment by

Chance's expression. A mixture of admiration, sadness and something she didn't want to identify but hoped like hell wasn't guilt etched the handsome planes of his face. He met her gaze, but he blinked first.

His hand captured one of hers again while the other cupped her cheek. "Dammit, Cassie. I...care about you. I don't want you to get hurt."

"Too late for that." He winced at her cutting tone, but she didn't care. Much. Tired of feeling alone, she leaned into his palm. "Help me, Chance. Help me make everything right again."

His expression softened, and his fingertips caressed her skin but he didn't say anything as he dropped his hand.

Exasperated, she pulled away from him. "You can help me or get the hell out of my way, Chance." When he remained silent, she shrugged. "Fine. Thanks for dinner, but I need to get home. I've got a lot of work to do to get ready for the trail drive."

The uncomfortable trip home couldn't end fast enough. Cass had the passenger door open before Chance put the truck in Park. She hopped out, slammed the door and trotted toward the barn, hoping he'd get the hint and just leave. She still had evening chores to finish.

Aware that Chance had cut the motor on the pickup and now followed her, she did her best to ignore him. Every time she thought their relationship held some promise, he dashed cold water on the whole idea by his actions. Fine. She could deal with that. By not dealing with him. She wouldn't think about him, wouldn't plan on him ever being a part of her future. She could stand on her own two feet, and she would.

Cass climbed up to the loft and dragged a bale of alfalfa hay to the edge. She shoved it over and waited a heartbeat before calling out, "Heads up." She snickered when Chance stumbled backward out of the way.

Back on the main floor, she snagged a pair of wire cutters and snipped the baling wire. After splitting the bale into blocks, she grabbed an armful and paced the length of the barn, putting hay into the mangers of each stall. When she got to the colt's stall, she glanced in. He lay on his side and didn't raise his head as she clucked to him.

"Doc?" He still didn't respond so she whistled sharply. The horse merely flicked an ear. She fumbled with the latch, frantic to get into the stall to check on him.

"Cass? What's wrong?" Chance covered her hands with his and stilled them. "Here. I'll do it."

A moment later, he had the door open, and she rushed in. Doc's legs had brushed back and forth so hard, the horse had cleared the straw down to the dirt floor. She dropped to her knees and stroked his neck. Running a hand across his withers and then his belly, she stilled. This was bad. Really bad. His belly felt hard and looked bloated.

"We need to get him up on his feet." She stood and bent over, tugging on Doc's halter but nothing happened. "Chance, help me!" Her voice broke, revealing her helplessness.

"Easy, baby. Calm down. Let me get a look."

She backed away, but hovered close. "What's wrong with him?" Her stomach tightened and the fried food from dinner was a queasy lump threatening to choke her. She swallowed then shoved her hands in her pockets to keep from wringing them.

"I think it's colic, Cass, and he doesn't look good. I'm going to call the vet."

She shook her head. "Oh damndamndamn. I…I don't think you can get one to come. I can't pay."

"It's okay, Cass. We'll figure it out. Stay here with him. I'll make a couple of calls."

Chance backed out of the stall as she knelt in the hay, petting the colt and crooning softly. She seemed oblivious to him. Even so, he stepped outside the barn before he dialed the first number. As soon as he had the information he needed from his brother, he ended the call before Cord could launch into all the reasons his presence at the Crazy M was a bad idea.

Besides, he had a good reason—one even his father might applaud, given the old man wanted the colt for his own. If Doc died, no one would profit. He kept telling himself that's why he was dialing the emergency large animal vet. He gave his full name, directions and a description of the colt's symptoms. He also guaranteed payment.

He'd just finished the call when Boots arrived. Chance squared his shoulders and prepared to do battle with the other man. He didn't have to wait long for Boots to fire the first shot.

"What are you doing here?"

"Cass got hurt." He held up his hand. "It's not serious. She got caught in some barbed wire and needed a ride so she could get a tetanus shot. But when we got back, she found the colt down in his stall. I've called the vet." Boots glared at him, and Chance worked to remain calm.

"You haven't answered my question. Why are you here?"

Why *was* he here? Because he couldn't stay away from her? Because she had rubbed a raw spot right over his heart? He gave the only answer he had. "I don't know, Boots. There's something about her. Something special. I just can't stay away."

"Your daddy is behind all her troubles, ain't he."

As Chance had suspected, Boots knew the truth. Since the man hadn't asked a question, no answer was required.

"You gonna let him get away with this? With hurtin' her like he's doin'?"

Chance glanced over his shoulder and lowered his voice. He wasn't ready for Cass to discover the truth. Not yet. Not until he had an opportunity to explain things to her.

"There's nothing I can do, Boots. The old man holds all the cards in this game."

"Game? This is a game to you?"

He shook his head, adamant in his denial. "No. That's not what I meant. Dammit. Have you ever known Cyrus Barron to lose at anything?" Boots stared at him and, while it took some effort, Chance steadily returned the man's gaze.

"Yeah. I have. Her name was Colleen. A damn finer man wooed that woman, married her and produced that little girl in there."

"Uncle Boots!" Cass's panicked shout cut off any retort Chance might have made. He beat the older man to the stall by a few strides, then waited in the doorway while Boots eased through and knelt beside her.

"It's gonna be okay, baby girl. Chance called the emergency vet."

"How can we pay, Uncle Boots? The vet'll put him down instead of treating him if we can't pay."

Her anguish slammed into Chance's chest. "I'll take care of it, Cass. Don't worry."

"You? How can you afford it? This could cost thousands of dollars."

He bit back his first answer—that he had a credit card with no limit. Hell, he had a sports car sitting in his garage that cost as much as some people's houses. He'd always worked, but he'd never had to worry about getting paid, or having to save up money to buy something, or pay a bill.

"I have it covered, Cass. I promise." He recognized the argument she started to raise by the look on her face. "And we'll work out a way for you to pay me back. Not charity. A loan. Okay? Right now, let's just get the little guy fixed."

Boots had a stubborn look on his face—one Cass was extremely familiar with—but he didn't say anything. After a staring match with Chance, Boots turned his gaze to her. "I'm goin' up to the house to get a few things. I'll be back before the vet gets here." The look he leveled at Chance as he backed out of the stall spoke volumes. Problem was, Cass couldn't translate it.

"Do the right thing, son."

And what the heck did Boots mean by that parting shot? Wrung out emotionally and on edge already, she waited until she heard the barn door close before she broached the subject. "What's he talking about, Chance?"

With a weary sigh, he squatted in the straw across from her and took his own sweet time getting settled with his back against the wall. "It's a long story. And it doesn't really matter right now anyway."

She stared at him from under furrowed brows. "I've got nothing but time at the moment."

Buddy lay down beside Chance and rested his chin on the man's thigh. The dog closed his eyes as Chance ruffled his ears.

"Traitor." She muttered the word but both dog and man seemed to chuckle at her. "Why did you come back tonight?"

"I didn't come *back*. I just…I never left, Cass. Not in the sense you mean. I have a job. I have bills to pay, too."

Heat flushed her face. "I will pay you back."

Chance shook his head. "That's not what I meant. I have the vet bill covered."

She tilted her head. "Why doesn't Boots trust you?"

He wouldn't look at her. "He has his reasons."

"What are they?"

"Look, I don't really want to get into it right now, okay?"

She blinked, taken aback by the vehemence in his voice. Even Buddy raised his head to stare up at the man. "Well, I do. Maybe I shouldn't trust you, either."

"Maybe you shouldn't."

His muttered admission shocked her, even as his stony expression revealed nothing and completely shuttered any emotions he might be feeling.

"Fine. Just…fine."

She continued to stroke the colt's neck and shoulder. Two could play that game, so she steadfastly ignored Chance. The problem with ignoring him, though, was that it left her mind free to wonder. Boots wasn't a suspicious man by nature, but he was a smart man and a good judge of both horses and men. He clearly did not like Chance. Hadn't almost from the first, truth be told. Come to think of it, she'd been leery of him, too, that first time he showed up unannounced and knew all about the colt.

The longer she stewed about the situation, the more suspicious she became. Chance had emerged from the barn when she rode up. How long had he been there? Had he done something to Doc? He'd been pretty dang insistent she go to the ER, which would have taken hours. After she'd insisted on going to the minor care clinic, he'd persisted until she agreed to dinner. Had he done that to stall her? Was he buying time so she'd come home to a dead colt? Had he poisoned Doc? And then called in his own vet? So the vet could finish the job…or fix the colt so Chance didn't get caught?

She pushed to a sitting position and stared at Chance. He leaned against the wall, his legs sprawled in front of him, eyes closed. But she seriously doubted he was asleep.

"What did you do to him?"

Chance didn't bother to open his eyes. "I didn't do a damned thing."

"You were in the barn, Chance. Alone. And he was fine when I left to mend the fence." He opened his eyes and leveled a look at her that might have chilled her to the bone if she hadn't been so full of righteous anger.

She kept pushing. "You show up here all solicitous and

kind and wanting to help. Who the hell are you, Chance? Why do you care? You obviously have money. You drive a brand-new truck. You live in that fancy condo down in Bricktown. Hell, I don't even know what you do for a living. You aren't a cowboy. As much as you might pretend to be, you aren't."

"I'm a lawyer."

That stopped her cold, her mouth hanging open just as she was about to start a new tirade. She snapped her jaw closed and stared at him in consternation. "A lawyer?"

He shrugged. "I've been a cowboy, too. I used to rodeo. A long time ago."

Something about his expression triggered a memory, but she shoved it aside. "So what? You play at being a cowboy now? And how did you know my dad? Why were you at his funeral?"

"I was there to see you."

That shocked her silly. "Me?" Her voice squeaked, and she swallowed around the frog in her throat. The colt stirred, as if he sensed her upset, so she roped in her emotions. After several deep breaths, she continued, her voice calm now. "I'd never met you before Chicago. Why were you looking for me?"

"I...just was."

She grimaced. "That's certainly cryptic. Can you be a little more specific?"

"No. The reason doesn't matter. But *this* does. Do you really believe I would hurt the colt? Hurt any animal?" His face remained expressionless but for a narrowing of his eyes and a slight jut of his chin. His voice sounded cold, and she decided right then she never wanted to be on the wrong side of the courtroom from him.

"I don't get you, Chance. I don't know why you're here. I...jeez. We've had some good times. Sex. Granted, the sex was fantastic but—"

"But what? We didn't have sex, Cassie. I made love to you. I…" He choked off whatever he was going to say but stayed on the offensive. "Is that all you can manage? Just sex? What's your deal? Relationships too sticky for you?"

She rocked back from the anger in his voice. "Whoa, dude. Back right the hell up. You're the one who didn't return my calls."

"I couldn't."

"Couldn't? What? You flushed your phone down the toilet? Your dog ate it? Oh, wait, you don't have a dog." She glared at Buddy. "You just steal mine."

"There are…extenuating circumstances." He clenched his jaw, and the words gritted out between lips stretched tight across his teeth.

"Extenuating circumstances? What's that? Legalese for I can't be bothered?"

Chance rubbed his temple, eyes closed. When he spoke, he seemed to have leashed his temper. "That's not fair, Cass. You have no idea what's going on. What's at stake."

She wanted to throw her hands up in the air and scream but Doc was restless again. She bridled her emotions though her angry response hissed out. "How the hell am I supposed to know if you don't tell me!"

He ground his teeth together. "I can't tell you. Not right now." He dragged the fingers of one hand through his hair and sighed. His gaze caught and held hers. "Please. Can you just trust me? For a little while longer?"

So many replies popped into her head. *Why should I? How can you ask that? Oh, hell no!* But as she looked at his face, recognized the pleading for understanding in his eyes, the grim set of his mouth, which all showed a crack in the emotions he did his best to stonewall deep inside, none of those admonitions worked. Between one thudding beat of her heart and the next, she knew the answer.

"Yes."

Twelve

By the time the vet left, Cass felt exhausted. Her arm still ached from the booster, and the bandages over the deeper cuts on her arm itched. Chance walked the man out, and only then did she stop to wonder why there'd been no mention of the bill at all. She stroked the colt's neck, hoping her touch would keep him calm. The vet had done what he could, telling her to watch him for further signs of distress and to call if Doc wasn't better in a few hours. They'd have to get him on his feet every hour or so and walk him to help ease the blockage in his intestines.

Colic. One of the worst things that could happen to a horse. The little guy snuffled as he labored to breathe, and her eyes prickled with tears as she listened to him wheeze. She'd considered selling him as a way to get money, but she knew she couldn't, especially not now. Buddy crept into the stall and curled in beside her, his head on her knee. The dog whined softly and stared up at her with big brown eyes as if to say, *I have faith in you. You're my human. You'll make it right.* She ruffled his ears.

"I hope so, Buddy. I hope so."

Chance reappeared moments later, Boots a few steps behind. The older man carried a couple of quilts and a pillow. Chance had mugs of coffee and handed her one. She accepted the cup and stared at its contents. Muddy brown.

Just the right color when cream and coffee achieved the perfect blend.

"One sugar, right?"

She nodded dumbly. The man remembered how she drank her coffee?

"Thought you might as well be comfortable, baby girl." Boots's voice broke her rumination. He spread out one quilt after shooing Buddy away and left the other folded on top with the pillow. "Gonna be a long night." He turned toward Chance, and Cass recognized a look of distrust crossing Boots's face.

"I'll stay up with Cass, Boots. I'll call if we need help."

There was that look again. Cass's attention ping-ponged between the two men. There was definitely defiance and dismissal in Chance's voice, along with a hint of challenge, but Boots didn't rise to the occasion. Instead, he focused on her.

"You need anything at all, baby girl, you just holler. I'll come running."

Cass made a show of straightening the quilt and getting settled on it as the older man shuffled out. She stretched out on her side, the pillow bunched under her head, one hand stroking the colt's neck. An uncomfortable silence descended on the stall, but she wasn't going to be the one to break it. She fidgeted but couldn't get comfortable. After thirty minutes, she gave up.

"We should try to get him on his feet and walk him."

Chance said nothing as he stood and helped her push and pull the colt. Only a yearling, the little guy wasn't close to being full grown, but he was big enough the two of them had trouble. He wobbled on his legs but managed a few tentative steps as Cass led him from the stall. She walked him up and down the center run of the barn so many times she lost count but by the time her legs started to ache, the colt walked a little easier. Once back in the stall, though, he flopped in the straw with a distressed whinny.

Chance had rearranged the blanket and pillow, and now sank down on the quilt before Cass could say anything. He patted the space next to him. She made a face but joined him, realizing too late that he'd raised his arm, and she was now snuggled up against his side. Her nostrils flared at the scent of his cologne, and her stomach did a darn good impression of a bowl of gelatin.

Why did this man tie her up in knots physically and emotionally? What would be so terrible about just letting go, letting him take some of her troubles? Not forever. No, not that. She could never relinquish control forever, but what was the harm in sharing the burden just for a little while? Just long enough to get back on her feet.

"I don't think I'm going back to Chicago." She felt him stiffen.

"Oh?" He said the word carefully.

"I can't leave here. Not yet anyway. I had my neighbor box up or sell all my stuff. It might not be much, but this is home." Something shifted in her heart. Home. This had always been home, and she'd been too blind to realize it.

"That's not true, Cass." She started to bristle, but his hand squeezed her shoulder and she realized he'd relaxed. "This place is a helluva lot. Your dad worked hard to build the Crazy M and to make a home for you. You might not have wanted to be here, but you knew you could always come back."

She nodded, her cheek rubbing against the soft material of his shirt. "I tried to run away. Then I tried to stay away. And then I felt guilty because I hated this place. But I really didn't." She squiggled her nose to chase away the burn of forming tears. "Do you think Daddy understood? Did he know why I wasn't here?"

Chance dropped a kiss on the top of her head. "Did you get to say goodbye?"

Cass inhaled and held her breath to ease the pain in her chest. Exhaling slowly, she shook her head. She had to swallow before she could speak. "Sort of. I was on the phone with him when he passed." She felt Chance wince, and she brushed her palm along his abdomen. "That night at the hotel. In Chicago. I waited too long and got caught by that blizzard. Boots put the phone by Daddy's ear. He…he told me cowgirls don't cry. They just get back on and ride. He used to say that when I was little." She snuggled closer to Chance, seeking his warmth and the gentleness of his embrace. "I guess I've been doing that ever since I got here."

He tilted her head and leaned down to kiss her. His lips, full and firm, danced across her mouth as if seeking permission. She pressed into the kiss, her lips parting in invitation. His hand caressed her side and his fingertips teased the swell of her breast before his palm cupped her fully. Her breath hitched as she sighed.

Cass trailed her hand down those firm, rippled abs of his and found what really interested her. Oh, yeah. He was glad to see her. She stroked him through his jeans and he arched against her hand.

"Damn, girl. I want you."

Not the most romantic of declarations, yet it went straight to her core. She wanted him with a fierceness she'd never experienced. She freed her other arm and fumbled with his buttons.

"Here, let me."

While he dealt with his buttons, fly and boots, she did the same. She kicked off her boots, peeled out of her jeans and T-shirt and was down to her bra and panties when he growled, "No. Mine." She stopped as he took over. He was already naked, but she didn't have time to admire him. His mouth covered hers as he unhooked her bra and slipped its straps off her shoulders.

"You are so beautiful, Cassidy Morgan." He whispered it against her skin as his mouth dipped to find a nipple.

She bowed her back and threaded her fingers through his hair. Oh, the things this man could do with his tongue. She squirmed, pressing her thighs together. One of his hands dipped low, and his strong fingers found her wet and ready. He groaned against her breast, and his erection pressed against her thigh.

Cass wrapped her fingers around his shaft and he groaned again, only this time, he tried to say something. He raised his head to gaze at her, his face flushed and his eyes radiating desire and regret.

He inhaled sharply and finally managed a complete sentence. "I want to be inside you, darlin', but I don't have a condom."

She was so with that program because that's exactly where she wanted him. Until he admitted he wasn't a Boy Scout. "Oh." That one syllable was filled with disappointment. But at the same time, she had to respect him. She stroked his erection and offered a little smile. "We go to Plan B?"

He blinked at her, his confusion showing in his expression. She wiggled loose and kissed her way down his chest. The moment he figured out her intentions, all the air whooshed from his lungs. Gripping him in one hand, she held him still as she wet her lips with her tongue, her eyes glued on his face. He gulped and held his breath. She dipped her head, and her lips glided over him. His hands clutched her head, fingers fighting her ponytail until her hair fell around her shoulders. He held her still for a moment as he throbbed against her palm.

"Easy, baby. I'm already primed."

She raised her head but not before giving him a swirl

with her tongue. "I'll be gentle." She didn't hide the smirk on her face, and after a wink and a cheeky grin, she went back to work.

Chance thought he might die before she finished him off. Cassie had tricks he'd never experienced, and he'd experienced a lot. Sated and lazy, he managed to pull her up to lay next to him, her head just below his shoulder. He hugged her loosely with one arm as her hand alternated between playing with the hair on his chest and places lower.

He was not a man who kept a woman in his bed overnight, but he wanted to spend the night with this woman in his arms—wanted to spend every night with her. He hadn't dated anyone else since he'd first seen her in Chicago; hadn't even looked at other women. He had feelings for her but couldn't define them. The Barrons didn't exactly have a great track record when it came to long-term relationships. Yet this woman touched something deep inside him—a place he wasn't aware of until she came into his life.

He kissed the top of her head and breathed her in. Her hair smelled faintly of sweat and citrus, and his stomach tightened. She nuzzled his skin in a sleepy kiss, and he settled in just to hold her. He'd make sure she was as satisfied as she'd made him when she woke up. For now, she seemed as content as he was.

A few minutes later, the colt stirred but didn't try to get up. Cass awoke instantly but Chance tightened his arms around her. "He's just moving around, darlin'. It's okay. We'll walk him here in a few minutes. First, though, I have my own Plan B to implement."

Her lips curled in a cat-and-cream smile, and her eyes twinkled. He slid down her body until he found a breast. With lips and tongue, he started a slow, sweet assault, gratified when her breath hitched and her legs twitched. He smoothed a hand down her side and cupped the curve of her ass for a gentle squeeze before he pulled her knee over his hip. His fingers dipped lower, finding her sweet spot. Her sharp exhalation ruffled his hair and he smiled, his tongue still flicking over her pebbled nipple. He pushed one finger inside her, and her inner muscles gripped him with wet ferocity. He added a second and she rocked against his hand. He let her set the pace. This time was for her. All her. He wanted her to come saying his name.

Cass panted, and each breath pushed her breast against his tongue. He discovered that his own breathing matched hers, and even as her heart thundered beneath his ear, his heart galloped along. He hardened to the point of pain but didn't care. His fingers caressed and teased, driving her hips to thrust harder and faster. He found her magic button with his thumb and savored her gasp.

"Yes. Yes…oh, yes." She didn't shout it, she whimpered. And that was even sweeter to his ears.

His erection throbbed in time to the clenches her muscles made around his fingers. He rubbed against her firm thigh, the friction making him even harder.

"C'mon, baby. That's my girl. Come for me. Show me how beautiful you are."

"Oh, Chance." His name sighed across her lips and he felt himself tighten. Damned if he wasn't going to come again, with her this time.

"That's it, honey. Yes. C'mon." His hips surged against her, rocking with the same rhythm as hers.

She whimpered, and a soft cry escaped right before she inhaled. A shudder rocked her body, and he exploded as she called his name. "Chance!"

Her fingers dug into his shoulders, and he lifted his head, seeking her lips. He kissed her. Long and hard and deep, his tongue sweeping across hers, his lips branding hers.

"I love you."

The words hung in the dusty air between them. Had he said them out loud? Her body quivered with little aftershocks, and she sighed, her warm breath both tickling and cooling his heated skin. His heart seemed to hesitate between beats as he waited for her reaction.

"Me, too, you."

His heart started again, steady this time, and he breathed. Those three words were enough for now. He cradled her against his side and let her doze. He'd get up and dressed in a few minutes and walk the colt. Until then, he wanted nothing more from life than this woman in his arms.

Now that he'd admitted his feelings aloud, Chance needed this respite from his guilt—and his indecision. He could follow his heart, betray his family and love the woman in his arms. Or he could betray her. The choices sucked, and the devil sitting on his shoulder whispered that he'd resent Cassie for driving a wedge between him and his brothers. He cursed softly even as he tightened his arms around the woman who was becoming his everything.

An hour later, he had the colt up and moving. Cassie watched him, her face pale, and the corners of her mouth drawn down.

"This is all my fault."

Chance continued walking the colt, but he glanced over his shoulder to study her. Her jeans hung low on her hips because she hadn't fastened the top button. The T-shirt she'd pulled on sans bra showed every curve, and he was glad he hadn't fastened his own fly.

"No, it's not. Horses colic, Cassie. I checked the grain bin and the hay. It's all good. No mold. He didn't get sick from eating it. Besides, he's been grazing on grass in the pasture and probably not drinking enough water. You did not do this to him."

She looked so miserable he felt compelled to do something—anything to make her feel better. He'd made love to this woman—*his* woman. And wasn't that a kick in the pants. He hated seeing her so emotionally beaten. As he returned, he paused long enough to gather her into his arms. He kissed her forehead and laid his cheek on the top of her head for a moment. A feeling of rightness settled somewhere in his chest. Despite all the roadblocks, he wanted her—in his bed and in his life.

"I repeat, Cass. This is not your fault. And we'll get him through it. I promise." He planned to promise her so much more, too.

"Don't make promises you can't keep, Chance."

Thirteen

"Shut up, Cord."

Chance's brother was waving a piece of paper in his face. "Have you seen these fliers? Every store in Cowtown has one stuck to the door." He used the local nickname for the area known as Stockyard City.

Chance brushed Cord back with a wave of his hand. "I've seen it. So what?"

"So what? All hell would break out if the old man was here. You better be glad he and Cash flew to Vegas to pull Chase's butt out of the fire over the deal with that showgirl."

He vaguely remembered something about a blackmail scheme and a showgirl at the Barron Crown Casino, and being glad at the time they hadn't dragged him into it. "What do you want me to do about the fliers, Cord? Go door to door and rip them down?"

"I want you to fix this. Before the old man gets back and has a stroke."

"I can't stop her, Cord."

"You can't? Or you won't?"

"Does it matter? Either way, I'm not getting involved."

"You're already involved, Chance. You can't have your cake and eat it, too. Not this time. Do what you always do. Take the bitch—"

Before he knew what happened, Chance had surged from his desk chair and wrapped his fist in his brother's shirtfront. "Don't call her that. Cassidy Morgan is not that kind of woman." Cord grabbed his wrist and squeezed, but Chance didn't loosen his grip.

Cord stared at him, his arched brow speaking volumes.

With studied care, Chance released his brother and leaned back in his chair. Cord retreated to the far side of the desk and tried to look nonchalant as he lounged in one of the armchairs. They stared at each other as the clock ticked off several minutes. Cord finally broke the silence.

"So what are you going to do?"

"Nothing."

"Nothing? What does that mean?"

"Just what it sounds like. Nothing. I'm not going to stop her. I'm not going to help her. I don't think she can pull this thing off. If she does, I'll be surprised, but damn proud of her. It won't matter what we do. She's not giving up." He scrubbed at his forehead with his fingers and willed his headache away. "If the old man had listened to me in the first place, we could have bought her out, and she'd be back in Chicago, safe."

"Safe?"

"Safely out of our hair."

"Yeah. Right. I'm sure that's what you meant. But the old man doesn't work that way, Chance. You know it. I know it. The world knows it. If he finds out about this, it's your ass."

"I'm aware of that, Cord. But…"

"But what?"

"She trusts me."

"Well…crap."

Cass leaned on the stall door and watched as Doc dipped his muzzle in the water trough. She'd just emptied it and refilled it with fresh. She'd meticulously picked over the hay and grain she put in his manger. Chance had been right. No mold. She rubbed at eyes gritty from lack of sleep. Chance had been right about the colt, too. Doc was fine this morning, seemingly no worse for the wear. She'd have to muck out his stall soon, but this was one time she wouldn't complain. Not one bit.

Boots joined her. His appraising eye roamed over the horse and the stall. "He's gonna be fine, baby girl." He nudged her with his shoulder. "And I have news about your flyers. We'll have some help with the herd."

She glanced at him as he continued.

"The agriculture teacher over from the high school called. He's got some FFA boys comin' to round up the herd and get 'em gathered here in the big pasture today. Some of 'em are gonna make the ride with us, too. They get extra credit."

Future Farmers of America. Now that was a group she hadn't thought about in years. She'd been the FFA queen one year and sold a bunch of World's Finest Chocolate to help with votes. "What goes around comes around," she chuckled.

"We need to get those cows started tomorrow, Cassie. Big sale is on Friday mornin'. The cattle need to be penned and ready in the stockyards by Thursday night."

She rubbed her eyes again and rolled her head, listening to the familiar snap and crackle as vertebrae ground together at the top of her spine. "I got all the permits for Canadian County. And the commissioner from Oklahoma County says he'll have a set ready today."

"Nadine's offered to feed everyone. She's shuttin' down the Four Corners and is gonna drive her RV. She'll set up camp for us and have food ready for the crew mornin' and night."

"But…she can't close the diner. She'll lose too much money, Uncle Boots."

He patted her shoulder, his grin adding more crinkles to his weatherworn cheeks. "Honey, she wouldn't miss this for the world. She closes a week for vacation ever year anyway, so this is her vacation."

Cass rubbed her chest to ease the tightness forming there. "This is going to work, Uncle Boots."

"Yup."

Boots could be a man of few words. "I guess I'd better go pick up those permits, huh?"

"Yup." He dug in his pocket and handed over the keys to the truck.

Cass perched on the tailgate of Boots's truck and tried not to laugh. She really did. But the sight of the group of high school kids flapping their arms and waving their hats as they tried to funnel the herd through the gate while on foot had her doubled over. She lightly punched Boots's arm as he leaned next to her.

"That's just mean."

"Yup."

The ag teacher laughed along with her. "They need to taste a little vinegar. Ranching is hard. The sooner they learn that, the better. This life isn't a glorified Western movie."

"Boy, isn't that the truth!"

"Still, I'm always reminded of that speech John Wayne makes in the movie *McClintock*. The one where he's talking to his daughter about how he didn't plan to leave her the whole ranch, just a little start-up place. There's a whole lot of growing a person has to do to become a rancher."

Cass stared at the teacher, struck dumb by the revelation. She watched the kids work, sober now in her reflections. In many ways, her dad had given her that same speech—but in his actions, not his words. She ran off to the world and forgot the lessons she'd learned here in this place. She'd forgotten what home felt like. And now she remembered. Thanks to Boots. And Chance.

Her heart burned with fierce pride for the first time in ten years. She turned her head slightly to look at Boots, and a small smile hovered at the corner of her mouth. Squeezing the old man's arm, she leaned in and planted an impulsive kiss on his cheek.

"What was that for?"

"For helping me realize that I'm home." She laughed as a boy tripped and face-planted in the pasture. A girl helped him up, and the two of them jogged after a steer refusing to go through the gate. "God help me with that bunch, but by golly, we're going to get this herd to market!"

Chance's absence kept this from being perfect. She knew he was busy. Lawyers with their own law firms were. Her feelings for him were still new enough she hadn't figured out the rules. Cass did know that what she felt for Chance was all tied up with her feelings of coming home.

Early the next morning, Nadine's RV idled in the front yard. She'd arrived at the crack of dawn and already had coffee and doughnuts ready for folks as they arrived. Horse trailers and pickups littered the yard and people milled about. Saddled horses stood tied, swishing desultory tails at the occasional fly, heads down as they dozed in the early-morning light.

Cass hadn't slept much. Keyed up, nervous and scared she'd fail, she'd paced the floor of her bedroom in between bouts of tossing and turning. She wished Chance was there—even if Boots would have a conniption over Chance sharing her bed. She wanted the comfort of his arms. He would have kissed her, told her she was doing the right thing and that everything would be all right.

He's busy, she told herself, but part of her resented the fact he wasn't there. He'd said the words, told her he loved her, but everything was still new enough, she didn't know whether to believe or not. Especially when it seemed that if she needed him, he couldn't, or wouldn't, make time.

She had four days to go just over twenty miles with five hundred head of prime grass-fed beef. At current market rates, they were selling for almost a hundred and fifty dollars for a hundredweight. Even if they brought less, she'd make enough to pay off the mortgage and her dad's medical bills.

Nadine pressed a steaming cup of coffee in her hand. "I made it good and strong this morning, honey. Y'all are gonna need a kick in the britches today."

Without thinking, Cass took a sip and sputtered. She managed to swallow the hot, black liquid without spitting, but it took supreme effort on her part.

"Cream and sugar is over there, hon." Nadine patted her on the back in an effort to ease her coughing spasm.

"Thanks." The word came out choked but at least she could still talk. Movement down at the gate caught her eye. The big Ford pickup maneuvered through the congestion and inched up the drive. Chance. Had he come to help after all? She waited until he parked before walking over. She arrived just as he stepped out.

He wore boots, but he sure wasn't dressed for cowboy work. Dress slacks and a starched button-down shirt made him look more like a male model than ever. Or a lawyer. But what she wanted right then was a cowboy. She schooled her expression before greeting him.

"Hi, cowboy, fancy meeting you here." She kept her voice light and teasing despite the disappointment churning inside her. That whole fantasy of the two of them riding off into the sunset was just that. A fantasy. For now at least.

"I have court today, Cass. I'm sorry. I couldn't get the docket changed." He didn't step away from the shelter provided by the open door and the bulk of the truck cab. Truth be told, she was glad for the privacy.

She lifted one shoulder in a lopsided shrug. "Hey, work happens. Thanks for getting up so early to come see us off."

He gazed around and seemed surprised by the hustle and bustle and the number of people. "Looks like you have a lot of help."

"Yeah. We even have places to camp out along the way. Once the word got out about what I'm doing, all sorts of people stepped up." She inhaled, feeling very pleased with herself. "This will work, Chance. I'm going to get the herd to the stockyards and get them sold. Then I can pay off Daddy's debts."

"What will you do then?"

His voice sounded peculiar, and she cut her eyes in his direction. He looked odd, the expression on his face unreadable. She tilted her head and turned to face him. "I'm staying here. Daddy's dying gift to me was that colt down in the barn. I'm not a rancher. I don't know squat about cows, but horses? Horses I know. I'll use any money left over from the sale to get a couple of mares and when Doc is old enough, I'll breed him. And I'll train horses. I may have been out of the game for ten years, but I went out on top. I was the national champion cowgirl."

Cass watched his Adam's apple bob as he swallowed then lifted her gaze to his eyes. He looked almost…haunted for a moment, and she wondered why. He blinked, and his expression changed. What lurked behind the smile he now wore?

"So you *are* a cowgirl at heart."

His teasing sounded forced to her ears, but she returned his smile with a hesitant one of her own. "Guess I always was. Just took coming home—and a certain cowboy—to make me remember that."

She glanced to the eastern horizon where the top curve of the morning sun had cleared the tree line. "Time to get this party started." She rocked up on her toes and brushed her lips across his, her palm braced against his chest for balance. "Thanks for coming to see me off."

There was nothing forced about his smile as his arm circled her waist and hugged her a bit closer. "I wouldn't have missed this for the world." He kissed her back, deeply, his lips nibbling hers as his tongue eased into her mouth to tease her.

A bit breathless when he released her, she rocked back on her heels and figured she looked either bemused or just plain stupid because wow. That man could kiss her right out of her boots.

Chance laughed, obviously pleased by her reaction. He placed his hands on her shoulders and turned her around. "Head 'em up, cowgirl."

In less time than she anticipated, her drovers had the herd lined up and ready to move out of the pasture and onto the road. Boots had cut part of the fence to install a temporary gate, and one of the neighbors would restring the barbed wire once the herd was well on its way. The old man sat on his horse at the opening, waiting to lead the herd. Cass held Red's reins, and was about to mount and give the order to move out when a car flew up the road scattering a dust cloud in its wake. The vehicle, with no apparent attempt to brake, careened into her drive.

"What the hell?" She dropped the reins and marched toward the car, which had stopped. She noticed that Boots was riding up at a gallop.

The white, four-door sedan looked like an unmarked police car. The vehicle even had a spotlight mounted above the driver's-side mirror. She stopped a few feet away, fists planted on her hips as she waited for the driver to emerge. She expected to see a uniform. She got a nondescript man wearing cheap khaki pants and a blue short-sleeved shirt that looked in desperate need of an iron.

"I'm lookin' for Cassidy Morgan!" The man bawled out her name at the top of his lungs. All eyes turned in her direction.

"That would be me. Who are you?"

He walked up and waved an envelope under her nose. "Here."

She refused to take it. "What's that?"

He stuffed it down the front of her shirt. "You've been served."

"What?" Cass dug the envelope out of her shirt and tore it open. She read the heading, "In the District Court of the County of Oklahoma, State of Oklahoma." Her eyes skipped down, caught her name and the name of the bank, followed by the words "wholly owned subsidiary of Barron Enterprises" before focusing on the first paragraph. "What the hell?"

"That, Miss Morgan, is a foreclosure notice. Everything on this ranch now belongs to Barron Enterprises by way of Stockmen's Bank and Trust."

She stared at him, her mouth gaping. She shook her head and bit back the curses she wanted to spew in his direction. Instead, she read the notice. "This is bull. It says there's a hearing set for next Monday. I have until then to present collateral assets or to pay off the loan." She thought. The legal terms were jumbled in her head and then she remembered. Chance! He was an attorney.

Before she could call him over, the process server called out. "Mr. Barron! I didn't see you, sir."

Mr. *Barron*? There was a Barron on her property? She whipped her head around to see who the man was talking to.

One look at Chance's face and she knew.

Oh, God. His last name—the one she'd assumed was Chancellor—was Barron. Her heart shriveled in her chest, and she couldn't breathe. Only sheer stubbornness kept her standing.

"Chance?" His name tumbled out before she could stop herself. "Please...tell me this isn't happening." But she knew. Her head knew even as her heart tried to hide from the pain. His expression said it all. Her stomach knotted, and she swallowed hard to keep the bile rising in her throat at bay.

"Cassidy." Her name, a whisper from his lying lips, sighed on the morning breeze.

God, but she was stupid. Chance. Chancellor Barron. Even in Chicago she'd heard the names of all the Barron brothers. How had she not recognized him? Would it have mattered? She'd wanted him that night in his condo, and again in the barn and every other time they'd been together. She'd wanted him, and she'd allowed herself to fall in love with him.

"Please, Cassie…" Her name dripped off his tongue like honey, and he tried to look sincere and repentant but she didn't buy his act for a minute.

"Please Cassie what? Please Cassie let me steal your home? Or please Cassie let me screw you one more time?" She wadded up the paper in her hand and threw it at his face. She scored a direct hit, but he didn't even flinch. "Get the hell off my land."

He grabbed her forearm and squeezed just hard enough she couldn't jerk away. Cass stared down at his hand—tanned, strong and belonging to a liar. She was such a fool. One night of mind-blowing sex with him and he'd gotten under her skin—and into her heart. And that one night had turned into so much more. She'd started dreaming—of him, of life with him here on the ranch. She loved him. Or did. Before he betrayed her. Her face flushed with anger as she raised her gaze to collide with his.

"Please, Cassie. Let me explain."

"Move it or lose it, Mr. *Barron*."

If anything, his grip tightened, and for a moment, she got lost in his amber eyes. Then she remembered he was nothing more than a predator. A snake. A…she didn't want to malign innocent members of the animal kingdom so she called a spade a spade. "Let me go, you bastard. You lied to me. And you cheated me. I...I thought you cared. About me. About the ranch. God, how could I have been so damned wrong about you? About...us."

Her voice cracked, and his grip loosened slightly. She jerked her arm out of his grasp, no longer caring that her voice quivered. "Get away from me, Chance. I hate you. I hate everything you stand for. I'll put a certified check for the full amount of the loan on your desk by five o'clock Friday afternoon. I have a herd of cattle to get to market so get the hell out of my way."

She turned on her heel and marched over to Boots where he stood holding the reins of her horse. She snatched them and stood glaring at him.

"You knew." Oh yeah, he knew all right. "Why didn't you tell me?"

"I was waitin' for him t'do the right thing."

"Seriously? He's a friggin' Barron, Uncle Boots." She dashed at her eyes with the back of her hand. She'd be damned if she shed tears over Chance Barron. Not now. Not ever. "He wouldn't know the right thing if it walked up and bit him on the ass."

Cass swung up on the big sorrel, and settled into the saddle. Boots touched her knee.

"I'm sorry, baby girl."

She closed her eyes and fought for control as Boots mounted his horse. The man never did anything without a good reason. Someday, maybe she wouldn't hurt so much, and she could talk about it. Not now. Now she had a herd to deliver.

Buddy barked and quivered with excitement. She glanced at her handful of drovers and though she tried not to, she had to glance at Chance. He hadn't moved and his face looked as if it had been carved from granite for all the emotion he showed. Fine. She didn't need him. Twenty miles from the ranch to the stockyards with five hundred head of cattle. If she pulled this off, it would be a miracle. She had to be as crazy as a grasshopper sunbathing on a red ant pile.

Fourteen

Chance recognized the stubborn jut of her chin and had to admire her despite the fact he pretty much hated himself as much as she claimed to hate him. She'd mounted her horse with controlled elegance and didn't take out her obvious anger on the sorrel. The grim set of her mouth didn't diminish her beauty. She wheeled Red around to face the people who'd gathered.

Despite angry looks from other bystanders, he stepped back to the front fender of his truck to watch. This moment belonged to Cassie. He might have destroyed any hope for a relationship but he still cared, still loved her. Cyrus Barron would never be able to take his feelings for her away. Chance had wanted her to have this moment of glory, even if it turned into a last hurrah. He would track down who tried to rob it from her.

"This is it," she called. "Cyrus Barron has decided I'm public enemy number one. Some of you might not want to get on his bad side. I'll understand if you drop out. No hard feelings. But I'm mad as hell, and I'm going to prove to that old bastard that he can knock me down, but I won't stay in the dirt."

She straightened her shoulders and stood in her stirrups. "My daddy didn't know what giving up meant. I'm not about to let him down now. I have four days to get these cows to the stockyards and by God, I'm gonna get 'em there come hell, high water or the damned Barron family!"

Cheers answered her, and he couldn't suppress the feeling of pride welling inside him. And apprehension. If he knew his father, she would have both hell and high water to deal with.

She laughed, but it sounded mirthless in the fading echoes of the shouts of the drovers. "I've always wanted to say this! Head 'em up! Move 'em out!"

Chance waited until the last steer and the drag riders disappeared up the road. Two men patched the fence, and Nadine rolled up the awning on her RV. She walked over and leaned on the truck fender next to him.

"You should'a told her." The woman gazed eastward where a red haze still hung in the still air.

"Probably." He watched the same dust cloud.

"You care about her."

"Probably." Hell, yeah, he cared. He loved her. But he couldn't admit it. Not out loud. He'd told Cass and look what happened. He hung his head and refused to meet Nadine's knowing gaze.

"So what are you going to do about it?"

"Damned if I know, Nadine."

She chuckled and smacked his arm. He resisted the urge to rub the spot. For a woman her age, she still carried quite a punch. "Then it's high time you figured it out, Chancellor Barron. She's worth fightin' for."

Nadine walked away before he could reply. He watched her climb into the big RV then maneuver it over the rutted yard. Once she had the nose of the vehicle pointed in the right direction, she tooted the horn and waved at him as she headed off.

His phone vibrated on his hip. Tempted to ignore it, he checked the caller ID anyway. His brother Cash.

"What?"

"Did I catch you in the middle of something?"

"What do you want, Cash?"

"If I'd known you were going to be at the Morgan place this morning, I could have saved money on the process server."

"You're the one who sent him out here?"

"Well…yeah. The old man said you were busy. Since you hadn't done it yet, he had the papers filed yesterday and wanted them served first thing."

"Yeah, I just bet he did."

"Whoa, Chance. You sound pissed."

"I am."

"Hey, I was just following the old man's orders. You want to tell me what's going on?"

"No. But fair warning, Cash. You ever again go behind my back to serve papers without my go-ahead, you'll regret it." He stabbed the end button on his phone and tossed it onto the center console of the truck. Within seconds, it danced across the leather. He ignored it. Gazing around, he realized his family might have more money than many small countries, but Cass Morgan was far richer.

After three days on the trail, Cass would give just about anything she owned for a hot shower lasting longer than five minutes. It was hard to do much more than sluice off the surface dust in the tepid water and confined space of the tiny shower in Nadine's RV. Her hair hung dull and limp when she removed the ponytail holder.

A new set of volunteers had arrived each day to help as drovers and outriders. The nightly camps had a holiday air as folks visited and relaxed once the herd was settled for the night. She wished she could unwind and enjoy their camaraderie. But she couldn't. Not until the herd was delivered, sold, and she had the check in her hand.

The RV was parked on the expansive lot of a suburban

acreage. A catering truck from a local BBQ restaurant was on site with a smoker. The scent of roasting beef wafted in the open window. With a grimace at how nasty her hair felt as she combed it with her fingers, she smoothed it back and refastened it into a ponytail. Navigating down the narrow aisle, Cassie smiled at the cowboy chic decor and squeezed past the older woman puttering at the stove. The motorhome was pure Nadine.

Cass pushed the screen door open, stepped out and ran smack dab into a very masculine body.

Chance's hands steadied her until she regained her balance. She scowled at him. "What the hell are you doing here?"

"We need to talk, Cass."

"No, we don't."

"Yes, we do. I had to take care of some things or I would have been here sooner."

She wanted to thump his chest with her fist. Or slap him. "Go away, Chance. I don't need or want you."

"Look, you have every reason to be upset—"

"Ya think? You lied to me."

"No. Not technically speaking."

"What? You lied about your name."

"No, I didn't."

"Yes, you did."

"No. When I first introduced myself, I said my name was Chancellor. *You* jumped the gun and assumed it was my last name."

"Well, you weren't in any hurry to correct that assumption, were you?" He flushed at that, and she pressed home her point. "And you never made any attempt to set me straight."

"Technically, you never asked for clarification, Cass."

She blinked at him, opened her mouth and closed it, at a loss for words for a moment. "Technically? Freaking lawyer. I shouldn't have had to. You led me on, Chance. You let me believe you were somebody else. Somebody I could—"

She snapped her jaw shut. She would never admit to this man how much she had trusted him, how much he had hurt her. She let him hurt her by caring about him. By…no. She refused to acknowledge that she loved him.

Chance hung his head and looked penitent. She didn't believe the pose for a New York minute. "Cass, please? I can explain. Things are different now."

"Different? You mean you didn't actually file a foreclosure action for your father? That you don't mean to steal the ranch from me? Throw me out on my butt? Jeez, Chance. You can't even admit that I was nothing but a piece of ass to you." Her eyelids prickled, but she'd be damned if she'd cry.

"Don't be mad, Cass. Just listen to me."

"Mad? I don't get mad, Chance Barron. I get even."

She pushed past him with a growl, ignoring his outstretched hand, and stomped over to the campfire where Boots and the volunteer wranglers sat. Only Boots had the guts to look at her. She stamped her foot, her face flaming from anger. "Ooh. That man makes me crazy, Uncle Boots."

He patted the folding chair next to him. "Take a load off, honey. I get the feeling that situation goes both ways. You make Chance Barron a little crazy, too."

Cass dropped into the chair and stretched her legs out. Inhaling slow, measured breaths, she glanced at the old man from the corner of her eye and caught a flicker of movement. Chance actually had the nerve to walk closer. She reached for the shotgun lying across the ice chest beside her chair and placed it across her thighs. Not that she'd actually use it. Chance took another step, and she checked the breach to see if the gun was loaded.

Boots chuckled as Chance retreated without turning his back. "Discretion is the better part of valor, I guess."

She watched Chance retreat. "What the hell does that mean, Uncle Boots?"

"It means you've got the man tied up in knots, honey. He wants you. Wants you enough to stand up to his daddy to get you." Boots inclined his head toward the picket line, the rope stretched between two trees where the trail horses were loosely tied for the night. He watched her face to make sure she paid attention. A television reporter and cameraman interviewed one of her volunteers, who was brushing his horse, for the evening news. "Who do you think alerted the media? Why do you think we suddenly got all this attention and more riders?"

"Ha! I don't believe that at all."

Nadine stuck her head out of the RV. "Well, you better believe it, Cassie. They got a call from Chance's office, least ways that's what the producer feller told me. Your story is all over the news. Here and nationally. All the networks picked it up. Considering Cyrus Barron owns the newspapers around here and a bunch of TV and radio stations, just how else do you think the national folks tumbled to this little shindig?"

Cass leaned back in the chair and swiveled her head just far enough to keep track of Chance. He'd walked back to his pickup truck and leaned against the front fender talking to another man just as tall, dark and handsome. Had to be one of his brothers but for her life, she didn't know which one.

"Why would he do that?"

"He loves you."

"He's in love."

Boots said it first, but Nadine's assertion echoed a half beat later. No. Nonononono no! This wasn't happening. Chance Barron didn't love her. He couldn't. He just wanted the ranch so his father could erase all memory of Ben Morgan from the face of the earth.

Cass had finally finagled the full story out of Boots—

how Cyrus had pursued her mom but she'd married her dad instead. She couldn't fathom why a man as rich and powerful as the senior Barron carried such a long-standing grudge. Three hard days in the saddle had rubbed the furious off her temper, though she remained miffed at the old man for not telling her Chance's real identity.

Boots's revelation over Chance's feelings left her own unsteady. When she realized her hand was still curled around the shotgun, she carefully placed it back on the ice chest.

"No. I can't deal with this. Not now. I have five hundred head of cattle to get to market. And one more day to get it done."

"We've made good distance, Cass. We only have about five miles to go."

She closed her eyes and laid her head back against the chair. "It might as well be a thousand, Uncle Boots. We hit the county line tomorrow. You know Cyrus Barron will have every deputy in Oklahoma County lined up to keep us out. Even though I managed to get the permits from Oklahoma County, I don't believe for a second they'll be worth the paper they're printed on. Even if the sheriff and his deputies don't stop us, there'll be the whole Oklahoma City Police Department waiting at the city limits. The Barrons always get their way."

"You forget, hon. The media will be there, too. Sheriff Wallace is up for reelection. You're a huge story." Hands on her ample hips, Nadine climbed down the steps and stopped right in front of Cass. "You're the underdog. The pretty little girl takin' on the big bads with a ragtag group of volunteers. From the information the national outlets are reporting? You can bet someone on the inside spilled the beans. Mr. Chance Barron, in fact."

Cass shook her head, unable to believe Chance would stand up to his father. "What's in it for him?"

Nadine chuckled. "A pretty little blonde who hog-tied his heart."

"No. There's something more. He doesn't love me. If he loved me, he wouldn't have lied. And he damn sure wouldn't have betrayed me like he did."

The rumbling bass thrum of a diesel engine caught her attention. Chance and the man he was with had climbed into the pickup. She watched as Chance carefully backed the truck onto the road and headed east. The bright lights of Oklahoma City shone like jewels scattered on a pair of faded jeans.

Yeah. He loved her all right. He'd tucked his tail between his legs and slunk off like the dirty dog he was.

Buddy whined, almost as if he'd read her thoughts. She dropped her hand to his head and scratched his ears. "No offense, Buddy," she murmured.

The dog growled softly in reply but dropped his chin to the toe of her boot and settled in for a nap. He'd worked hard, and she was going to buy him the biggest steak Cattlemen's Cafe had on the menu once the herd was delivered to the stockyards. She had the cash in her pocket to buy that steak—and one for Boots and Nadine, too.

Chance ignored his brother as he gunned the big diesel engine of his Ford F250. "I know what I'm doing, Cord."

"No, Chance. You don't. The old man is already stroking out from this mess. How the hell did the national media get this story?"

"I told them."

"You what? Damn, little brother. Do you have a death wish? The old man is going to cut you off at the knees."

"He can try, Cord." He moistened dry lips with a tongue resembling sandpaper and loosened his white-knuckled grip on the steering wheel. "Look, we all know he's being a jerk about this. And he can't get his hands on the ranch anyway."

"Oh? You're that sure she's going to get those cows to the stockyards and sold?"

"Doesn't matter if she does or not. I paid off the mortgage and put the deed solely in her name."

"Oh, hell, son. Tell me that ain't so. The old man will shoot you dead right where you stand." Cord scrubbed fingers through his hair. "Does she know?"

"Not a chance. She'd fight me all the way, Cord. Besides, this is something she has to do on her own. She needs to find out what's important. That what's *here* is important." *That I'm important to her.*

"Do you truly believe she'll be so grateful she throws herself into your arms, kisses you all over and falls in love?"

Chance squirmed in his seat remembering Cassie's kisses. "She's already in love with me, Cord. She just hasn't admitted it yet."

"Dammit, Chance. Are you really going to throw away everything for that girl?"

He didn't hesitate a moment. "Yeah. I am."

Fifteen

Her wristwatch read five minutes after five. Cass sipped the cup of coffee Nadine handed her and watched the sky in the east lighten from cobalt to lapis. Wisps of cloud looked like watercolor brush strokes in shades of sangria and salmon.

"Red sky at morning, sailors take warning." Cass recited the old weather adage.

A voice rumbled behind her. "Well, it's a good thing we aren't on the water, then."

She chuckled as the man stepped up beside her. "G'morning, Uncle Boots."

Nadine handed him a cup, and Cass noticed how their fingers lingered against each other. She'd seen this coming, and it lightened her heart. Nadine and Boots made a good match. Maybe she should just turn over the ranch to the Barrons. Boots and Buddy could move in with Nadine. Cass could choose any city in the country and pick up the pieces of her life.

Not far away, a horse whickered, answered by the low-ing moo of one of the cows. She inhaled. The aroma of the coffee in her mug mingled with the hot, acrid smell of dust. Leather, trampled grass and the dry sweet scent of Bermuda hay all hit her nose. And it smelled like home. No. She couldn't give up the ranch. Not now. Not after all the battles she'd fought.

The camp stirred around her. Quiet voices as people finished quick breakfasts were punctuated by the stamp of horses' hooves as they were saddled, the creak of leather and the jangle of bridle bits as riders mounted. An occasional whinny as horses and humans worked to gather the herd added to the music of Buddy's happy barks.

Cass swallowed the last bit of liquid in her cup. "I'll saddle our horses, Uncle Boots. You finish your coffee."

The first vivid scarlet of the sun's curve poked above the horizon. Cass looked at the knot of riders awaiting her signal. This was it. About six miles to the end of her rainbow. She needed a big pot of gold when she reached it. Her throat closed, and she couldn't breathe for a long moment.

Boots nudged his horse up beside hers. "What's up, baby girl?"

Her smile wavered. "Just a memory." At his arched brow and curious head tilt, she continued. "Do you remember the spring Momma died?" He nodded, and she swallowed around the lump. "Lot of storms that year. There was a double rainbow after one of them and Daddy loaded me up in the truck to go chase the end of it. We drove all over three counties, me pointing and shouting out the way. I swear that thing stayed in the sky for a couple of hours. I was so disappointed when it faded away. Daddy held my hand on the way home, even when he had to shift gears. When we got out, he told me that Momma gave me that rainbow— to show me that chasing my dreams was never a waste of time. And to remind me that she'd always watch over us."

Boots cleared his throat then coughed softly. "For such a hard man, Ben was just an old softy when it came to you and your momma, baby girl."

She inhaled and exhaled, her chest rising and falling, but the constriction only lessened slightly. "Daddy's watchin' over me now, Uncle Boots. And I want him to be proud of me." Cass rose in her stirrups and addressed the riders. "Head 'em up, folks. Time to move 'em out."

Buddy barked and raced to the back of the herd. The others reined their horses into position and remained quiet while the drag riders pushed the herd forward. Amid moos and bleats, the cattle milled around then moved forward. Outriders funneled them through the gate of the field where they'd camped. Boots led the way, setting the pace. With fences on either side of the section line road, it was more a matter of keeping the herd moving. They wanted to stop and graze in the right-of-way.

This was their fourth day on the drive, and folks had settled into the rhythm. The occasional whoop and slap of work-gloved hands on leather chaps punctuated the still summer air. Four thousand hooves kicked up a lot of Oklahoma red dirt. Cass wondered how far off the dust cloud could be seen. In less than a mile, they'd hit the Oklahoma County line. The front of the herd was already on paved road, but she seriously doubted she could sneak past the border.

A helicopter buzzed overhead. A few of her volunteers looked up to track its movement. A couple of them waved. National news reporters or local? She shook her head, still surprised by the coverage. She might fail miserably but at least she'd go out in a blaze of glory. She thought of the Bon Jovi song and chuckled.

"Oh, yeah. Cyrus Barron definitely wants me dead or alive. Preferably dead, I'm sure."

Cord led two horses out of the trailer and handed the lead rope of one to Chance. "I can't believe all the legal hoops you've jumped through. Getting recused from the suit and then you got Judge Reynolds to sign the order that'll really put a twist in the Old Man's shorts."

"You don't have to come, Cord. I'm not twisting your arm."

His brother laughed. "No, you aren't. I'm doing it because it'll piss off the old man. Plus, I want to see if this gal is good enough for you."

Chance smoothed the blanket across his horse's withers, grabbed his saddle and tossed it up. He loosely cinched the girth then slipped the halter down as he bridled the animal. "The question is whether or not I'm good enough for her. I screwed this one up royally."

Cord clapped him on the shoulder. "I still can't believe you got Judge Reynolds to sign that order."

He shrugged. "I caught him in the bar at the club. Heidi will file it as soon as the court clerk's office opens, and then she'll deliver a copy to the sheriff's office." He glanced at the expensive watch on his wrist. "I just hope Cass got a late start this morning. She's been driving those cattle from can see to can't see."

Cord chuckled. "You've been reading Louis L'Amour again." He glanced toward the west. A few stars still sparkled faintly against an indigo backdrop. Behind them to the east, the sun was banked by clouds and fiery red rays grabbed at the dark sky. "Red skies, Chance. I hope the weather holds. Getting caught out in a thunderstorm will be a very bad thing."

They tied their horses to the trailer, and Cord grabbed a stainless-steel thermos. He poured coffee into travel mugs and handed one to Chance. "This girl is riding you hard. I'm not sure that's a good thing."

Chance stared off toward the horizon. "She makes me want to be a better man than I am, Cord."

"How's that working for you?"

"Hurts like hell, but I'm going to prove myself to her. I'm going to be that man, come hell or high water."

* * *

Cass put her heels to the big sorrel, and the horse trotted up to join the dun Boots rode. Red whickered, and Lucky answered back. The horses didn't care what was up ahead. She couldn't see over the low rise in front of them, but she knew what waited on the other side. County Line Road. The helicopter still droned overhead, and she could see media trucks set up for remote telecasts. So far she'd declined comment but didn't stop any of her volunteer riders from answering reporters' questions. She rolled her neck. At the snap, crackle and pop, Boots turned to watch her.

"Problem with your neck?"

Her laugh sounded as dry as the red dust coating the weeds lining the road. "Naw. Just stress."

They rode in relative silence but for the thud of hooves, Buddy's excited bark and a few indignant moos. Her horse tossed his head and pulled against the reins. Cass realized she had a death grip on them and loosened her fingers. Red stretched his nose out and shook his head again, which jangled the rings on the bit in his mouth.

"It'll be okay, honey."

"I'm glad you think so, Uncle Boots. Me? I figure I'm on my way to jail as soon as we top that rise."

Before he could reply, two horsemen appeared silhouetted for a moment before they cantered up the road. Her mouth straightened into a grim slash. "Is that Chance? What the hell is he doing here?"

"Don't go jumpin' to conclusions, Cassidy. Let the man talk before you bite his head off."

"And who's with him? Is he wearing a uniform? Is that a deputy?"

"I never knew a deputy to wear a shirt like that, hon."

She shaded her eyes. Chance wore a faded chambray shirt, but the man riding with him wore a bright red plaid with fancy stitching, fringe and pearl buttons. "Okay. That's the worst Western shirt I've ever seen."

"I heard that," the other man called.

The men reined in and waited. When Cass and Boots came even with them, they turned their horses and fell in, Chance riding knee-to-knee on her right and the other man beside him.

"My brother Cord. Cord, Boots Thomas and Cassidy Morgan."

Cord tipped the brim of his hat and pretended to pout. "I dressed up special for this rodeo. I can't believe you're dissin' my shirt."

She had to bite her lip. Cord definitely got all the charm in the family. Working her mouth to keep from grinning, she cast an arch look in their direction. "So why are you here?"

"I have a signed injunction, Cass."

"You what?" She twisted in her saddle and nailed his arm with a fist. "Of all the low-down, cowardly, despicable, low-life…" She sputtered and spit, so angry she couldn't even talk. Without warning, Chance grabbed her, hauled her out of her saddle and settled her across his thighs. His arms pinned hers to her sides but she struggled anyway.

"Dammit, hold still, Cass."

"Let. Me. Guh-uh-uh." His lips sealed on hers, cutting off her last word. She fought him, but as his mouth pressed against hers and his tongue teased her lips open, her struggles lessened, and she relaxed—if pressing against him as her tongue entwined with his could be called relaxing.

With a ragged gasp, he broke the kiss. "Please listen, Cass. The injunction is against the sheriff and the city police. Judge Reynolds signed it so you can continue to drive the herd to Stockyard City."

If someone were to ask later, she'd vow that was not a sob bubbling in her throat. When his arms loosened enough that she could move, she bunched his shirt into her fists and stared at him nose to nose. "Swear you mean that. Swear I'm going to get the herd to the stockyards today so they can go in the sale tomorrow."

"On my honor, Cass. I know my word means nothing to you, but give me a chance to prove myself. That's why Cord and I are here." He kissed her again. "Give me a chance to be the right man for you. To prove how much I love you."

"Oh, hi, Cass. I'm Cord. Chance's older, saner brother. Nice to meet you."

She laughed, unable to stop the swing of emotions from anger to giddy relief with a pit stop at *Ohmygoshhereally-lovesme!* She glanced over at Cord but returned her gaze to stare at Chance, her head slowly shaking from side to side. "Hi, Cord. Nice to meet you. I think." Then she thumped her fist against Chance's chest. "Put me back on my horse, buster. We have a herd to deliver."

"Yes, ma'am!"

A moment later, Chance's strong arms slid from around her, and she was back in her saddle. Behind her, cheers rose in sharp crescendo to the soothing lows from the herd. Did she have a chance to make her dad proud? She didn't dare hope. Not until she'd closed the gate on the last pen at the stockyards. Chance reached over and took her hand, gave it a little squeeze and winked. Her heart danced a two-step in her chest. Then they topped the rise, and her heart stopped. The road was blocked by black sheriff cruisers, the emergency lights on top blazing red and blue.

Sixteen

"Stop right there!" The voice echoed through the bull-horn.

"Keep riding."

She didn't need Chance's urging. "Let's get this over with." She touched her spurs to Red's sides, and the big horse surged to a canter. Chance's horse stayed right beside her. The next thing she knew, Cord had galloped up on her other side. "Gee, we're one horseman short of the Apocalypse." She couldn't resist the quip.

Cord blew out a snort of laughter. "We'll just have to try harder."

She glanced to her left and studied Chance's brother for a long moment. Of similar build, with the same dark hair and brown eyes, they shared some amazing genetics. He rode with a reckless ease even though his expression looked grim and determined. She was suddenly glad these two men rode at her side.

Peeking at Chance, she noticed he was scanning the crowd gathered in the intersection behind the barricade of sheriff's office vehicles. His face lit up, and she followed his gaze to find a petite brunette waving madly. Jealousy twisted in her stomach.

"There's Heidi." Chance stood up in his stirrups to see better. The woman waved again and held up a manila folder.

"She got the filing done. We're good to go. I know it's not your style, Cass, but let me do the talking this time?"

The corner of her mouth quirked in a little grin. He hadn't made that an order but a request. He was learning. "Who's Heidi?" She wanted to bite off her tongue as the question slipped off its tip.

"My paralegal. She filed the injunction and delivered copies first thing this morning."

The constriction in her chest lessened. His paralegal. Just his paralegal. Nobody special. Well, she amended, nobody special to his heart. "Tell her thanks?"

"You can tell her yourself when I introduce you. In the meantime…" He paused and blew out a breath. "I've probably been presumptuous but I'm on file with the court as your attorney. Let me deal with the deputies. Okay?"

"Okay."

Chance rode past Heidi, grabbed the envelope but didn't dismount when they stopped in front of the roadblock. He delivered the signed, if slightly crumpled, order to the deputy with the bullhorn. Words were exchanged, followed by radio transmissions between the deputies and the sheriff's office. Cass sat stiffly, pressing her lips together.

"Easy, Cass. Chance knows what he's doing."

She cut her eyes to Cord. "I sure hope so."

His knee bumped hers as his bay sidled closer to her horse. "You did something to him, Cass. Something good. Don't let pride mess this up for either of you."

She rolled her eyes. "That's easy for you to say."

Chance reined his horse around and rejoined them. "It's done. They're moving their cars. We'll still need to deal with OCPD when we hit the city limits. The good news is, Bethany PD is shutting down traffic and giving us an escort through town. That'll help. I doubt we'll get the same consideration from the OKC cops."

Cass wanted to kiss him again but didn't. Cameras of

every sort were aimed in their direction and had been recording every moment of the confrontation. She turned and raised her hand. "Move 'em out!"

The outriders pushed the herd slowly, and like a lumbering black wave, the cattle shuffled forward. The cruisers moved out of the way, and the deputies turned to crowd control to keep zealous onlookers safe. The herd lined out, and the trail drive continued. As the lead riders neared the flood plain leading to Lake Overholser, Cass doubled back to check with each rider.

"We'll take them around the lake road to the spillway and down the riverbed. It's mostly dry. We can cross under I-40 that way."

The herd moved without incident. A Bethany police car led the way while other units shut down intersections to traffic so they could pass safely. The lead cows balked at the dip down the riverbank, but the smell of water overcame their fear. They plunged over, and the rest of the herd followed. The riders allowed the cattle to drink their fill and then pushed them down the wide, sandy river bottom.

The sun climbed overhead, passed zenith, and the herd kept moving. They needed to find a place to move the cattle out of the riverbed and back up to a surface street. Cord and Chance rode ahead to find a spot and a few minutes later, Cord galloped back. He joined Cass, and the expression on his face left her worried.

"Chance is talking to the Oklahoma City cops. They say we can't use Fifteenth Street to push the herd through."

"What? How the hell are we going to get them across I-44 then? We can't swim them down the river, and the first dam is just past Meridian. If we don't push them out of the river soon, we'll be stuck."

"Duh. Chance is negotiating with them. I'm thinking we take them just past MacArthur. They're dredging the river there, and it's a construction zone. We can drive the herd to the start of the riverside park and use the bike and running trail. That gets us under I-44. If we go all the way to Agnew, we can take them straight under the Stockyard City arch and to the stockyard pens. With the publicity you're getting, all the merchants are lined up ready to help." He held up his cell phone. "My contact at the chamber of commerce says they're ready to block the intersections with their private vehicles if that's what it takes." He passed the phone to her so she could read the text for herself.

"I…this is just crazy."

"And?"

She laughed. Cord seemed convinced they could do this. And Chance was a white knight fighting battles for her. "I say we unleash some crazy."

They managed a steady speed of almost two miles an hour. Chance hadn't returned, and she hoped he hadn't been arrested. Cord assured her his brother wouldn't let that happen, but she noticed he looked worried and checked both his phone and the view downriver every few minutes for some sign of Chance.

When the herd reached the construction area, the lead riders turned up the gently sloping bank. Cass topped out and reined in her horse. A cluster of police cars, with lights flashing, lined up to block any sort of egress to the street. She was relieved to find Chance, dismounted and talking to a policeman. Chance waved his hands to make some point and while she couldn't hear his words, his posture and every gesture indicated how angry and frustrated he was. The cop responded with a jutted chin and hands stiff at his side as if he had to keep them there with effort.

She waved her riders and the herd on to the east. They wouldn't try the street, instead opting for Cord's suggestion. They would follow the upper riverbank, crossing under the roads between them and the stockyards. There was only undeveloped land until they hit Meridian Avenue. Any problem would likely crop up once they hit the bike trails and developed area between there and the stockyards where the land narrowed.

Cass couldn't help but glance over her shoulder to keep an eye on Chance. And then all hell broke loose. Staccato pop-pop-pops sounded like gunfire. Her horse reared. The cattle panicked and surged every which way. She struggled to stay in the saddle as cops drew their weapons. Chance yelled and shoved the cop he'd been talking to out of the way as a knot of cows stampeded in their direction. He managed to hang on to his horse's reins, leaped up on the animal and rode into the melee.

She heard Buddy barking wildly as he darted this way and that, nipping at the heels of the cattle, herding them away from the street. Two steers darted past the police line headed for a cluster of onlookers. She kicked her sorrel into a gallop to head them off. Buddy raced past her, nothing but a gray blur. Then everything went into slow motion.

A police car swerved in front of the cows to stop them. The driver slammed on his brakes when he realized he was going to hit them, and he twisted the wheel. The car went into a slide, the tires screaming in protest. Cass's horrified yell was lost in the confusion. Buddy, intent on the steers, never saw the car. Despite all the yelling, the sirens, the mooing of panicked cattle, she still heard the sickening thud of metal meeting flesh and bone. Buddy yelped as he went flying. Forgetting everything but her dog, she jumped down and ran to the injured animal.

"Oh, Buddy, Buddy, Buddy." She sobbed, tears streaming unchecked down her cheeks, leaving red streaks in the dust coating her skin. "Easy, boy. Easy. Just lie still. It's going to be okay. Oh, please, God, let him be okay." She touched his head, and he licked her wrist.

A warm hand gripped her shoulder with gentle fingers.

"We'll get him to the vet's, Cass." Chance's voice cracked but he cleared his throat. "Heidi! Get a blanket!"

Cass didn't hear Heidi's reply but moments later, the woman appeared, her stylish heels sinking into the red Oklahoma dirt. She dropped to her knees, unheedful of her stockings and tailored linen skirt. The woman clutched a baseball-print fleece blanket and spread it out next to Buddy.

While Cass stroked the dog's head and crooned to him, Chance carefully checked for injuries. With the gentleness of a father handling a newborn baby, he lifted Buddy just enough so that Heidi could slip the blanket beneath him. The dog whined but didn't move. A police officer appeared, and before Cass could tell him off, he picked up one edge of the blanket.

"My car is this way, Mr. Barron. I'll take the dog to the emergency vet's."

"I'm going, too." She stood up and bent to take a corner of the blanket.

Chance pulled her against his chest. "No, love. You can't. You need to get the herd back together and get them to the stockyards. Cord will help. I'll go with Buddy. I promise he'll be okay. I won't let Buddy out of my sight." His arms tightened around her, and he kissed the top of her head. The only way to beat the old man was for her to lead a triumphant parade into the stockyards. She had to do this. For herself. And for the two of them. "Now go do what you have to do. You have to finish this."

He cupped her cheeks as she tilted her face up, and he dipped his head to kiss her. His thumbs caressed her skin, smearing tears and dirt. "Cowgirls don't cry, Cass. And you are the finest damn cowgirl I've ever had the honor to meet. Now get your pretty ass back in that saddle and ride. Do this for you. For your dad. For the Crazy M Ranch." *For us,* he added silently.

Cass drew in a long, shuddering breath. Her chin came up even as she leaned her forehead against Chance's very solid chest. "Take care of Buddy, Chance. I'll see you on the other side."

She stepped back, but he didn't release her. Not yet. Not until he claimed her mouth again. She clung to him through the kiss and for a moment longer. As his arms fell away, she turned on her heel and strode into the middle of the chaos, her back straight, her head held high.

Red waited nearby, one front foot stuck in the loop of the reins. He stood still as she approached and freed his foot. Grabbing up the reins, she shoved her boot in the stirrup, mounted and settled into her saddle. In less time than she anticipated, all the cattle were rounded up. Several of her riders had been injured, two seriously. A few of the cops suffered cuts and bruises but they were all on their feet. Cass was down to a handful of drovers, the herd was skittish, and they still had just over three miles to go.

One of the cops yelled and waved to her. She recognized him as the man Chance had been speaking with, so she waited as he approached. He grabbed one rein and stared up at her.

"Firecrackers. Some idiot let loose with a package of Black Cats." The cop shook his head and spit on the ground. He glanced around and winced at the scene. "Keep to the riverbank and the park. We'll patrol the overpasses, Miss Morgan. No one else will disrupt your trail drive. I didn't want it to come to this, that's for sure. But I had orders, ma'am." As they watched, one of her riders was loaded into the back of an ambulance. "No sirree, I sure didn't want it to come to this."

"Neither did I."

"Good luck, Miss Morgan." He turned loose of her horse and stepped back as she put her heels to the sorrel.

Someone called her name, and she glanced back. A bevy

of reporters clamored for her attention but she ignored them. The squad car with Chance and Buddy had already disappeared. The ambulance with her drover also pulled away, lights flashing, though the driver waited until the vehicle was well past the cattle herd before the sirens blared.

With the herd back in some semblance of order, she returned to work. She would finish this. Come hell or high water, she'd get these cattle to the sale and get the money she needed to pay off the mortgage. Cyrus Barron damn sure wasn't getting her ranch. For a brief moment, she wondered what the man would do when he discovered two of his sons had defected to her side in this private war of theirs.

Cord trotted up beside her and handed her a wet bandanna. "You might want to give your face a swipe, especially before we hit Stockyard City. At the moment, you look like you've been ridden hard and put up wet."

"Gee, Cord. I bet the girls just swoon when you give them a compliment."

He laughed. "I like you, Cassidy Morgan. Too bad my little brother met you first."

She wiped her face and winced when she saw the dirty streaks staining the bandanna. "When this is done, I'm going to stand in the shower until there's no hot water left in the tank."

"I'd offer to scrub your back, but I have the feeling Chance will volunteer first."

Up ahead, a cow broke ranks and before she could react, Cord urged his horse forward and charged after the miscreant steer. She watched the expert way he worked. Chance sat a horse just as well. And he'd helped her restring barbed wire fence like he'd done it all his life. Neither of these men acted as she expected. The Barrons were the closest thing to royalty in Oklahoma—in fact, one media wag had dubbed them Red Dirt Royalty. One brother was a US Senator. Another presided over a media empire that included newspapers, TV stations, resorts and an amusement park. A Barron and the senior partner in his own law firm, Chance hobnobbed with the rich and powerful.

But when he came to her place, when he wore his jeans and work shirt like he was born to them, Chance became a different man. He sat on the porch with her, holding her hand and petting Buddy...

At the thought of the beloved dog, her chest threatened to cave in. Buddy had to be okay. Chance would take care of him.

A steer ambled away from the herd, and she shook her head. This was no time to be daydreaming—especially about a man like Chance Barron declaring his love for her. "Yaw," she yelled at the cow, urging Red after the critter.

The herd passed under Meridian without incident. Even though the riverside park system began here, there was little open space behind the hotels and office complexes. Land between "civilization" and the river narrowed. Her riders strung out in a thin line. The next hurdle would be Portland Avenue and then the I-44/I-40 interchange. She shuddered at the thought of any of the cattle making it up onto the interstate highway. Two miles. Two miles to the stockyards. She needed things to stay quiet for two more miles. She managed a deep breath. Chance was right. She would succeed.

She continuously rode back and forth, encouraging her drovers, chasing steers back into line and trying not to get her hopes up. They passed Portland Avenue. Just as with the Meridian corridor, a large police presence kept traffic and onlookers at bay. A couple of the officers even offered surreptitious thumbs-up gestures as she passed beneath them.

The strip of land they traversed widened, and the herd bunched up a little more. Ahead, an office building and huge parking lot would choke them down into almost single file. Red whickered and shook his head. His lathered neck proved how hard he'd been working. All the horses, and their riders, too, looked worn out.

Boots, still riding at the head of the herd, let out a whoop. She stood in her stirrups to see what new problem they faced. To her surprise, a knot of riders advanced from the east. Clicking her tongue, she eased Red into a trot and headed to meet them. She reined in as she reached Boots and let the riders approach.

The lead rider stopped and tipped his hat. "Miz Morgan? We're members of the Stockyard City Sheriff's Posse."

She cringed. What now? She thought the sheriff's department had accepted Chance's injunction. Before she could respond, he continued.

"We heard about that dust up back down the way. We'd have been here sooner to help but some of us needed to go get our horses."

She blinked and then blinked again. "Help? You're here to help?"

"Yes, ma'am, we are. Some of these boys might look like city slickers, but we know how to ride and work cattle." Since the man wore dress pants and a button-down shirt with a loosened tie, he likely qualified as one of those city slickers.

Her eyes burned, and she blinked hard. "Help." She glanced at Boots and answered his big grin with one of her own. She finally remembered her manners. "Uh…thanks!"

The ten riders headed west and circled around to fill in blank spots along the herd. She twisted in her saddle so she could watch, and relaxed after a few minutes. Yeah, even though that one guy probably left his suit coat in his office, he sat his horse with ease. Beside her, Boots grinned like the Cheshire cat.

"What?"

He laughed. "If you could see the expression on your

face, sugar. You look like you just walked into a glass door, thinking it was open."

"Gee, thanks, Uncle Boots. But…yeah. I guess the description fits. I feel like I've been sucker punched. I…I just can't believe all these people want to help. The media. The cops." Another word hovered on the tip of her tongue, but she didn't voice it.

"Chance."

Yeah. That was the one. "He's a Barron, Uncle Boots. His father is the cause of all of this. I—" She huffed out a breath. "How can I trust him?"

They rode in silence for a few minutes before Boots spoke up. "Look inside his heart, baby girl. Tally up all the things he's done to help you. Despite his father. Sometimes blood is thicker than just about anything. But sometimes, a woman loves a man so much she's willing to give up everything for him because she knows he loves her more than anything in the world."

She glanced at him. "That sounds like you're talking about Momma and Daddy."

"I suppose I am, Cassie. Even way back then, Cyrus Barron was a man on the way up. He had a big ranch with lots of cattle, and the horses he bred were some of the finest in the country. He didn't lease his oil and gas royalty rights. He started his own drilling company. And that eventually became Barron Oil. If your momma had married him, she'd have been a rich woman."

Boots took off his hat and wiped his forehead with a bandanna before continuing. "Your daddy was a rodeo cowboy without a pot to piss in. But after that beating, layin' there in the hospital, your momma holdin' his hand and tellin' him how much she loved him, he figured he'd better do something with his life. He scraped together every bit of cash and credit he had and bought the home place. He knew rodeo. And he knew rodeo stock. He started small, but the rodeo folks knew they'd get quality if they hired him. Your momma was there each step of the way, keepin' the books, cleanin' out pens, whatever it took. Until she got sick."

Cass nodded and swallowed hard against the nausea. Her mother had been so sick from pneumonia and despite the breathing tubes and everything else, she couldn't fight the disease.

"You find a love like what your momma and daddy shared, baby girl, you grab on with both hands and never let go." He dipped his chin and stared forward. "Highway's just up a ways. We'd better get ready."

Cass reined Red to a stop on the slope leading up to the interstate right-of-way. A line of riders flanked the road on each side of the overpass. To her now-practiced eye, the herd looked as worn out as her drovers and their horses. Just about a mile now. She exhaled in relief when the last drag rider passed by and disappeared under the overpass. She followed.

On the other side, the herd had bunched tightly again and moved forward like some weird amoeba. Cass could only imagine what the scene looked like from above. Maybe someday, she'd catch a news report to see the footage shot from a helicopter. In the meantime, she had cows to get to market. She rode up the line, urging tired riders and cattle onward.

The news helicopter disappeared, heading west. Cass glanced over her shoulder hoping it wasn't focusing on something bad happening to the drag riders. It kept flying straight and as she watched, lightning flickered in the clouds massing on the western horizon.

"I knew it," she muttered. "Red skies in the morning, sailors…and cowboys take warning." She glanced at her watch. With luck, she'd have the herd delivered to the stockyards, and they'd all be safely in their pens by the time the storm moved in. Nothing to panic over. Yet.

Seventeen

The new bridge with the fancy streetlights loomed ahead. Agnew Avenue. If Chance was right, the street would be blocked to traffic, and she could bring the herd right down the middle of the street. Cord cantered up to her and slowed his horse to match hers.

"About time for you to move up, Cass. You should be at the head of this parade."

She shook her head. "I didn't do this for attention, Cord. If your father had stayed out of things, I'd be back on the ranch with the loan paid." She felt her face flush as her blood pressure spiked.

"Yeah, he's a real sonofabitch. And I figure he's probably not quite done yet. Chance will do everything he can to stop whatever the old man has up his sleeve."

"But...?"

"But?"

"Yeah, I heard a *but* on the end of that sentence." She turned to stare at him, and more than her blood pressure hammered in her ears. "He's going to turn Chance against me, isn't he?" She muttered a string of cusswords but didn't smile when Cord laughed at her. "Damn the man!"

"Which one?"

His quiet question surprised her. "Your..." She blinked and shut her mouth while she considered her answer, which came in the form of a question. "Will he succeed?"

Cord wouldn't look at her, but his shoulders rose in what might be a negligent shrug. "Yesterday, I would have said yeah. The old man always gets what he wants. But today? I don't know." He reined his horse around and headed toward the rear of the herd before she could reply.

She touched spurs to Red's sides, and the big horse quickened his pace. If Cyrus Barron was waiting to stop her at the end of this, by golly she'd be front and center to confront him.

Boots glanced at her as she joined him. "About time you got up here."

She laughed, but it sounded mirthless. "How did this get so out of control, Uncle Boots?"

"People, honey. People always complicate matters. But we're almost there."

Their horses' hooves clopped on the asphalt as they stepped off the curb. Sheriff's cruisers had the street blocked at the off ramp from I-40, and the way was clear to the south. Almost as if sensing the end was near, horses and cattle all picked up the pace. The gateway arch stretched above the street ahead of them. A cowboy on horseback and a long-horned steer bracketed the words "Stockyard City" displayed across the metal span. As she passed beneath it, Cass breathed again. This was it. They'd done it. People lined the street while cameras—digital, phone and video—all preserved the moment for posterity.

"Cass!"

She glanced over in the direction the voice came from. Chance! He stood on the bumper of a pickup truck waving at her. And then the sweetest sound in the world reached her ears—Buddy's excited barks. Her chest swelled with so much happiness she might burst wide open. Her grin spread from ear to ear. She probably looked like a complete idiot but didn't care.

Cord trotted up from behind her and rode past, tipping

the brim of his hat as he went by. He stopped in front of Chance and dismounted. The brothers exchanged places, Chance mounting the horse, and Cord taking charge of Buddy. The men shook hands. Cord said something Cass couldn't hear, but it must have been about her because Chance turned to look at her. Then he smiled, and nothing else mattered.

Police and the fire department had Exchange Boulevard to the east and Agnew to the south blocked off. The cattle had no place to go but turn right and head straight to the National Stockyards. Cheering people lined both sides of the street and surprisingly, the cattle didn't seem bothered by all the hoopla. Cass tamped down her excitement. Until those steers were penned, went through the auction tomorrow morning and she had a check to give Cyrus Barron, she couldn't celebrate.

Chance risked a quick touch on her arm as he rode knee to knee with her. Buddy woofed and wagged his tail, his head hanging out of the pickup truck window as Cord carefully drove by them.

"The pup had some bruised ribs, and his right hip is tender where he landed on it. The vet says as long as Buddy takes it easy, he'll be fine."

She inhaled and blew out a little puff of air. "Thank you."

He glanced at her. "For what?"

"For everything. For taking care of Buddy. For helping despite everything…" Her voice trailed off and left hanging just what that *everything* comprised. In her head, she finished the thought—despite her mistrust, her anger, her accusations.

"You had every right, Cass. I wasn't completely honest with you. And I'm truly sorry for that. I won't lie to you again. Not ever."

She flashed him a cocky grin. "Can I have that in writing and notarized, Mr. Lawyer Guy?"

He chuckled but choked off the sound as he stared at the knot of people waiting ahead. A beefy man in Western clothes, his sleeves rolled up to reveal brawny forearms, his hat pushed back off his forehead, argued vehemently with a tall, distinguished man wearing a tailored suit that cost more than many people made in a month.

Damn. The old man was back from Vegas. He glanced at Cass and offered her a smile. Things were going to get ugly in a heartbeat.

"Are you going to tell me everything will be all right?"

"No."

"Good. So what *are* you going to tell me?"

"That's my father up there. I suspect the other man is the sales manager of the stockyards. If the old man stays true to form, he's threatening all sorts of dire consequences about now."

"Then we'd better go face whatever those consequences are." She clucked to her horse and trotted forward.

Chance followed at a jog. Cord had parked nearby and Buddy was there, hackles raised, ears back. He could almost feel the growl forming in the dog's chest as he reined to a stop next to Cassie.

"I don't give a damn, Mr. Barron. The last time I looked, your name wasn't on the bottom of my paycheck. You can scream and cuss all you want but since you don't own this place, I'm not about to turn away any cattle brought here for sale."

Camera crews homed in on the altercation, and Chance winced. The family would need a lot of damage control after the news tonight. The old man, red in the face and sputtering, jabbed his finger in the man's chest.

"I will own this miserable excuse for a sale barn, and I will fire your insolent ass. I will shut this place down and fire everyone even remotely associated with the stockyards. Do you understand me?"

Cyrus Barron straightened to his full height and looked for all the world like some old revival preacher raining fire and brimstone on his congregation. No one had called his bluff in ages. He pulled out his phone, called his assistant and snarled terse instructions Chance didn't hear but could imagine. With a cold, calculating smile, Cyrus faced the sales manager, ignoring Cass and Chance. The standoff lasted what felt like an hour but was ten minutes in reality. The herd bunched up in the street, and people waited breathlessly.

The manager's cell phone rang. He answered, his face draining of color as he listened. He stammered and hemmed but in the end, he ducked his head and mumbled something. Turning on his heel, he walked back to his wranglers and told them to shut the gates and go home. The stockyards had closed for the day.

The old man turned his cold smile on Cass, and adrenaline surged through Chance's body, leaving his fingers and toes tingling and burning.

"I'm disappointed in you."

Chance straightened his shoulders as the old man focused on him. He was pretty sure the smirk he plastered on his face was a mirror image of the one his father wore. "Makes two of us. This has gone far enough, Cyrus."

"Indeed it has. I've already instructed my attorneys to remove you from the trust."

Cass gasped but he ignored her. If he broke eye contact now, the old man would think he'd won, and Chance wasn't about to let that happen. His expression didn't change. "It will be an interesting court battle, considering I'm the one who drew up the trust papers in the first place. Did you ever read them, Cyrus? Or did you just sign them?"

There. There was the flicker in the old man's eyes he'd been waiting for. He'd learned the art of confrontation from the master himself. He quirked one corner of his mouth.

"Oh, I forgot rule number one. If you can't trust family, you can't trust family. You should have remembered that one, Cyrus."

"It's too late for your little who—"

Lightning fast, his fists wrapped in the lapels of his father's suit. "Don't go there, Old Man. You say what's on the tip of your tongue, I'll happily spend the night in jail for knocking the crap out of you."

Cyrus glared but didn't finish the sentence. "It's still too late, *son*. She can't make the balloon payment on that loan unless she sells those steers by five o'clock tomorrow afternoon. And that will not happen."

"Yes, it will. I'll buy the cattle from her."

Chance and his father whipped their heads around at the new voice. The crowd grew silent as anticipation filled the air. The newcomer ignored Cyrus and walked over to Cass, where she'd remained mounted.

"Miss Morgan, I'm J. Rand Davis."

As his gaze darted between the man and Cass, Chance had to stifle a laugh. If there was a man Cyrus Barron hated even more than Ben Morgan, it had to be Joseph Randolph Davis. They'd been rival wildcatters back in the early days of the oil boom; now both of them were among the richest men in the country.

Cass dismounted and offered her hand. "Mr. Davis, I suspect it's going to be my pleasure to meet you."

"I certainly hope so." He glanced at his smartphone, checked a couple of screens then smiled at her. "According to the closing spot prices on the Chicago Commodities Exchange, prime grass-fed Black Angus cattle are going for a hundred and forty-seven."

Chance did a quick mental calculation. The price was per hundredweight and given the size and quality of Cass's steers, she'd make over five hundred thousand dollars. Cass looked stunned as she also did the math.

"I have trucks lined up, and we'll get a final weight on 'em but I'm prepared to hand you a certified check for three hundred thousand dollars as a down payment. Once the weigh-in is final, I will cut another check for the remainder."

Cass glanced over at Chance, her eyes wide with surprise. It was enough to pay off the note. He nodded to her. "It's a fair price, Cass. And I figure Mr. Davis is good for the rest."

She offered her hand, and Davis shook it. He handed over a check and she glanced at it, stared for a long moment, blinked and barely resisted doing a happy dance right there in the middle of the street.

Davis spoke up immediately. "Knowing Cyrus like I do, I didn't want to take any chances that he'd wiggle out of the deal." He reached for the inside breast pocket of his sport coat and pulled out some folded papers. "Here's the bill of sale with the terms and deadline for payment of the additional funds"

Cass accepted them and with a confused expression, glanced over at Chance. "Will you look it over?"

He took the papers and unfolded them as Davis added, "Look it over, Chancellor. If Miss Baxter agrees, she can sign it and we'll start loading these steers."

Chance read through them, his practiced eye picking out the important parts. Everything was just as Mr. Davis had outlined. He handed the sheaf of papers back to Cass as Davis passed his pen to her. She took the time to read every page, and Chance couldn't help the grin forming. She glanced at him finally and he nodded. She signed, using his back.

Chance had almost forgotten about his father until the old man snorted. "You wait, Rand Davis. You think you've won this time, but I guarantee this thing isn't over between us." Then he turned a baleful stare on Chance. "As for you, I'll deal with you later."

Davis offered a frosty smile. "Careful what you threaten, Cyrus."

The old man spun around and stomped off to his chauffeured Lincoln. In a matter of minutes, the stockyard wranglers reappeared, opened the gates to some loading pens, and the herd was moved off the street. A spontaneous celebration erupted behind them, but Chance and Cass remained with Mr. Davis, watching as the cattle were transferred up the chutes and loaded into the waiting trucks.

Chance watched one of the richest oilmen in the world chat with the woman he loved. Three months ago, on that snowy Chicago night, he would never have guessed he'd be standing on a dusty street in Stockyard City watching this scene.

But then, all of a sudden, Davis clamped his mouth shut in the middle of a sentence, and his eyes narrowed in anger. Chance turned around, thinking his father had returned.

To his surprise, Cord stood there like a deer caught in headlights. The two men stared at each other, and Chance couldn't help but compare the standoff to a scene from a Western movie—the gunfighters on Main Street, fingers flexing over the handles of their six-shooters, each waiting for the other to make a move. He'd never seen his brother look so unnerved.

After a long, tense moment, Davis turned his head and focused his attention on Cassie. "I'll have the certified check for the rest of the money delivered to you tomorrow, Miss Morgan."

She offered her hand again, after wiping it down her thigh. As dusty as her jeans appeared, she probably didn't clean much dirt off, but she made the effort. "Thank you again, Mr. Davis. I…" On impulse, she raised up on her toes and planted a quick kiss on his cheek. "I couldn't have done this without you."

Davis shook his head and glanced toward Chance. "No, honey. I think you had all the help you needed right there at your side." He offered his hand to Chance. "You take care of this little lady."

Chance shook hands with Rand. "I will, sir." He slipped his arm around Cassie's shoulders and hugged her closer to his side. "You did it, darlin'."

She smiled up at him. "No. *We* did it. I'm sorry I ever doubted you."

He shook his head. "Don't apologize. To be honest, I wasn't sure I could stand up to the old man. But you made me want to. Your belief in me, Cass. That's what gave me the courage."

He caught movement in the corner of his eye and turned just in time to see Davis stop in front of Cord. The two men exchanged what appeared to be heated words until Chance realized something was off about Cord's posture. His shoulders drooped a little, and while he hadn't bowed his head, he wasn't quite looking Mr. Davis in the eye, either.

"Now what the hell is that all about?"

Cass leaned around him to watch. "I…wow. Cord almost looks cowed. He's definitely on the defensive."

Davis walked away but Cord stood rooted to the spot. Chance wrapped his fingers around Cassie's hand and tugged her with him as he approached his brother. "Cord?"

"Don't."

"Don't what? What's going on?"

"Nothing."

"That didn't look like nothing to me."

"Leave it be, Chance. It's…"

Cass squeezed his arm before he could speak again. "Not now, Chance."

Cord flashed her an appreciative look then turned on

a high-wattage smile. Chance knew that look. Cord had dodged some sort of bullet, but that was okay. He'd eventually pin down his brother to find out what that discussion had been about.

The stockyards manager approached and cleared his throat. "Sorry to interrupt, folks, but the last cow has been loaded. Five hundred on the nose, Miss Morgan. Mr. Davis already paid the loading fees. If you'll just sign this receipt, we're all done." He thrust a battered aluminum clipboard in her direction, and she scribbled her name across the bottom. The man made a show of tearing off the receipt and handed it to her with a flourish.

"Congratulations, ma'am. We were all rooting for you."

Chance glanced at her upturned face, and his heart lurched. Damn but he loved this woman. "You did it, Cass. I am so freaking proud of you, I'm about to bust. I love you, darlin', with everything I am."

Cord punched him on the arm. "Well, don't just stand there, little brother. Kiss the girl."

Epilogue

Cass adjusted the blue garter on her thigh then slipped her foot into the Justin Western boot. She flounced the full skirt of her wedding dress and turned around. Her maid of honor and two bridesmaids had crystal champagne flutes in their hands ready to toast her nuptials. She glanced at the other person in the room. Boots had a finger stuck between his buttoned-up collar and his neck, trying to stretch the shirt. With a knowing smile, she adjusted his silver-and-black bolo tie. "As soon as you walk me down the aisle, Uncle Boots, you can unbutton. Promise."

The old man muttered something under his breath, and she had to bite back her giggle. She felt giddy, her thoughts scattered as her nerves thrummed in anticipation.

After selling the herd, Chance had handed over the deed to the Crazy M, admitting he'd already paid off the loan. She'd insisted on paying him back and did so five minutes before he dropped to a knee and asked her to marry him.

She smiled at the memory.

She squelched the one niggling thought that she was about to make the worst mistake of her life. She must be insane to join Cyrus Barron's family by her own free will. But if she was crazy, she didn't care.

"Answer me one thing, baby girl."

She shook the negative thoughts from her mind and focused on Boots. "Yes?"

"Would your life be better without him?"

A nervous laugh burbled up before she could catch it. "What? Are you reading my mind now?"

"Be honest, Cassidy Anne. With me, but most important with yourself. If you walked away now, would you look back in relief or regret?"

She stared out the window. Knots of people gathered on the lawn in front of the chapel. She glimpsed what looked like a rugby scrum—the Barron brothers. They'd all come to support Chance, and each one of them had privately offered her friendship and brotherhood. She couldn't breathe for a minute, and her vision fogged. When it cleared, she saw only Chance standing there surrounded by his family. Business-wise, he'd put his foot down. His law firm was his and not part of Barron Enterprises, though he continued to represent the family's various entities. Chance had talked things through with her before he agreed to remain as the Barron's legal counsel. He glanced toward the window almost as if he knew she watched.

"That answers my question."

Startled from her reverie she turned to stare at Boots. "What? I didn't say anything."

"You didn't have to, Cassie. The smile on your face said it all. Now let's get this rodeo goin' before I strangle in this monkey suit."

Chance stood at the front of the church looking outwardly calm, but he felt as if he was on a sinking life raft in a raging storm. Cord stood on his left, along with his other brothers. Heidi and her husband occupied the front pew of the small chapel, along with the caretaker couple who'd practically raised the brothers, Beth and John Sanders. Cyrus Barron hadn't bothered to attend, not that he was surprised. The rest of his family stood up for him, though, and that's all that mattered.

The front doors opened, and the congregation hushed. An ancient organ wheezed out music vaguely resembling something classical. Two bridesmaids and the maid of honor floated down the aisle. He squinted against the bright sun backlighting the door and made out Boots's stocky form. As the man stepped into the more sedate light of the nave, with Cass on his arm, Chance held his breath.

She looked beautiful. Absolutely, totally, completely stunning. His heart galloped then smoothed out its rhythm. Her gaze held his and any sense of foreboding dissipated. God, but he loved this woman with every ounce of his being. The feeling of rightness overwhelmed him, and he blinked away the sudden moisture gathering in his eyes.

Cass stopped in front of him, leaned up on her tiptoes and kissed his cheek. "Hey, don't you know cowboys aren't supposed to cry?"

He smiled and whispered. "I heard it was cowgirls never cry, they just get back on and ride." Yes, Chance Barron always knew exactly what he wanted. And he always got it.

* * * * *

Don't miss
the next book in Silver James's
RED DIRT ROYALTY *series*
THE COWGIRL'S LITTLE SECRET
Available April 2015!

MILLS & BOON®

Want to get more from Mills & Boon?

Here's what's available to you if you join the exclusive **Mills & Boon eBook Club** today:

◆ *Convenience – choose your books each month*
◆ *Exclusive – receive your books a month before anywhere else*
◆ *Flexibility – change your subscription at any time*
◆ *Variety – gain access to eBook-only series*
◆ *Value – subscriptions from just £1.99 a month*

So visit **www.millsandboon.co.uk/esubs** today to be a part of this exclusive eBook Club!

MILLS & BOON®

Need more New Year reading?

We've got just the thing for you!
We're giving you 10% off your next eBook or
paperback book purchase on the Mills & Boon
website. So hurry, visit the website today and type
SAVE10 in at the checkout for your exclusive

10% DISCOUNT

www.millsandboon.co.uk/save10

Ts and Cs: Offer expires 31st March 2015.
This discount cannot be used on bundles or sale items.

MILLS & BOON®

Desire™

PASSIONATE AND DRAMATIC LOVE STORIES

A sneak peek at next month's titles...

In stores from 16th January 2015:

- **His Lost and Found Family** – Sarah M. Anderson
  and **Terms of a Texas Marriage** – Lauren Canan

- **Thirty Days to Win His Wife** – Andrea Laurence
  and **The Texan's Royal M.D.** – Merline Lovelace

- **Her Forbidden Cowboy** – Charlene Sands
  and **The Blackstone Heir** – Dani Wade

Available at WHSmith, Tesco, Asda, Eason, Amazon and Apple

Just can't wait?
Buy our books online a month before they hit the shops!
visit www.millsandboon.co.uk

These books are also available in eBook format!

MILLS & BOON®

Why shop at millsandboon.co.uk?

Each year, thousands of romance readers find their perfect read at millsandboon.co.uk. That's because we're passionate about bringing you the very best romantic fiction. Here are some of the advantages of shopping at www.millsandboon.co.uk:

* **Get new books first**—you'll be able to buy your favourite books one month before they hit the shops

* **Get exclusive discounts**—you'll also be able to buy our specially created monthly collections, with up to 50% off the RRP

* **Find your favourite authors**—latest news, interviews and new releases for all your favourite authors and series on our website, plus ideas for what to try next

* **Join in**—once you've bought your favourite books, don't forget to register with us to rate, review and join in the discussions

Visit **www.millsandboon.co.uk** for all this and more today!